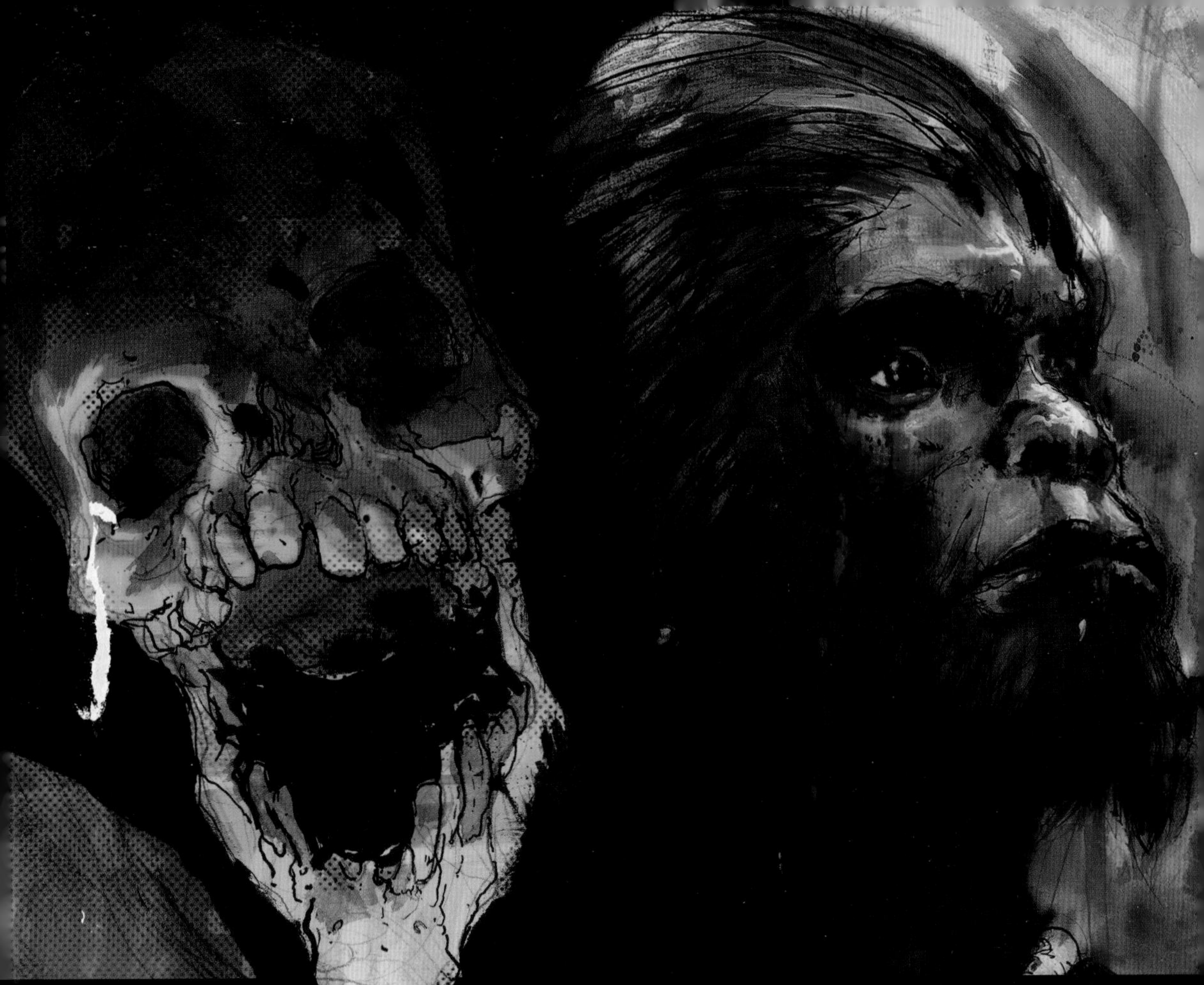

PROOF™ JULIA

CREATED BY ALEXANDER GRECIAN & RILEY ROSSMO

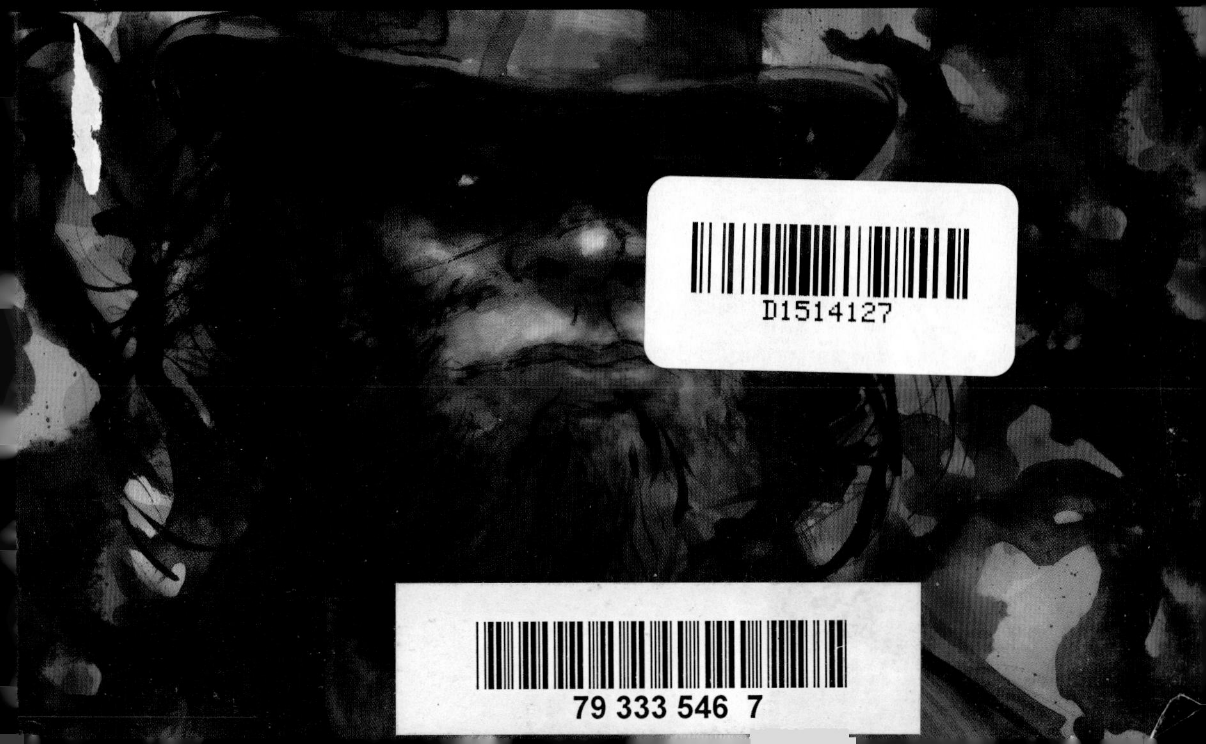

IMAGE COMICS, INC.

ROBERT KIRKMAN chief operating officer **ERIK LARSEN** chief financial officer **TODD McFARLANE** president **MARC SILVESTRI** chief executive officer **JIM VALENTINO** vice-president

ERIC STEPHENSON publisher **JOE KEATINGE** sales & licensing coordinator **BETSY GOMEZ** pr & marketing coordinator **BRANWYN BIGGLESTONE** accounts manager **SARAH deLAINE** administrative assistant **TYLER SHAINLINE** production manager **DREW GILL** art director **JONATHAN CHAN** production artist **MONICA HOWARD** production artist **VINCENT KUKUA** production artist

www.imagecomics.com

PROOF BOOK 4: JULIA
ISBN: 978-1-60706-285-1
First Printing

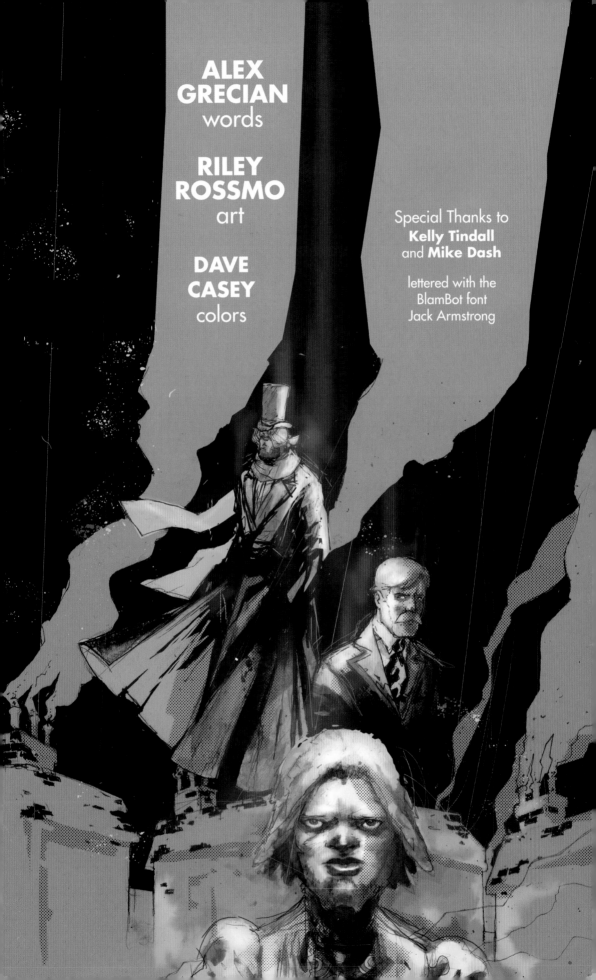

ALEX GRECIAN words

RILEY ROSSMO art

DAVE CASEY colors

Special Thanks to **Kelly Tindall** and **Mike Dash**

lettered with the BlamBot font Jack Armstrong

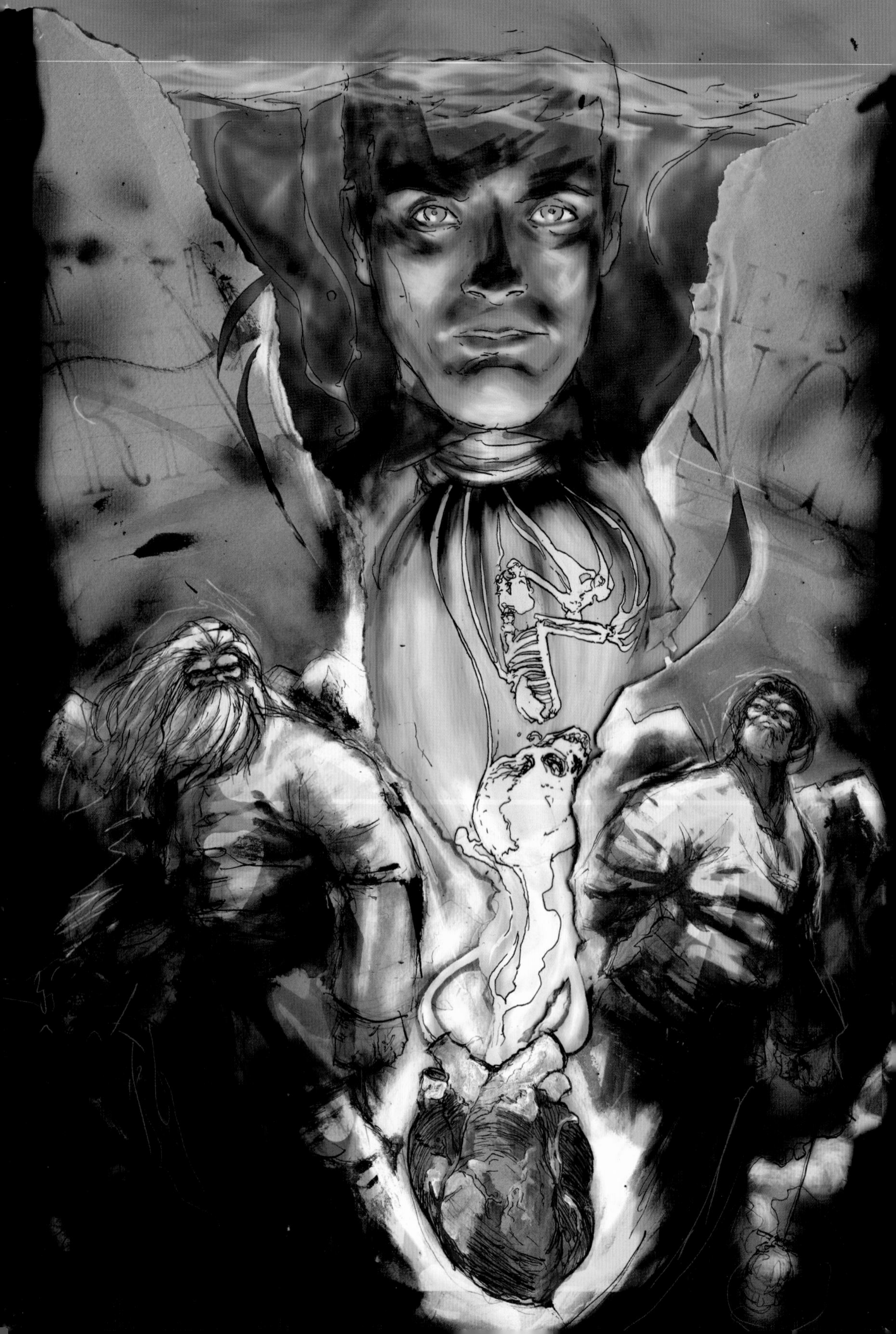

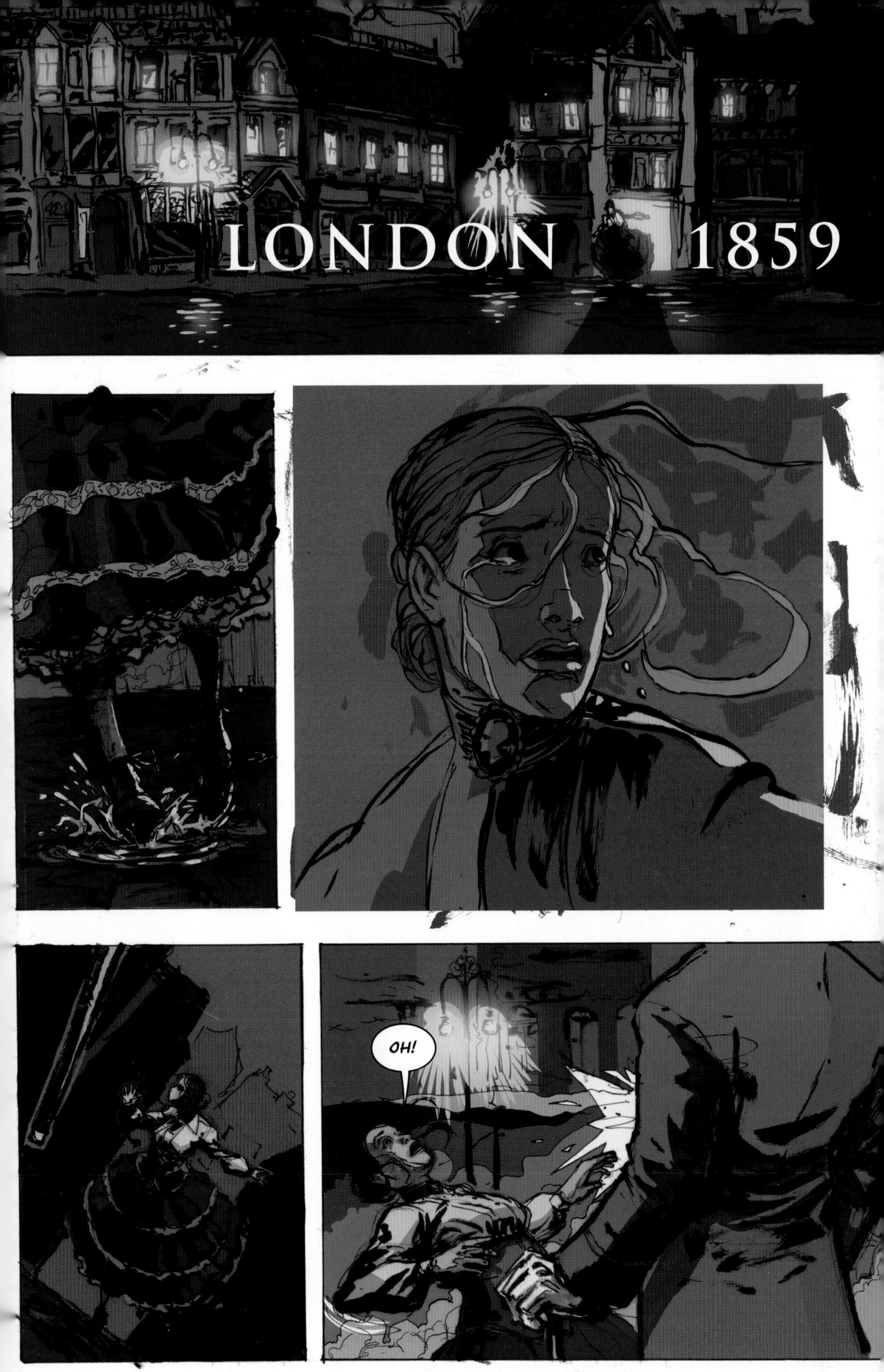
LONDON 1859
OH!

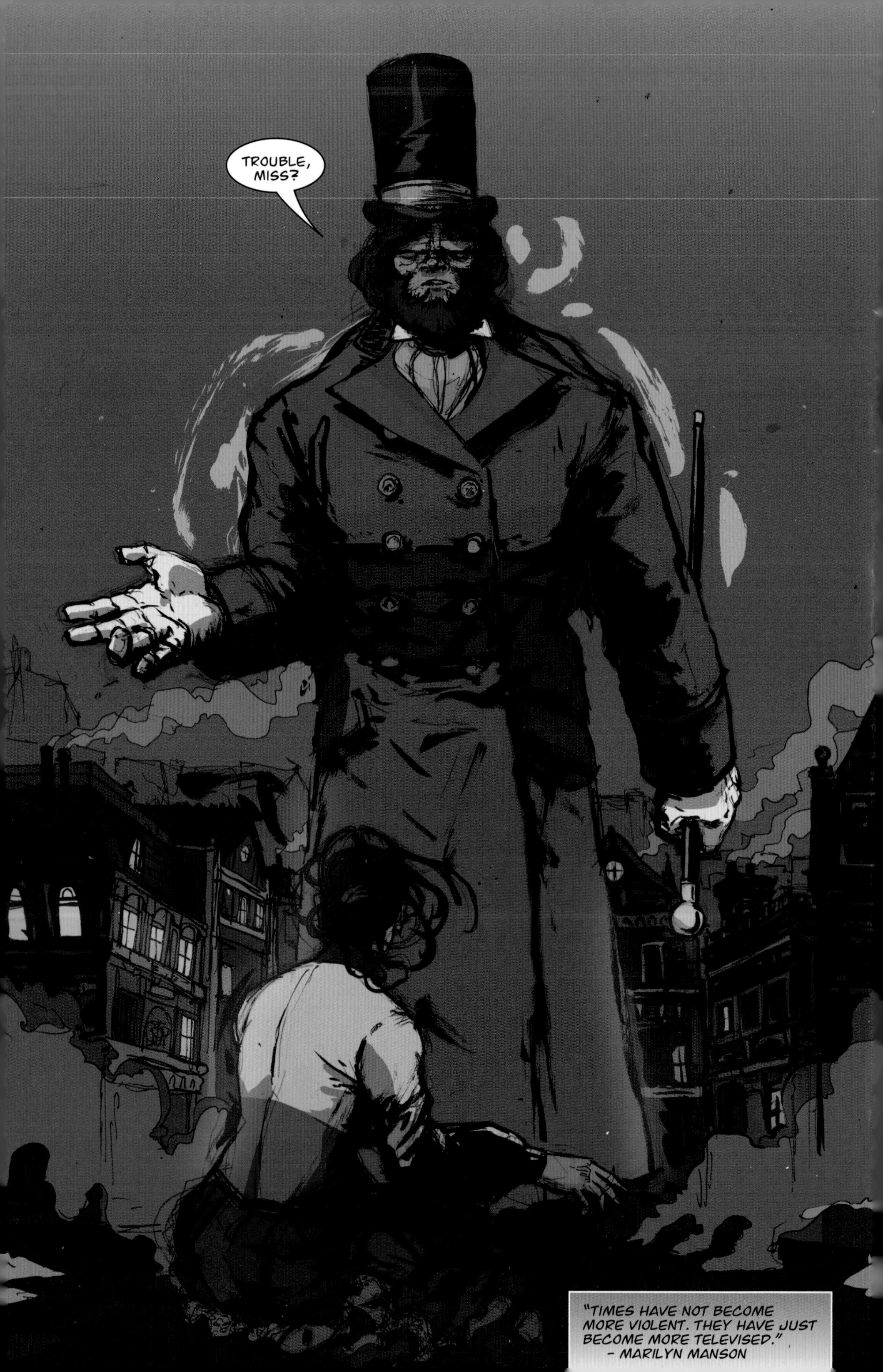
TROUBLE, MISS?
"TIMES HAVE NOT BECOME MORE VIOLENT. THEY HAVE JUST BECOME MORE TELEVISED."
– MARILYN MANSON

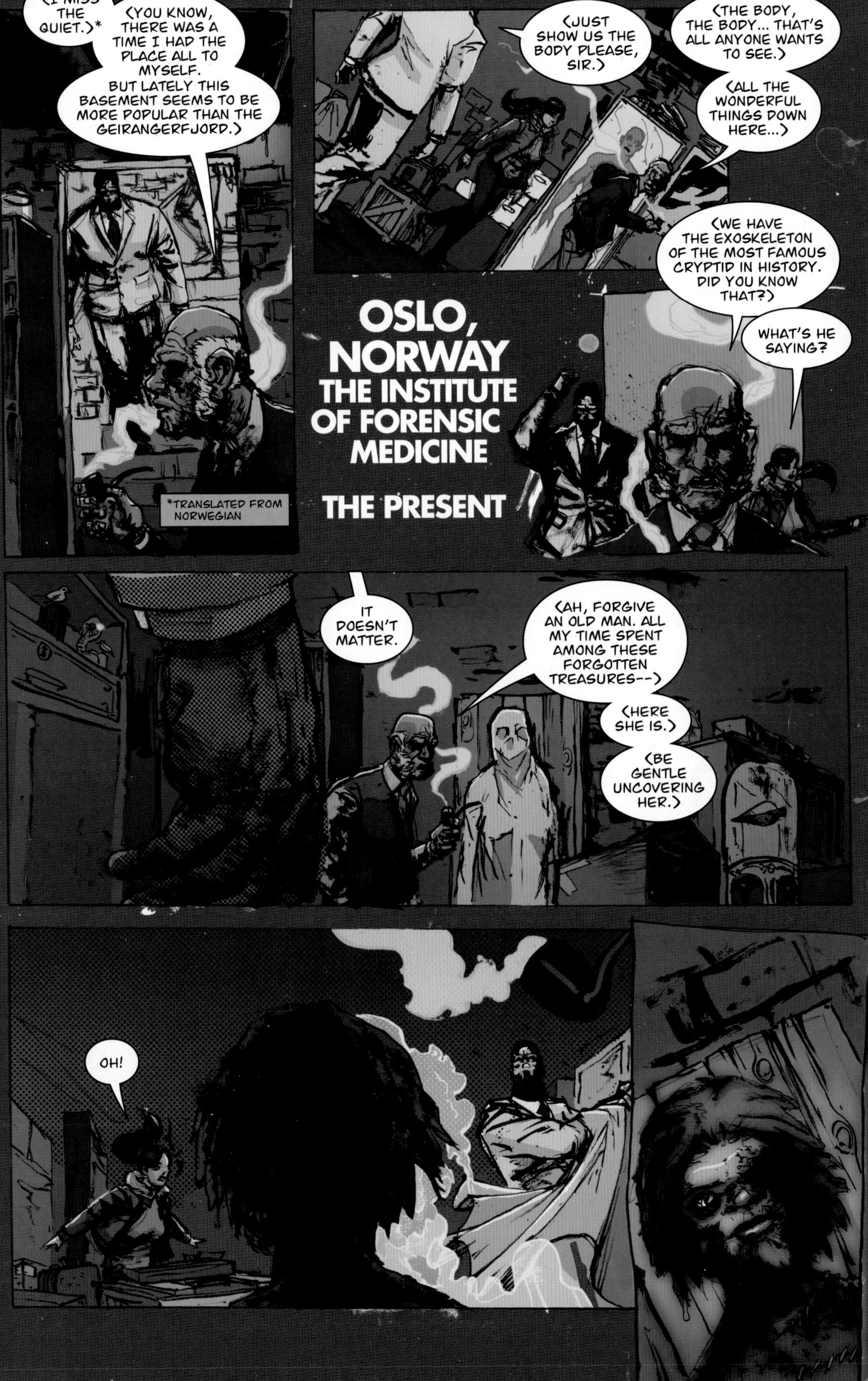

<I MISS THE QUIET.>*
<YOU KNOW, THERE WAS A TIME I HAD THE PLACE ALL TO MYSELF. BUT LATELY THIS BASEMENT SEEMS TO BE MORE POPULAR THAN THE GEIRANGERFJORD.>
*TRANSLATED FROM NORWEGIAN
<JUST SHOW US THE BODY PLEASE, SIR.>
<THE BODY, THE BODY... THAT'S ALL ANYONE WANTS TO SEE.>
<ALL THE WONDERFUL THINGS DOWN HERE...>
OSLO, NORWAY THE INSTITUTE OF FORENSIC MEDICINE
THE PRESENT
<WE HAVE THE EXOSKELETON OF THE MOST FAMOUS CRYPTID IN HISTORY. DID YOU KNOW THAT?>
WHAT'S HE SAYING?
IT DOESN'T MATTER.
<AH, FORGIVE AN OLD MAN. ALL MY TIME SPENT AMONG THESE FORGOTTEN TREASURES-->
<HERE SHE IS.>
<BE GENTLE UNCOVERING HER.>
OH!

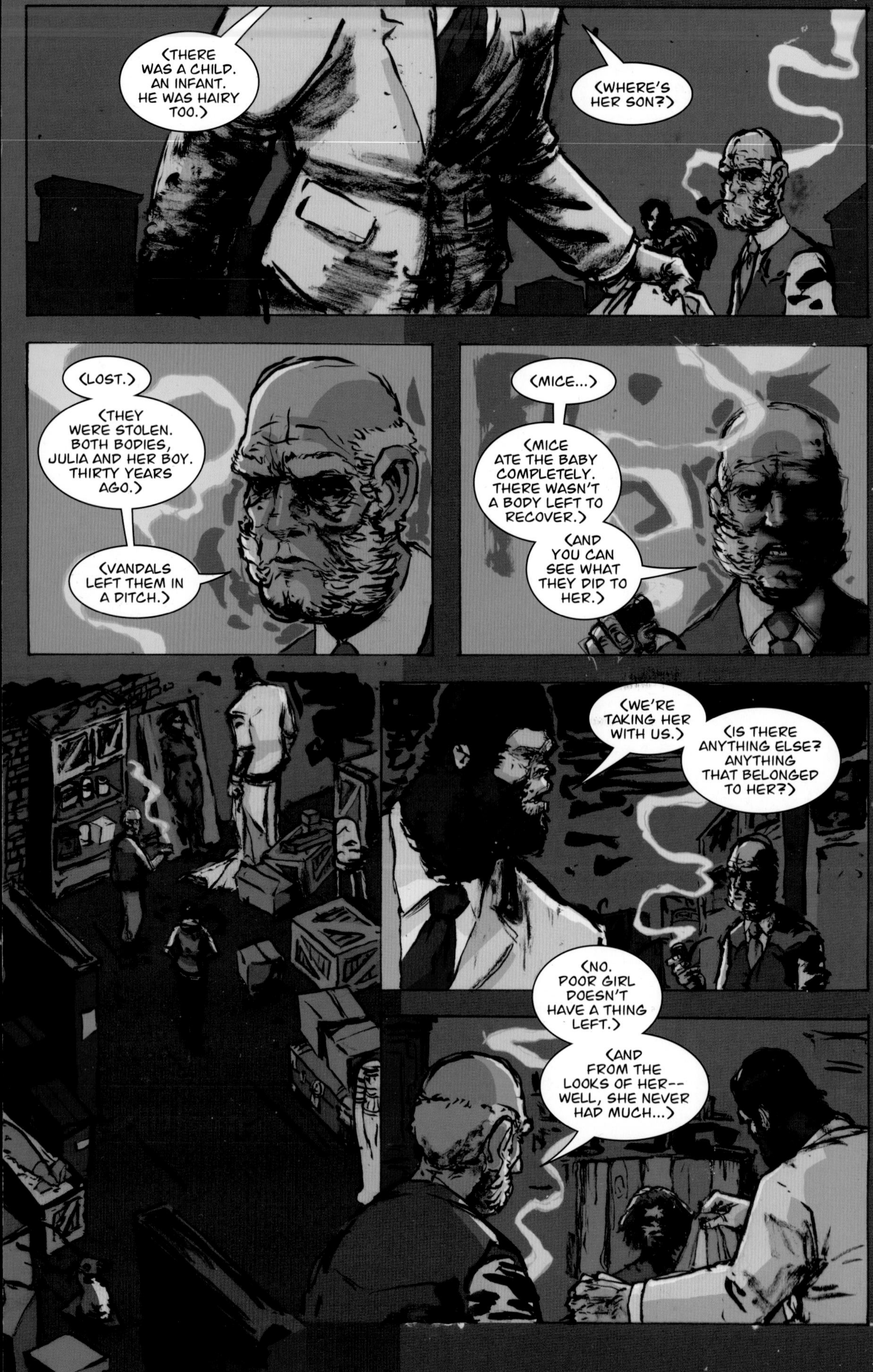
(THERE WAS A CHILD. AN INFANT. HE WAS HAIRY TOO.)
(WHERE'S HER SON?)
(LOST.)
(THEY WERE STOLEN. BOTH BODIES, JULIA AND HER BOY. THIRTY YEARS AGO.)
(VANDALS LEFT THEM IN A DITCH.)
(MICE...)
(MICE ATE THE BABY COMPLETELY. THERE WASN'T A BODY LEFT TO RECOVER.)
(AND YOU CAN SEE WHAT THEY DID TO HER.)
(WE'RE TAKING HER WITH US.)
(IS THERE ANYTHING ELSE? ANYTHING THAT BELONGED TO HER?)
(NO. POOR GIRL DOESN'T HAVE A THING LEFT.)
(AND FROM THE LOOKS OF HER--WELL, SHE NEVER HAD MUCH...)

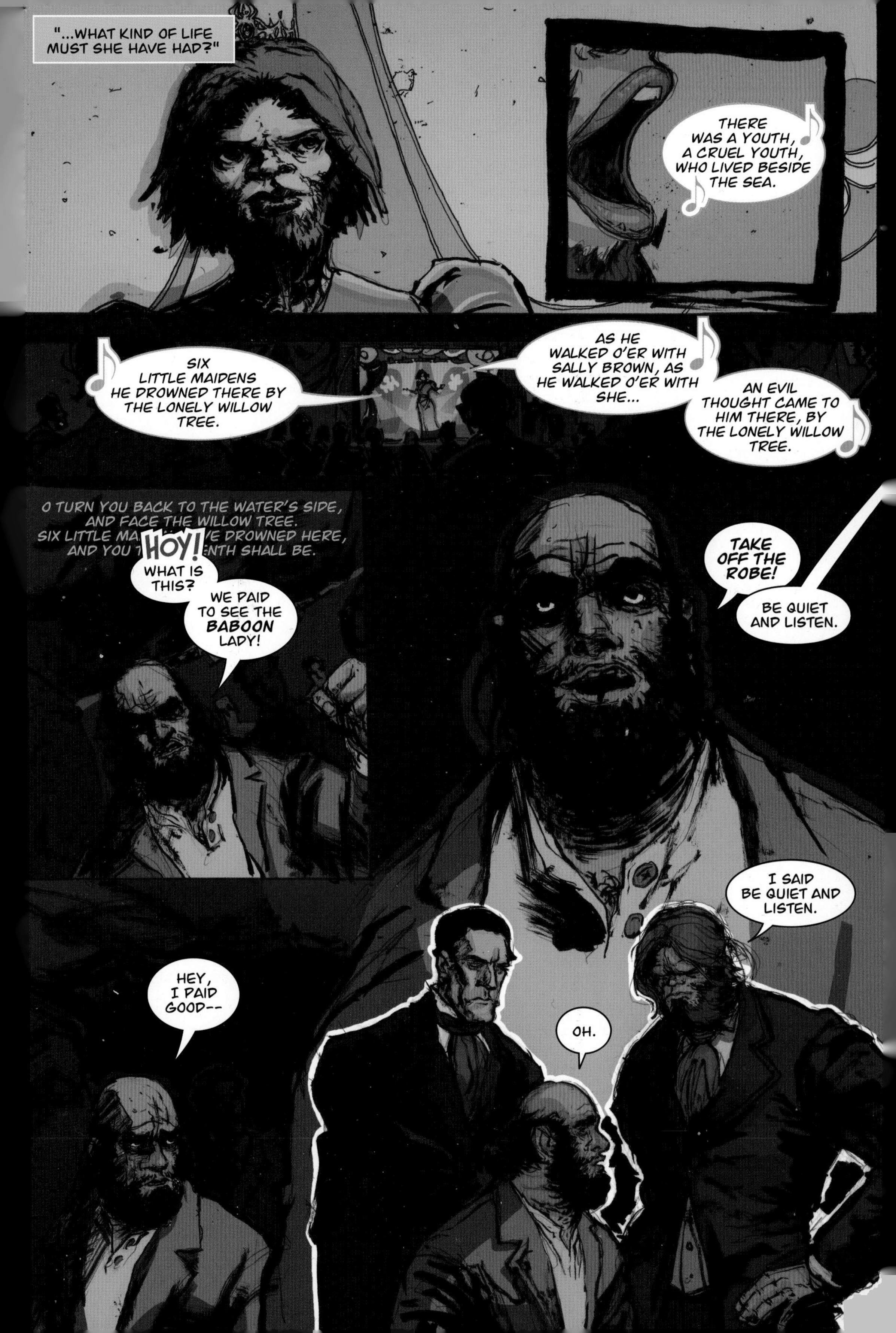
"...WHAT KIND OF LIFE MUST SHE HAVE HAD?"
THERE WAS A YOUTH, A CRUEL YOUTH, WHO LIVED BESIDE THE SEA.
SIX LITTLE MAIDENS HE DROWNED THERE BY THE LONELY WILLOW TREE.
AS HE WALKED O'ER WITH SALLY BROWN, AS HE WALKED O'ER WITH SHE...
AN EVIL THOUGHT CAME TO HIM THERE, BY THE LONELY WILLOW TREE.
O TURN YOU BACK TO THE WATER'S SIDE, AND FACE THE WILLOW TREE.
SIX LITTLE MA VE DROWNED HERE, AND YOU T ENTH SHALL BE.
HOY!
WHAT IS THIS?
WE PAID TO SEE THE **BABOON** LADY!
TAKE OFF THE ROBE!
BE QUIET AND LISTEN.
I SAID BE QUIET AND LISTEN.
HEY, I PAID GOOD--
OH.

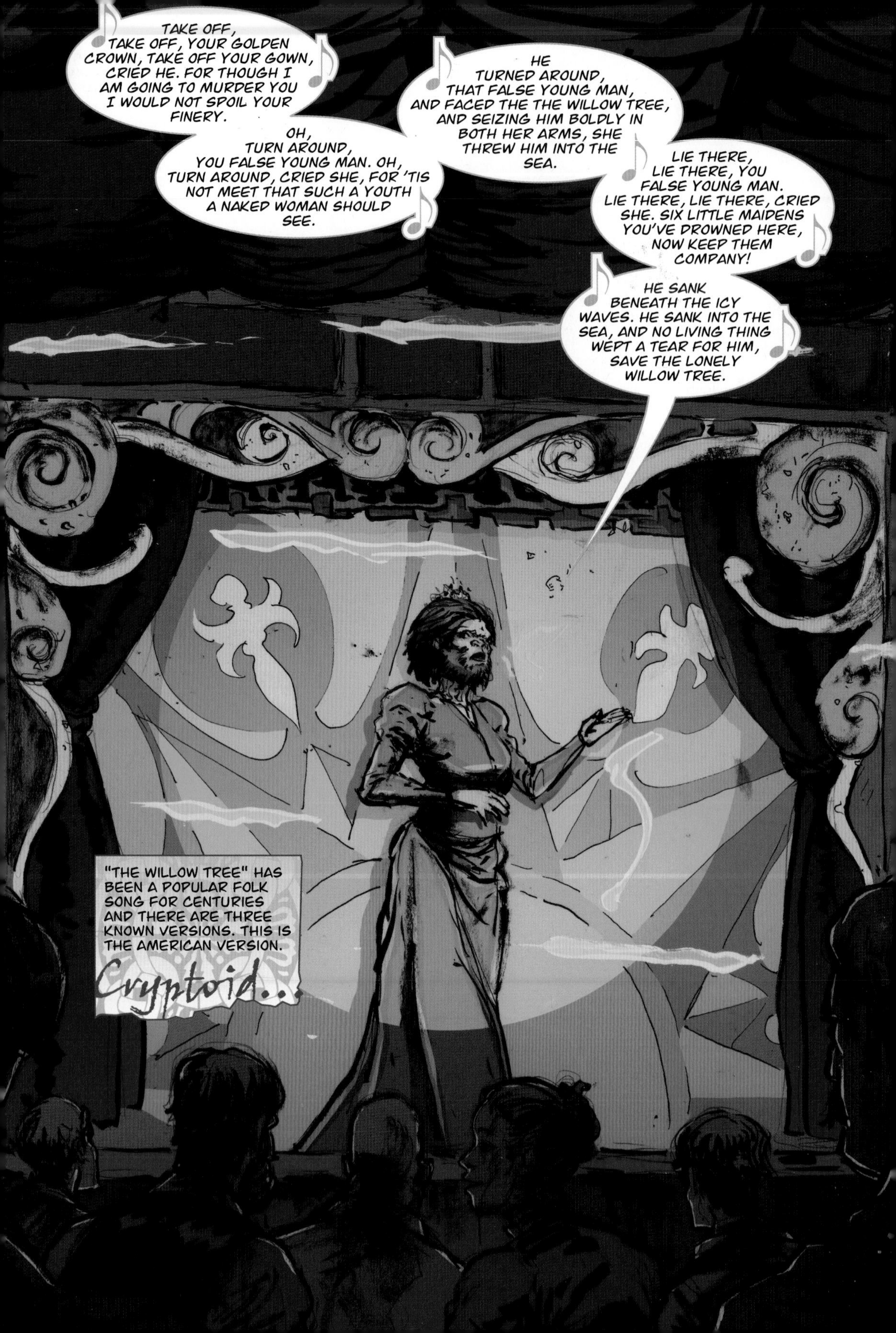
TAKE OFF, TAKE OFF, YOUR GOLDEN CROWN, TAKE OFF YOUR GOWN, CRIED HE. FOR THOUGH I AM GOING TO MURDER YOU I WOULD NOT SPOIL YOUR FINERY.
OH, TURN AROUND, YOU FALSE YOUNG MAN. OH, TURN AROUND, CRIED SHE, FOR 'TIS NOT MEET THAT SUCH A YOUTH A NAKED WOMAN SHOULD SEE.
HE TURNED AROUND, THAT FALSE YOUNG MAN, AND FACED THE THE WILLOW TREE, AND SEIZING HIM BOLDLY IN BOTH HER ARMS, SHE THREW HIM INTO THE SEA.
LIE THERE, LIE THERE, YOU FALSE YOUNG MAN. LIE THERE, LIE THERE, CRIED SHE. SIX LITTLE MAIDENS YOU'VE DROWNED HERE, NOW KEEP THEM COMPANY!
HE SANK BENEATH THE ICY WAVES. HE SANK INTO THE SEA, AND NO LIVING THING WEPT A TEAR FOR HIM, SAVE THE LONELY WILLOW TREE.
"THE WILLOW TREE" HAS BEEN A POPULAR FOLK SONG FOR CENTURIES AND THERE ARE THREE KNOWN VERSIONS. THIS IS THE AMERICAN VERSION.
Cryptoid...

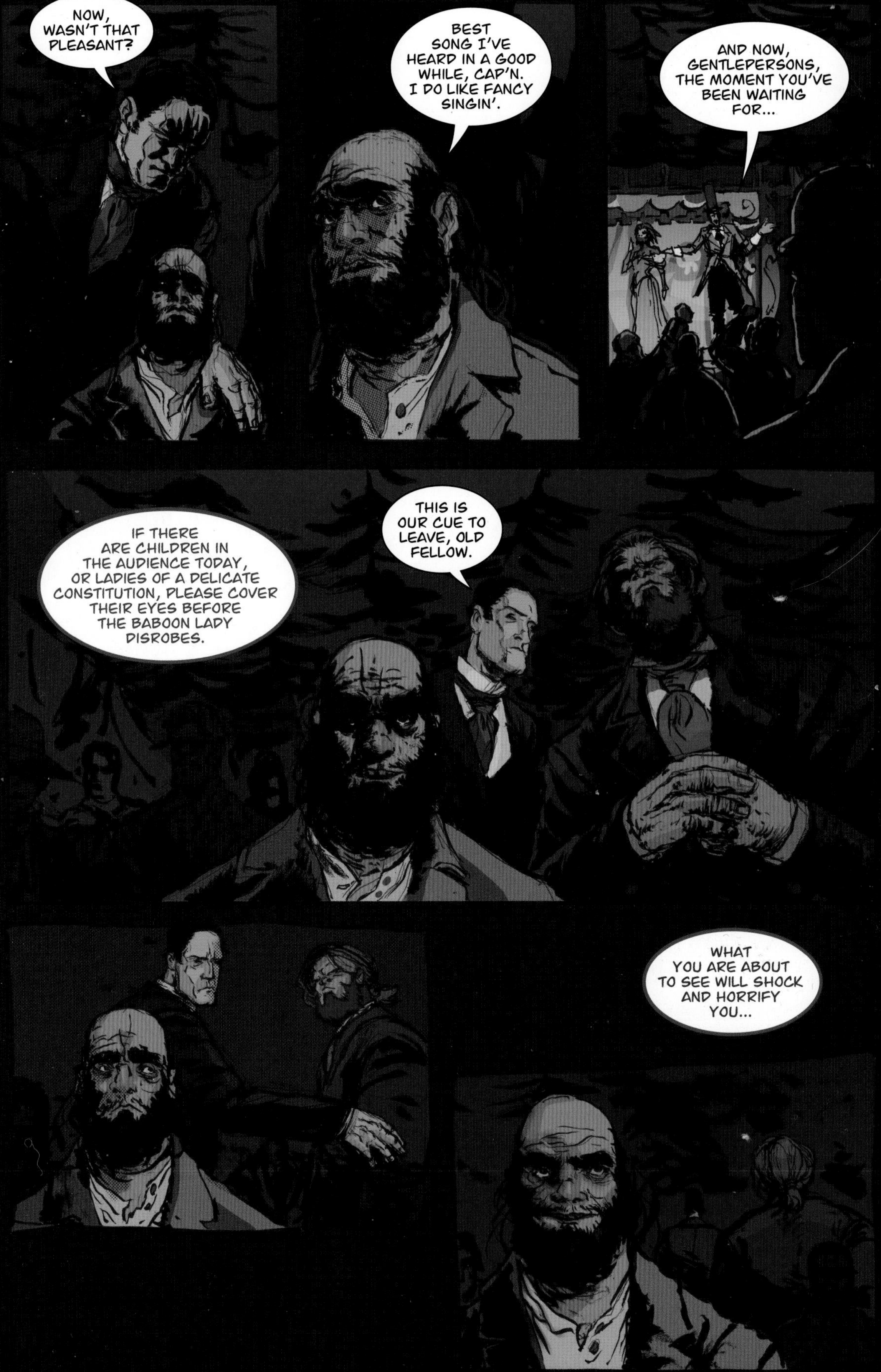
NOW, WASN'T THAT PLEASANT?
BEST SONG I'VE HEARD IN A GOOD WHILE, CAP'N. I DO LIKE FANCY SINGIN'.
AND NOW, GENTLEPERSONS, THE MOMENT YOU'VE BEEN WAITING FOR...
IF THERE ARE CHILDREN IN THE AUDIENCE TODAY, OR LADIES OF A DELICATE CONSTITUTION, PLEASE COVER THEIR EYES BEFORE THE BABOON LADY DISROBES.
THIS IS OUR CUE TO LEAVE, OLD FELLOW.
WHAT YOU ARE ABOUT TO SEE WILL SHOCK AND HORRIFY YOU...

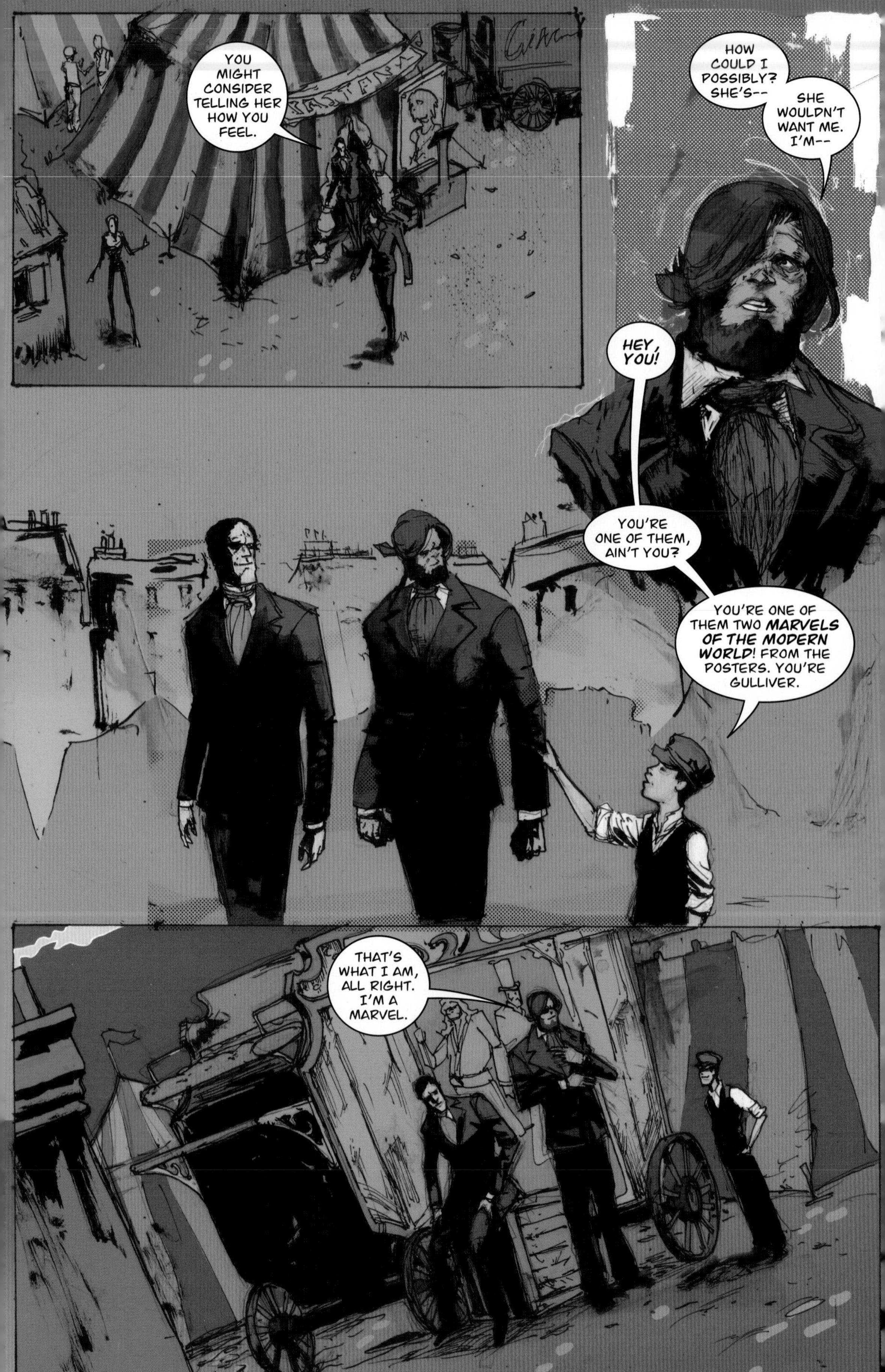

YOU MIGHT CONSIDER TELLING HER HOW YOU FEEL.
HOW COULD I POSSIBLY? SHE'S--
SHE WOULDN'T WANT ME. I'M--
HEY, YOU!
YOU'RE ONE OF THEM, AIN'T YOU?
YOU'RE ONE OF THEM TWO MARVELS OF THE MODERN WORLD! FROM THE POSTERS. YOU'RE GULLIVER.
THAT'S WHAT I AM, ALL RIGHT. I'M A MARVEL.

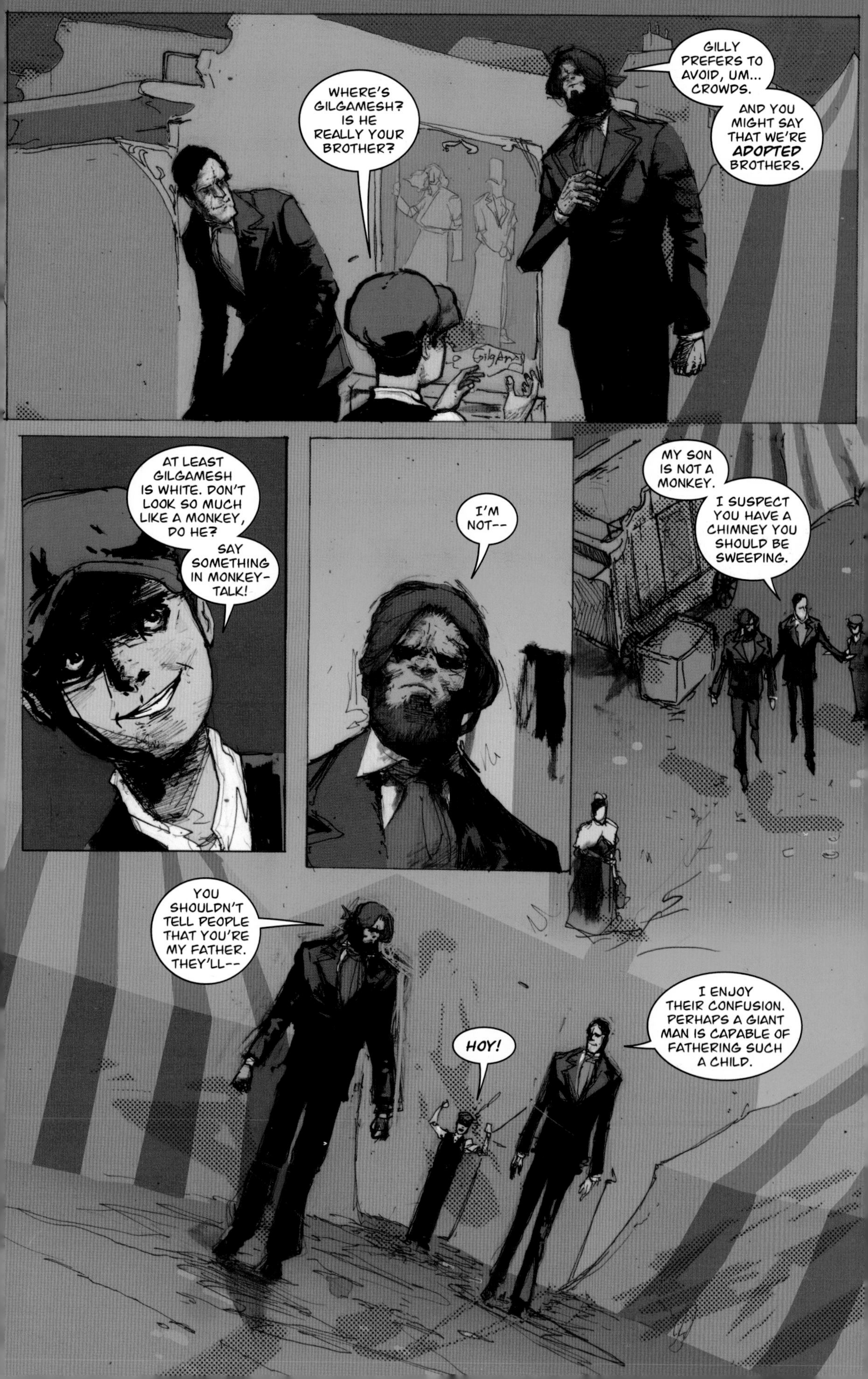
WHERE'S GILGAMESH? IS HE REALLY YOUR BROTHER?
GILLY PREFERS TO AVOID, UM... CROWDS.
AND YOU MIGHT SAY THAT WE'RE *ADOPTED* BROTHERS.
AT LEAST GILGAMESH IS WHITE. DON'T LOOK SO MUCH LIKE A MONKEY, DO HE?
SAY SOMETHING IN MONKEY-TALK!
I'M NOT--
MY SON IS NOT A MONKEY.
I SUSPECT YOU HAVE A CHIMNEY YOU SHOULD BE SWEEPING.
YOU SHOULDN'T TELL PEOPLE THAT YOU'RE MY FATHER. THEY'LL--
HOY!
I ENJOY THEIR CONFUSION. PERHAPS A GIANT MAN IS CAPABLE OF FATHERING SUCH A CHILD.

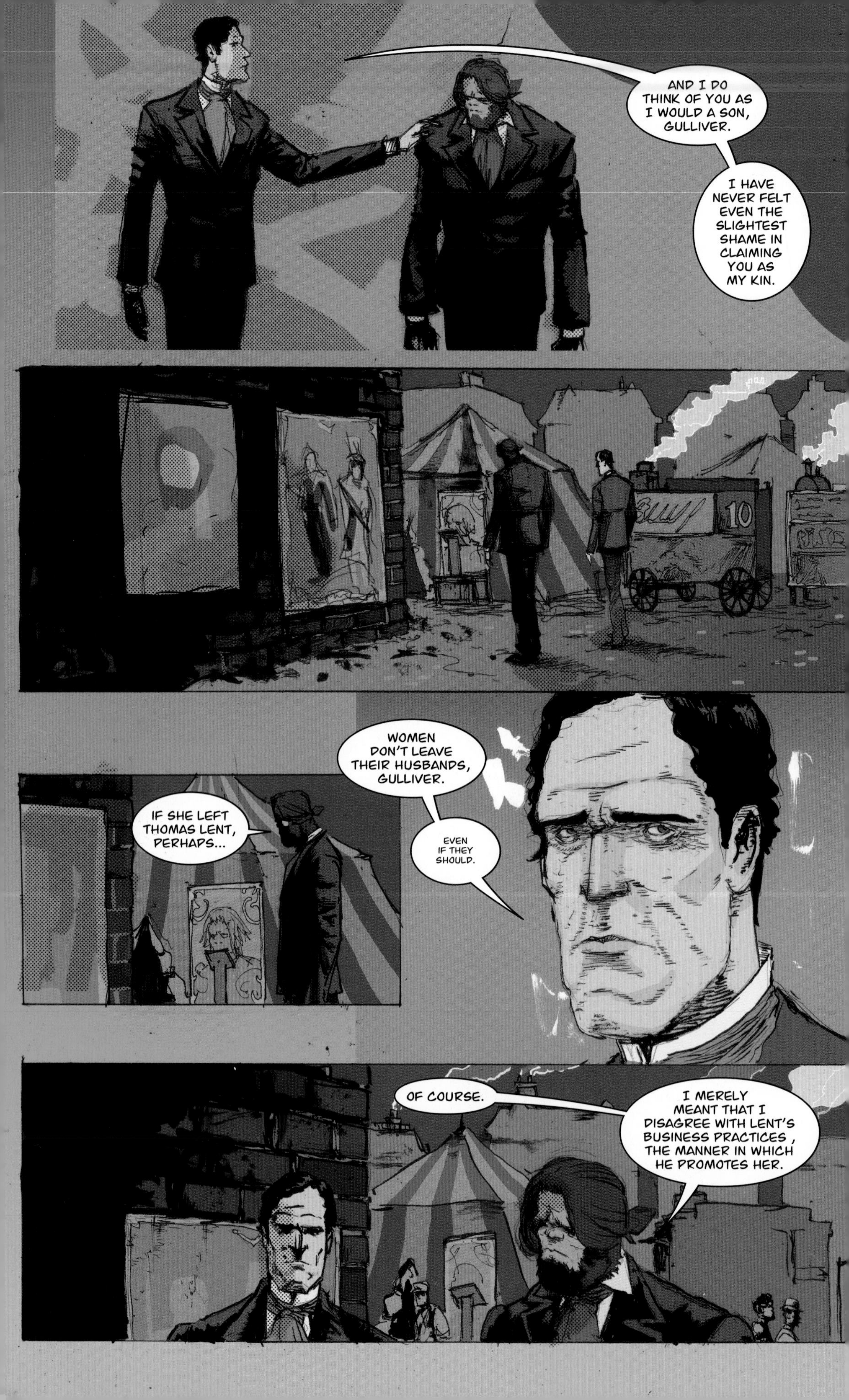
AND I DO THINK OF YOU AS I WOULD A SON, GULLIVER.
I HAVE NEVER FELT EVEN THE SLIGHTEST SHAME IN CLAIMING YOU AS MY KIN.
IF SHE LEFT THOMAS LENT, PERHAPS...
WOMEN DON'T LEAVE THEIR HUSBANDS, GULLIVER.
EVEN IF THEY SHOULD.
OF COURSE.
I MERELY MEANT THAT I DISAGREE WITH LENT'S BUSINESS PRACTICES , THE MANNER IN WHICH HE PROMOTES HER.

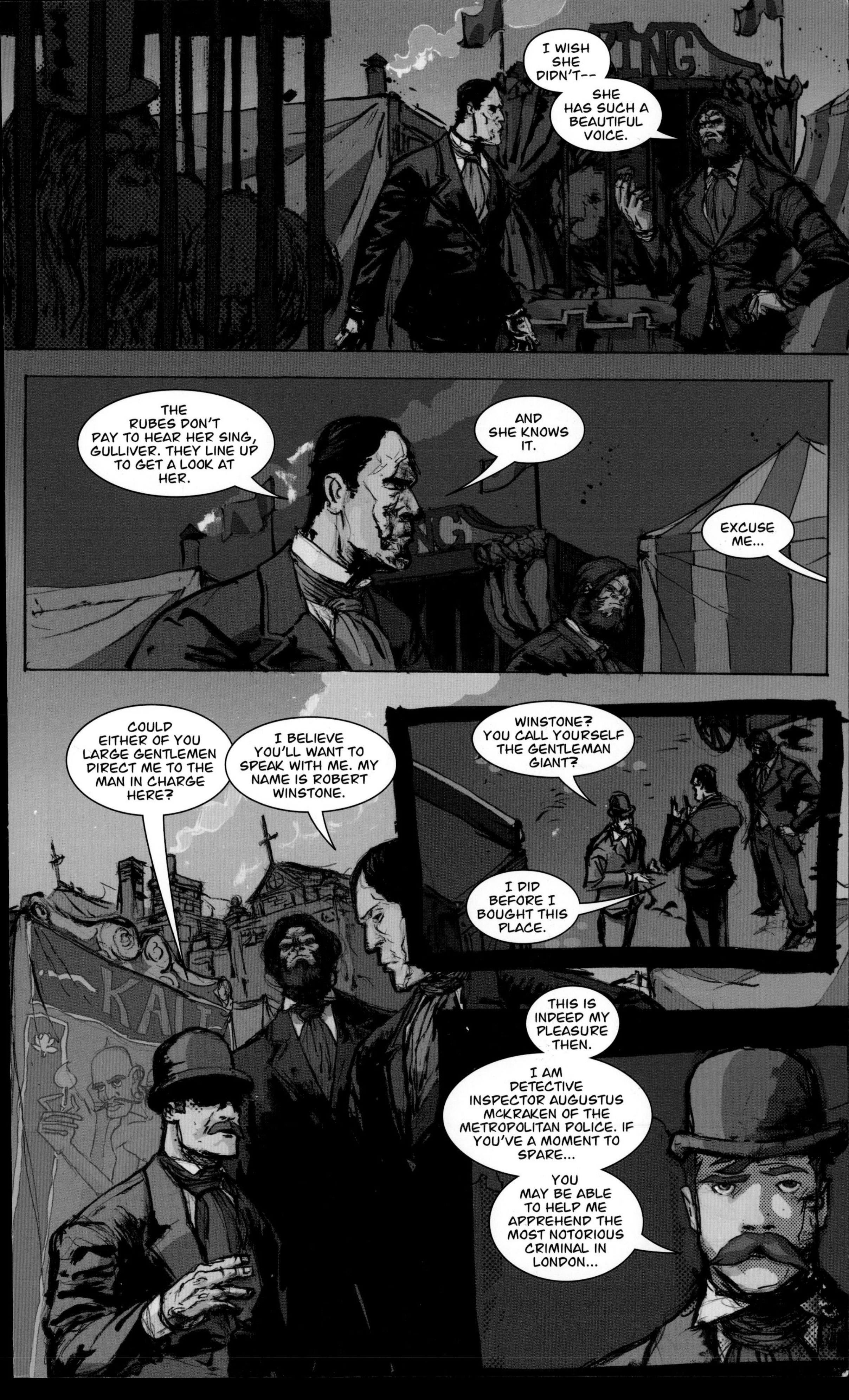
I WISH SHE DIDN'T--
SHE HAS SUCH A BEAUTIFUL VOICE.
THE RUBES DON'T PAY TO HEAR HER SING, GULLIVER. THEY LINE UP TO GET A LOOK AT HER.
AND SHE KNOWS IT.
EXCUSE ME...
COULD EITHER OF YOU LARGE GENTLEMEN DIRECT ME TO THE MAN IN CHARGE HERE?
I BELIEVE YOU'LL WANT TO SPEAK WITH ME. MY NAME IS ROBERT WINSTONE.
WINSTONE? YOU CALL YOURSELF THE GENTLEMAN GIANT?
I DID BEFORE I BOUGHT THIS PLACE.
THIS IS INDEED MY PLEASURE THEN.
I AM DETECTIVE INSPECTOR AUGUSTUS MCKRAKEN OF THE METROPOLITAN POLICE. IF YOU'VE A MOMENT TO SPARE...
YOU MAY BE ABLE TO HELP ME APPREHEND THE MOST NOTORIOUS CRIMINAL IN LONDON...

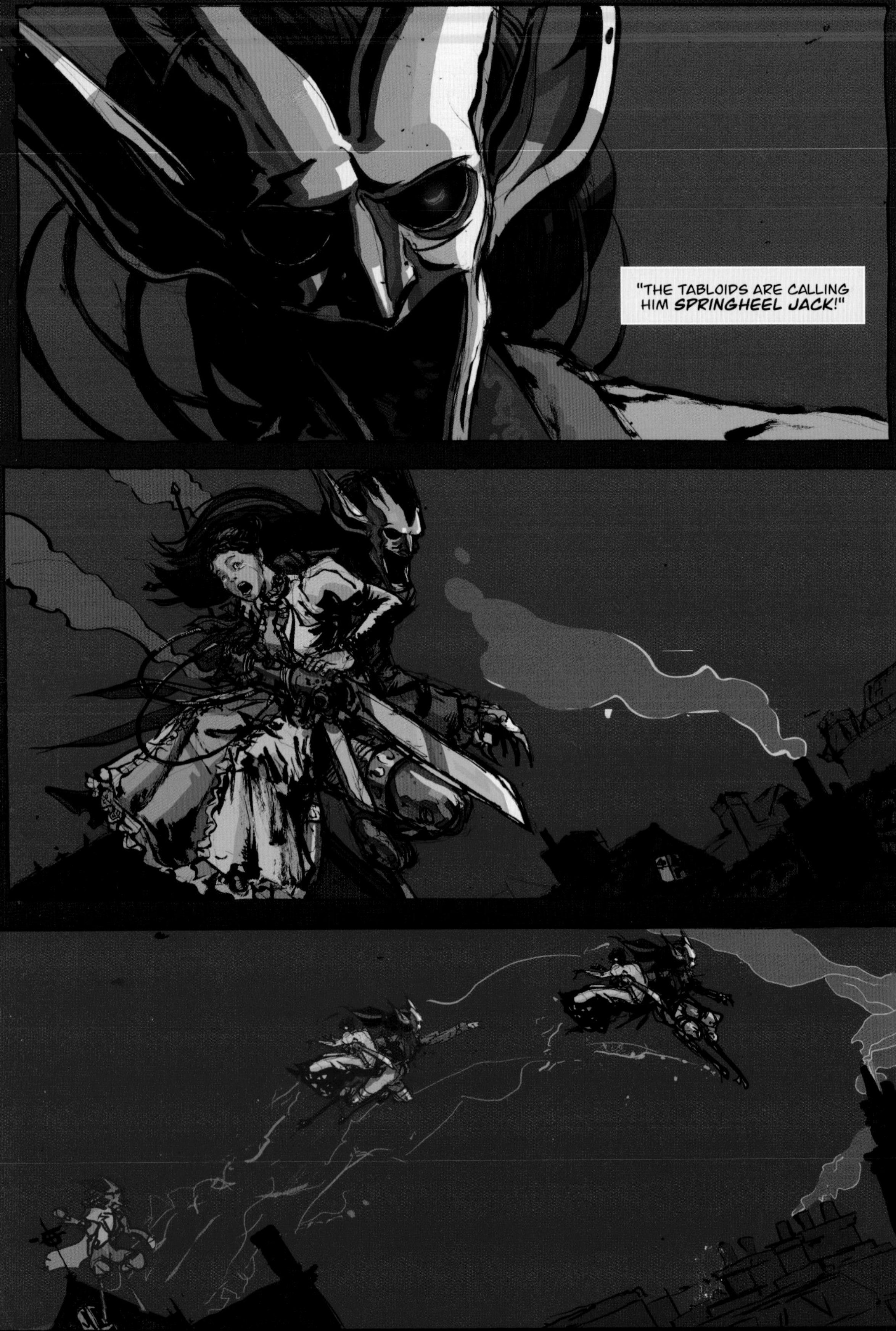
"THE TABLOIDS ARE CALLING HIM SPRINGHEEL JACK!"

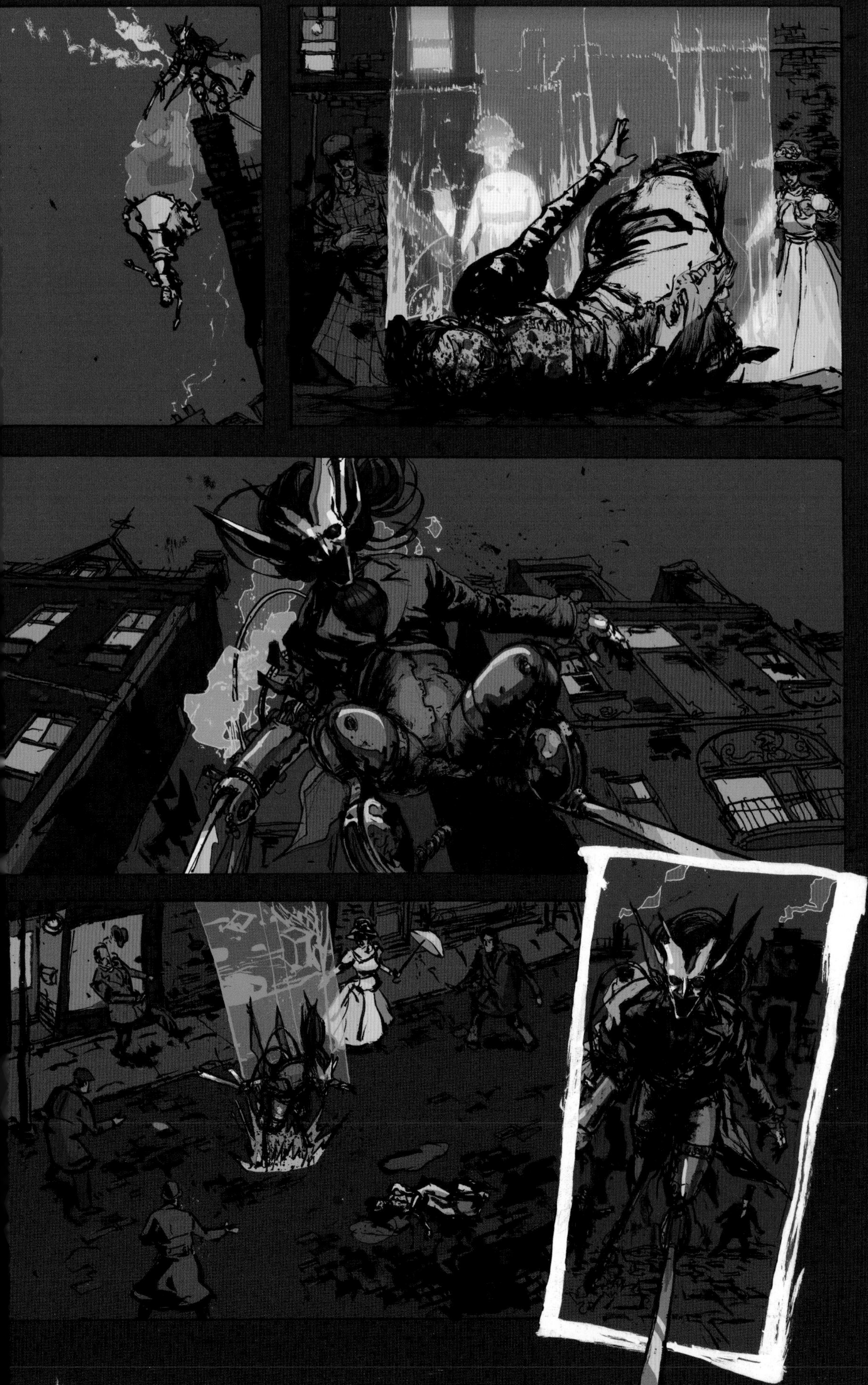

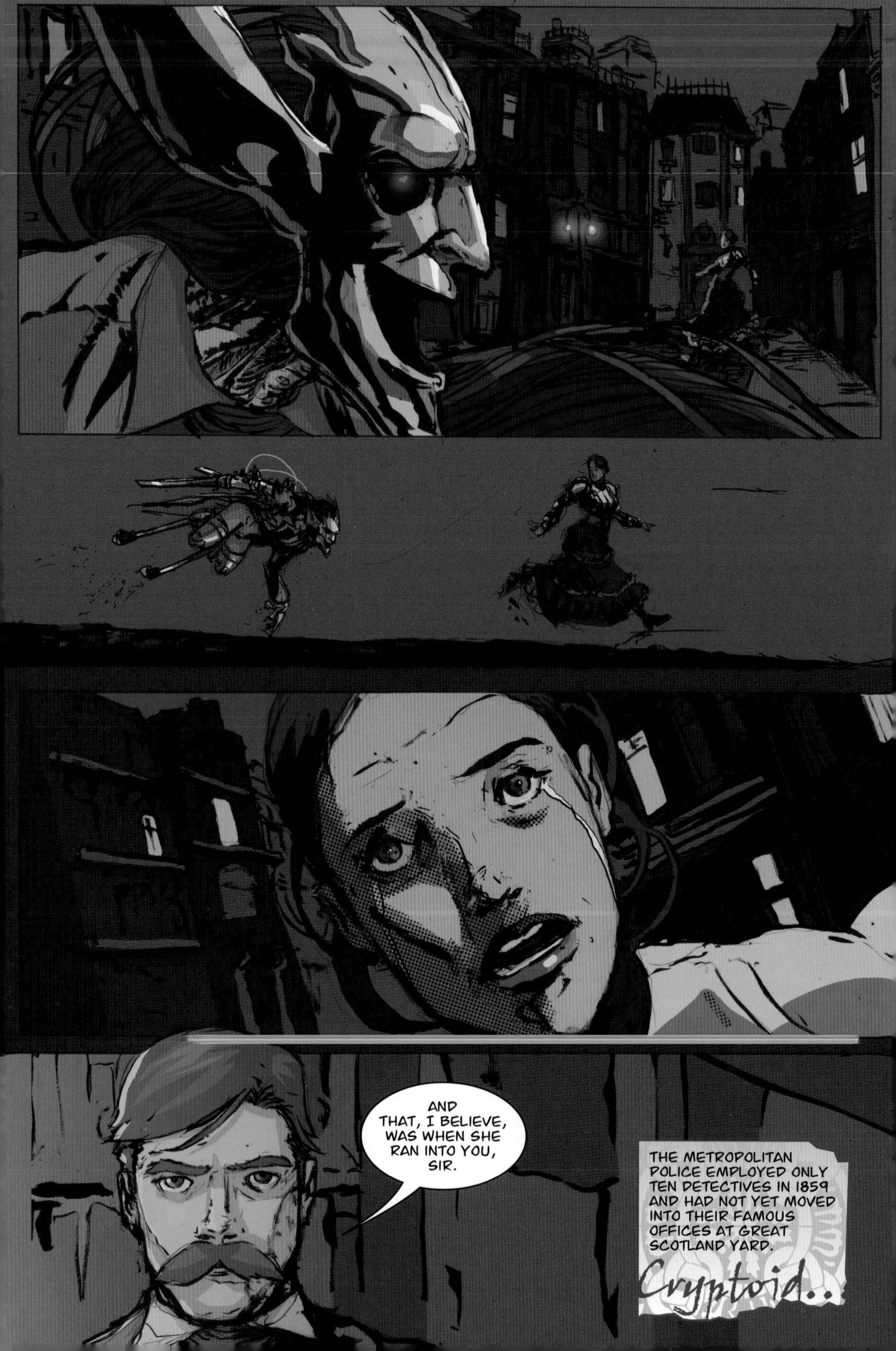
AND THAT, I BELIEVE, WAS WHEN SHE RAN INTO YOU, SIR.
THE METROPOLITAN POLICE EMPLOYED ONLY TEN DETECTIVES IN 1859 AND HAD NOT YET MOVED INTO THEIR FAMOUS OFFICES AT GREAT SCOTLAND YARD.
Cryptoid..

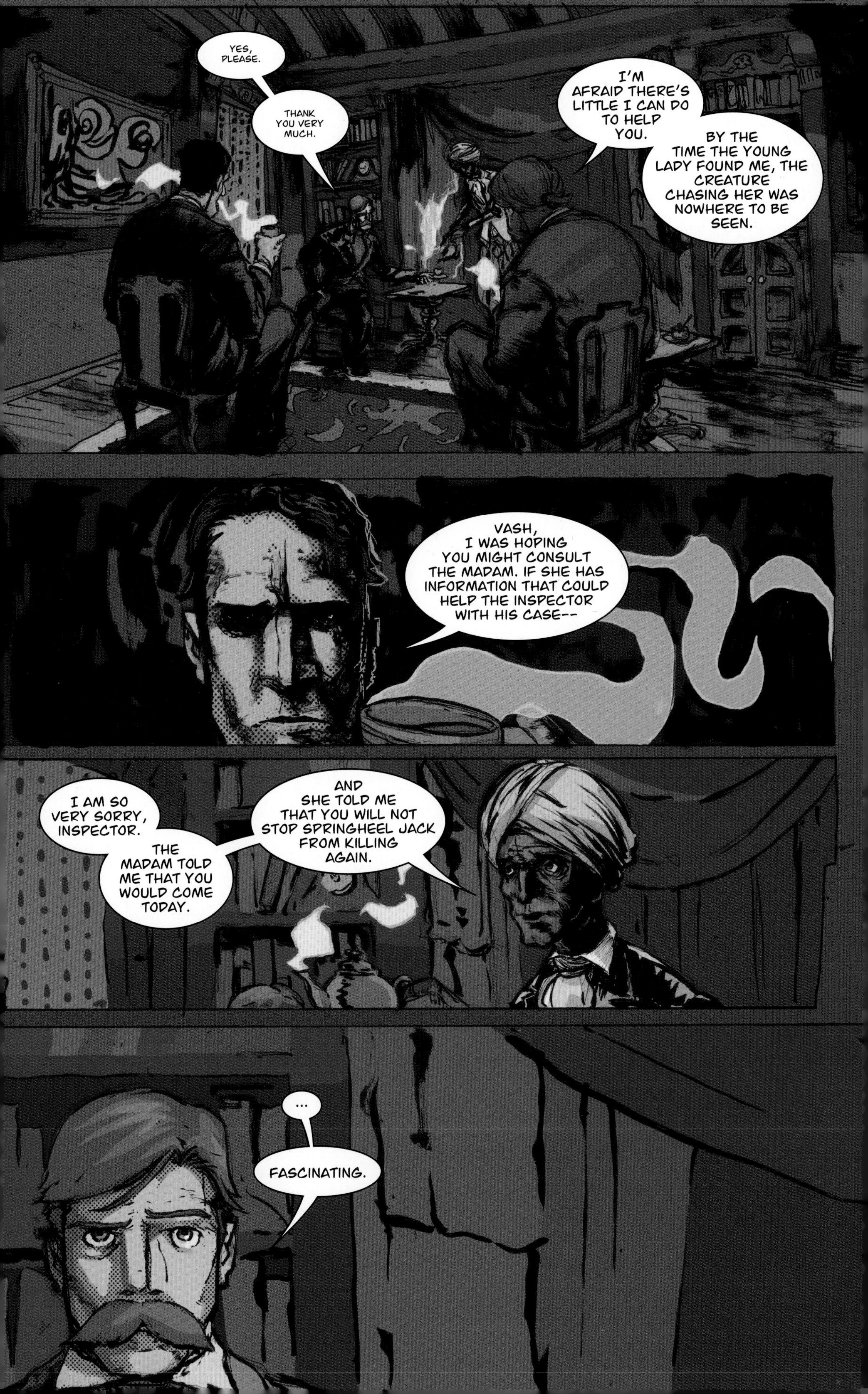
YES, PLEASE.
THANK YOU VERY MUCH.
I'M AFRAID THERE'S LITTLE I CAN DO TO HELP YOU.
BY THE TIME THE YOUNG LADY FOUND ME, THE CREATURE CHASING HER WAS NOWHERE TO BE SEEN.
VASH, I WAS HOPING YOU MIGHT CONSULT THE MADAM. IF SHE HAS INFORMATION THAT COULD HELP THE INSPECTOR WITH HIS CASE--
I AM SO VERY SORRY, INSPECTOR.
THE MADAM TOLD ME THAT YOU WOULD COME TODAY.
AND SHE TOLD ME THAT YOU WILL NOT STOP SPRINGHEEL JACK FROM KILLING AGAIN.
...
FASCINATING.

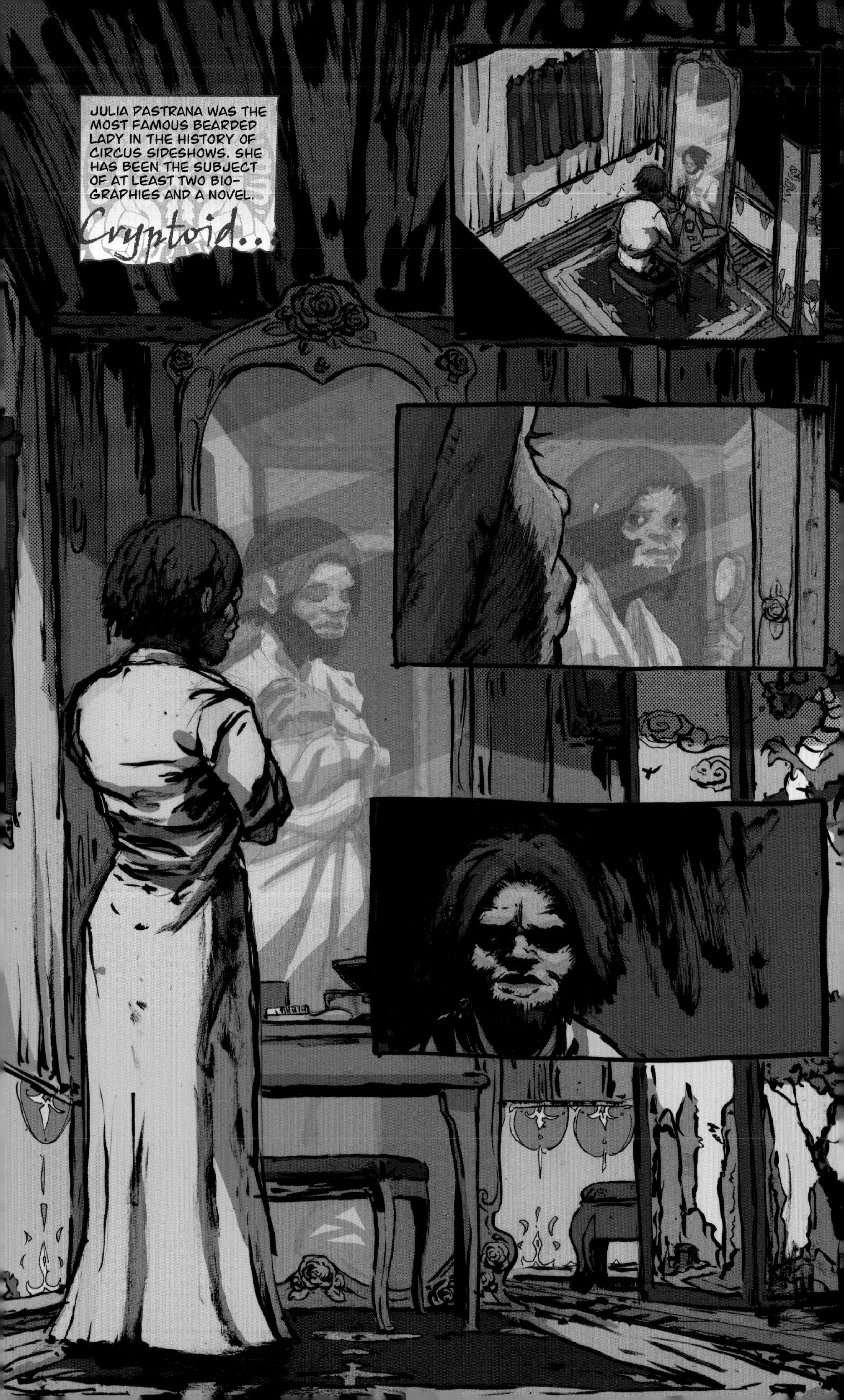
JULIA PASTRANA WAS THE MOST FAMOUS BEARDED LADY IN THE HISTORY OF CIRCUS SIDESHOWS. SHE HAS BEEN THE SUBJECT OF AT LEAST TWO BIOGRAPHIES AND A NOVEL.
Cryptoid..

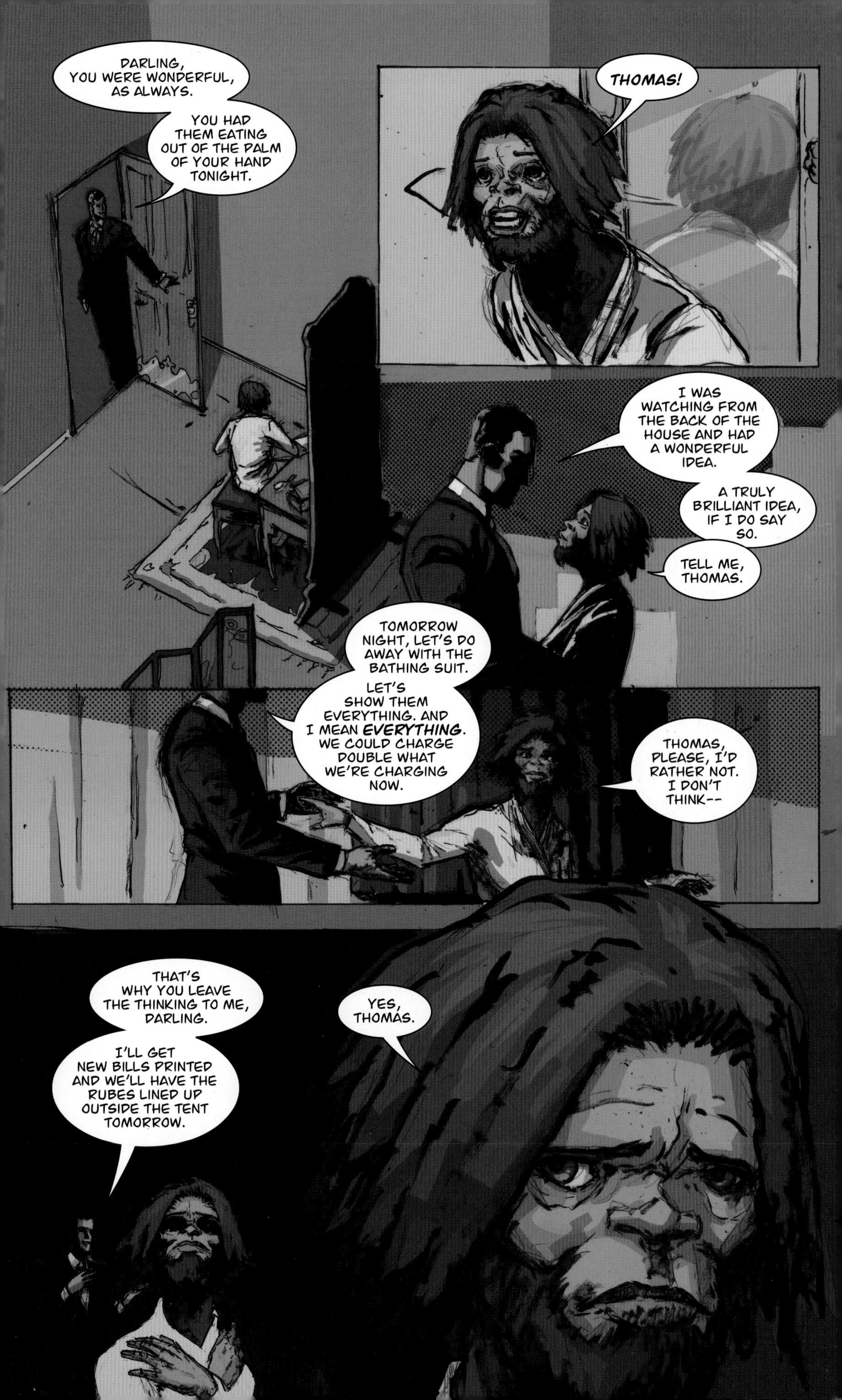
DARLING, YOU WERE WONDERFUL, AS ALWAYS.
YOU HAD THEM EATING OUT OF THE PALM OF YOUR HAND TONIGHT.
THOMAS!
I WAS WATCHING FROM THE BACK OF THE HOUSE AND HAD A WONDERFUL IDEA.
A TRULY BRILLIANT IDEA, IF I DO SAY SO.
TELL ME, THOMAS.
TOMORROW NIGHT, LET'S DO AWAY WITH THE BATHING SUIT.
LET'S SHOW THEM EVERYTHING. AND I MEAN EVERYTHING. WE COULD CHARGE DOUBLE WHAT WE'RE CHARGING NOW.
THOMAS, PLEASE, I'D RATHER NOT. I DON'T THINK--
THAT'S WHY YOU LEAVE THE THINKING TO ME, DARLING.
I'LL GET NEW BILLS PRINTED AND WE'LL HAVE THE RUBES LINED UP OUTSIDE THE TENT TOMORROW.
YES, THOMAS.

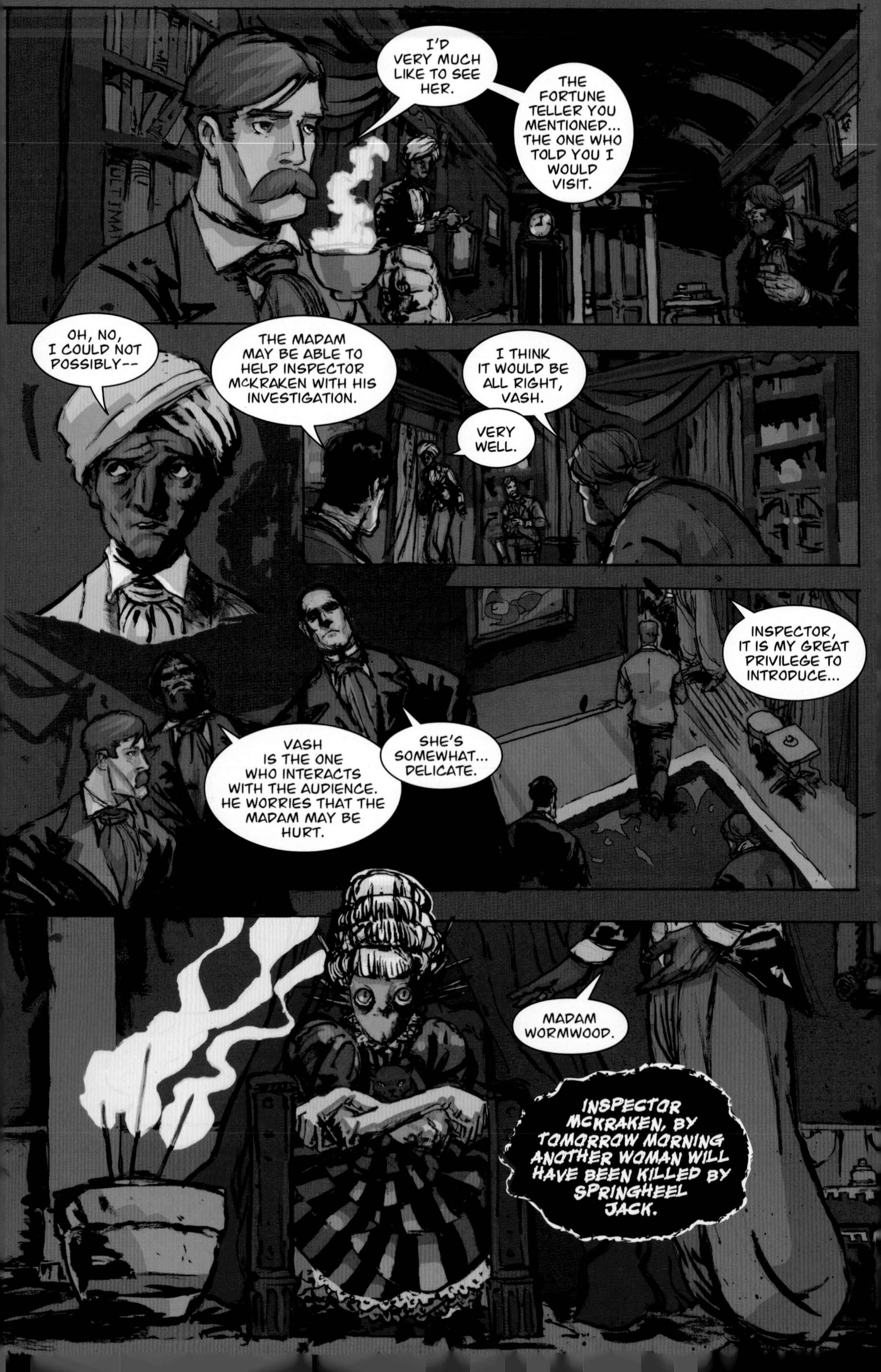
I'D VERY MUCH LIKE TO SEE HER.
THE FORTUNE TELLER YOU MENTIONED... THE ONE WHO TOLD YOU I WOULD VISIT.
OH, NO, I COULD NOT POSSIBLY--
THE MADAM MAY BE ABLE TO HELP INSPECTOR MCKRAKEN WITH HIS INVESTIGATION.
I THINK IT WOULD BE ALL RIGHT, VASH.
VERY WELL.
VASH IS THE ONE WHO INTERACTS WITH THE AUDIENCE. HE WORRIES THAT THE MADAM MAY BE HURT.
SHE'S SOMEWHAT... DELICATE.
INSPECTOR, IT IS MY GREAT PRIVILEGE TO INTRODUCE...
MADAM WORMWOOD.
INSPECTOR MCKRAKEN, BY TOMORROW MORNING ANOTHER WOMAN WILL HAVE BEEN KILLED BY SPRINGHEEL JACK.

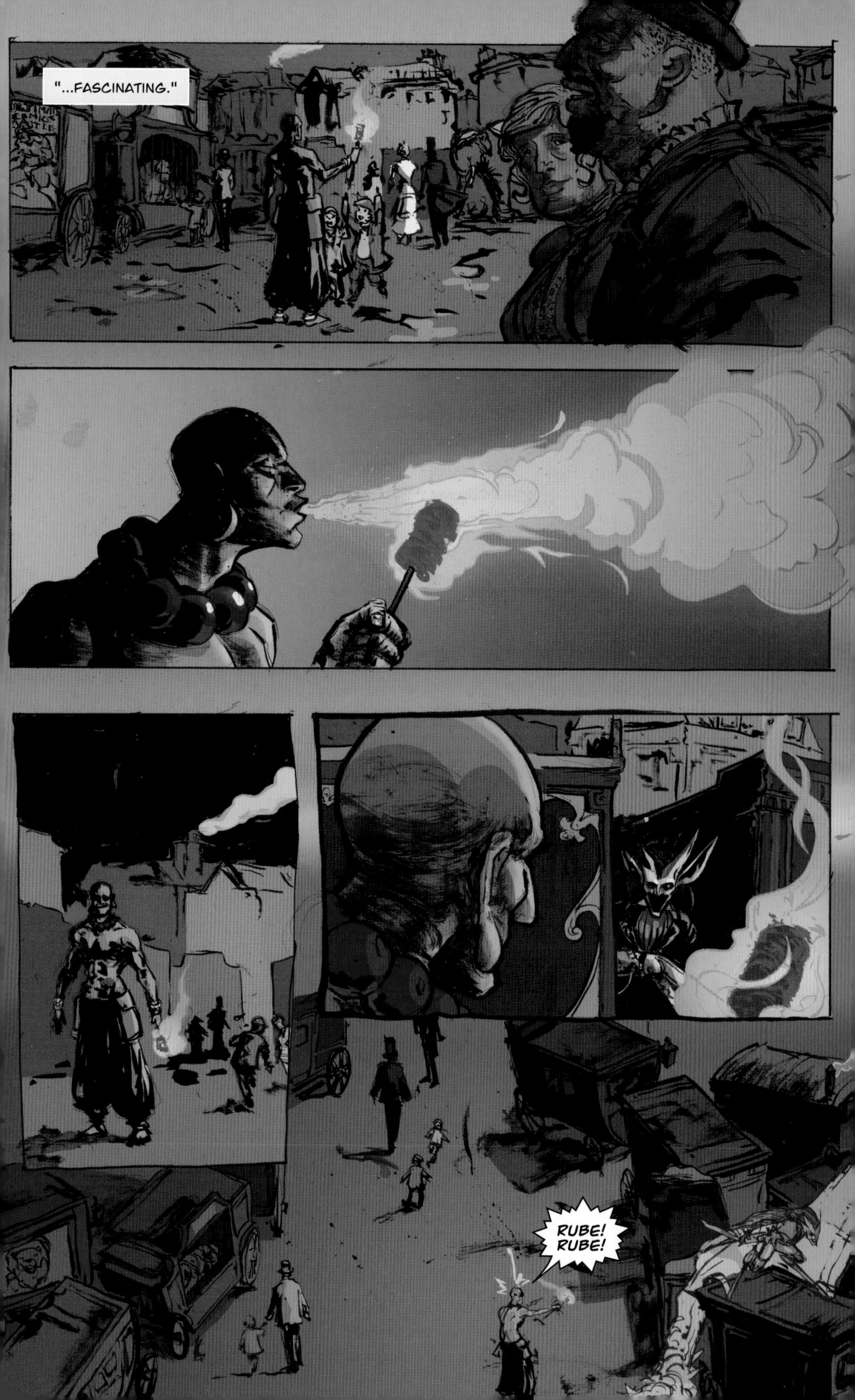
"...FASCINATING."
RUBE! RUBE!

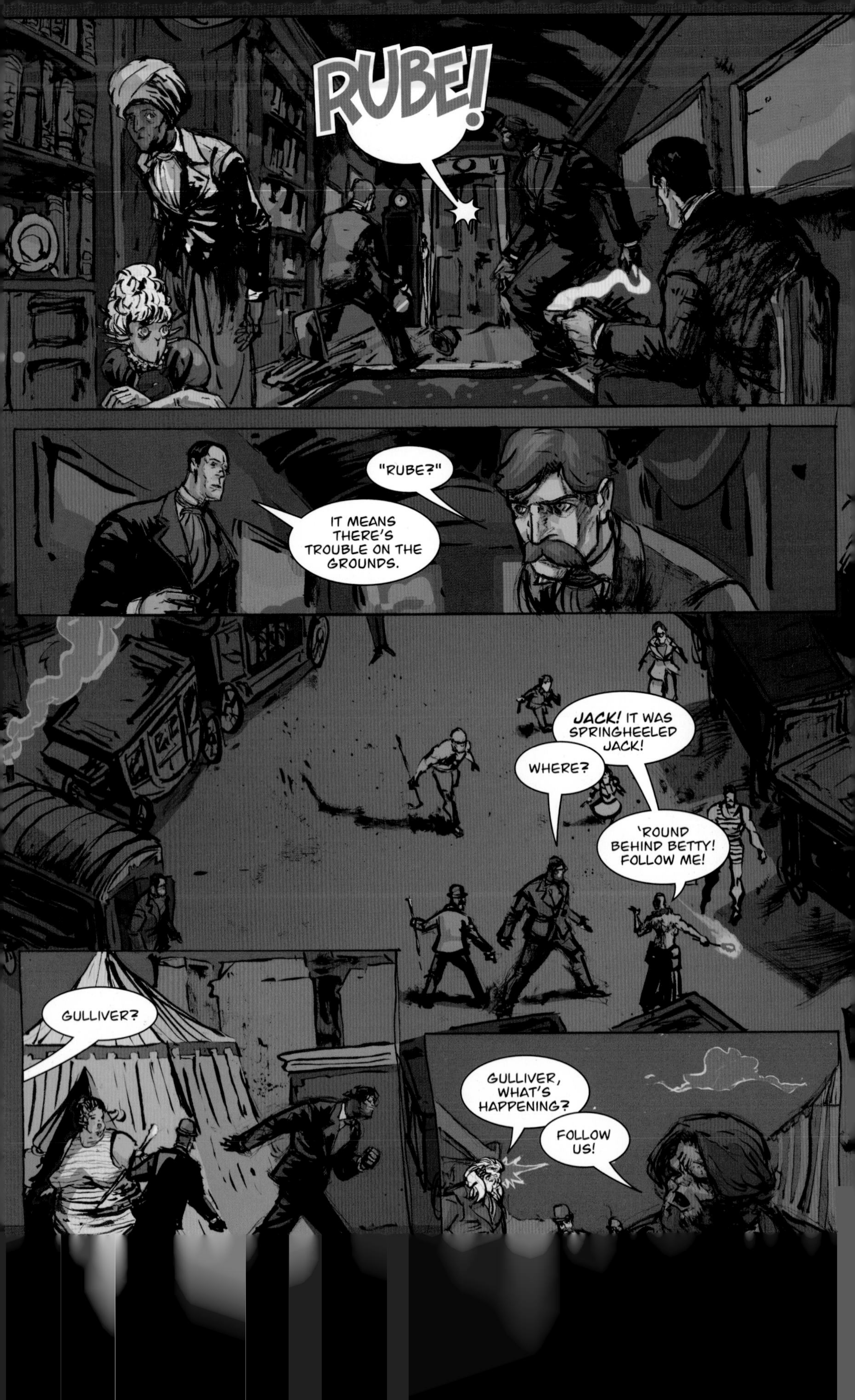
RUBE!
"RUBE?"
IT MEANS THERE'S TROUBLE ON THE GROUNDS.
JACK! IT WAS SPRINGHEELED JACK!
WHERE?
'ROUND BEHIND BETTY! FOLLOW ME!
GULLIVER?
GULLIVER, WHAT'S HAPPENING?
FOLLOW US!

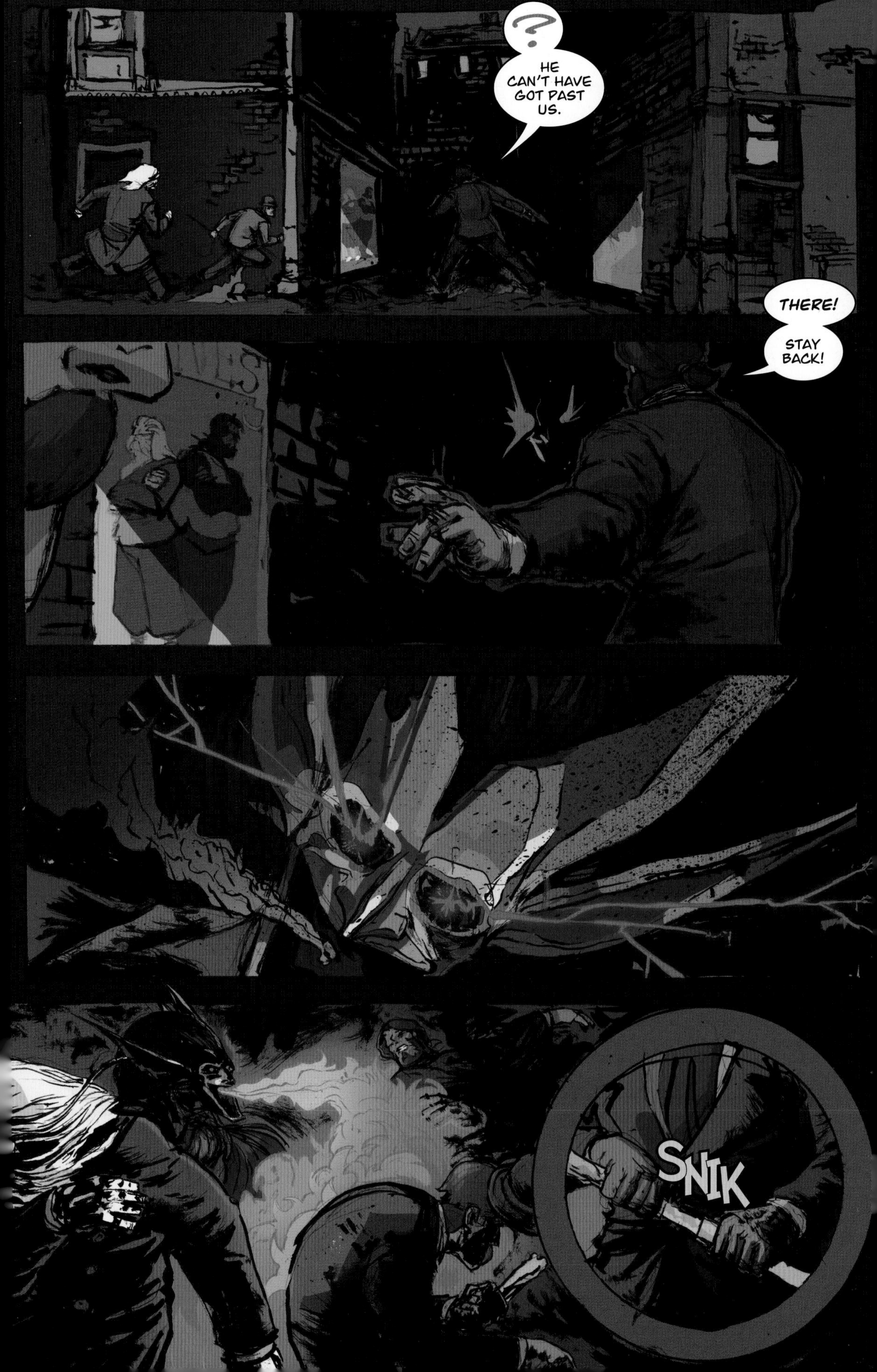
?
HE CAN'T HAVE GOT PAST US.
THERE!
STAY BACK!
SNIK

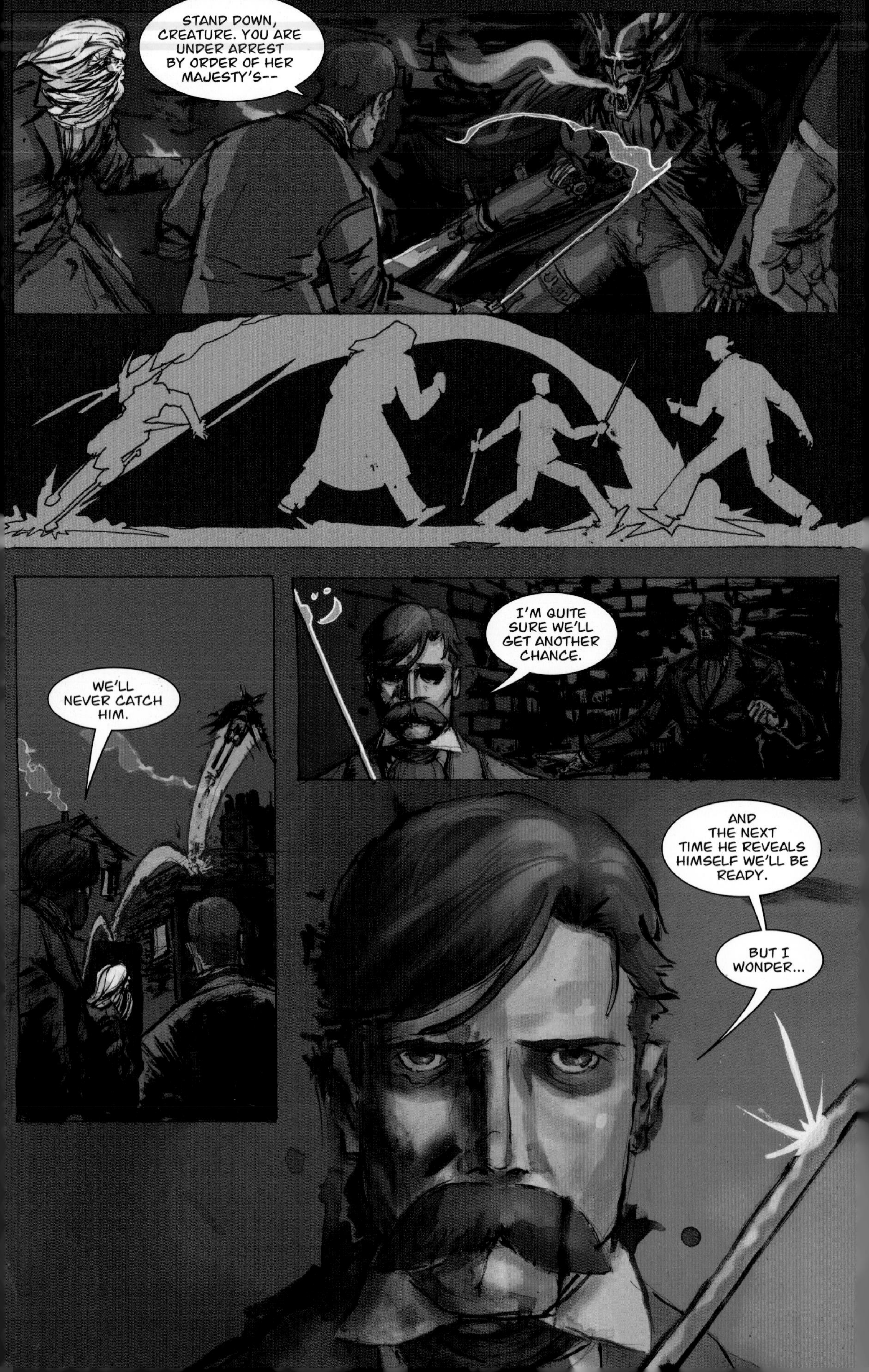
STAND DOWN, CREATURE. YOU ARE UNDER ARREST BY ORDER OF HER MAJESTY'S--
WE'LL NEVER CATCH HIM.
I'M QUITE SURE WE'LL GET ANOTHER CHANCE.
AND THE NEXT TIME HE REVEALS HIMSELF WE'LL BE READY.
BUT I WONDER...

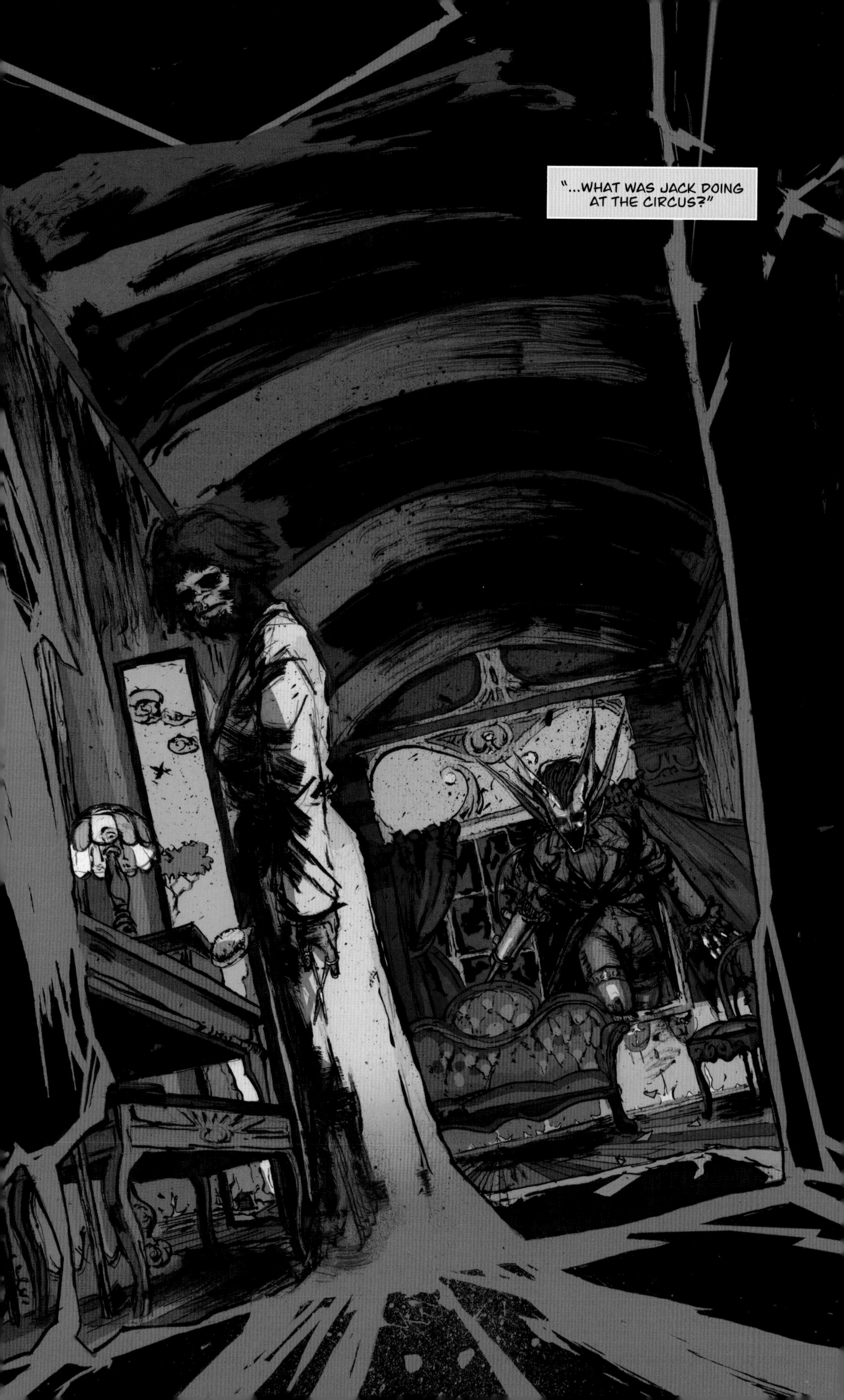
"...WHAT WAS JACK DOING
AT THE CIRCUS?"

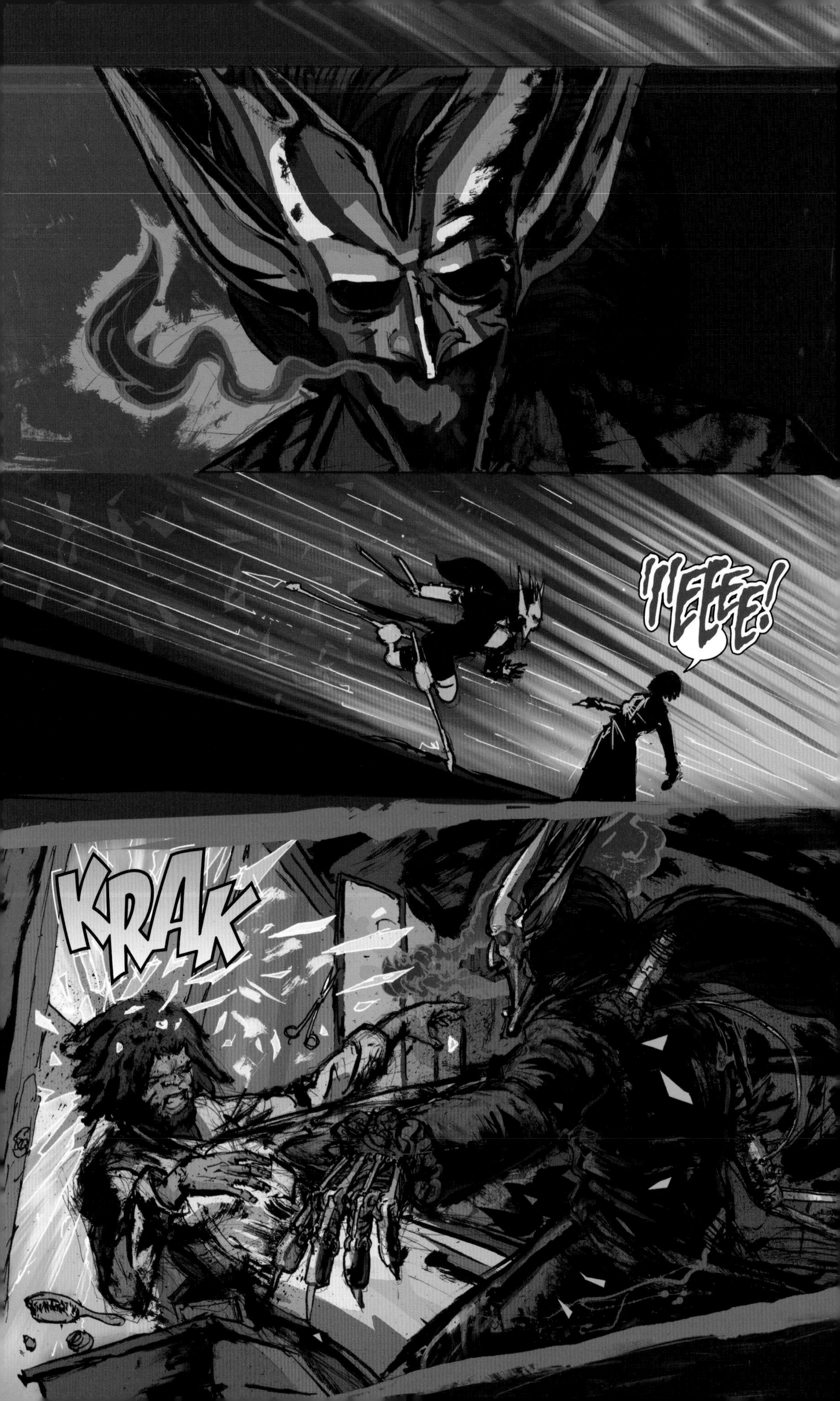
NEEEE!
KRAK

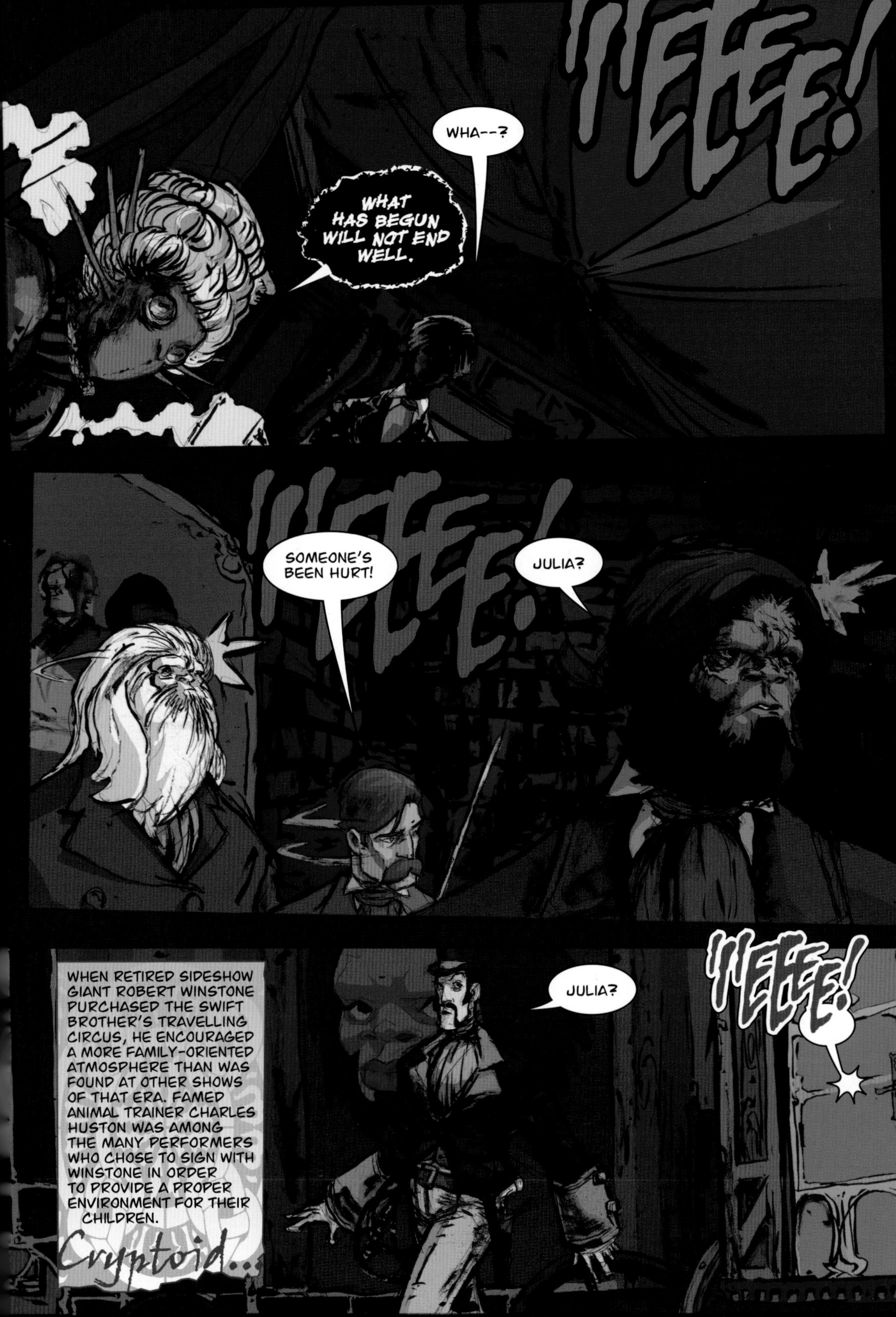
WHA--?
WHAT HAS BEGUN WILL NOT END WELL.
!!EEEE!
!!EEEE!
SOMEONE'S BEEN HURT!
JULIA?
WHEN RETIRED SIDESHOW GIANT ROBERT WINSTONE PURCHASED THE SWIFT BROTHER'S TRAVELLING CIRCUS, HE ENCOURAGED A MORE FAMILY-ORIENTED ATMOSPHERE THAN WAS FOUND AT OTHER SHOWS OF THAT ERA. FAMED ANIMAL TRAINER CHARLES HUSTON WAS AMONG THE MANY PERFORMERS WHO CHOSE TO SIGN WITH WINSTONE IN ORDER TO PROVIDE A PROPER ENVIRONMENT FOR THEIR CHILDREN.
Cryptoid...
JULIA?
!!EEEE!

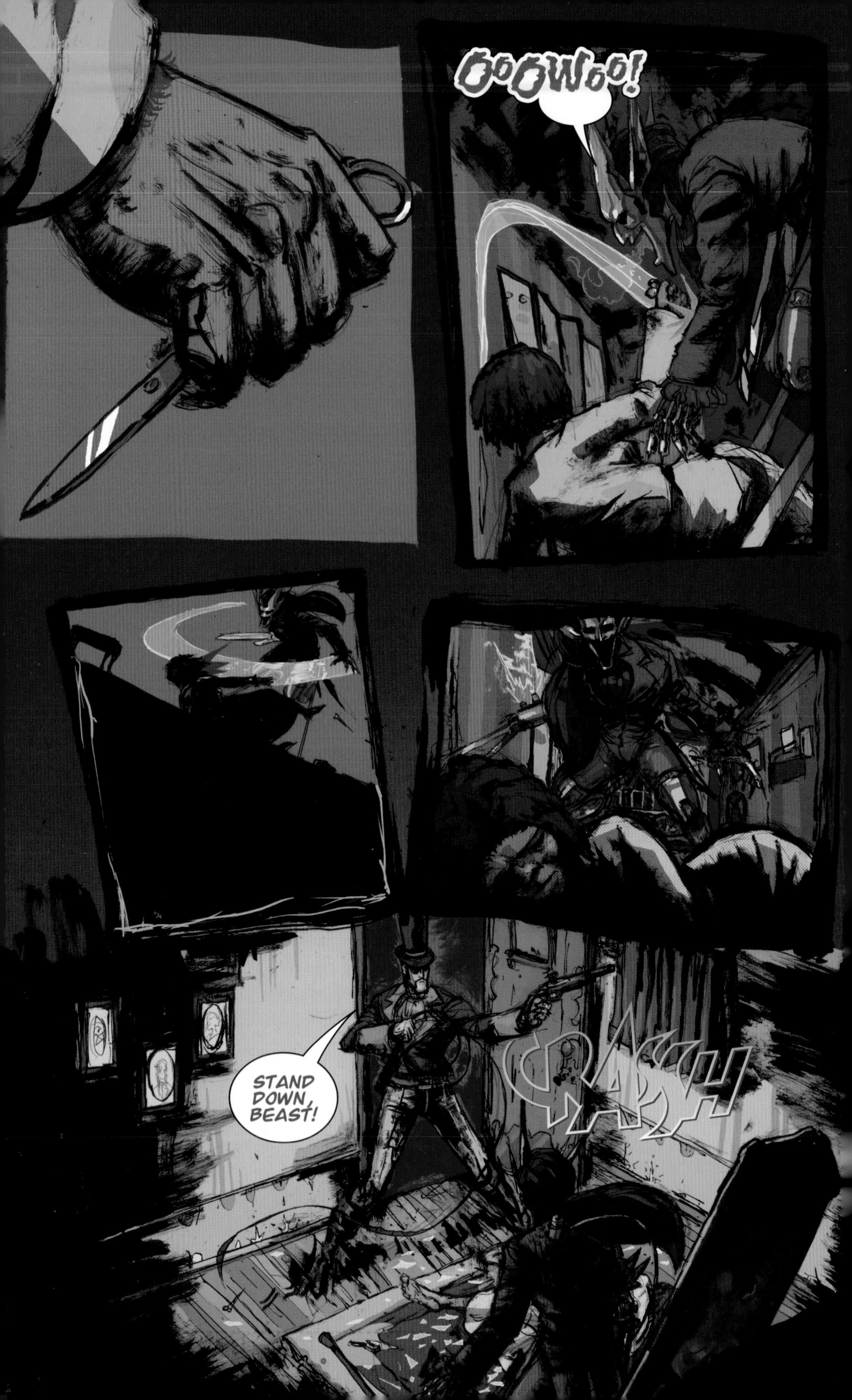
OOOWOOO!
STAND DOWN, BEAST!
CRASH

DON'T MAKE ANOTHER MOVE OR I'LL--

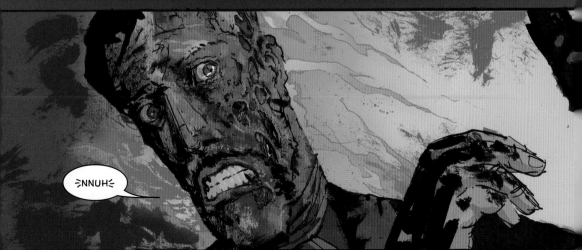

⇃NNUH⇂

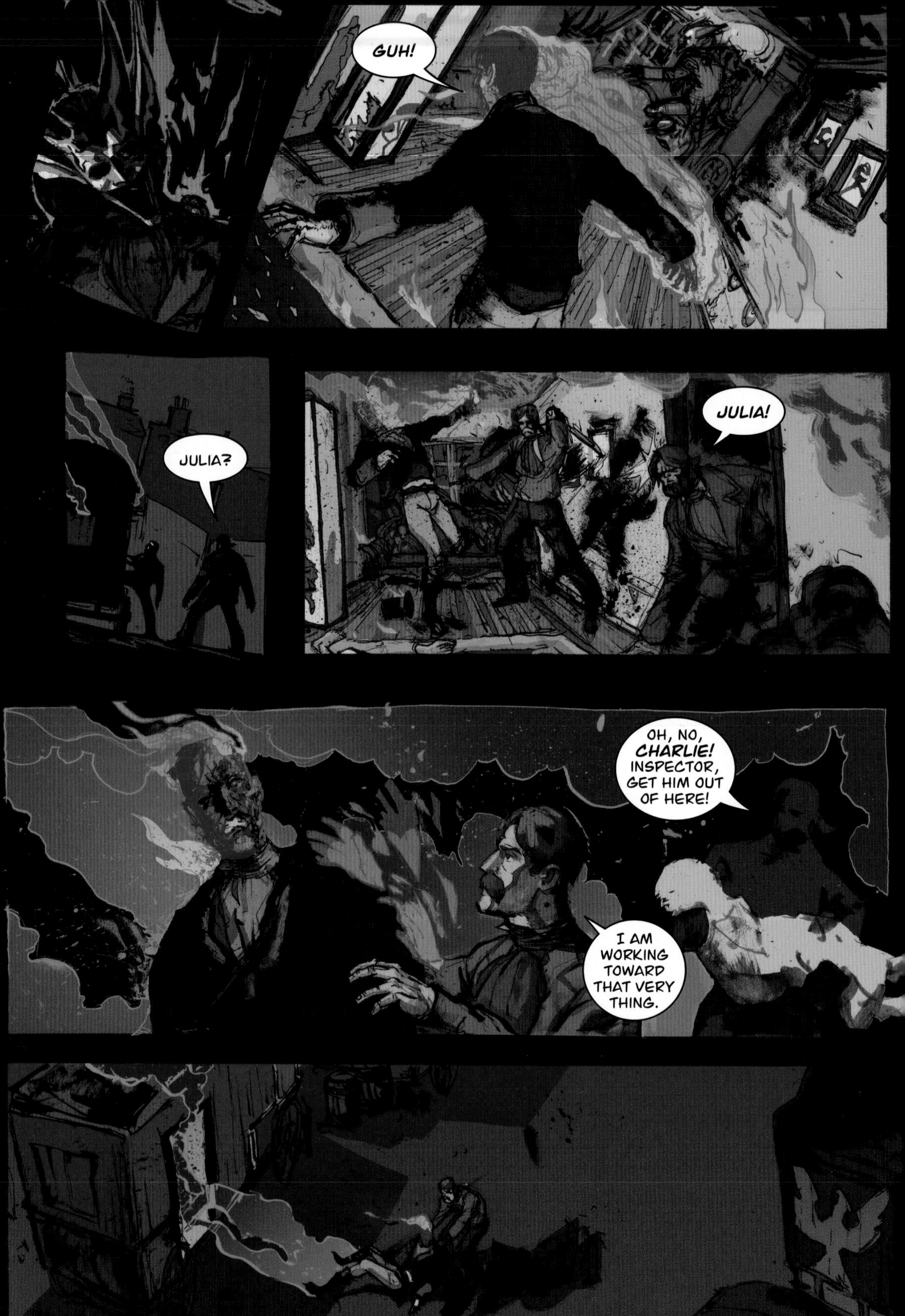
GUH!
JULIA?
JULIA!
OH, NO, CHARLIE! INSPECTOR, GET HIM OUT OF HERE!
I AM WORKING TOWARD THAT VERY THING.

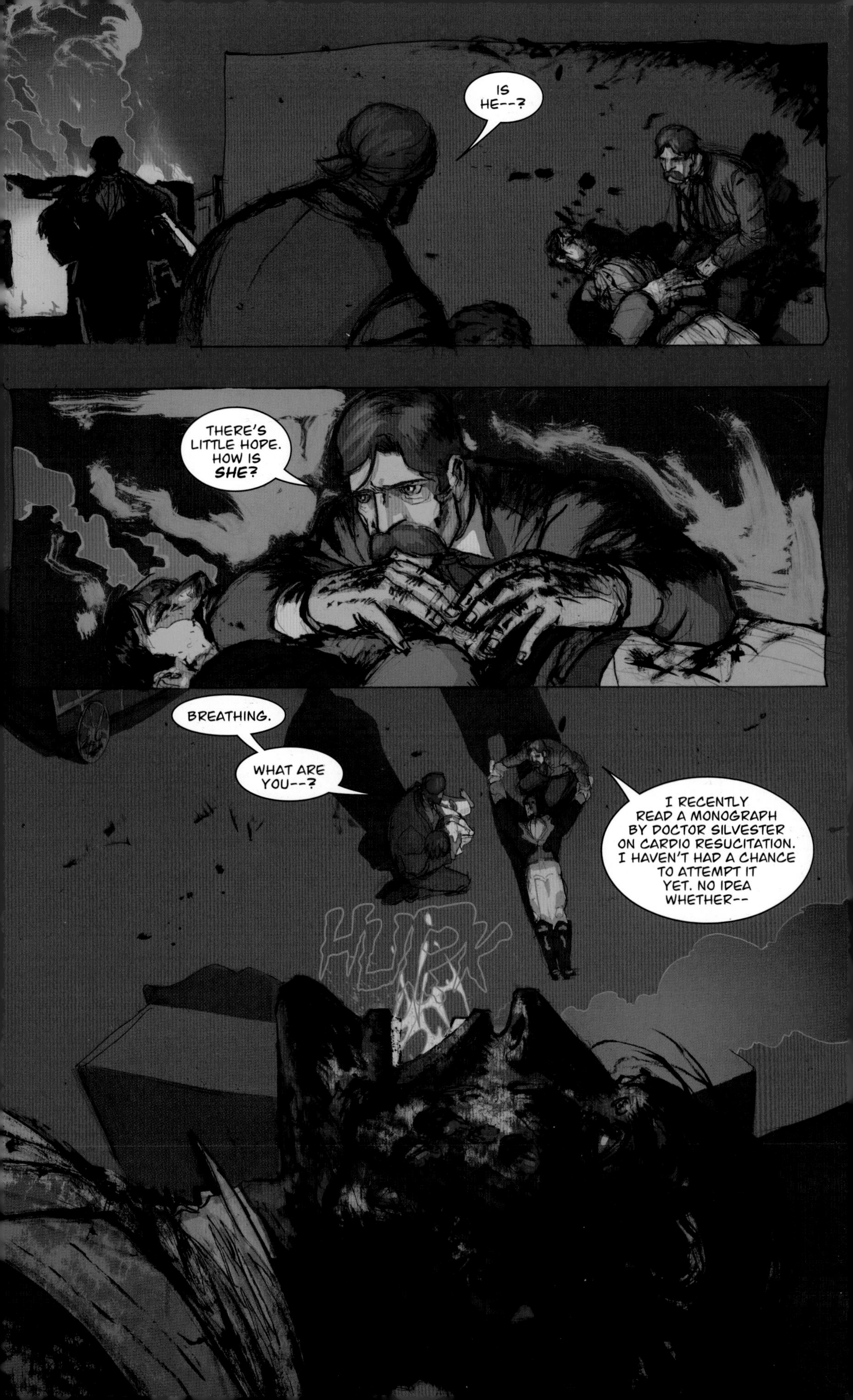
IS HE--?
THERE'S LITTLE HOPE. HOW IS SHE?
BREATHING.
WHAT ARE YOU--?
I RECENTLY READ A MONOGRAPH BY DOCTOR SILVESTER ON CARDIO RESUCITATION. I HAVEN'T HAD A CHANCE TO ATTEMPT IT YET. NO IDEA WHETHER--

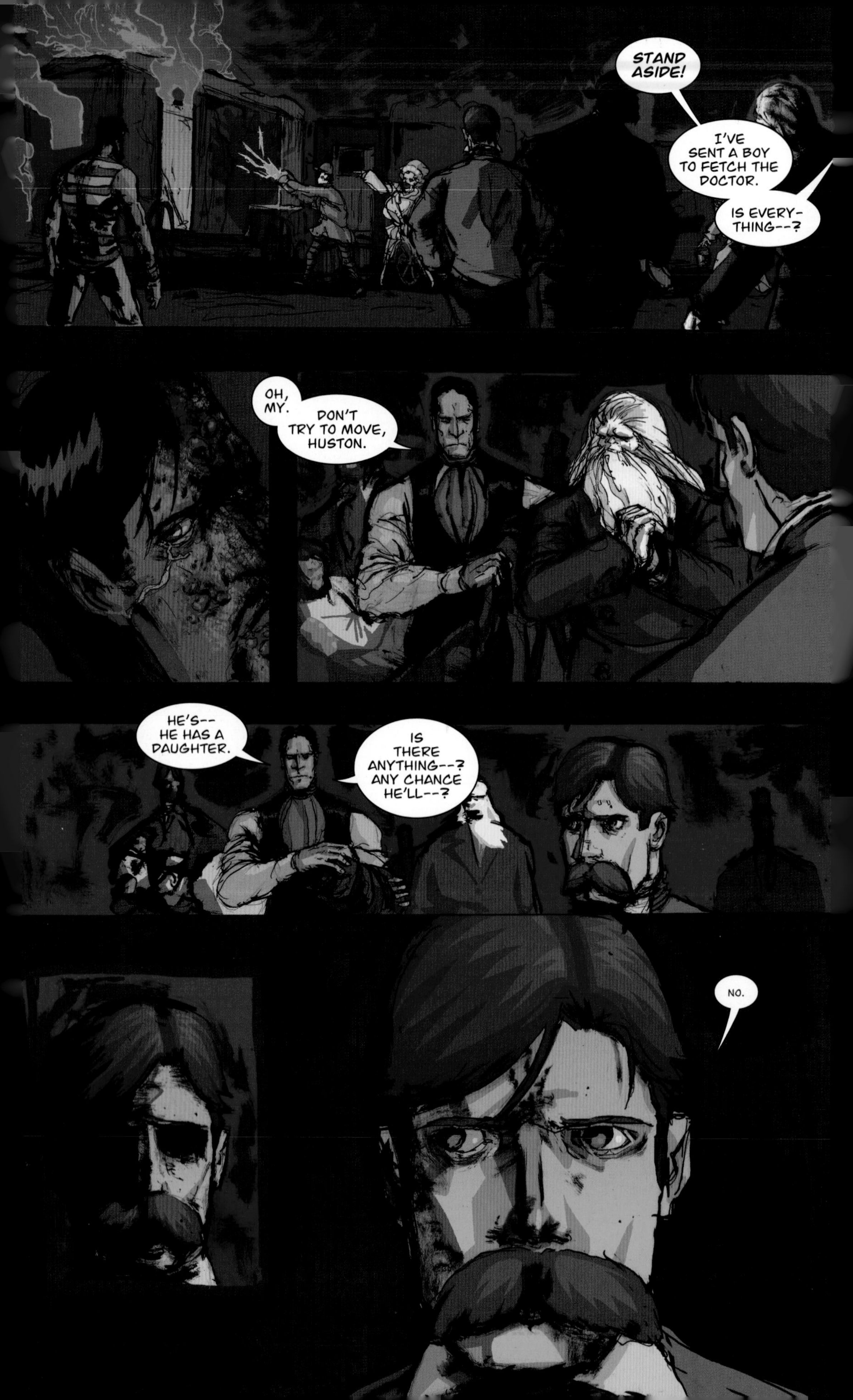
STAND ASIDE!
I'VE SENT A BOY TO FETCH THE DOCTOR.
IS EVERY-THING--?
OH, MY.
DON'T TRY TO MOVE, HUSTON.
HE'S-- HE HAS A DAUGHTER.
IS THERE ANYTHING--? ANY CHANCE HE'LL--?
NO.

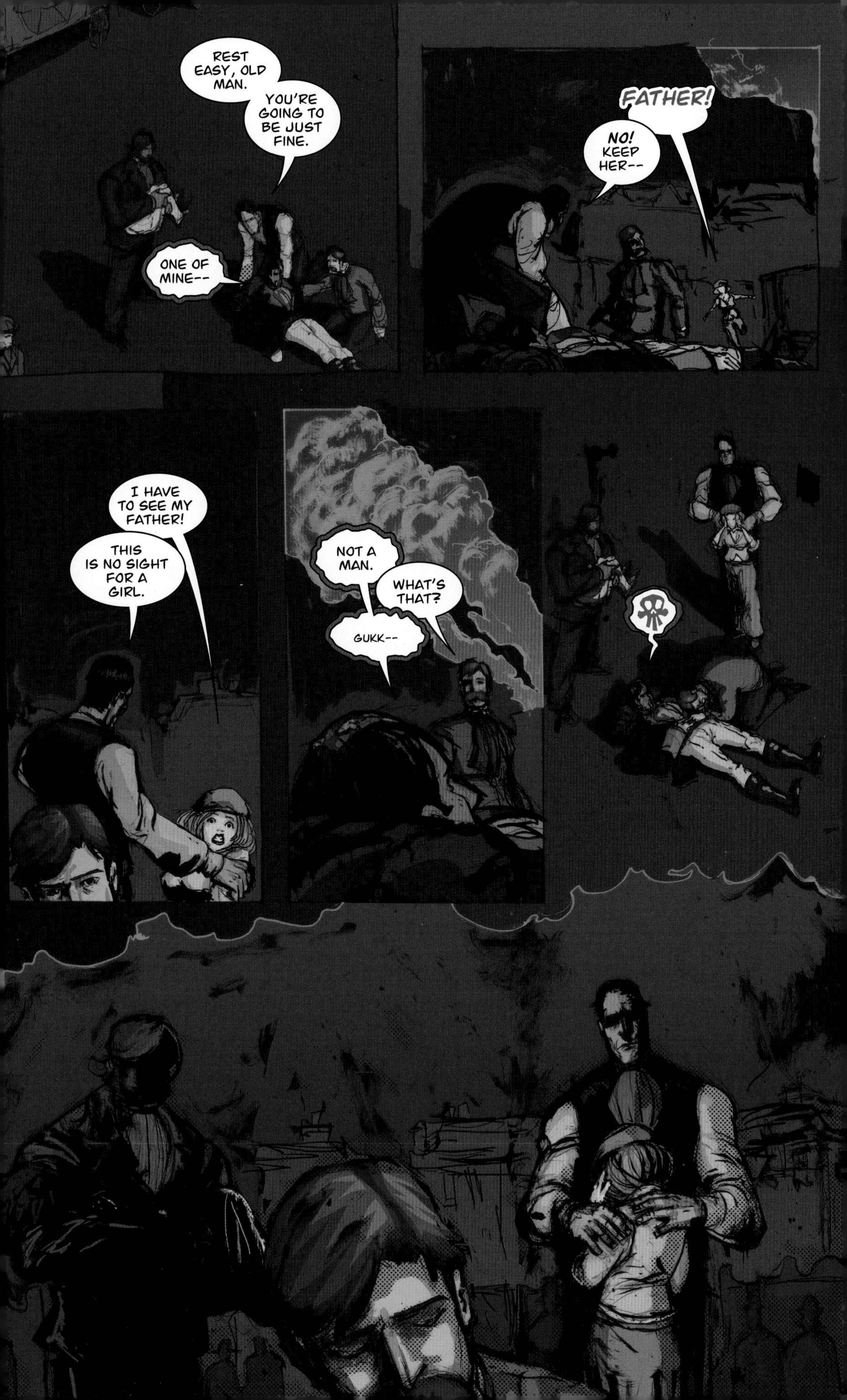
REST EASY, OLD MAN.
YOU'RE GOING TO BE JUST FINE.
ONE OF MINE--
FATHER!
NO! KEEP HER--
I HAVE TO SEE MY FATHER!
THIS IS NO SIGHT FOR A GIRL.
NOT A MAN.
WHAT'S THAT?
GUKK--

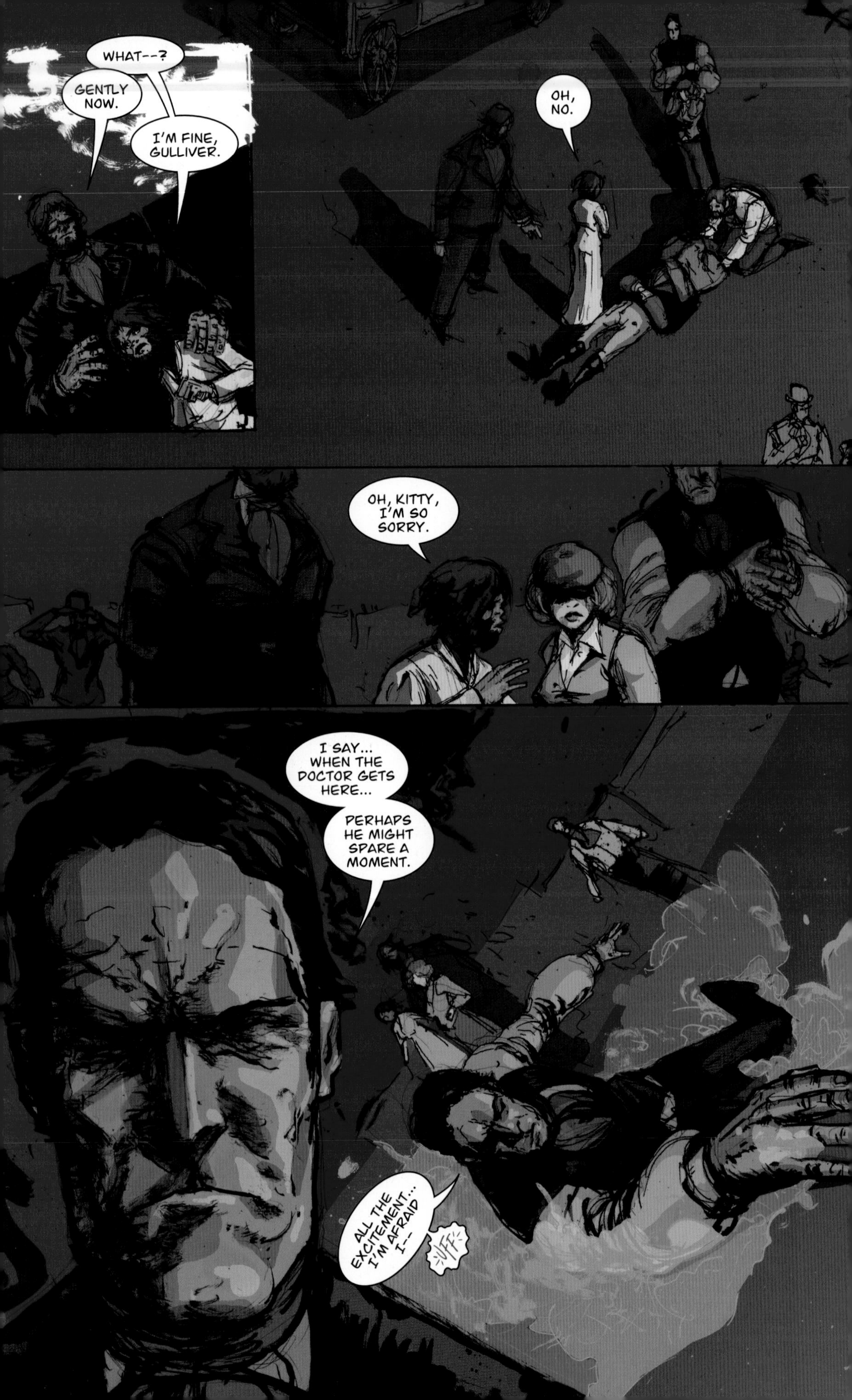
WHAT--?
GENTLY NOW.
I'M FINE, GULLIVER.
OH, NO.
OH, KITTY, I'M SO SORRY.
I SAY... WHEN THE DOCTOR GETS HERE...
PERHAPS HE MIGHT SPARE A MOMENT.
ALL THE EXCITEMENT... I'M AFRAID I--
UFF

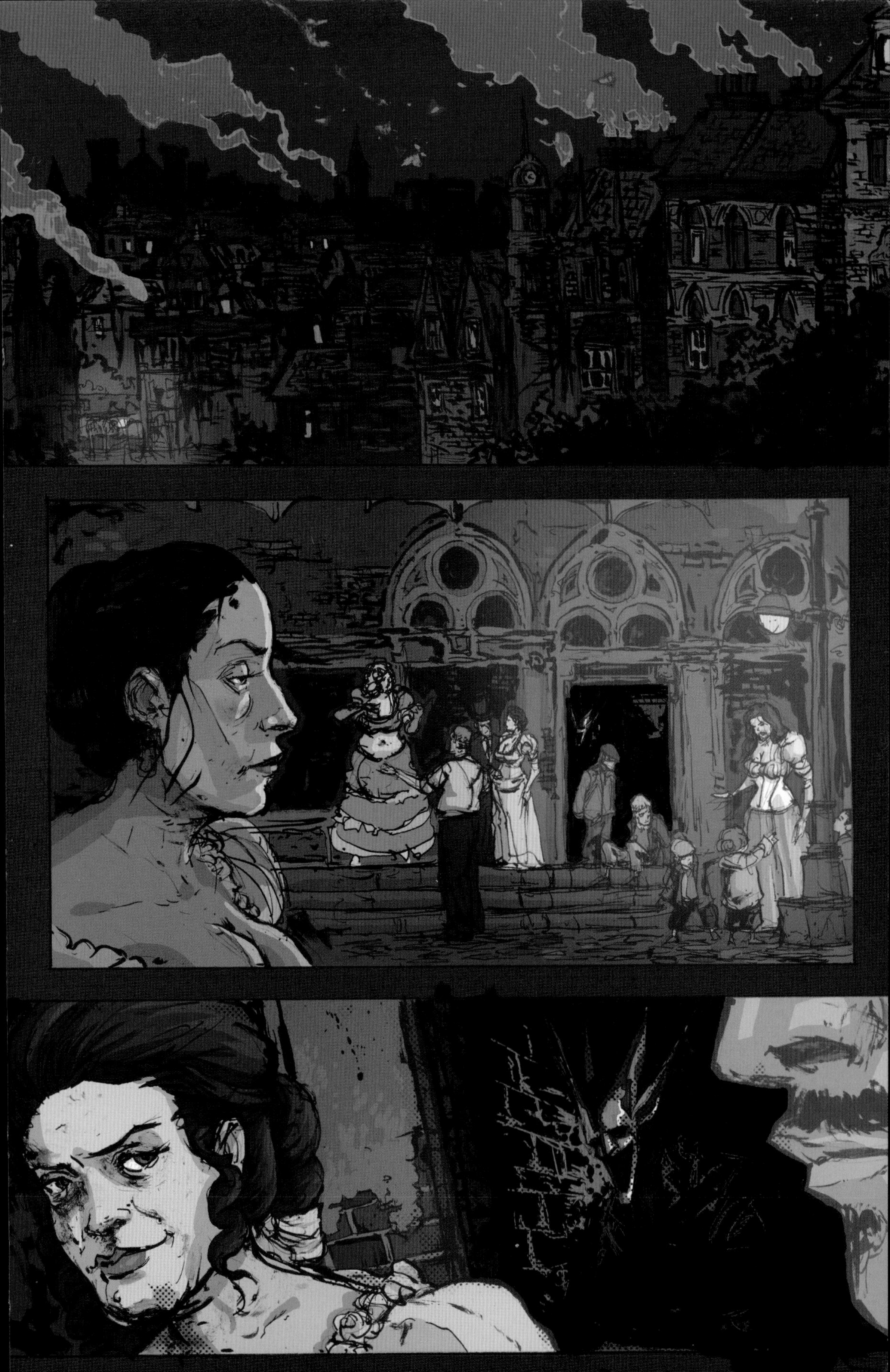

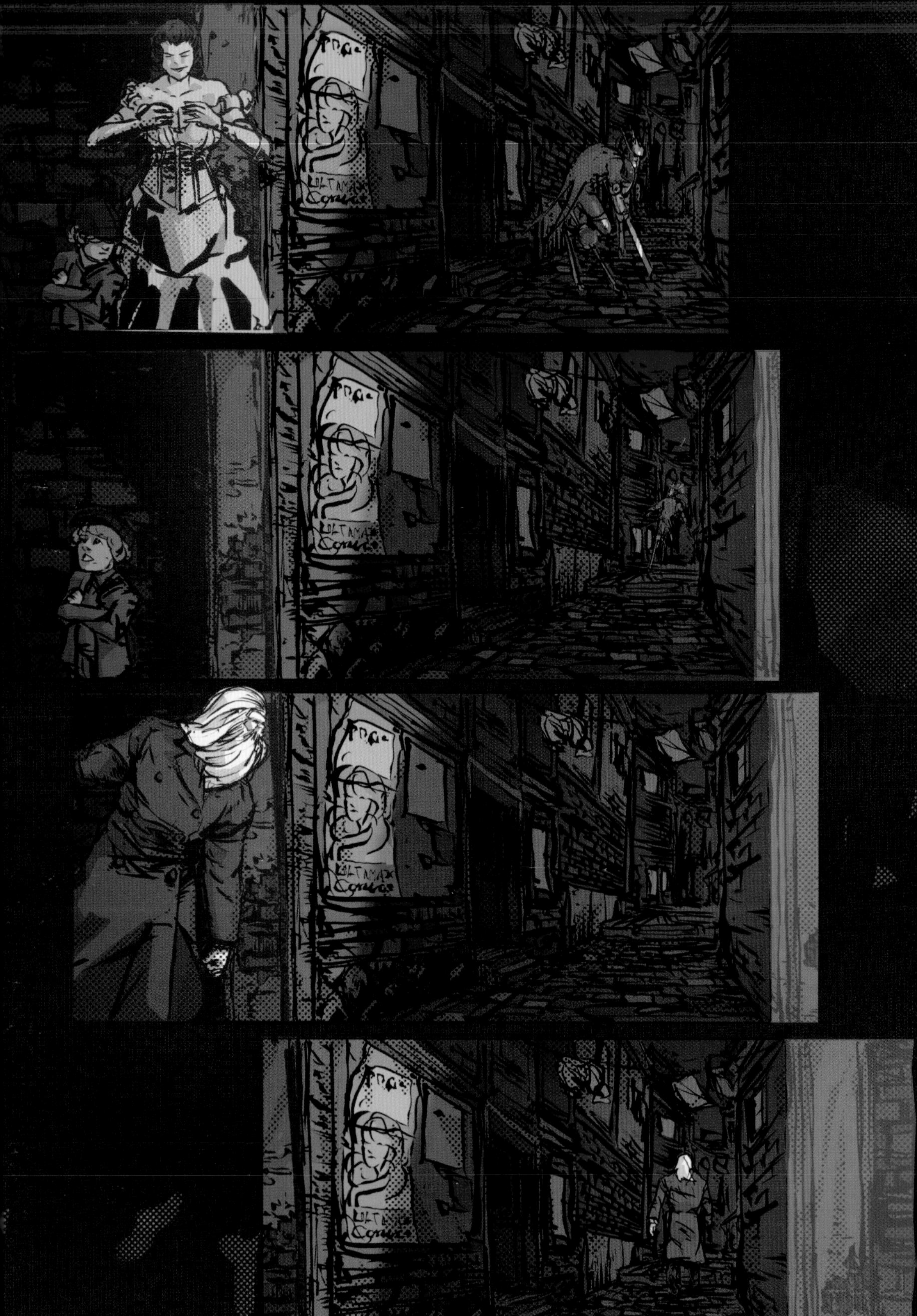

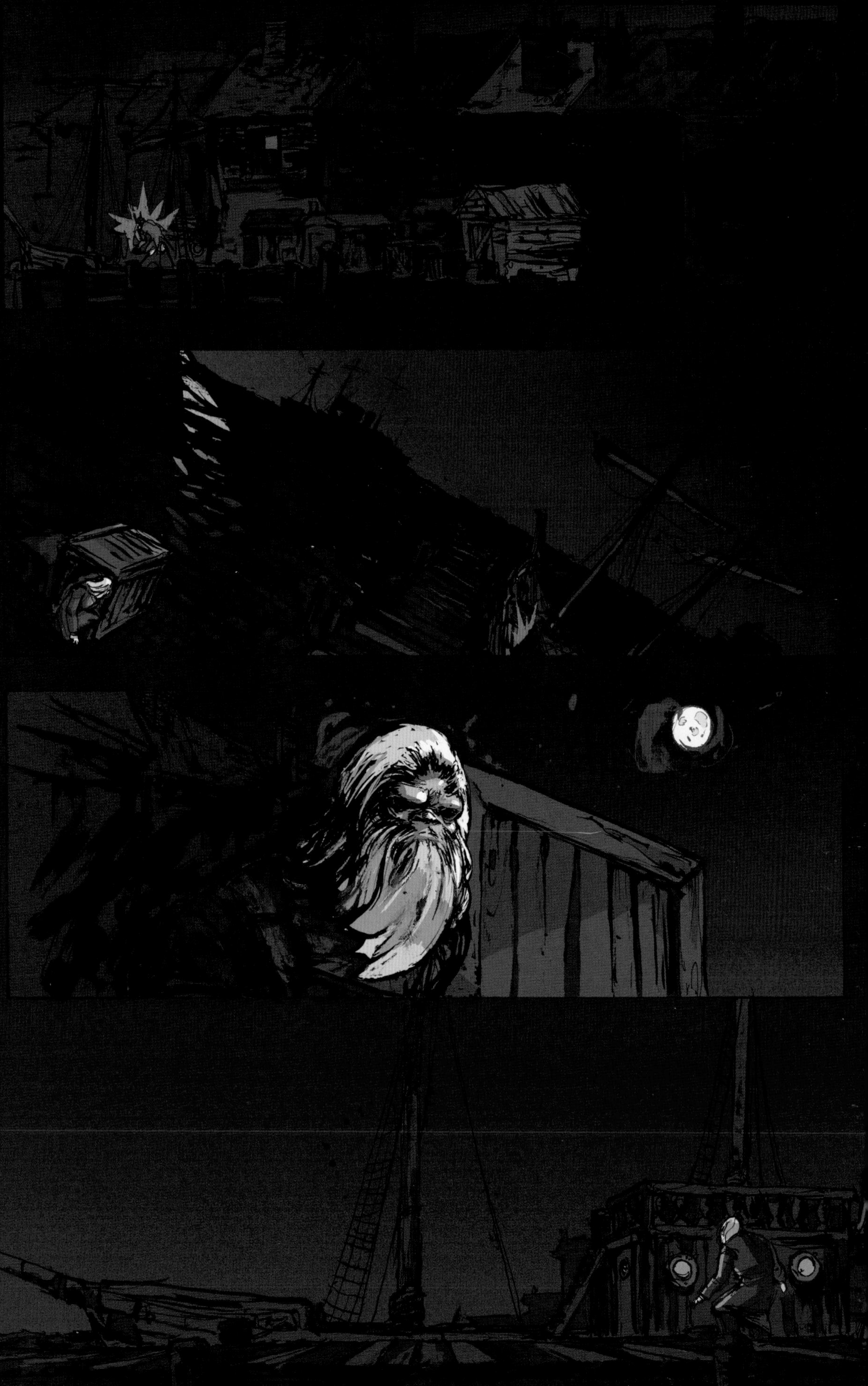

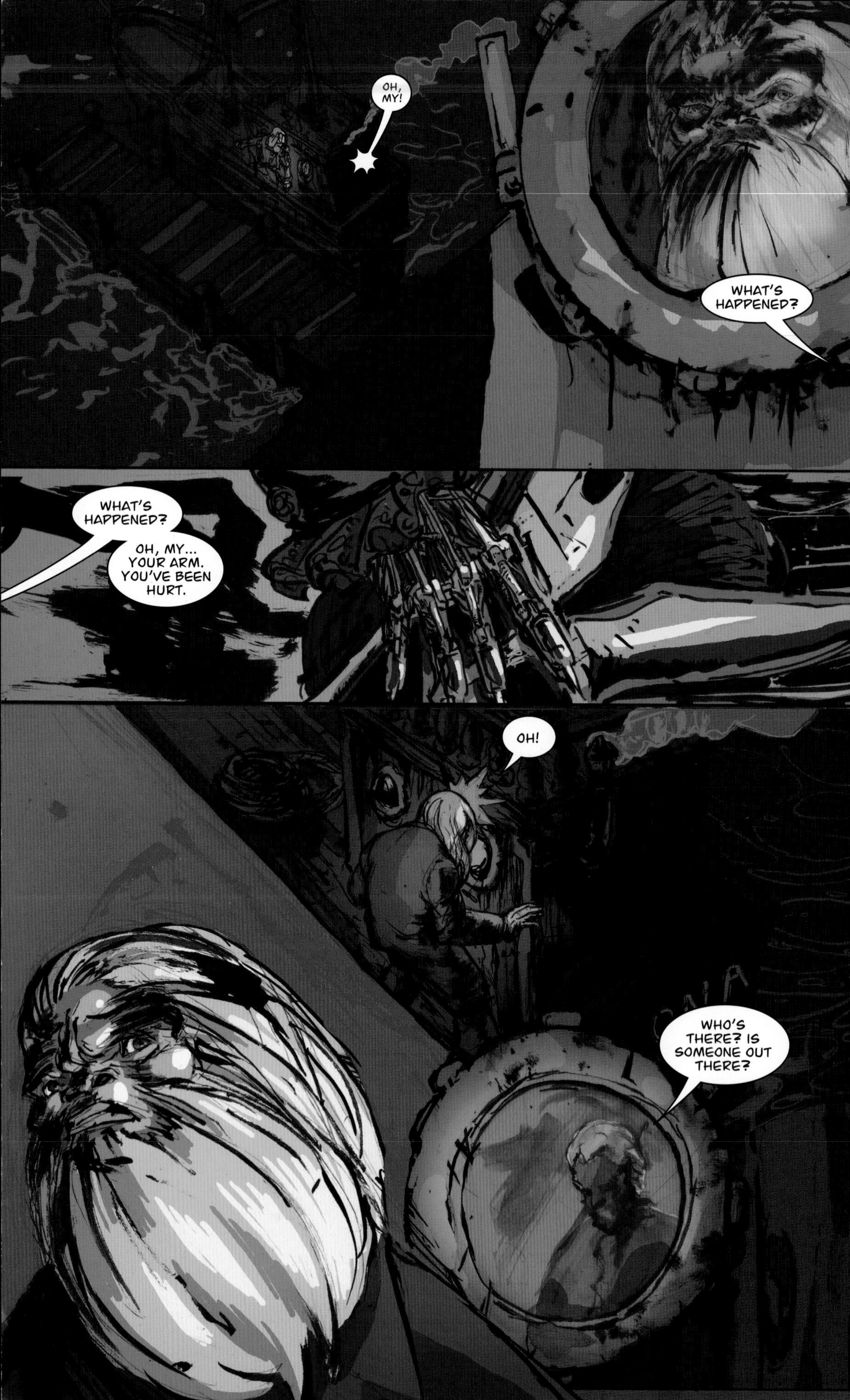
OH, MY!
WHAT'S HAPPENED?
WHAT'S HAPPENED?
OH, MY... YOUR ARM. YOU'VE BEEN HURT.
OH!
WHO'S THERE? IS SOMEONE OUT THERE?

IS THERE--?
ONLY THE WIND, I SUPPOSE. THE WIND AND THE WAVES.
LET'S TAKE A LOOK AT YOUR ARM. THE GASH DOESN'T LOOK DEEP.
I'LL HAVE YOU BOUNCING ABOUT IN NO TIME AT ALL.
NO TIME AT ALL.

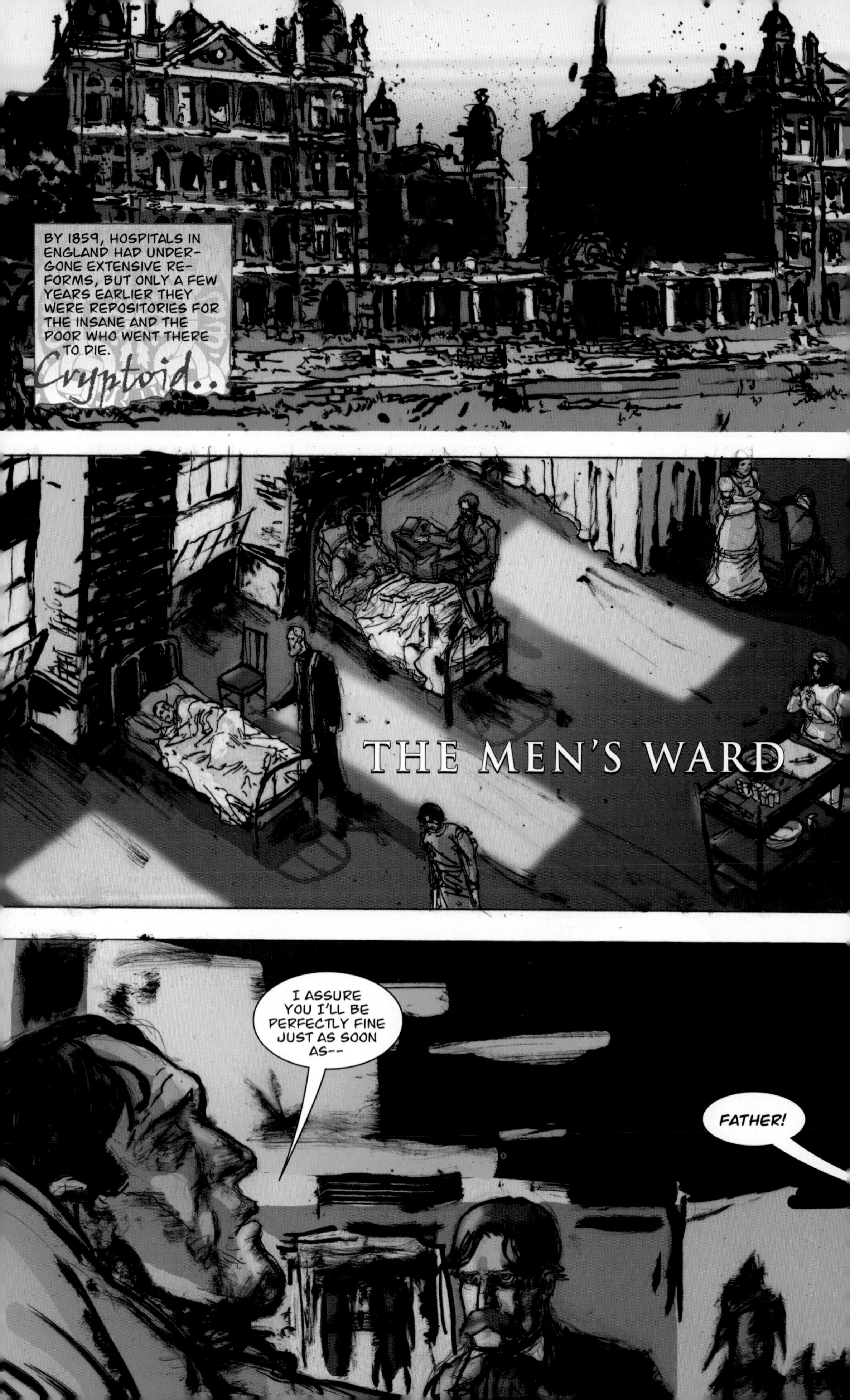

BY 1859, HOSPITALS IN ENGLAND HAD UNDERGONE EXTENSIVE REFORMS, BUT ONLY A FEW YEARS EARLIER THEY WERE REPOSITORIES FOR THE INSANE AND THE POOR WHO WENT THERE TO DIE.
Cryptoid..
THE MEN'S WARD
I ASSURE YOU I'LL BE PERFECTLY FINE JUST AS SOON AS--
FATHER!

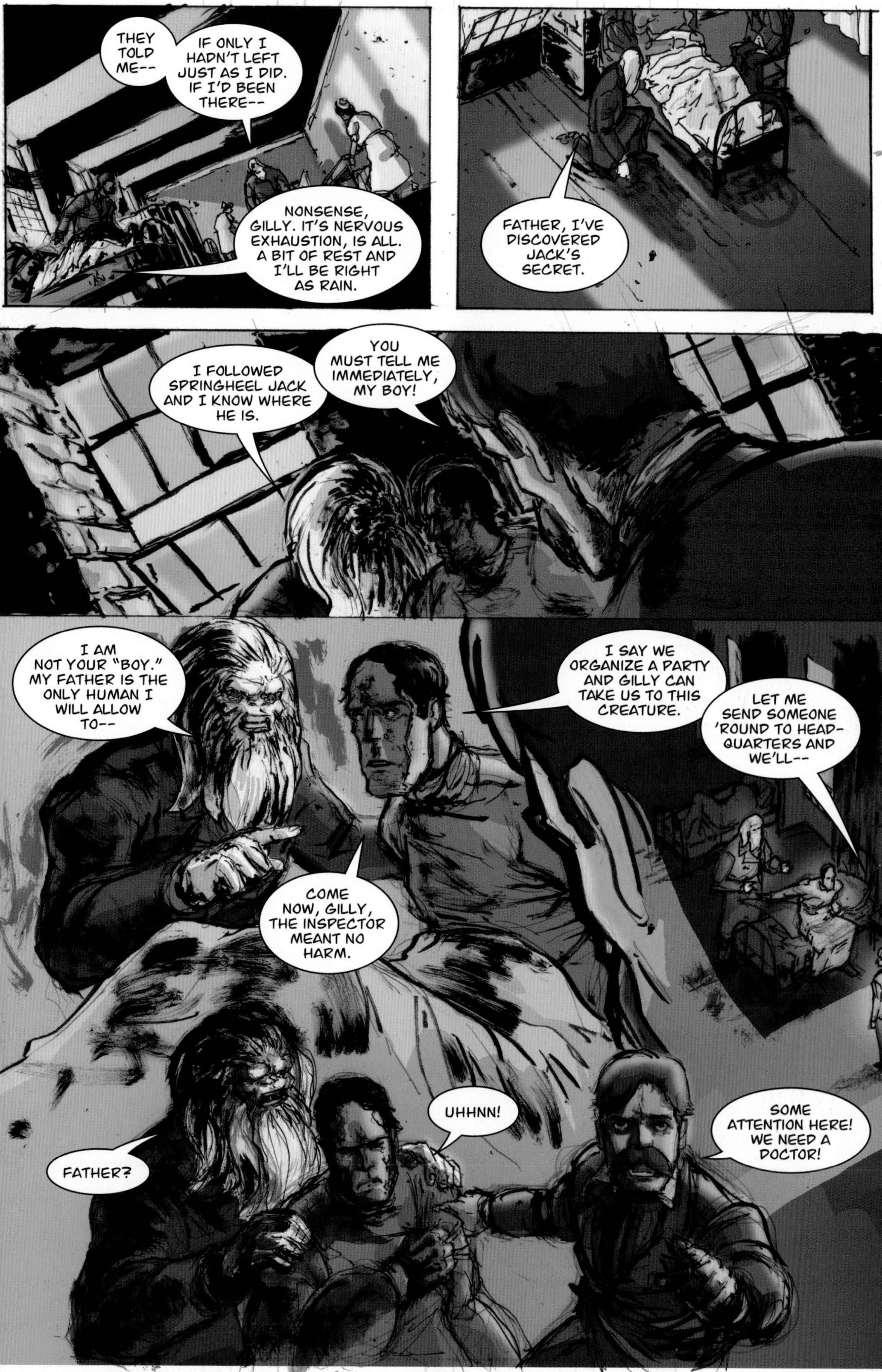
THEY TOLD ME--
IF ONLY I HADN'T LEFT JUST AS I DID. IF I'D BEEN THERE--
NONSENSE, GILLY. IT'S NERVOUS EXHAUSTION, IS ALL. A BIT OF REST AND I'LL BE RIGHT AS RAIN.
FATHER, I'VE DISCOVERED JACK'S SECRET.
I FOLLOWED SPRINGHEEL JACK AND I KNOW WHERE HE IS.
YOU MUST TELL ME IMMEDIATELY, MY BOY!
I AM NOT YOUR "BOY." MY FATHER IS THE ONLY HUMAN I WILL ALLOW TO--
I SAY WE ORGANIZE A PARTY AND GILLY CAN TAKE US TO THIS CREATURE.
LET ME SEND SOMEONE 'ROUND TO HEAD-QUARTERS AND WE'LL--
COME NOW, GILLY, THE INSPECTOR MEANT NO HARM.
FATHER?
UHHNN!
SOME ATTENTION HERE! WE NEED A DOCTOR!

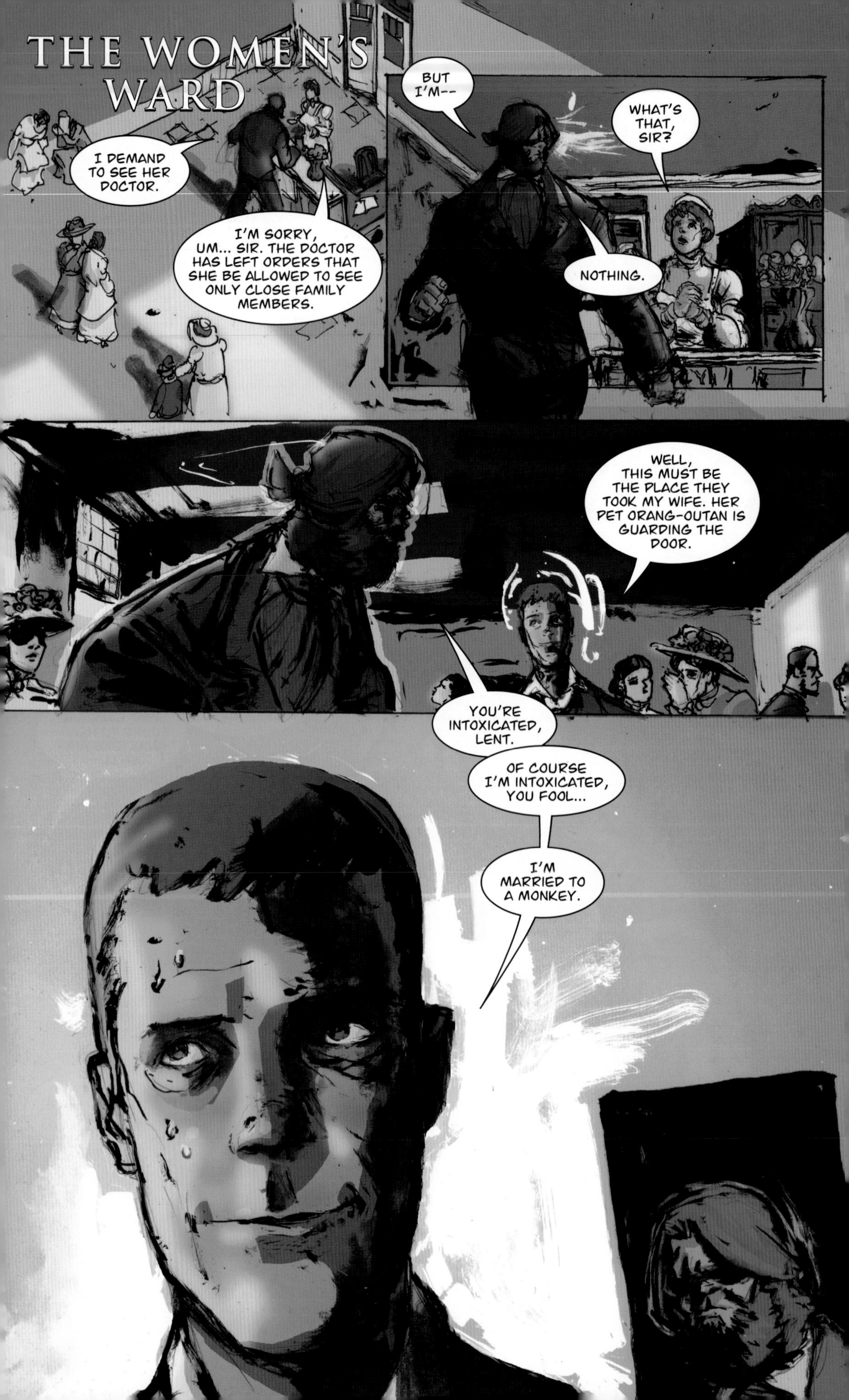
THE WOMEN'S WARD
I DEMAND TO SEE HER DOCTOR.
I'M SORRY, UM... SIR. THE DOCTOR HAS LEFT ORDERS THAT SHE BE ALLOWED TO SEE ONLY CLOSE FAMILY MEMBERS.
BUT I'M--
WHAT'S THAT, SIR?
NOTHING.
WELL, THIS MUST BE THE PLACE THEY TOOK MY WIFE. HER PET ORANG-OUTAN IS GUARDING THE DOOR.
YOU'RE INTOXICATED, LENT.
OF COURSE I'M INTOXICATED, YOU FOOL...
I'M MARRIED TO A MONKEY.

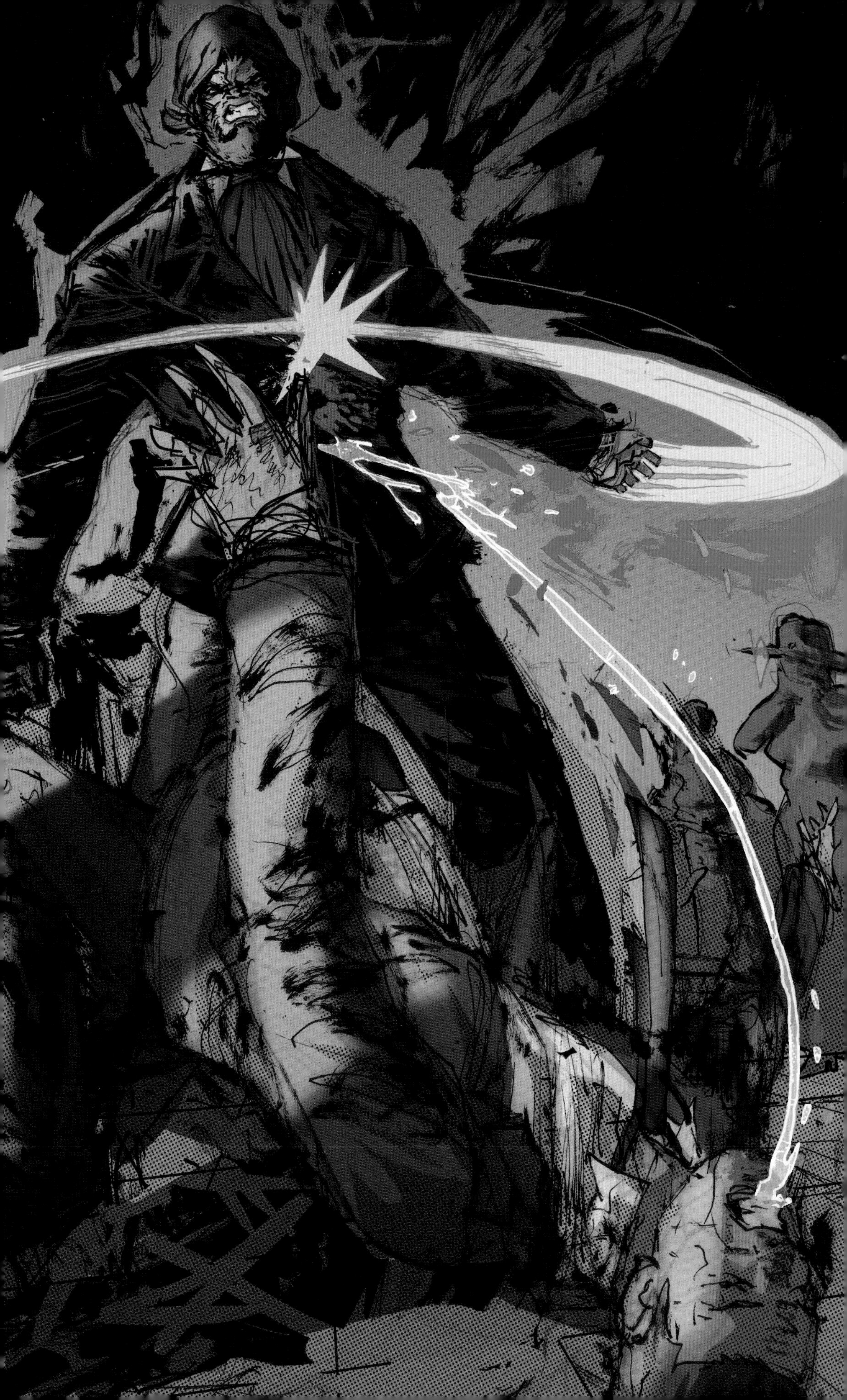

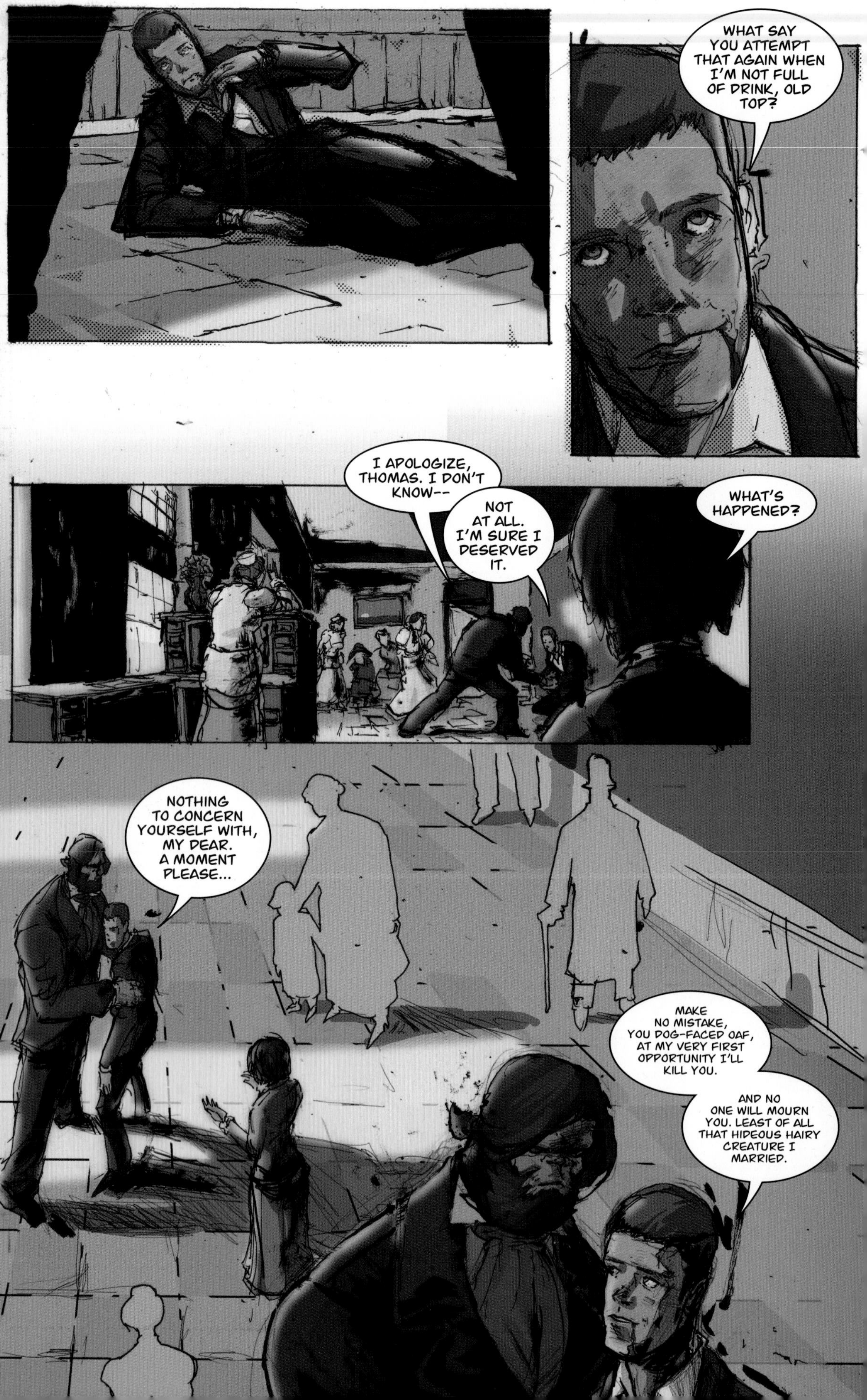
WHAT SAY YOU ATTEMPT THAT AGAIN WHEN I'M NOT FULL OF DRINK, OLD TOP?
I APOLOGIZE, THOMAS. I DON'T KNOW--
NOT AT ALL. I'M SURE I DESERVED IT.
WHAT'S HAPPENED?
NOTHING TO CONCERN YOURSELF WITH, MY DEAR. A MOMENT PLEASE...
MAKE NO MISTAKE, YOU DOG-FACED OAF, AT MY VERY FIRST OPPORTUNITY I'LL KILL YOU.
AND NO ONE WILL MOURN YOU. LEAST OF ALL THAT HIDEOUS HAIRY CREATURE I MARRIED.

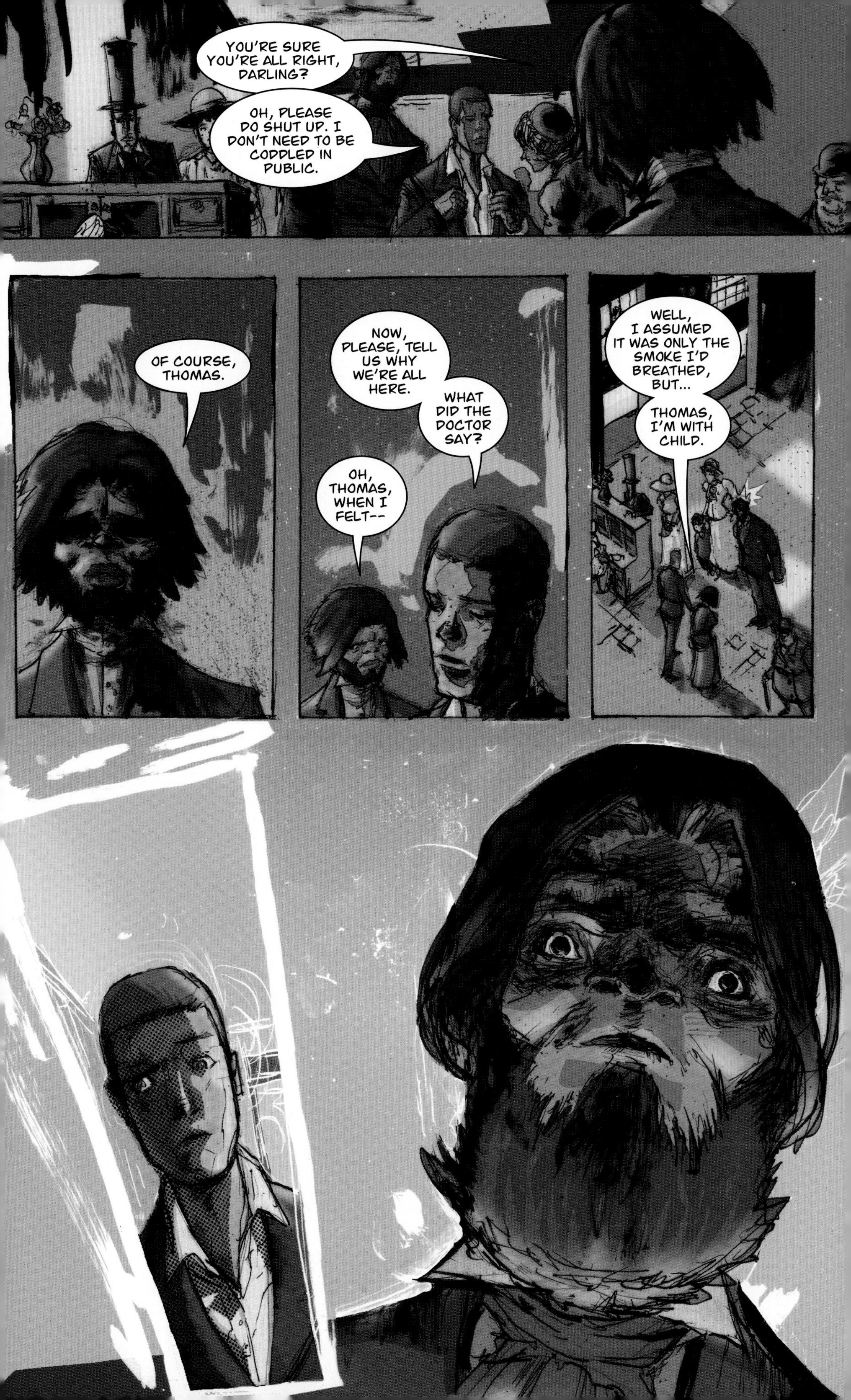

YOU'RE SURE YOU'RE ALL RIGHT, DARLING?
OH, PLEASE DO SHUT UP. I DON'T NEED TO BE CODDLED IN PUBLIC.
OF COURSE, THOMAS.
NOW, PLEASE, TELL US WHY WE'RE ALL HERE.
WHAT DID THE DOCTOR SAY?
OH, THOMAS, WHEN I FELT--
WELL, I ASSUMED IT WAS ONLY THE SMOKE I'D BREATHED, BUT...
THOMAS, I'M WITH CHILD.

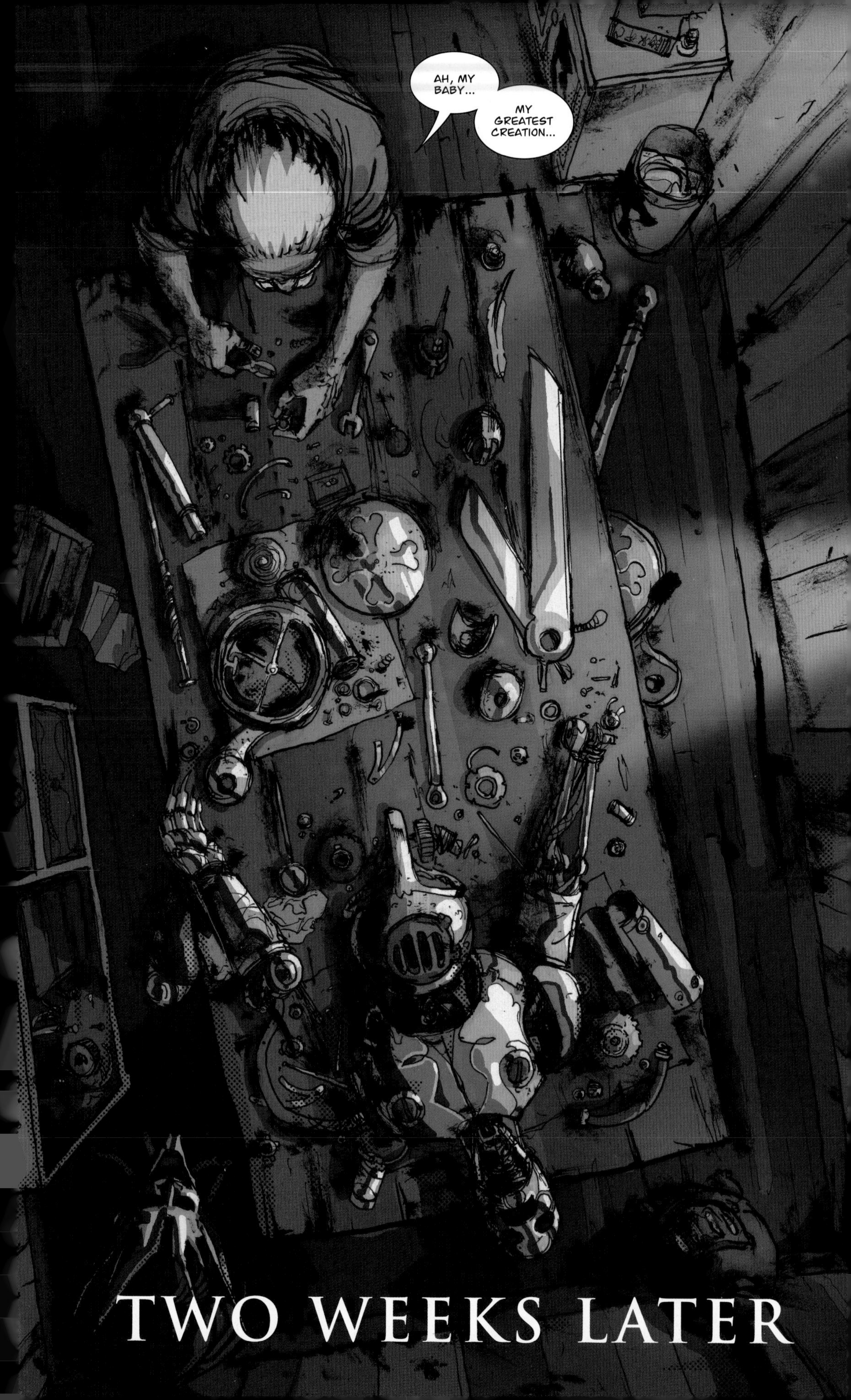
AH, MY BABY...
MY GREATEST CREATION...
TWO WEEKS LATER

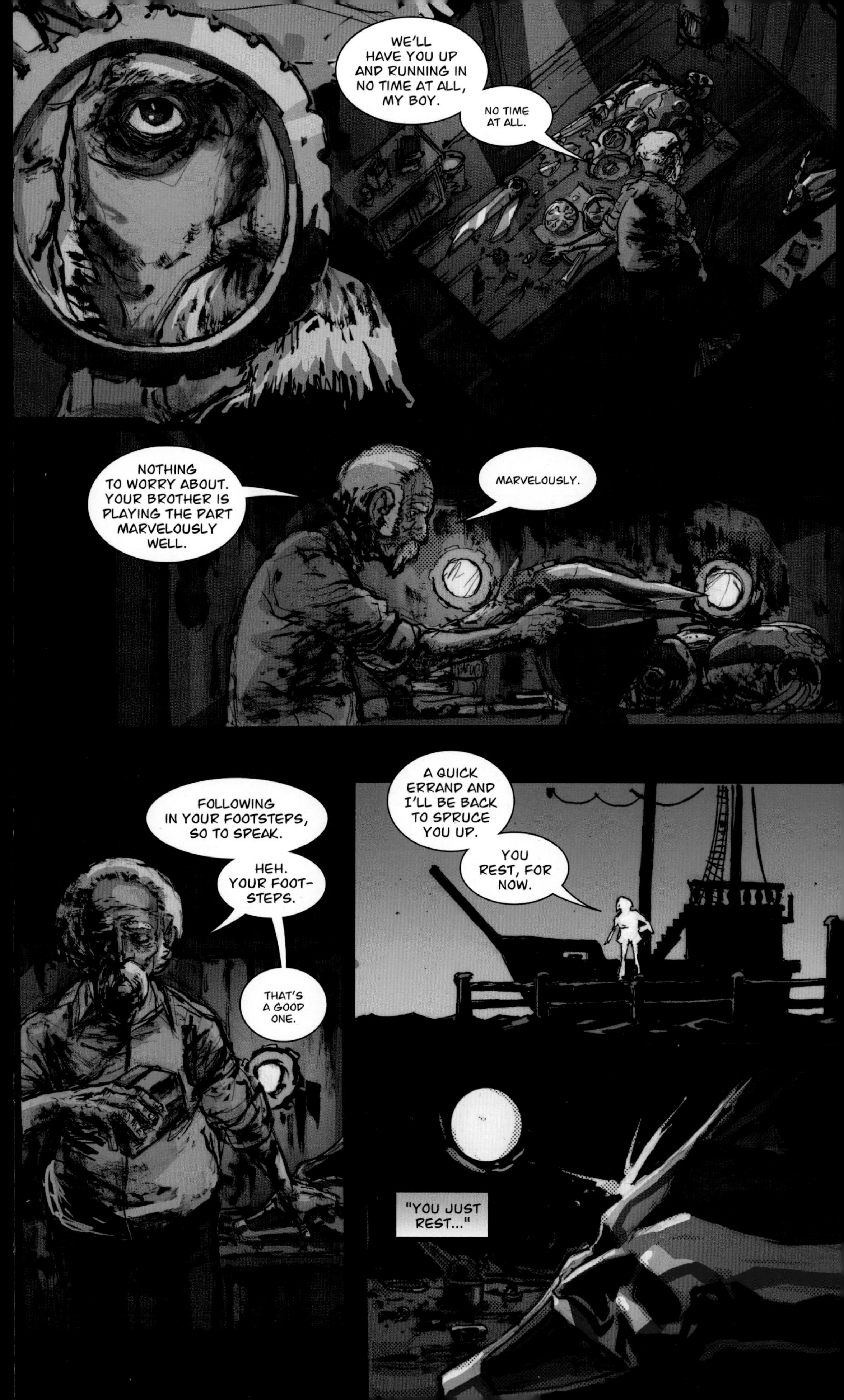
WE'LL HAVE YOU UP AND RUNNING IN NO TIME AT ALL, MY BOY.
NO TIME AT ALL.
NOTHING TO WORRY ABOUT. YOUR BROTHER IS PLAYING THE PART MARVELOUSLY WELL.
MARVELOUSLY.
FOLLOWING IN YOUR FOOTSTEPS, SO TO SPEAK.
HEH. YOUR FOOT-STEPS.
THAT'S A GOOD ONE.
A QUICK ERRAND AND I'LL BE BACK TO SPRUCE YOU UP.
YOU REST, FOR NOW.
"YOU JUST REST..."

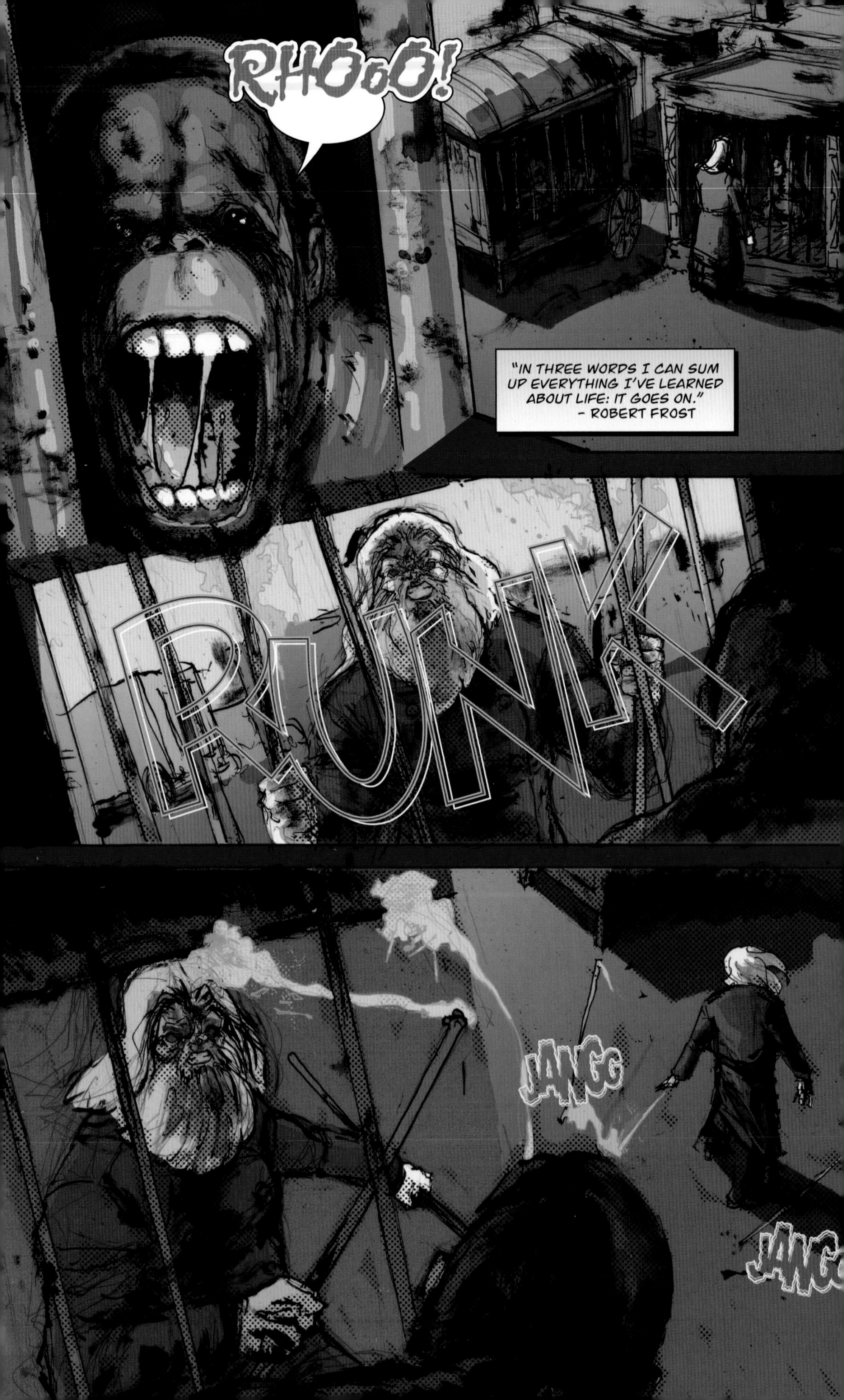
RHOoO!
"IN THREE WORDS I CAN SUM UP EVERYTHING I'VE LEARNED ABOUT LIFE: IT GOES ON."
– ROBERT FROST
RUNK
JANGG
JANGG

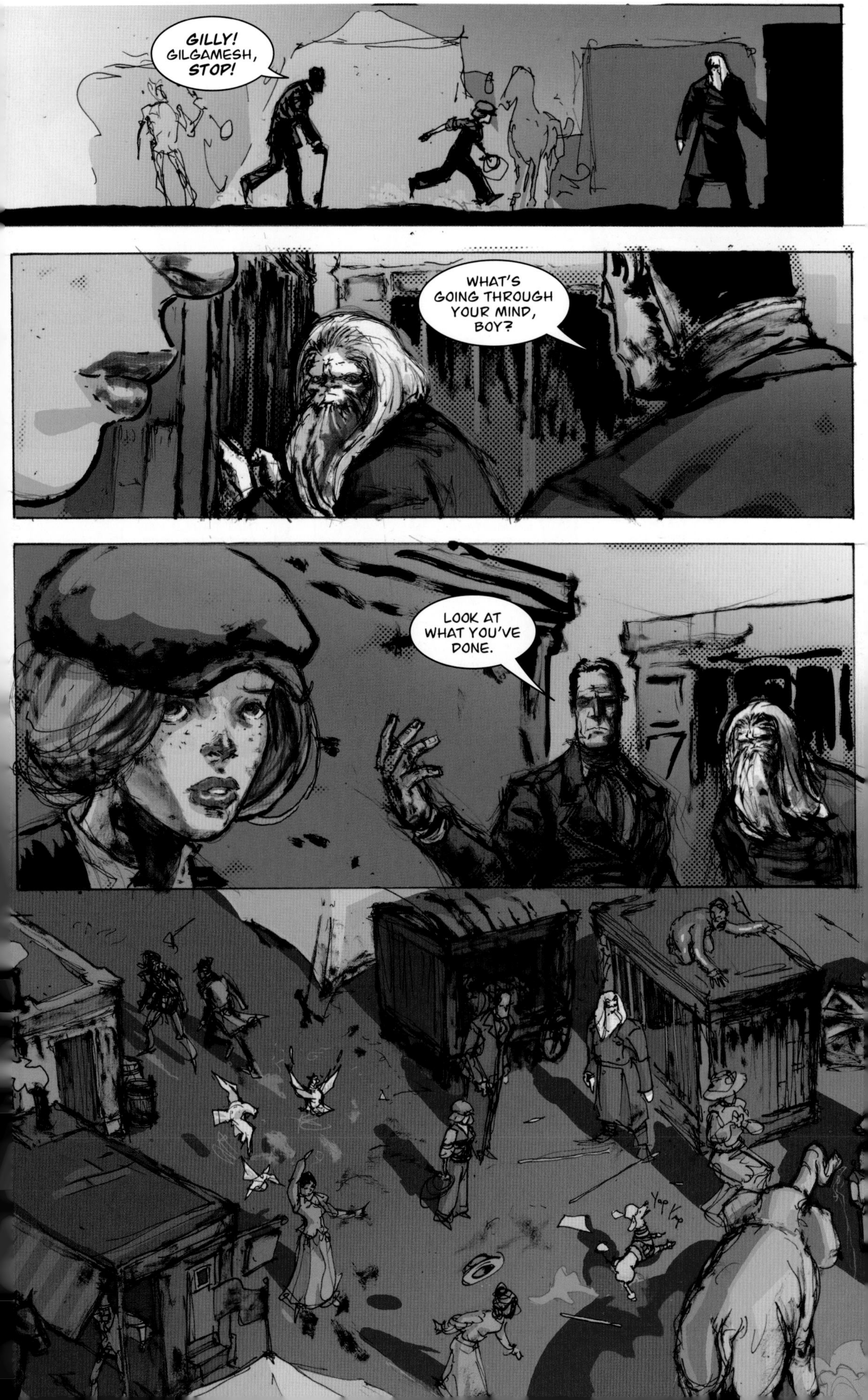
GILLY! GILGAMESH, STOP!
WHAT'S GOING THROUGH YOUR MIND, BOY?
LOOK AT WHAT YOU'VE DONE.
Yap Yap

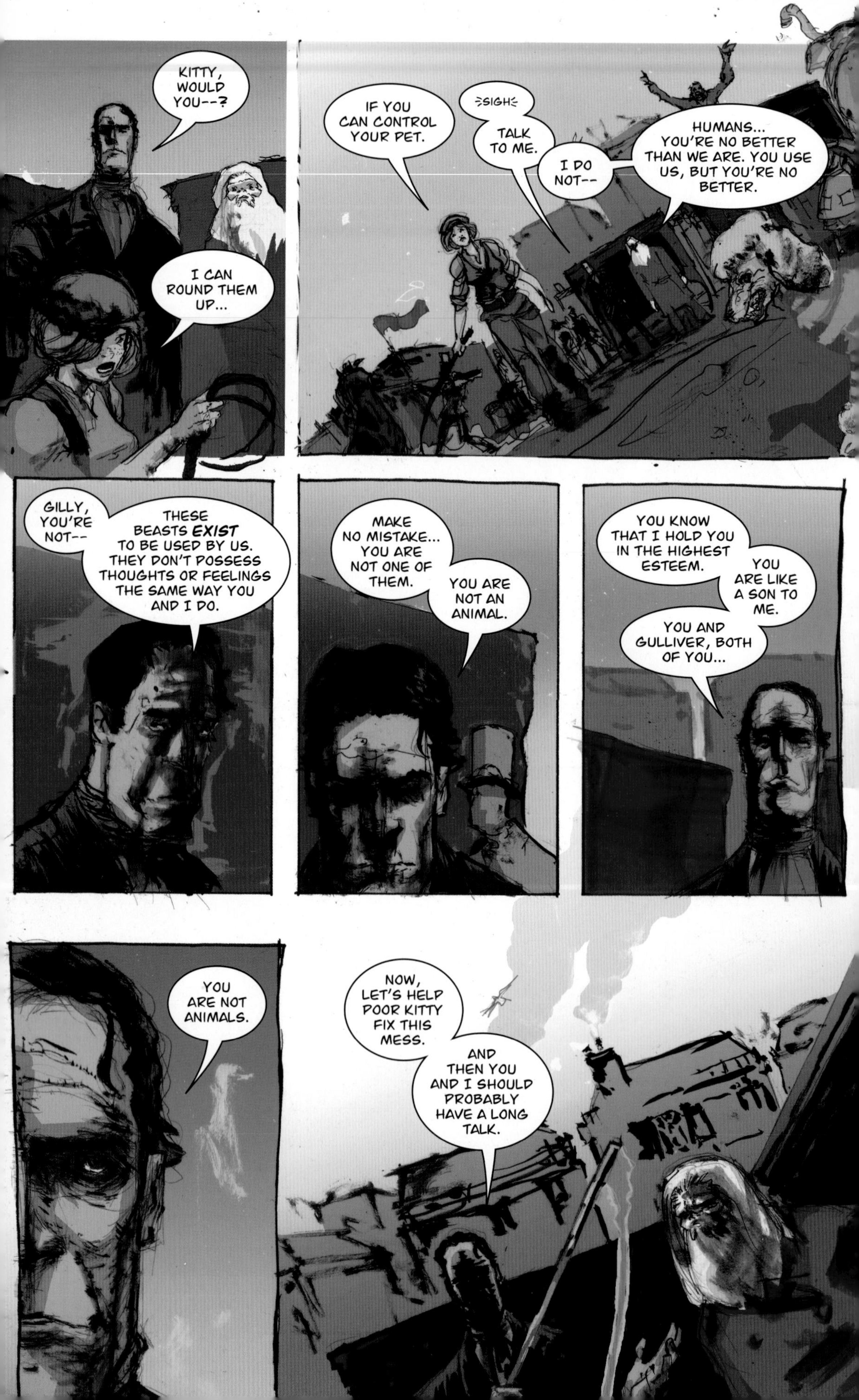
KITTY, WOULD YOU--?
I CAN ROUND THEM UP...
IF YOU CAN CONTROL YOUR PET.
SIGH
TALK TO ME.
I DO NOT--
HUMANS... YOU'RE NO BETTER THAN WE ARE. YOU USE US, BUT YOU'RE NO BETTER.
GILLY, YOU'RE NOT--
THESE BEASTS **EXIST** TO BE USED BY US. THEY DON'T POSSESS THOUGHTS OR FEELINGS THE SAME WAY YOU AND I DO.
MAKE NO MISTAKE... YOU ARE NOT ONE OF THEM.
YOU ARE NOT AN ANIMAL.
YOU KNOW THAT I HOLD YOU IN THE HIGHEST ESTEEM.
YOU ARE LIKE A SON TO ME.
YOU AND GULLIVER, BOTH OF YOU...
YOU ARE NOT ANIMALS.
NOW, LET'S HELP POOR KITTY FIX THIS MESS.
AND THEN YOU AND I SHOULD PROBABLY HAVE A LONG TALK.

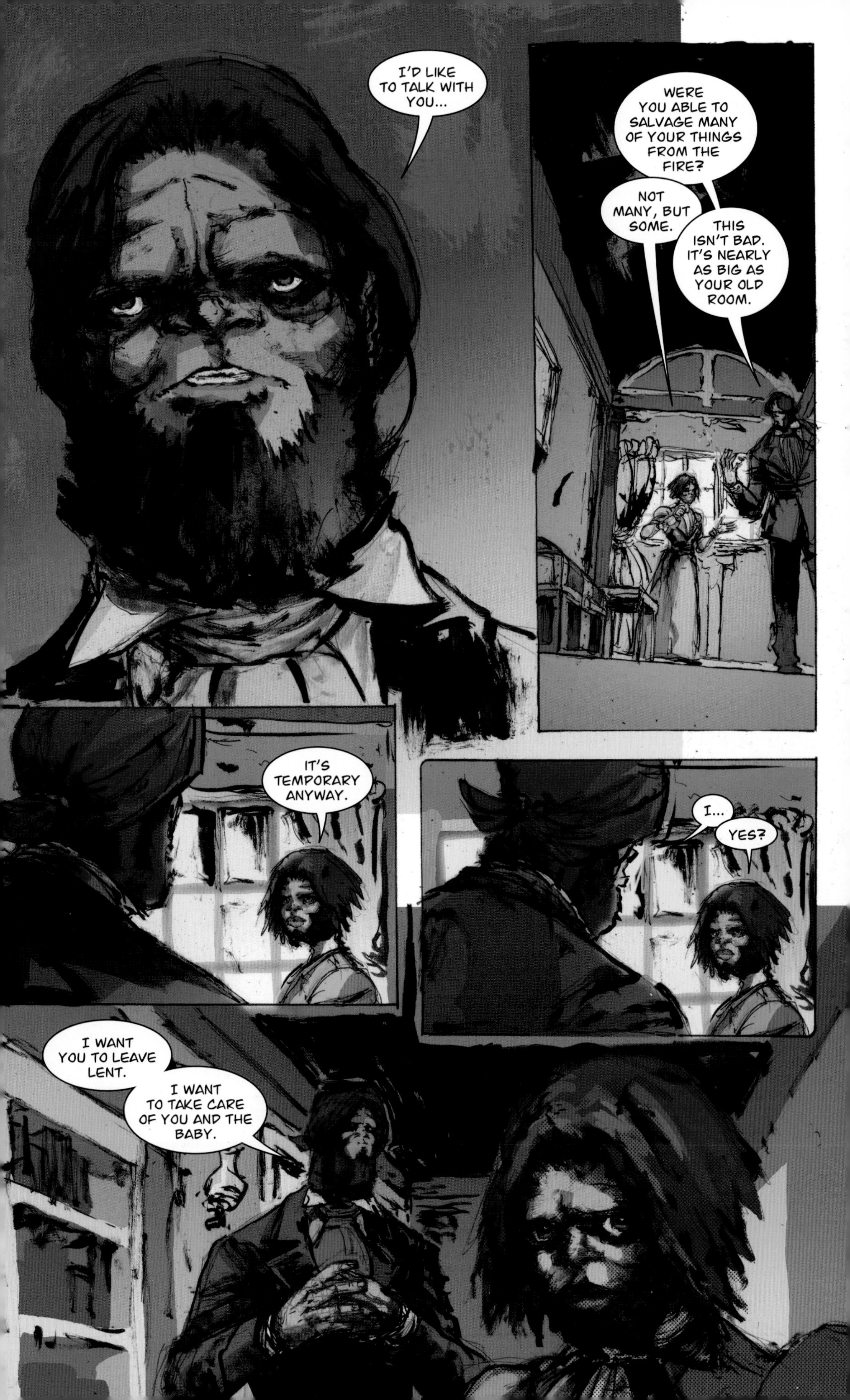
I'D LIKE TO TALK WITH YOU...
WERE YOU ABLE TO SALVAGE MANY OF YOUR THINGS FROM THE FIRE?
NOT MANY, BUT SOME.
THIS ISN'T BAD. IT'S NEARLY AS BIG AS YOUR OLD ROOM.
IT'S TEMPORARY ANYWAY.
I...
YES?
I WANT YOU TO LEAVE LENT.
I WANT TO TAKE CARE OF YOU AND THE BABY.

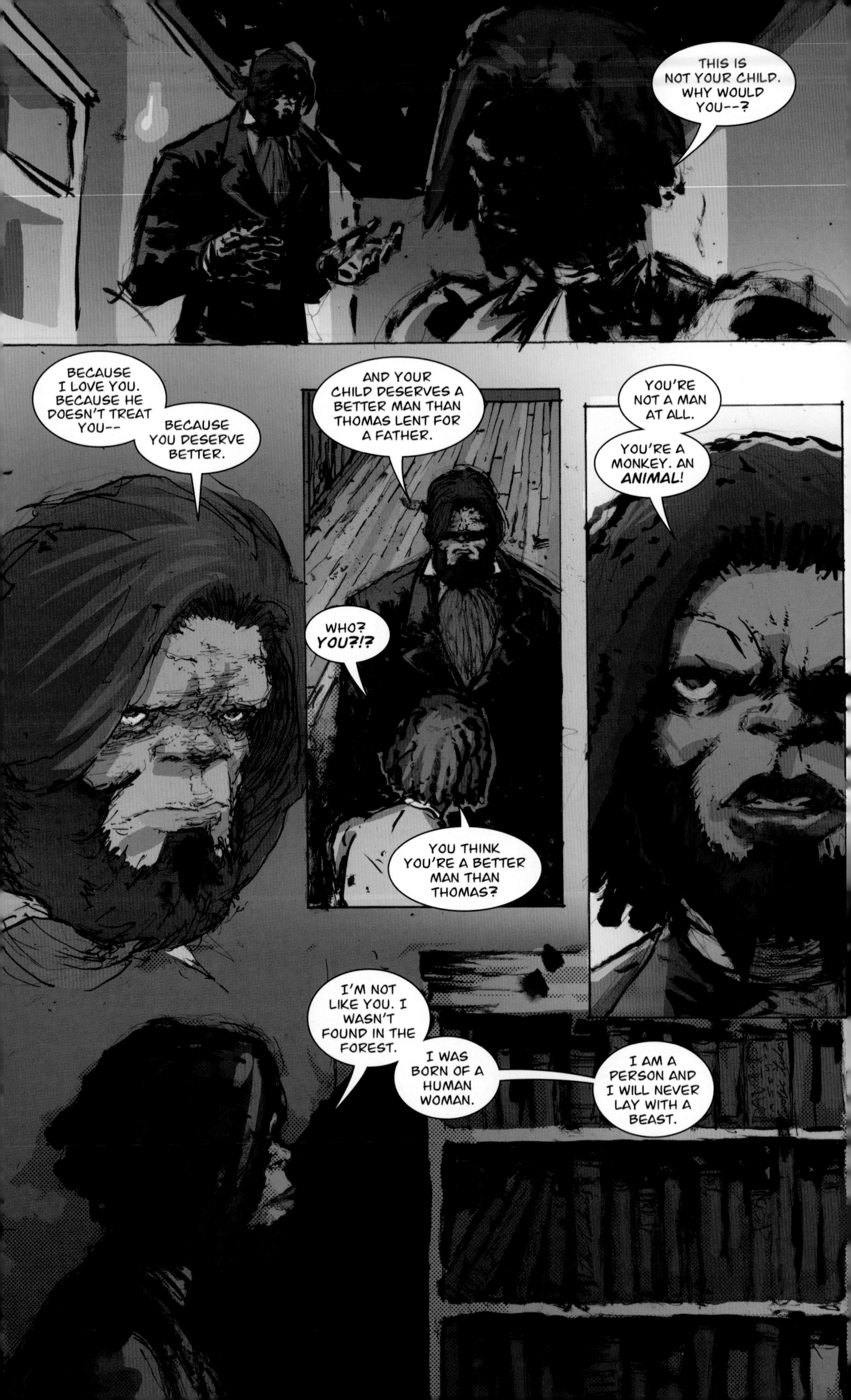
THIS IS NOT YOUR CHILD. WHY WOULD YOU--?
BECAUSE I LOVE YOU. BECAUSE HE DOESN'T TREAT YOU--
BECAUSE YOU DESERVE BETTER.
AND YOUR CHILD DESERVES A BETTER MAN THAN THOMAS LENT FOR A FATHER.
WHO? YOU?!?
YOU THINK YOU'RE A BETTER MAN THAN THOMAS?
YOU'RE NOT A MAN AT ALL.
YOU'RE A MONKEY. AN ANIMAL!
I'M NOT LIKE YOU. I WASN'T FOUND IN THE FOREST.
I WAS BORN OF A HUMAN WOMAN.
I AM A PERSON AND I WILL NEVER LAY WITH A BEAST.

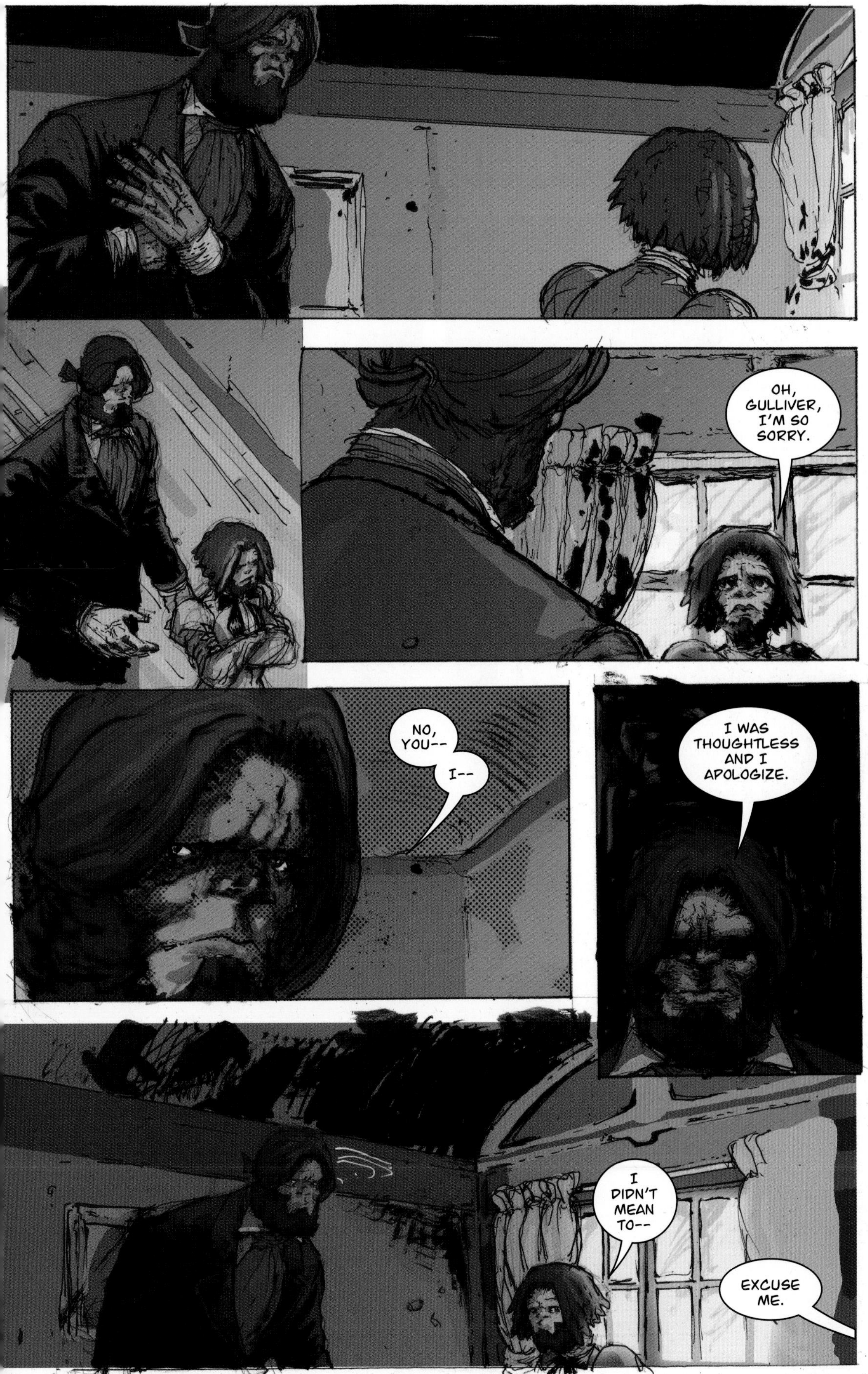
OH, GULLIVER, I'M SO SORRY.
NO, YOU--
I--
I WAS THOUGHTLESS AND I APOLOGIZE.
I DIDN'T MEAN TO--
EXCUSE ME.

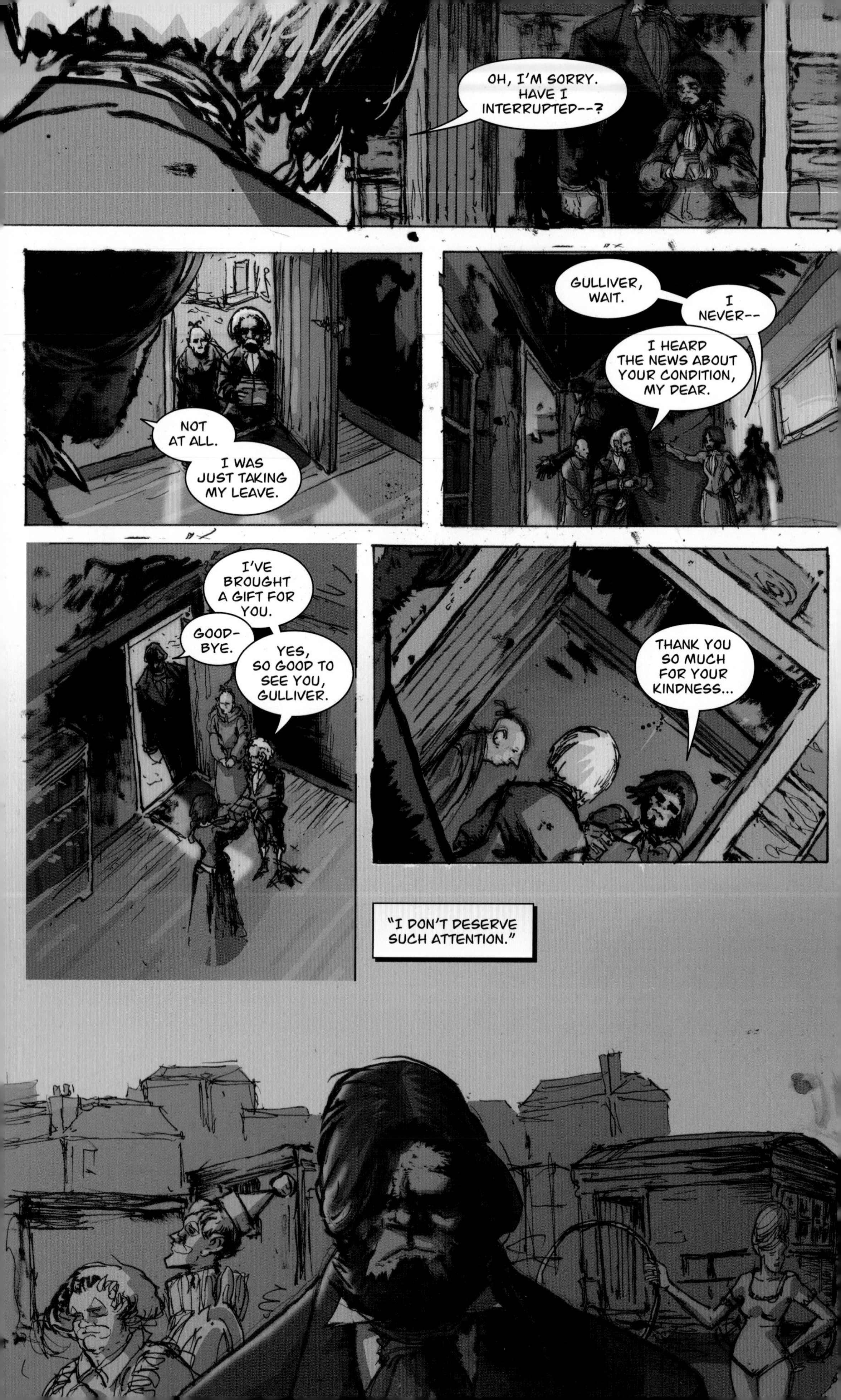
OH, I'M SORRY. HAVE I INTERRUPTED--?
NOT AT ALL.
I WAS JUST TAKING MY LEAVE.
GULLIVER, WAIT.
I NEVER--
I HEARD THE NEWS ABOUT YOUR CONDITION, MY DEAR.
I'VE BROUGHT A GIFT FOR YOU.
GOOD-BYE.
YES, SO GOOD TO SEE YOU, GULLIVER.
THANK YOU SO MUCH FOR YOUR KINDNESS...
"I DON'T DESERVE SUCH ATTENTION."

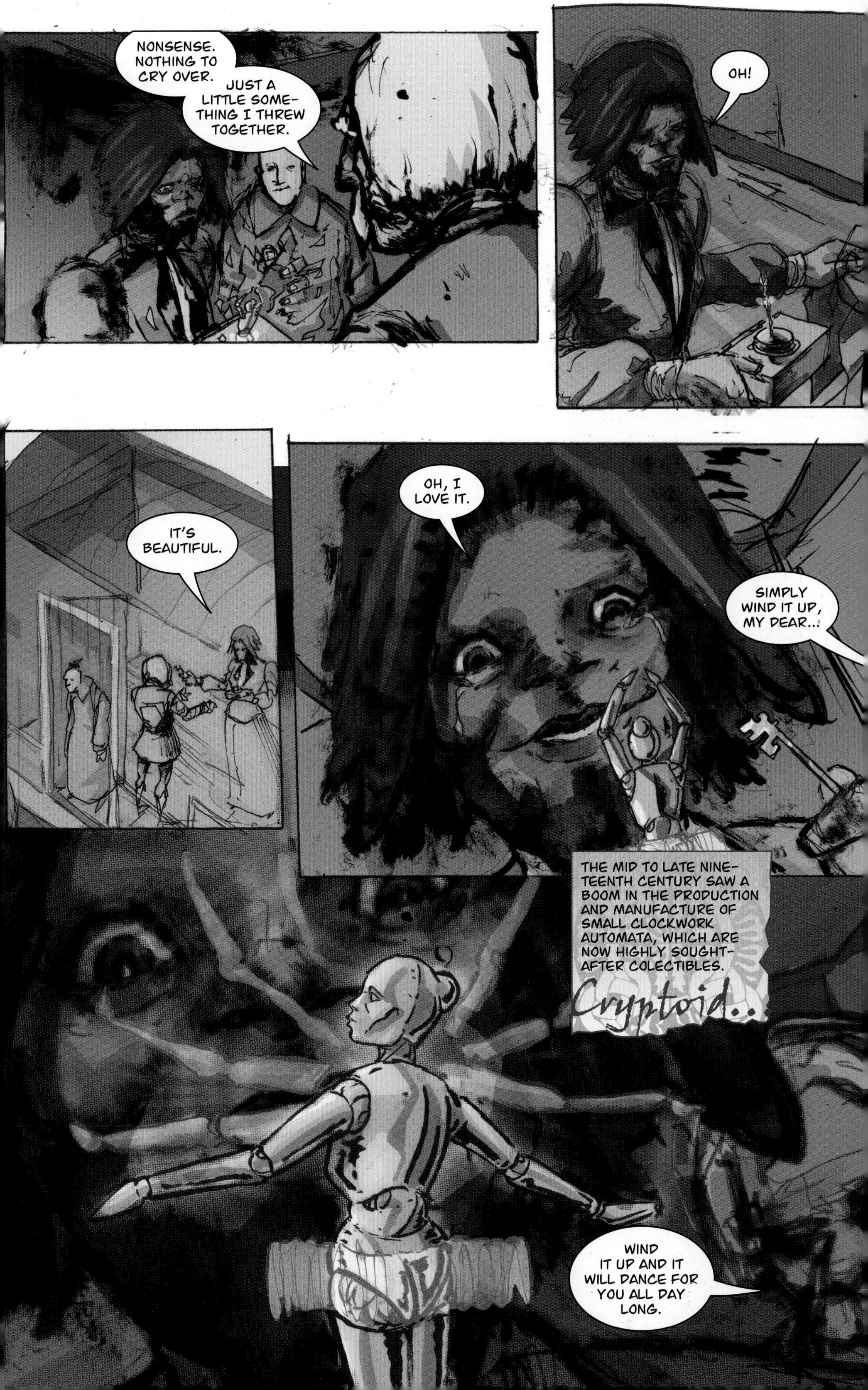
NONSENSE. NOTHING TO CRY OVER.
JUST A LITTLE SOME-THING I THREW TOGETHER.
OH!
IT'S BEAUTIFUL.
OH, I LOVE IT.
SIMPLY WIND IT UP, MY DEAR...
THE MID TO LATE NINE-TEENTH CENTURY SAW A BOOM IN THE PRODUCTION AND MANUFACTURE OF SMALL CLOCKWORK AUTOMATA, WHICH ARE NOW HIGHLY SOUGHT-AFTER COLECTIBLES.
Cryptoid...
WIND IT UP AND IT WILL DANCE FOR YOU ALL DAY LONG.

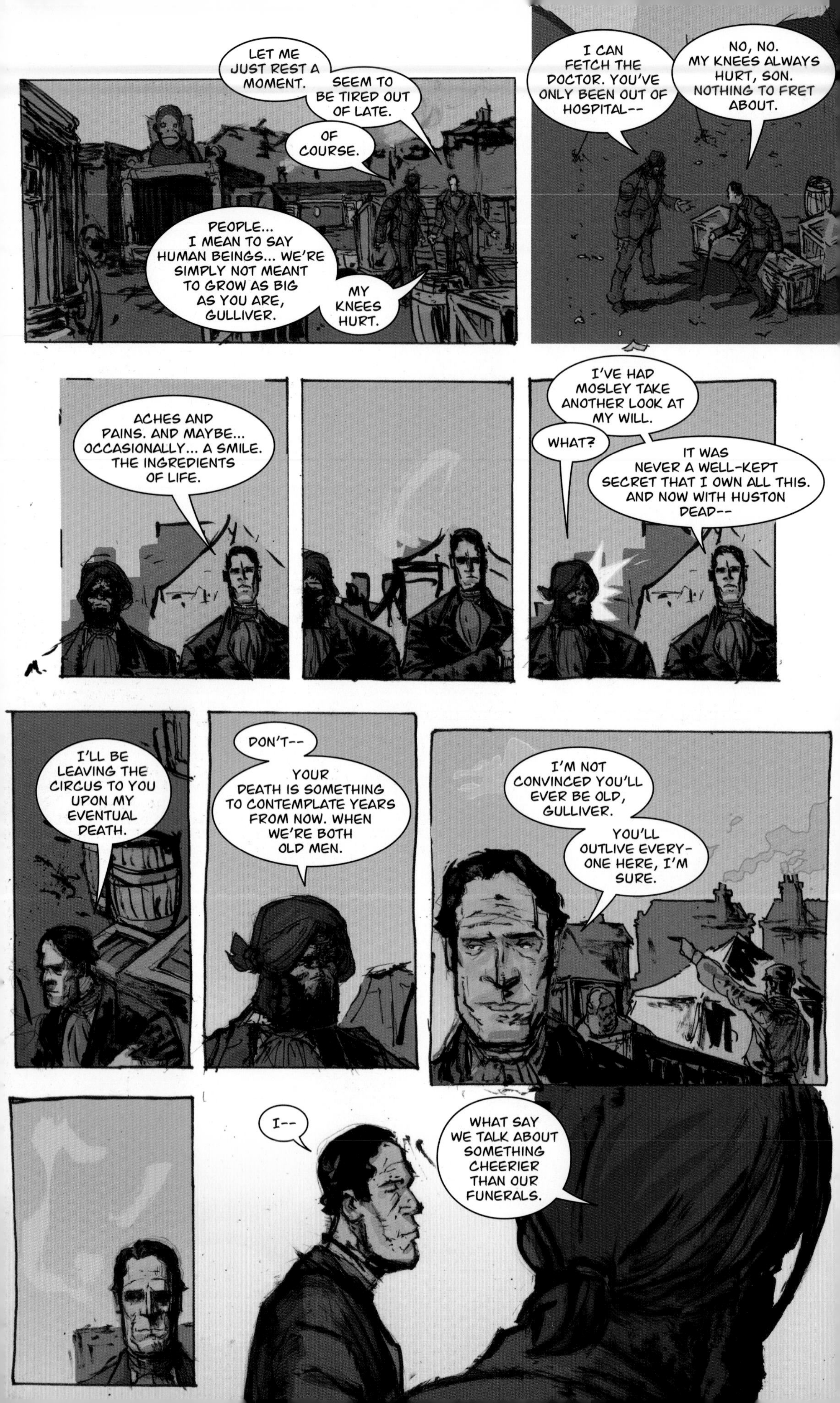
LET ME JUST REST A MOMENT.
SEEM TO BE TIRED OUT OF LATE.
OF COURSE.
PEOPLE... I MEAN TO SAY HUMAN BEINGS... WE'RE SIMPLY NOT MEANT TO GROW AS BIG AS YOU ARE, GULLIVER.
MY KNEES HURT.
I CAN FETCH THE DOCTOR. YOU'VE ONLY BEEN OUT OF HOSPITAL--
NO, NO. MY KNEES ALWAYS HURT, SON. NOTHING TO FRET ABOUT.
ACHES AND PAINS. AND MAYBE... OCCASIONALLY... A SMILE. THE INGREDIENTS OF LIFE.
I'VE HAD MOSLEY TAKE ANOTHER LOOK AT MY WILL.
WHAT?
IT WAS NEVER A WELL-KEPT SECRET THAT I OWN ALL THIS. AND NOW WITH HUSTON DEAD--
I'LL BE LEAVING THE CIRCUS TO YOU UPON MY EVENTUAL DEATH.
DON'T--
YOUR DEATH IS SOMETHING TO CONTEMPLATE YEARS FROM NOW. WHEN WE'RE BOTH OLD MEN.
I'M NOT CONVINCED YOU'LL EVER BE OLD, GULLIVER.
YOU'LL OUTLIVE EVERY-ONE HERE, I'M SURE.
I--
WHAT SAY WE TALK ABOUT SOMETHING CHEERIER THAN OUR FUNERALS.

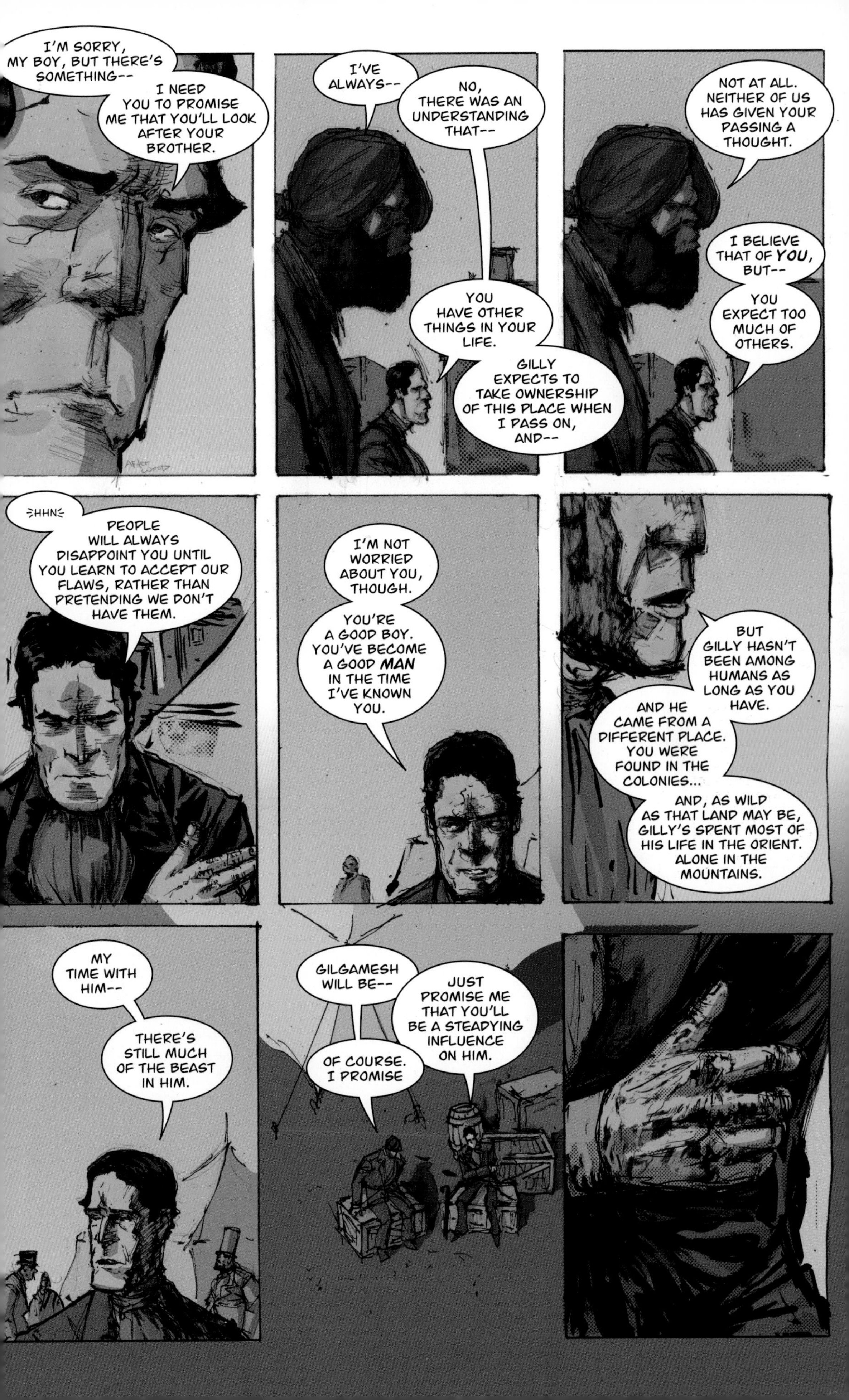
I'M SORRY, MY BOY, BUT THERE'S SOMETHING--
I NEED YOU TO PROMISE ME THAT YOU'LL LOOK AFTER YOUR BROTHER.
I'VE ALWAYS--
NO, THERE WAS AN UNDERSTANDING THAT--
YOU HAVE OTHER THINGS IN YOUR LIFE.
GILLY EXPECTS TO TAKE OWNERSHIP OF THIS PLACE WHEN I PASS ON, AND--
NOT AT ALL. NEITHER OF US HAS GIVEN YOUR PASSING A THOUGHT.
I BELIEVE THAT OF YOU, BUT--
YOU EXPECT TOO MUCH OF OTHERS.
HHN
PEOPLE WILL ALWAYS DISAPPOINT YOU UNTIL YOU LEARN TO ACCEPT OUR FLAWS, RATHER THAN PRETENDING WE DON'T HAVE THEM.
I'M NOT WORRIED ABOUT YOU, THOUGH.
YOU'RE A GOOD BOY. YOU'VE BECOME A GOOD MAN IN THE TIME I'VE KNOWN YOU.
BUT GILLY HASN'T BEEN AMONG HUMANS AS LONG AS YOU HAVE.
AND HE CAME FROM A DIFFERENT PLACE. YOU WERE FOUND IN THE COLONIES...
AND, AS WILD AS THAT LAND MAY BE, GILLY'S SPENT MOST OF HIS LIFE IN THE ORIENT. ALONE IN THE MOUNTAINS.
MY TIME WITH HIM--
THERE'S STILL MUCH OF THE BEAST IN HIM.
GILGAMESH WILL BE--
JUST PROMISE ME THAT YOU'LL BE A STEADYING INFLUENCE ON HIM.
OF COURSE. I PROMISE

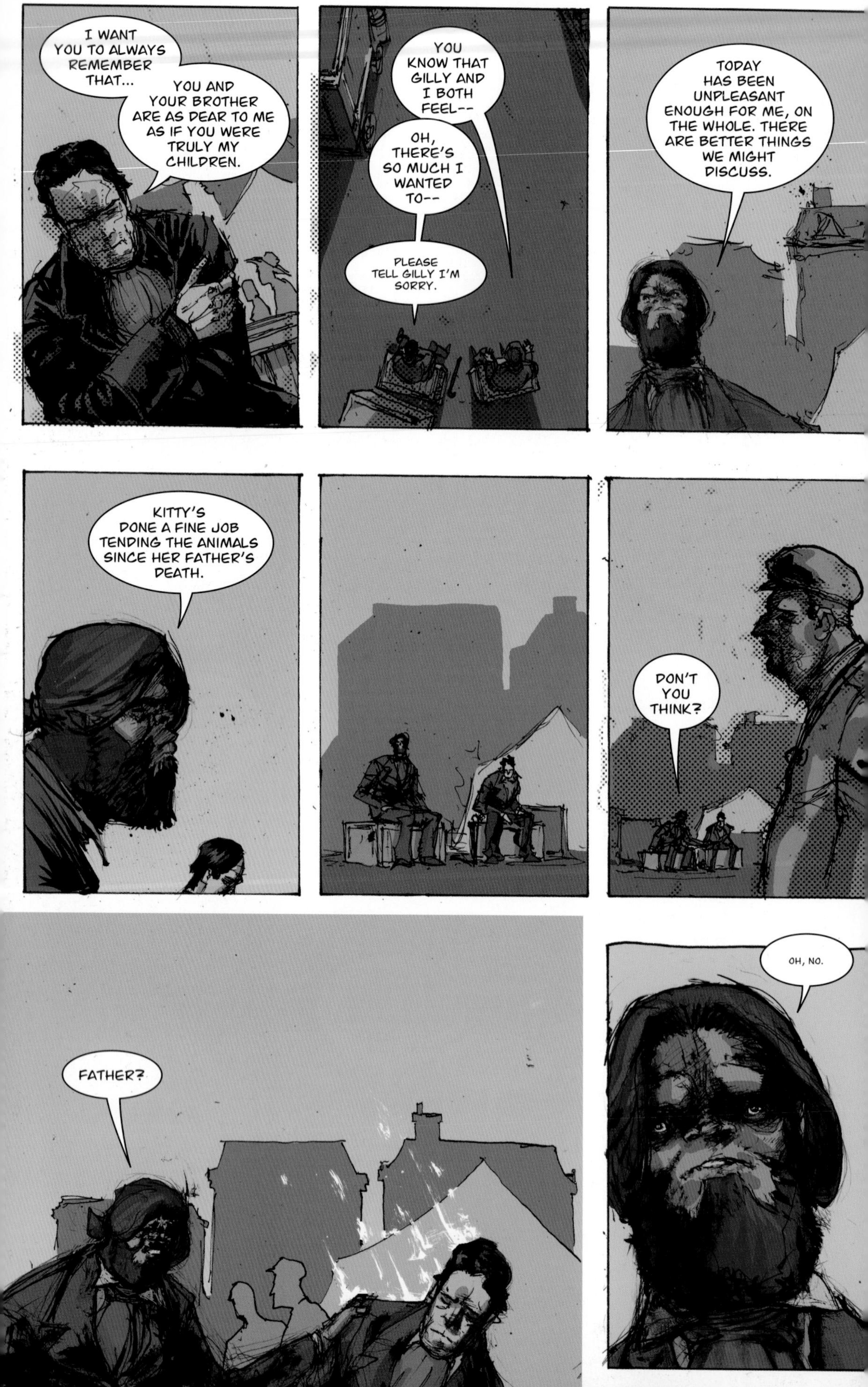
I WANT YOU TO ALWAYS REMEMBER THAT...
YOU AND YOUR BROTHER ARE AS DEAR TO ME AS IF YOU WERE TRULY MY CHILDREN.
YOU KNOW THAT GILLY AND I BOTH FEEL--
OH, THERE'S SO MUCH I WANTED TO--
PLEASE TELL GILLY I'M SORRY.
TODAY HAS BEEN UNPLEASANT ENOUGH FOR ME, ON THE WHOLE. THERE ARE BETTER THINGS WE MIGHT DISCUSS.
KITTY'S DONE A FINE JOB TENDING THE ANIMALS SINCE HER FATHER'S DEATH.
DON'T YOU THINK?
FATHER?
OH, NO.

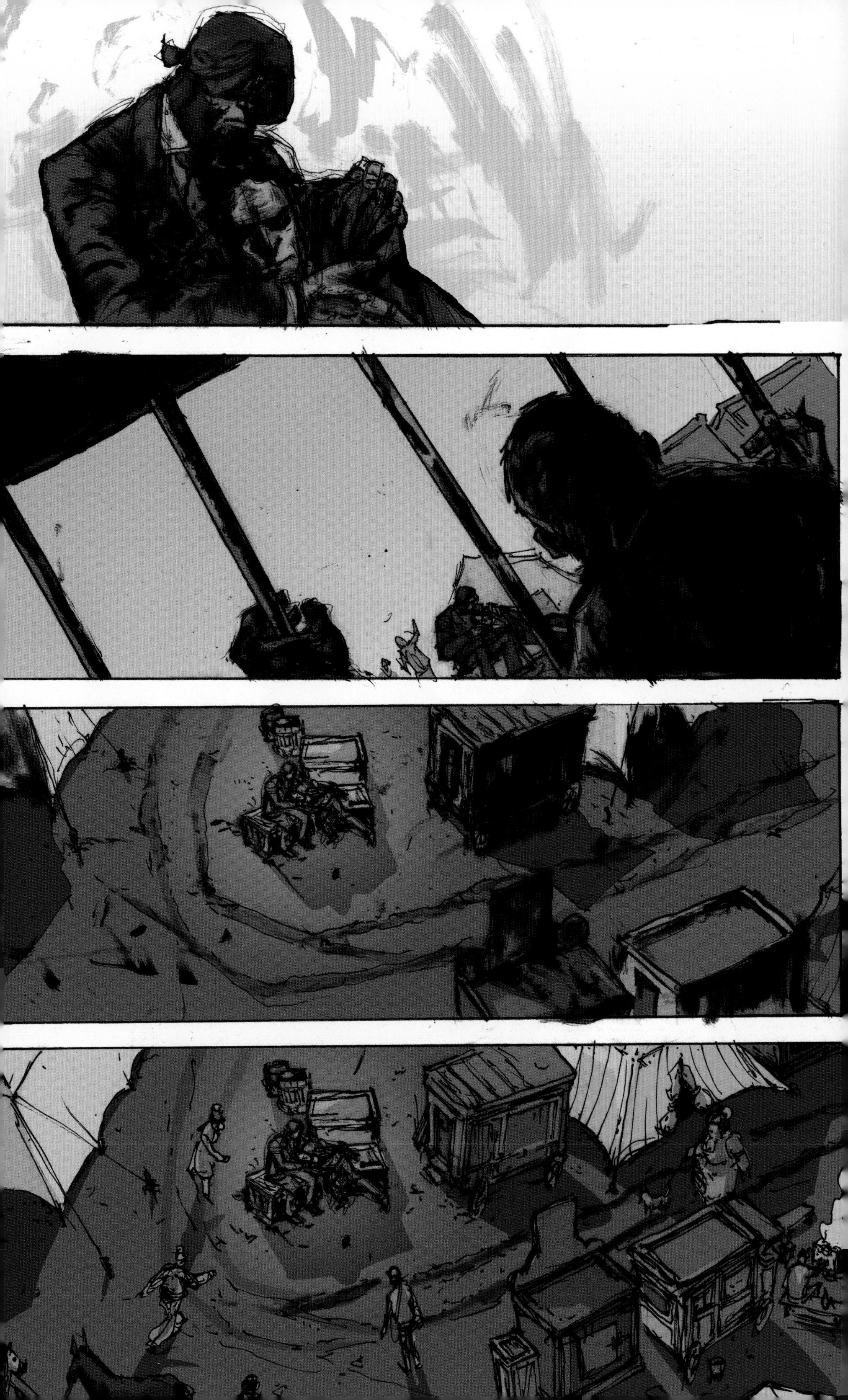

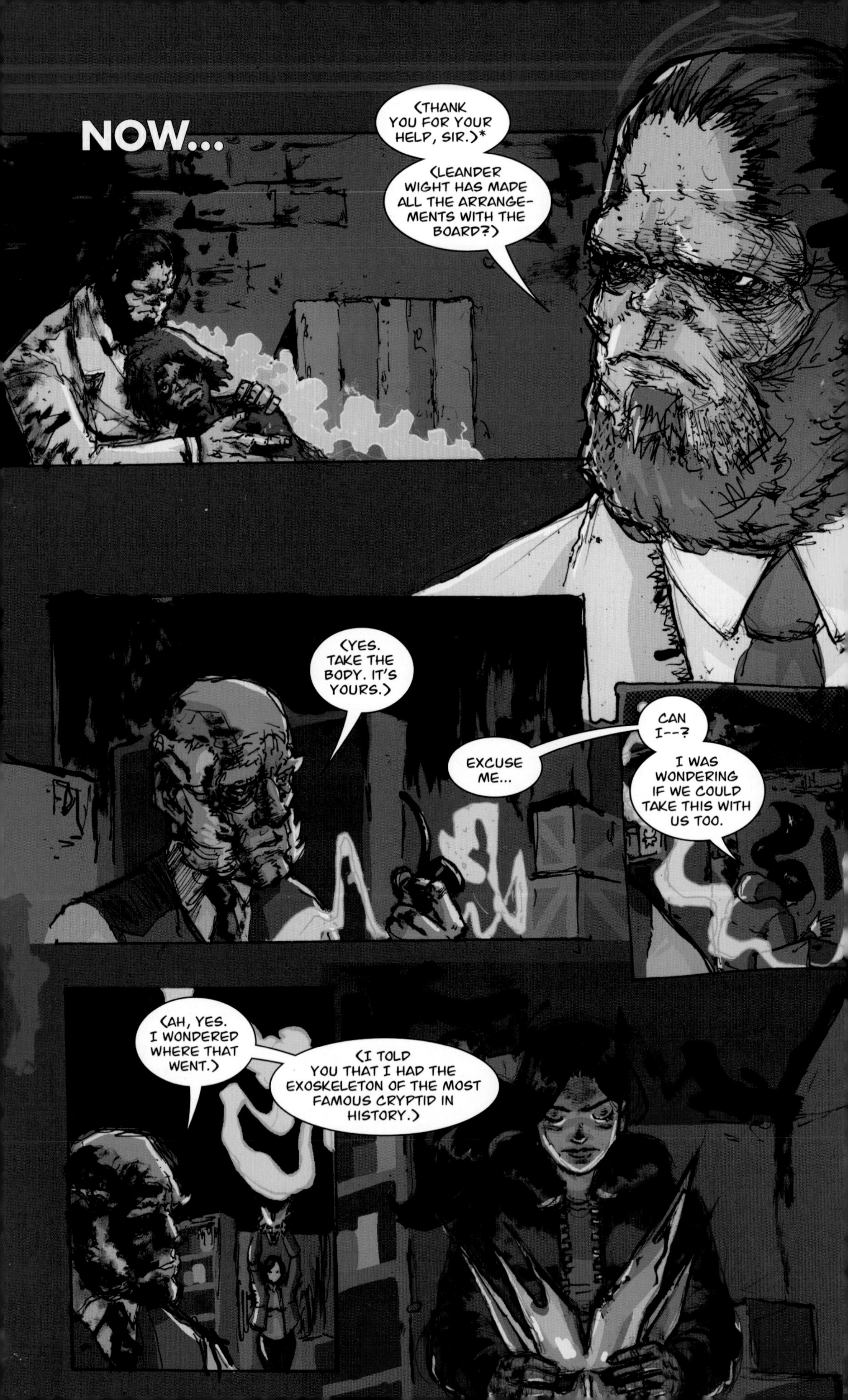
NOW...
(THANK YOU FOR YOUR HELP, SIR.)*
(LEANDER WIGHT HAS MADE ALL THE ARRANGEMENTS WITH THE BOARD?)
(YES. TAKE THE BODY. IT'S YOURS.)
EXCUSE ME...
CAN I--?
I WAS WONDERING IF WE COULD TAKE THIS WITH US TOO.
(AH, YES. I WONDERED WHERE THAT WENT.)
(I TOLD YOU THAT I HAD THE EXOSKELETON OF THE MOST FAMOUS CRYPTID IN HISTORY.)

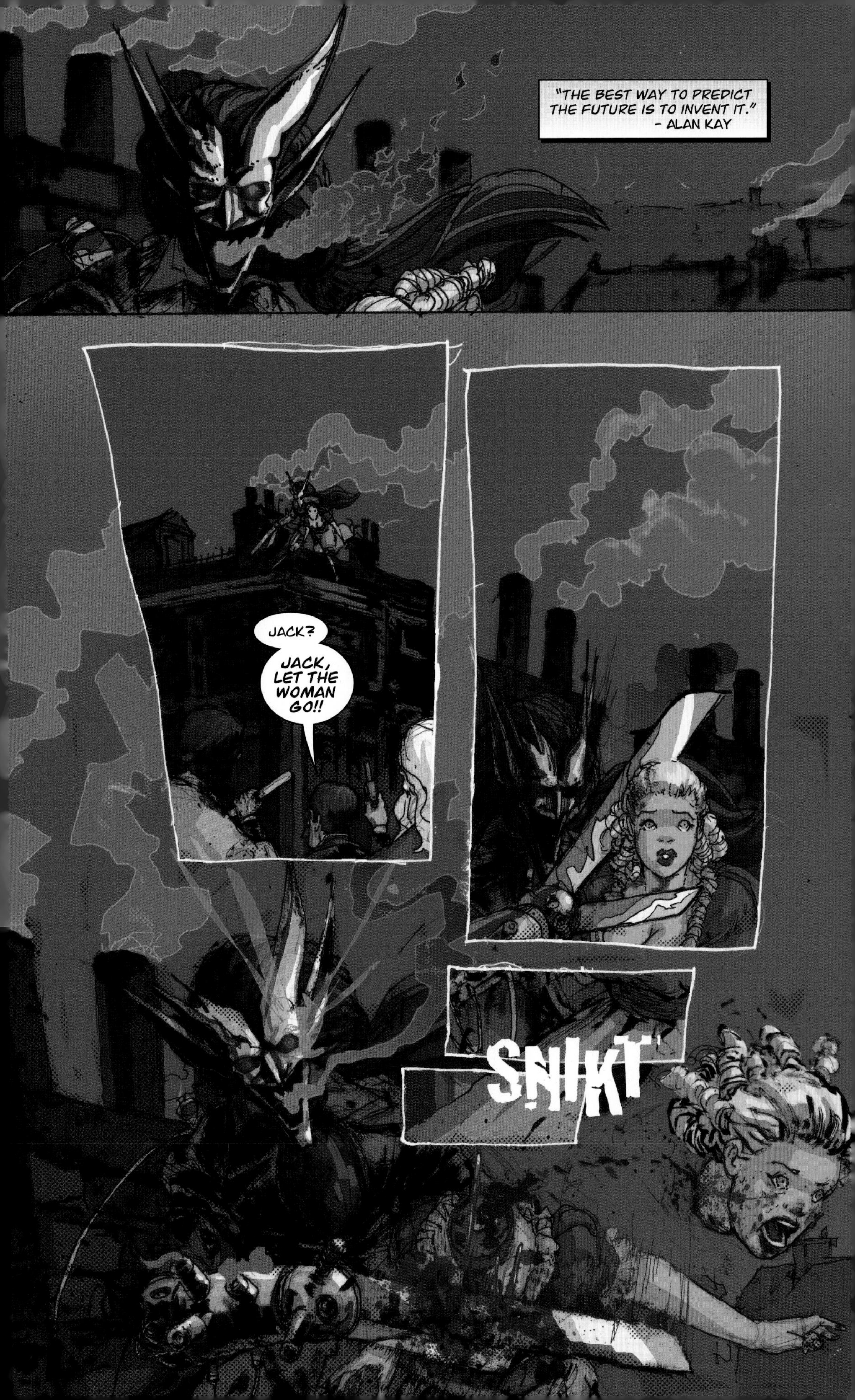
"THE BEST WAY TO PREDICT THE FUTURE IS TO INVENT IT." - ALAN KAY
JACK?
JACK, LET THE WOMAN GO!!
SNIKT

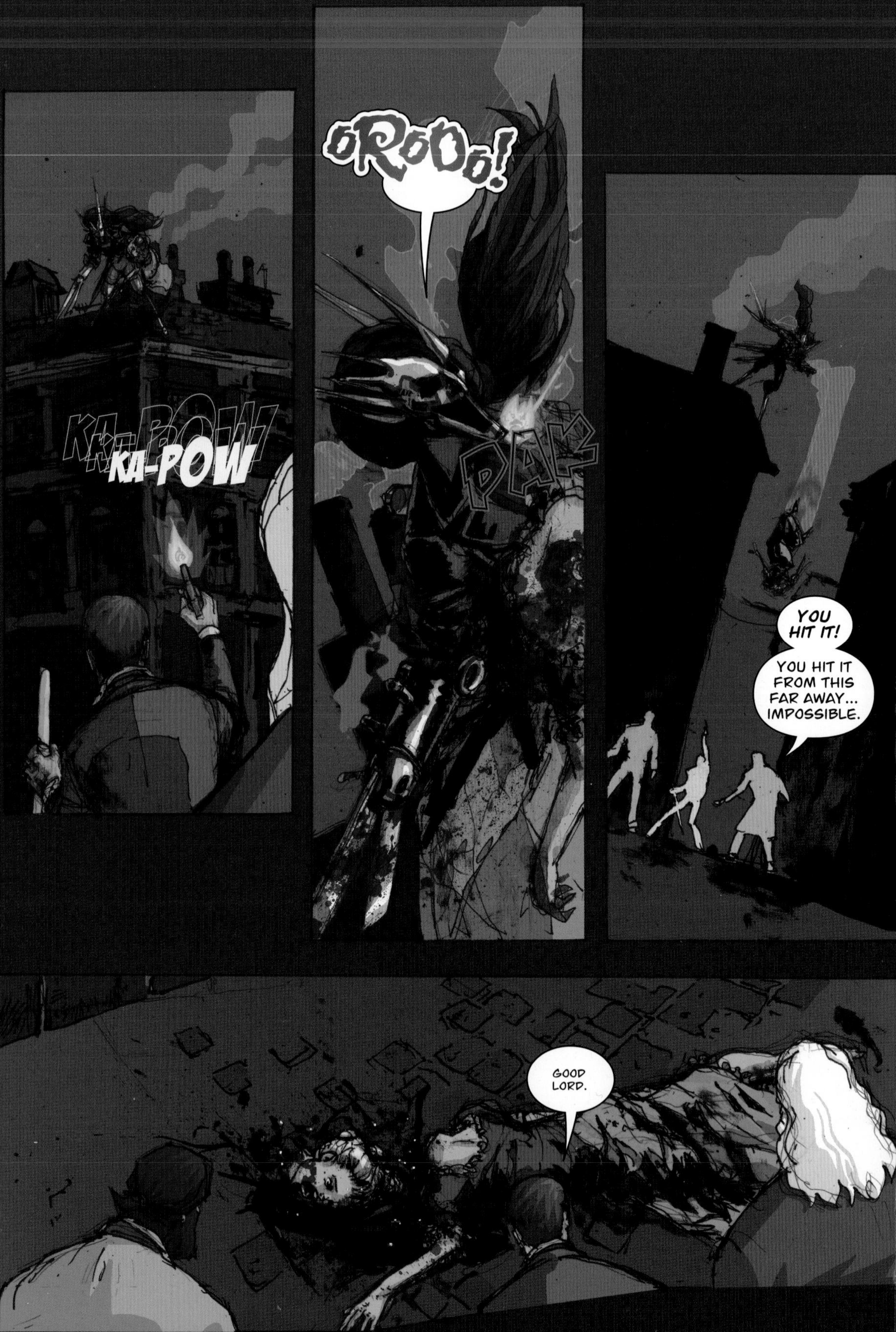

KA-POW
KA-POW
OROOOO!
PAK
YOU HIT IT!
YOU HIT IT FROM THIS FAR AWAY... IMPOSSIBLE.
GOOD LORD.

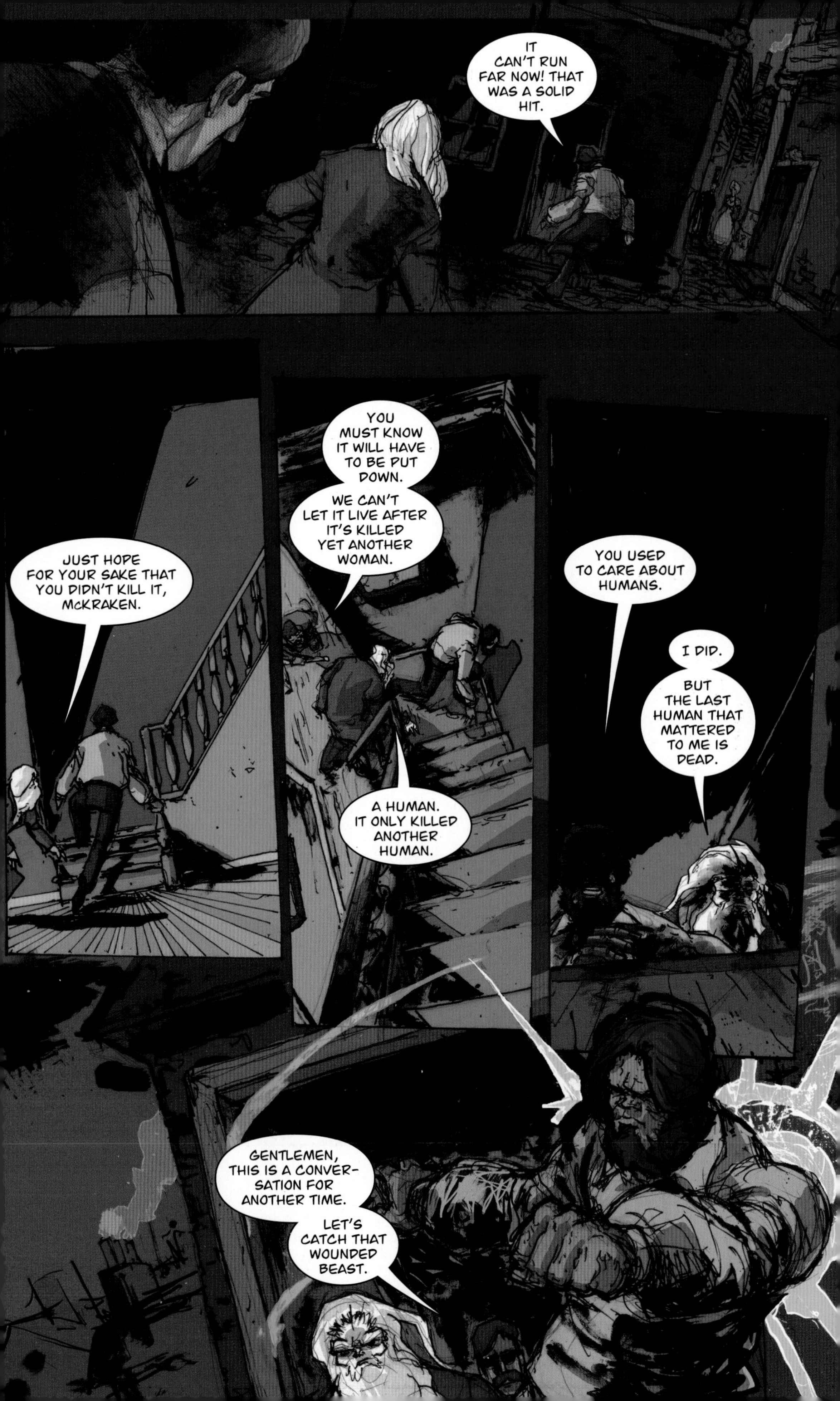
IT CAN'T RUN FAR NOW! THAT WAS A SOLID HIT.
JUST HOPE FOR YOUR SAKE THAT YOU DIDN'T KILL IT, McKRAKEN.
YOU MUST KNOW IT WILL HAVE TO BE PUT DOWN.
WE CAN'T LET IT LIVE AFTER IT'S KILLED YET ANOTHER WOMAN.
A HUMAN. IT ONLY KILLED ANOTHER HUMAN.
YOU USED TO CARE ABOUT HUMANS.
I DID.
BUT THE LAST HUMAN THAT MATTERED TO ME IS DEAD.
GENTLEMEN, THIS IS A CONVER-SATION FOR ANOTHER TIME.
LET'S CATCH THAT WOUNDED BEAST.

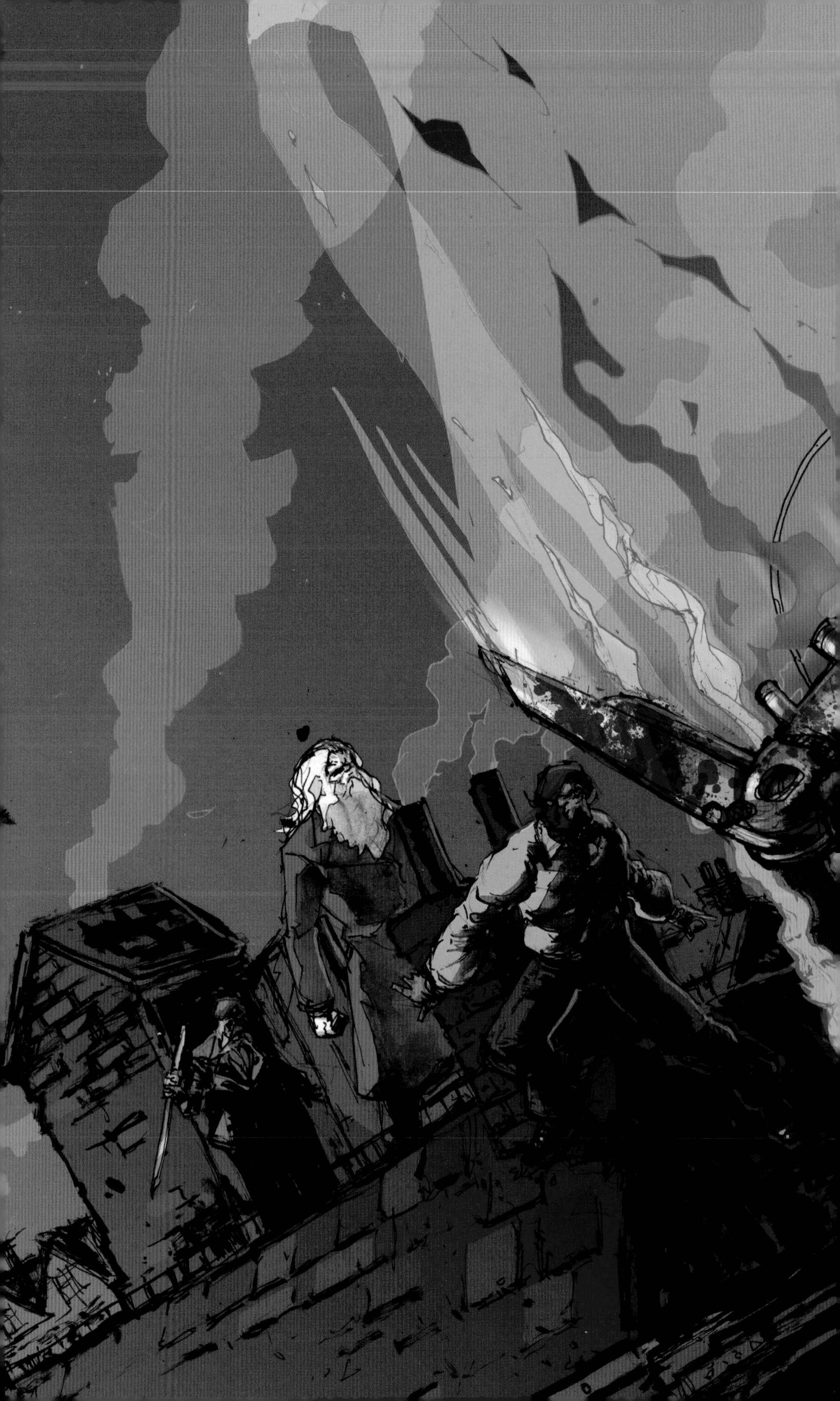

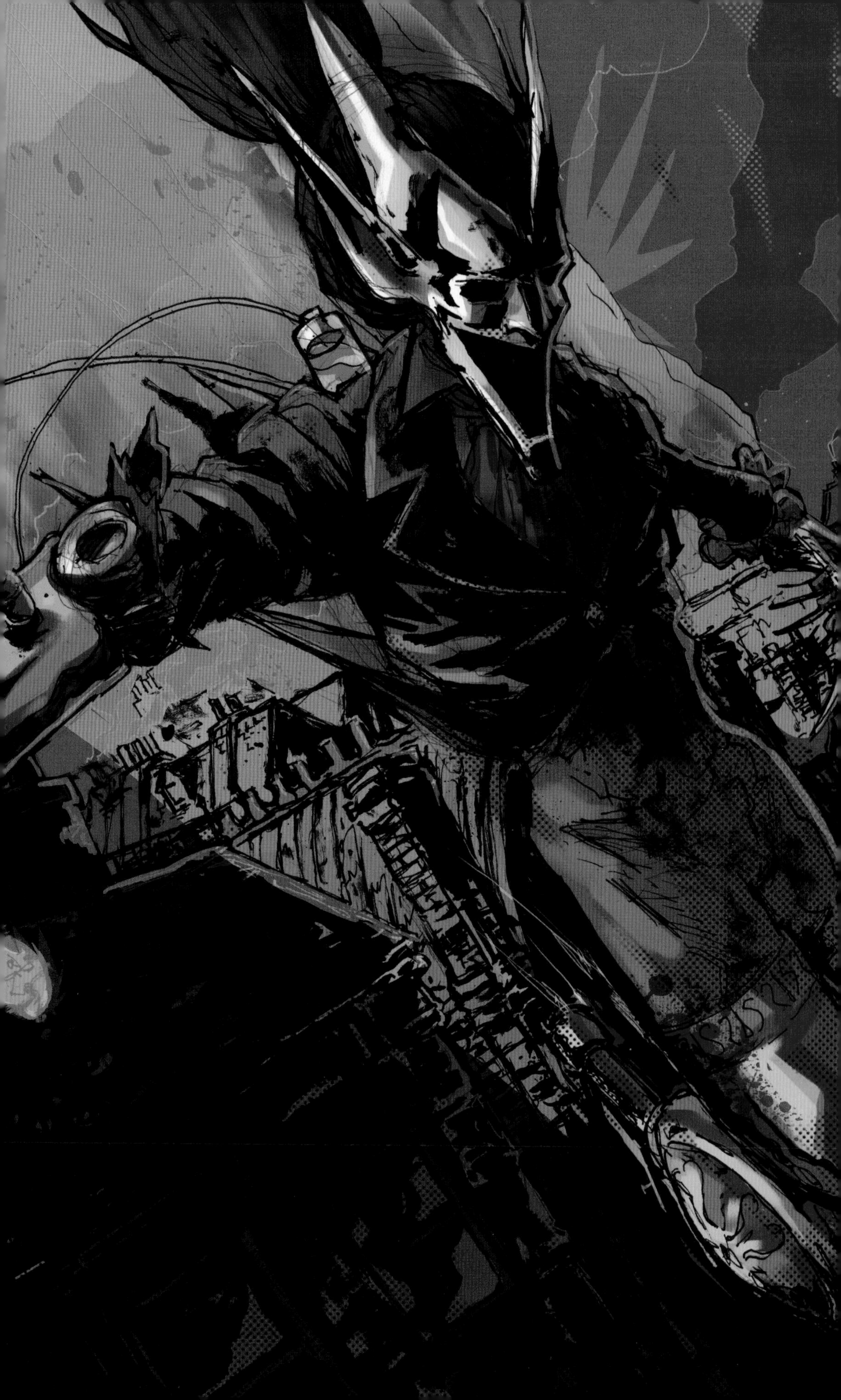

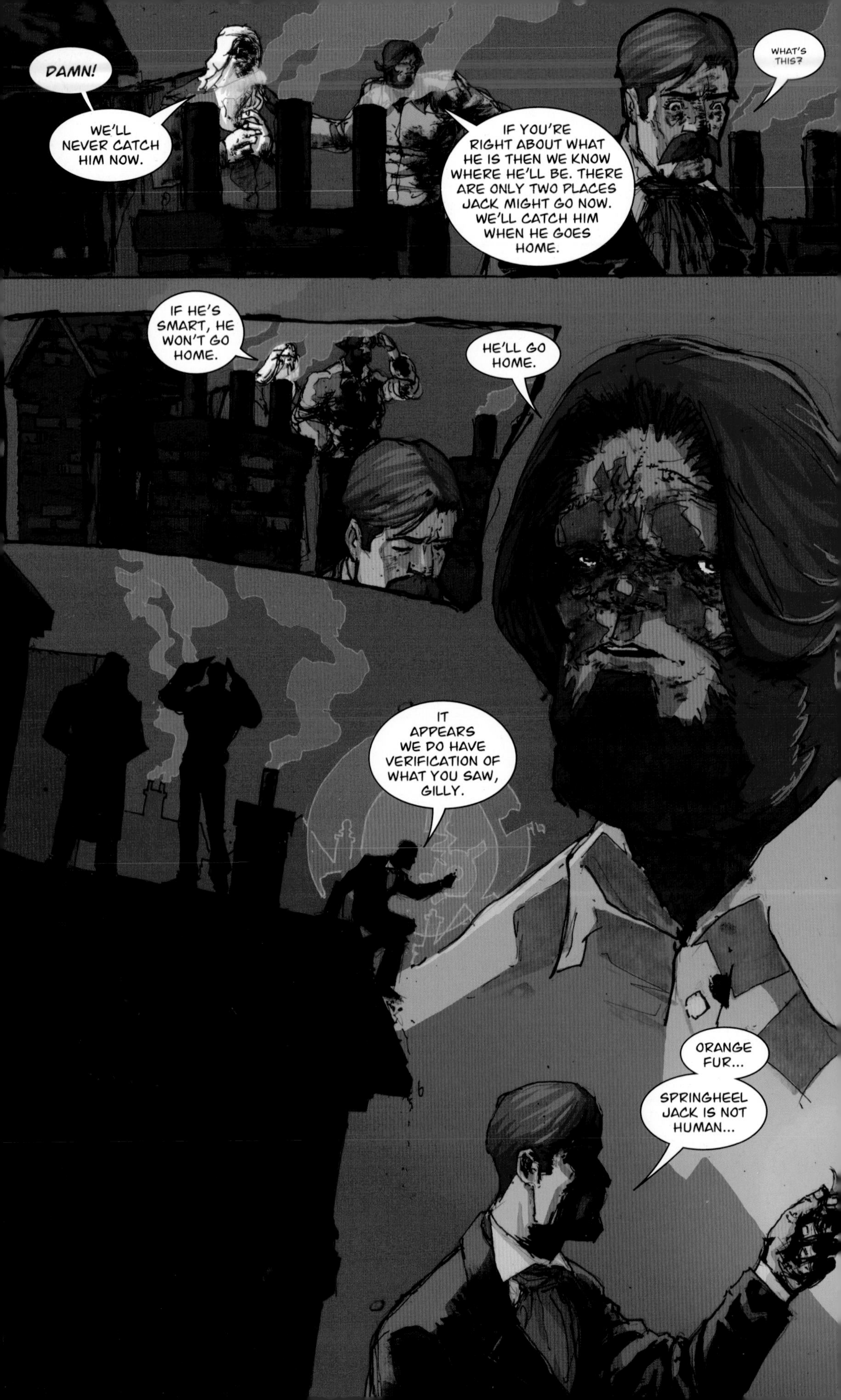
DAMN!
WE'LL NEVER CATCH HIM NOW.
IF YOU'RE RIGHT ABOUT WHAT HE IS THEN WE KNOW WHERE HE'LL BE. THERE ARE ONLY TWO PLACES JACK MIGHT GO NOW. WE'LL CATCH HIM WHEN HE GOES HOME.
WHAT'S THIS?
IF HE'S SMART, HE WON'T GO HOME.
HE'LL GO HOME.
IT APPEARS WE DO HAVE VERIFICATION OF WHAT YOU SAW, GILLY.
ORANGE FUR...
SPRINGHEEL JACK IS NOT HUMAN...

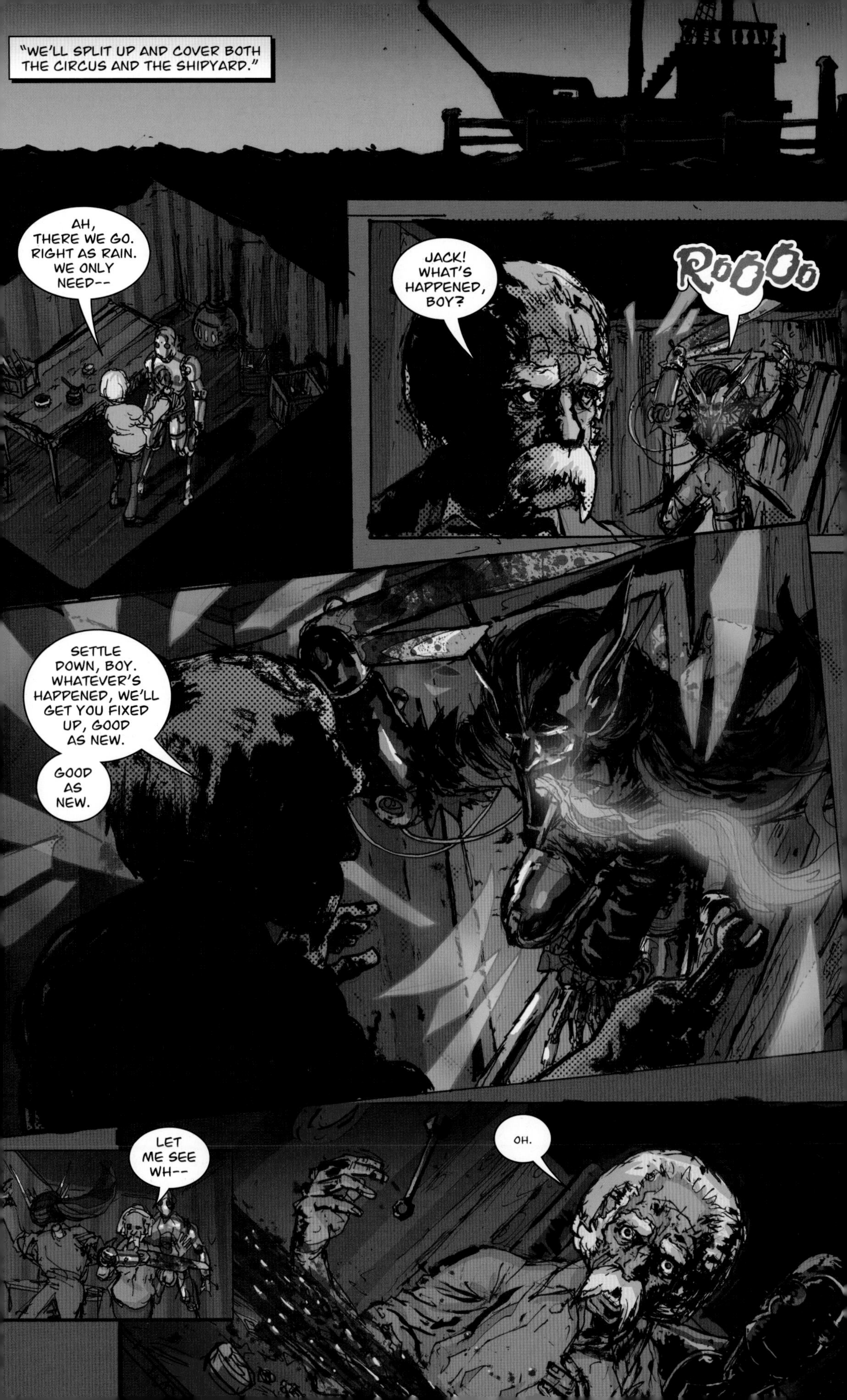
"WE'LL SPLIT UP AND COVER BOTH THE CIRCUS AND THE SHIPYARD."
AH, THERE WE GO. RIGHT AS RAIN. WE ONLY NEED--
JACK! WHAT'S HAPPENED, BOY?
ROOOOO
SETTLE DOWN, BOY. WHATEVER'S HAPPENED, WE'LL GET YOU FIXED UP, GOOD AS NEW.
GOOD AS NEW.
LET ME SEE WH--
OH.

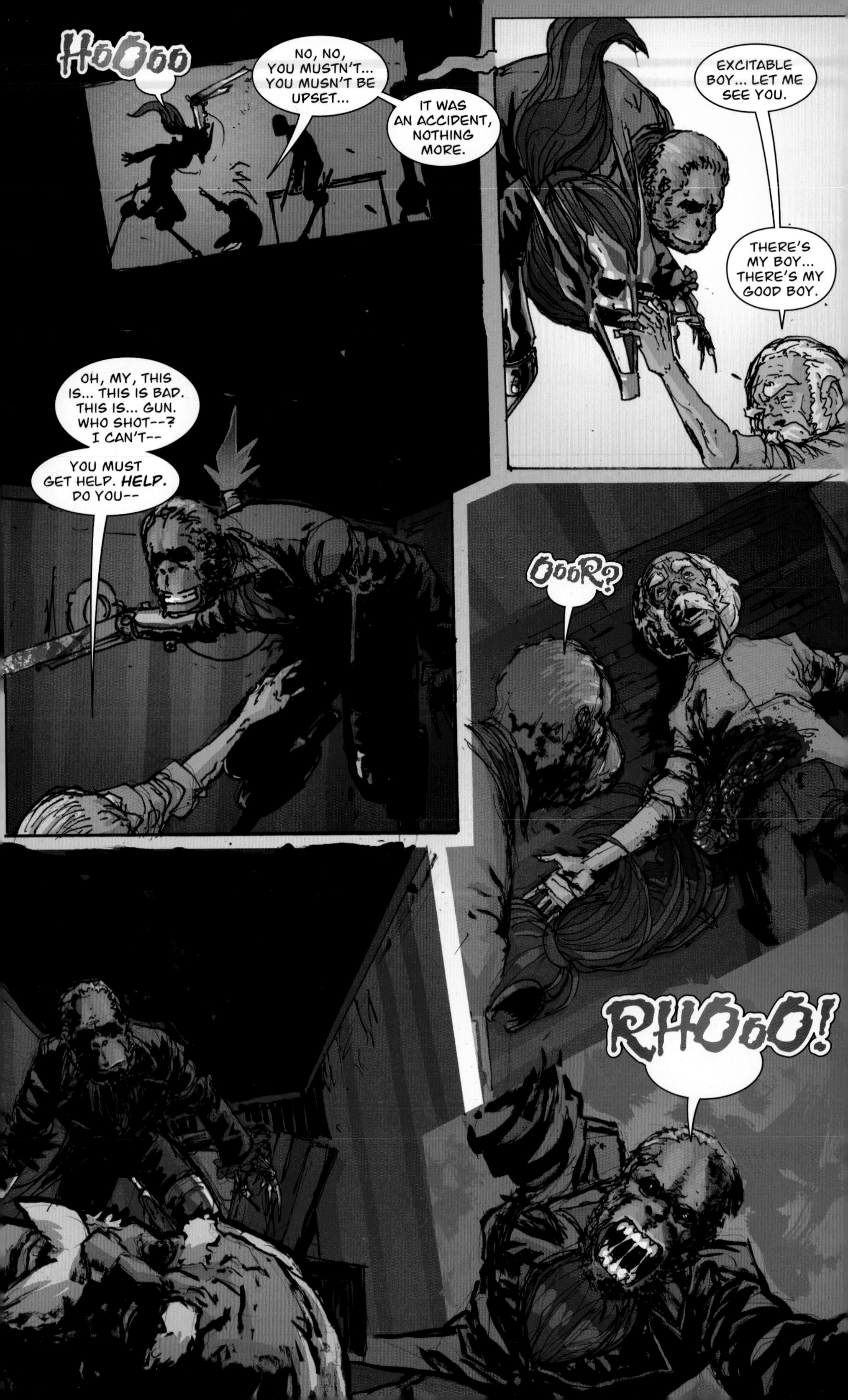
HOOOO
NO, NO, YOU MUSTN'T... YOU MUSN'T BE UPSET...
IT WAS AN ACCIDENT, NOTHING MORE.
EXCITABLE BOY... LET ME SEE YOU.
THERE'S MY BOY... THERE'S MY GOOD BOY.
OH, MY, THIS IS... THIS IS BAD. THIS IS... GUN. WHO SHOT--? I CAN'T--
YOU MUST GET HELP. **HELP.** DO YOU--
OOOR?
RHOOOO!

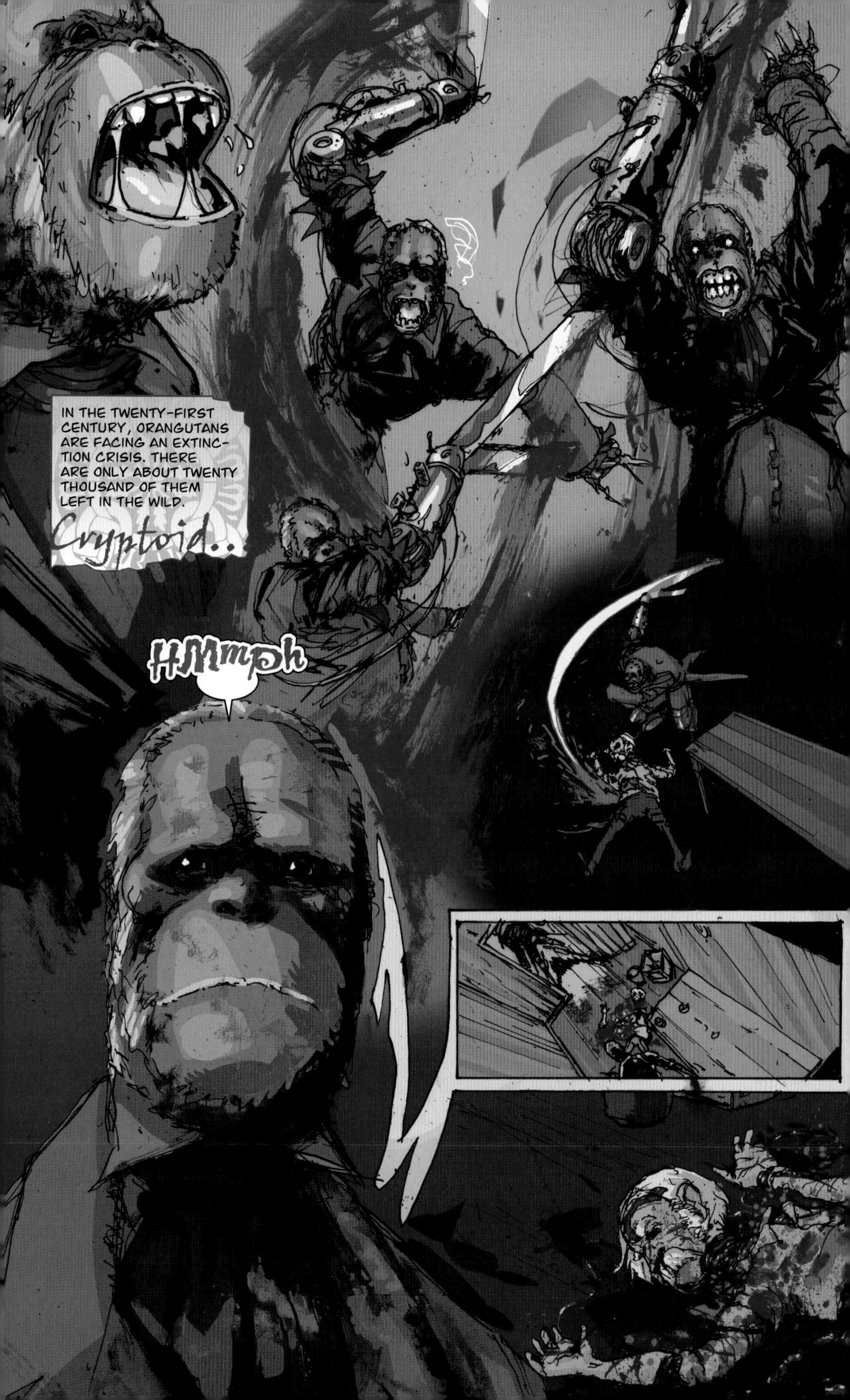
IN THE TWENTY-FIRST CENTURY, ORANGUTANS ARE FACING AN EXTINCTION CRISIS. THERE ARE ONLY ABOUT TWENTY THOUSAND OF THEM LEFT IN THE WILD.
Cryptoid..
HMmph

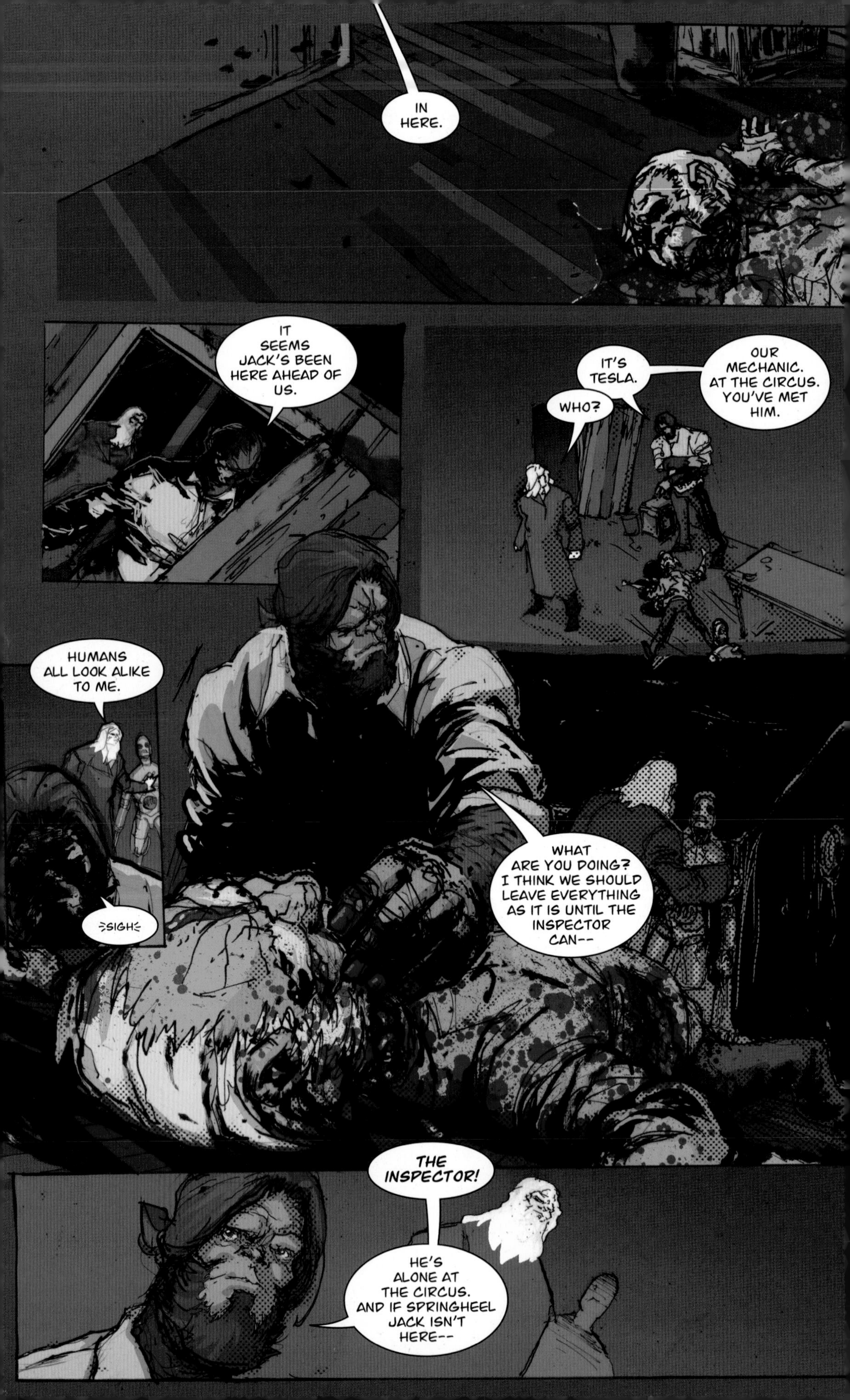
IN HERE.
IT SEEMS JACK'S BEEN HERE AHEAD OF US.
WHO?
IT'S TESLA.
OUR MECHANIC. AT THE CIRCUS. YOU'VE MET HIM.
HUMANS ALL LOOK ALIKE TO ME.
SIGH
WHAT ARE YOU DOING? I THINK WE SHOULD LEAVE EVERYTHING AS IT IS UNTIL THE INSPECTOR CAN--
THE INSPECTOR!
HE'S ALONE AT THE CIRCUS. AND IF SPRINGHEEL JACK ISN'T HERE--

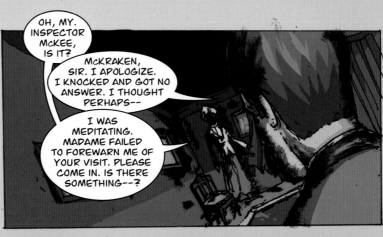

IS ANYONE IN HERE?

OH, MY. INSPECTOR MCKEE, IS IT?

MCKRAKEN, SIR. I APOLOGIZE. I KNOCKED AND GOT NO ANSWER. I THOUGHT PERHAPS--

I WAS MEDITATING. MADAME FAILED TO FOREWARN ME OF YOUR VISIT. PLEASE COME IN. IS THERE SOMETHING--?

IN FACT, I HAD A THOUGHT... I WONDERED IF YOUR--

I MEAN TO SAY THAT THIS AMAZING CREATURE MAY BE ABLE TO HELP ME FIND A DANGEROUS BEAST BEFORE IT KILLS AGAIN.

YES, I WILL GO WITH YOU.

FAREWELL, VASH. YOU WILL BE REMEMBERED FONDLY ON MANY FUTURE OCCASIONS.

WAIT A MOMENT--

OH, NO. NO!

I DON'T UNDERSTAND. ARE YOU LEAVING?

YOU WILL EXPIRE IN EIGHT MINUTES.

NOW IF YOU WILL ACCOMPANY ME, INSPECTOR, I WILL SHOW YOU WHERE TO CONFRONT THE APE THREE MINUTES FROM NOW.

YOU MUST TELL ME MORE. EIGHT MINUTES IS NO--

HOW MAY I PREVENT THIS?

THE APE IS ALREADY DYING FROM THE WOUND YOU INFLICTED, INSPECTOR...

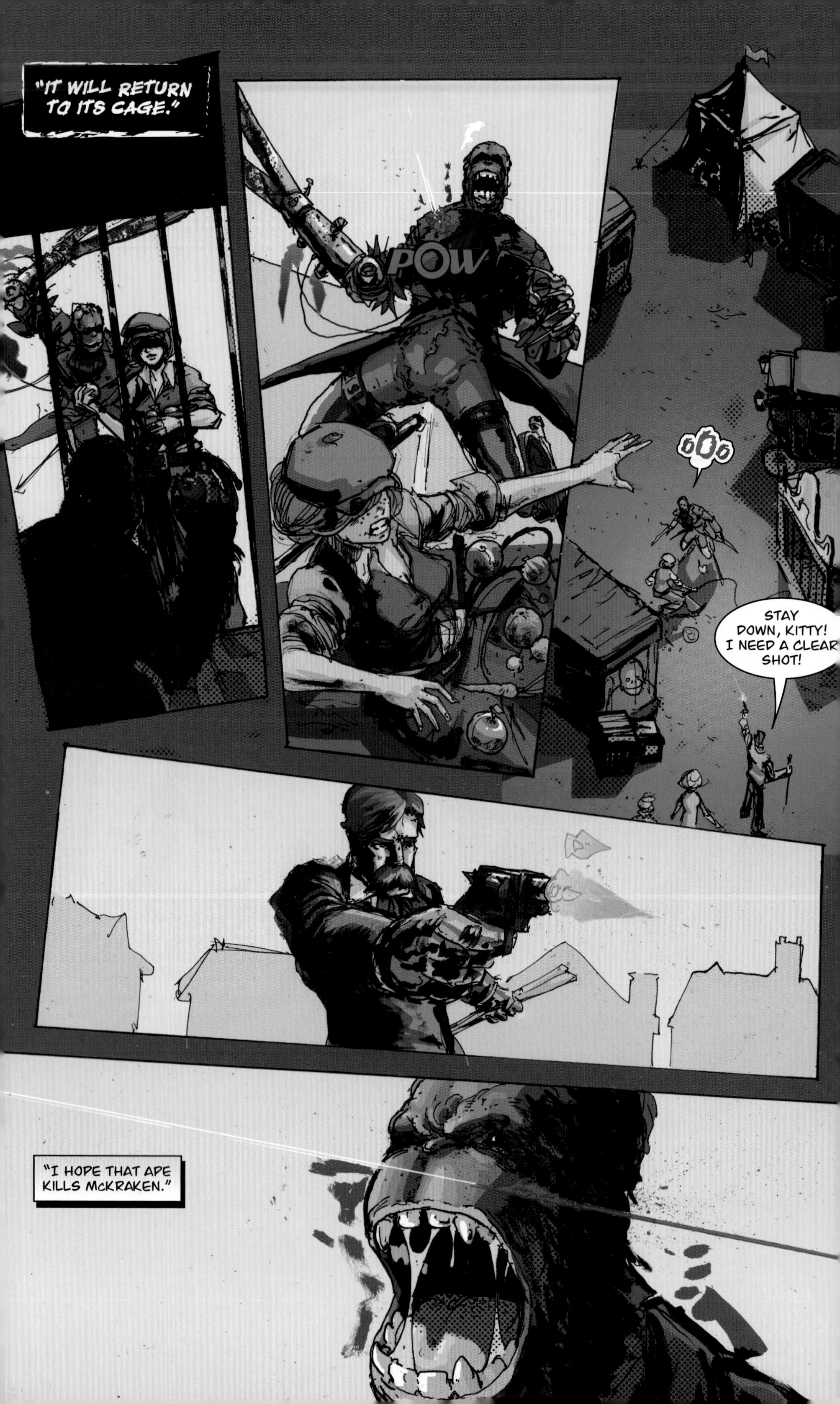
"IT WILL RETURN TO ITS CAGE."
POW
OOO
STAY DOWN, KITTY! I NEED A CLEAR SHOT!
"I HOPE THAT APE KILLS McKRAKEN."

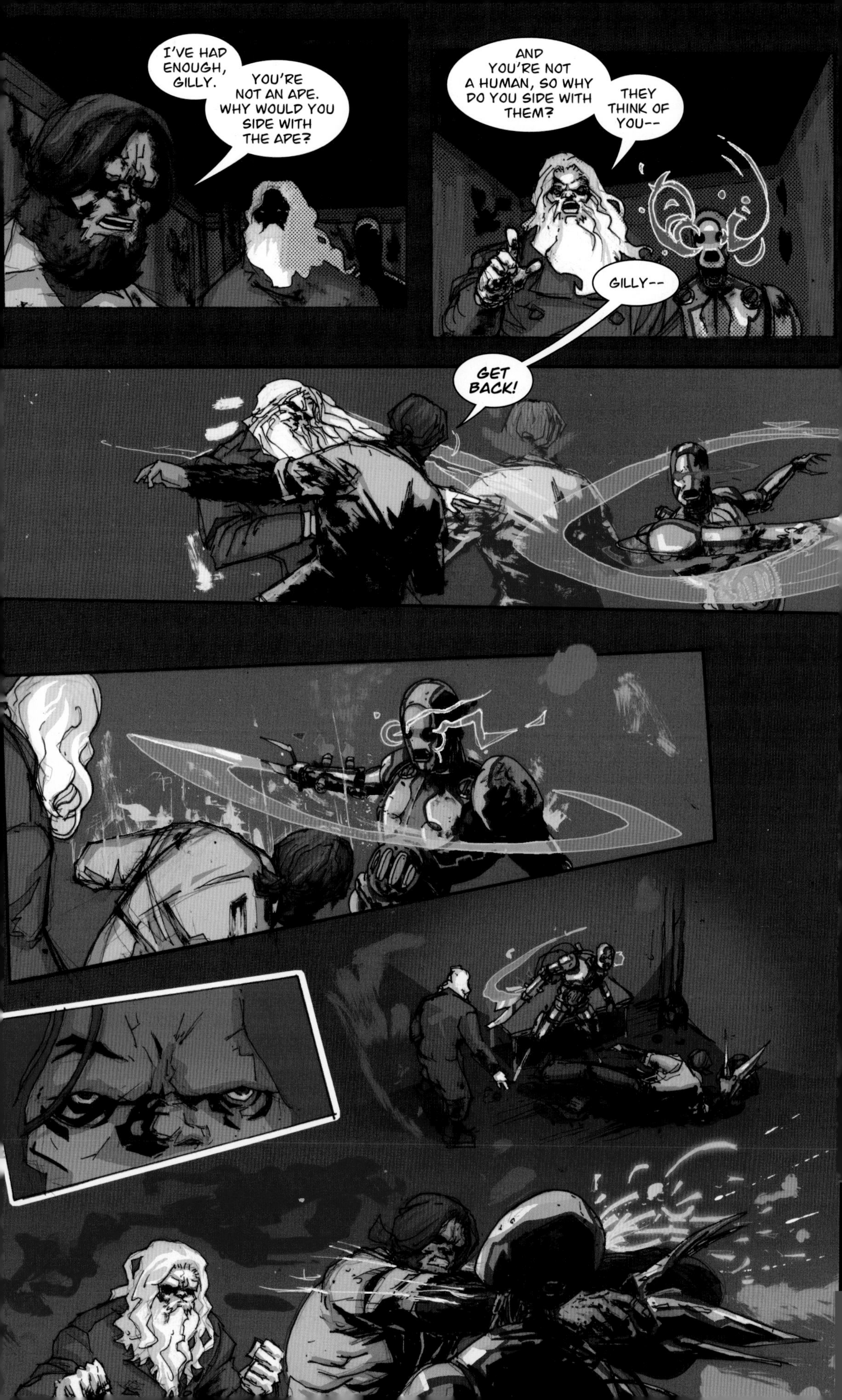
I'VE HAD ENOUGH, GILLY.
YOU'RE NOT AN APE. WHY WOULD YOU SIDE WITH THE APE?
AND YOU'RE NOT A HUMAN, SO WHY DO YOU SIDE WITH THEM?
THEY THINK OF YOU--
GILLY--
GET BACK!

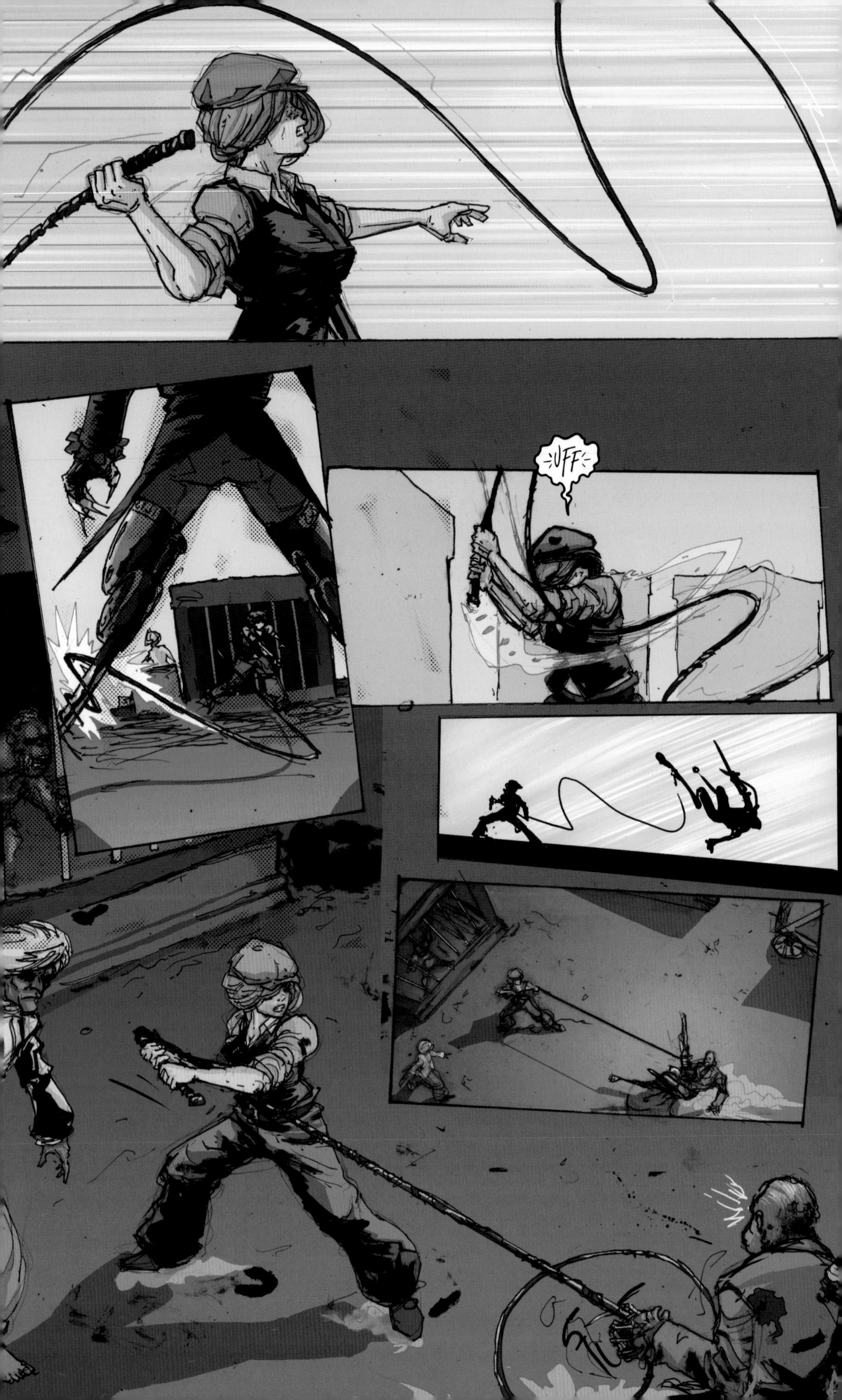
UFF

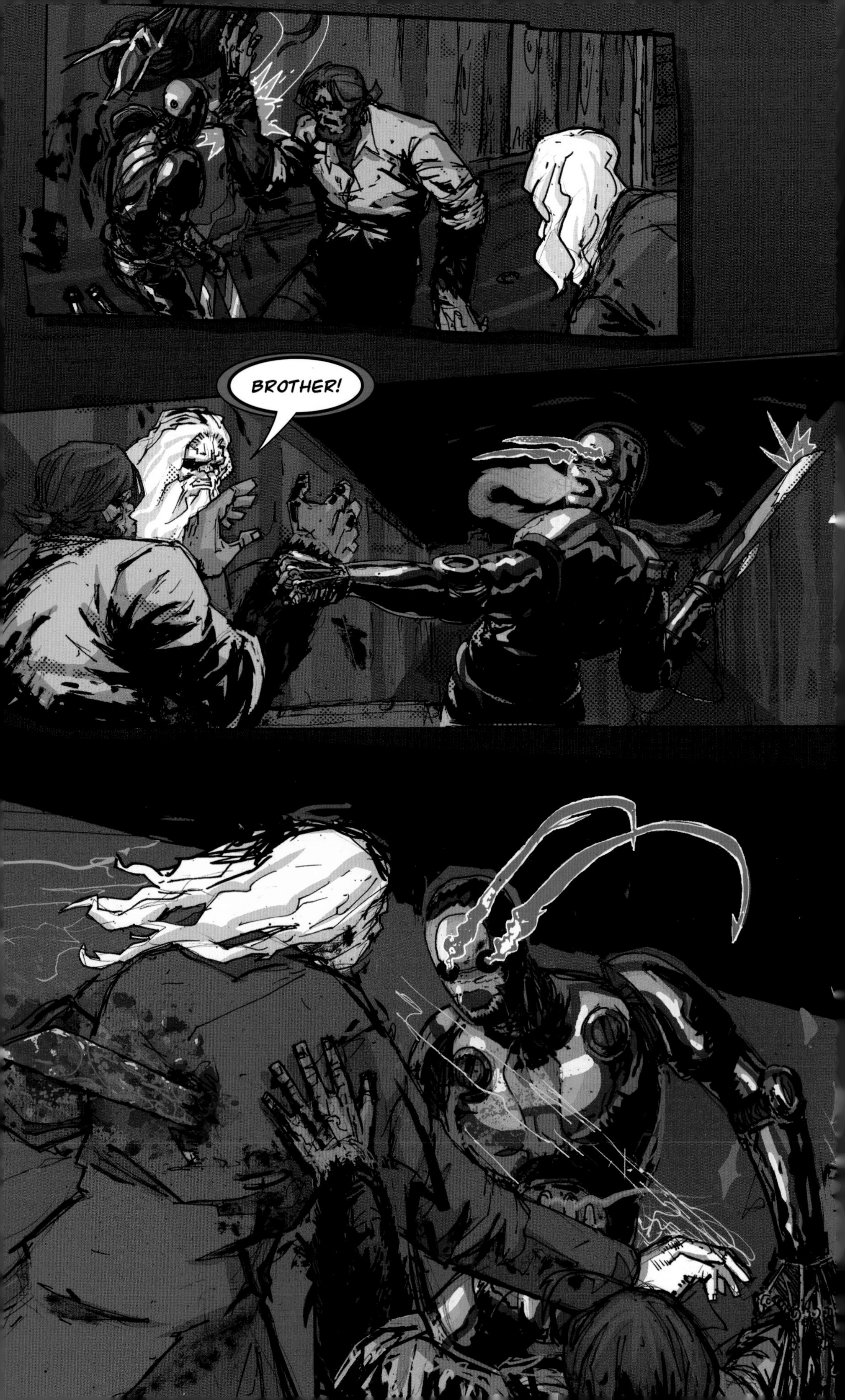
BROTHER!

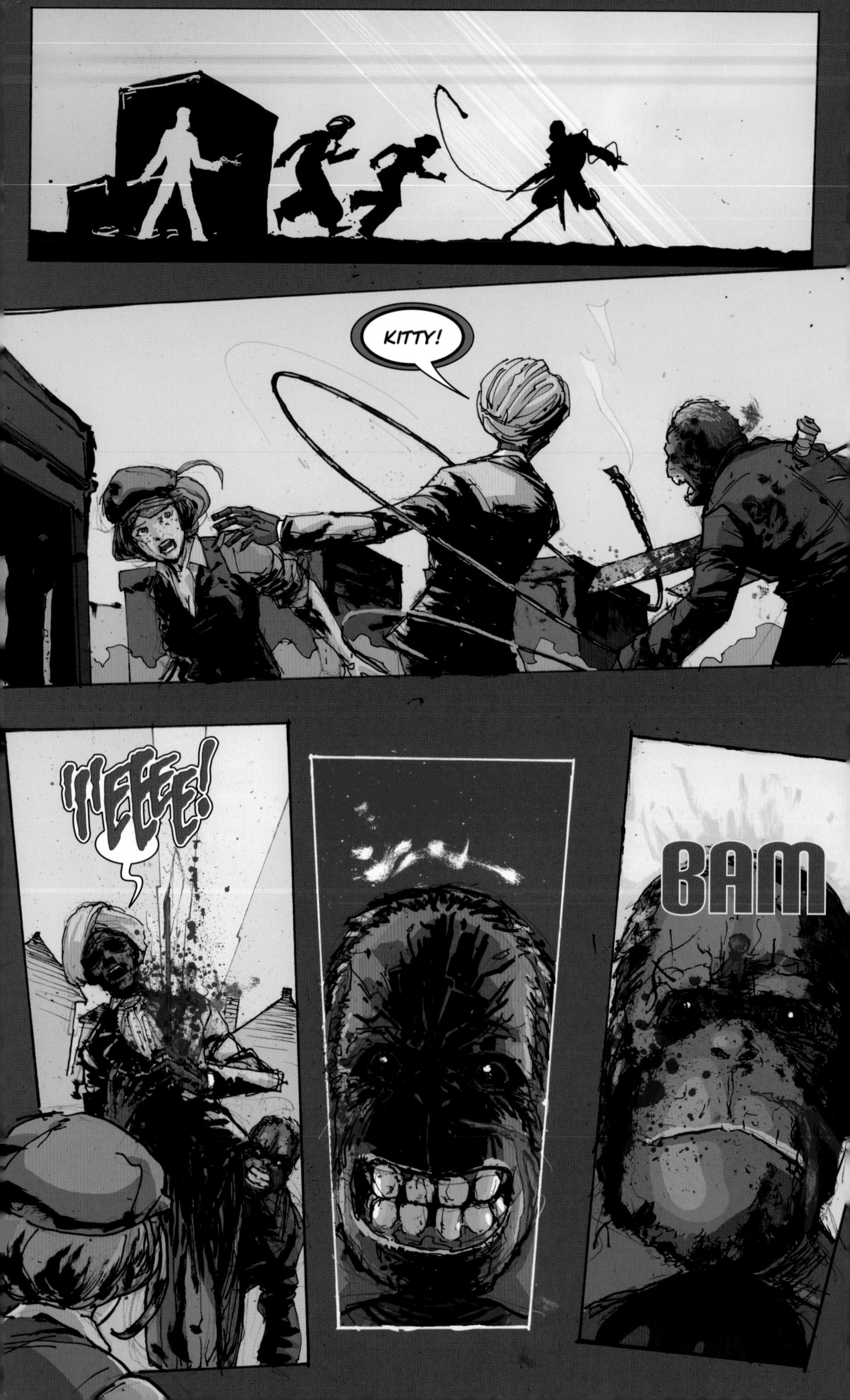
KITTY!
'I'EEEE!
BAM

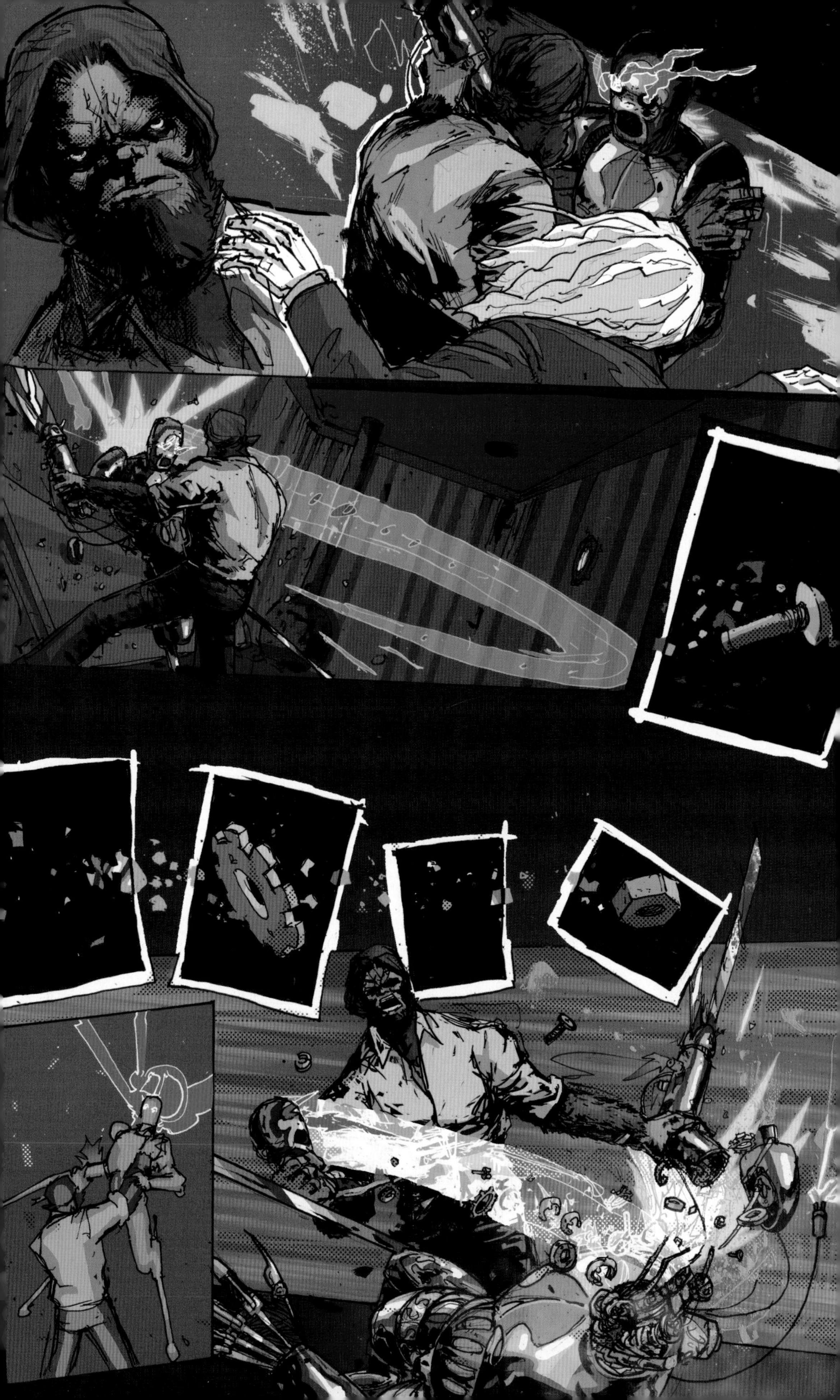

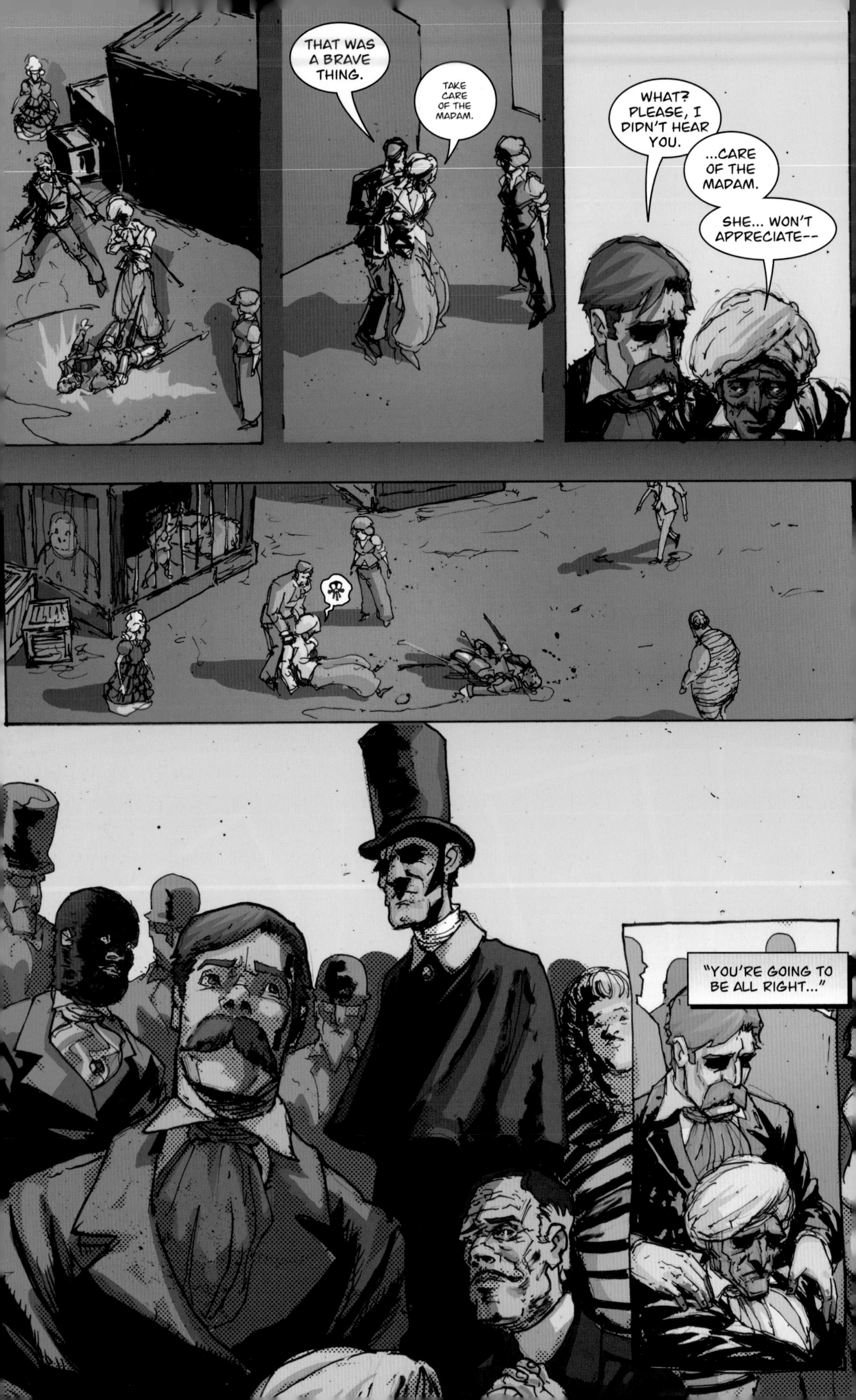
THAT WAS A BRAVE THING.
TAKE CARE OF THE MADAM.
WHAT? PLEASE, I DIDN'T HEAR YOU.
...CARE OF THE MADAM.
SHE... WON'T APPRECIATE--
"YOU'RE GOING TO BE ALL RIGHT..."

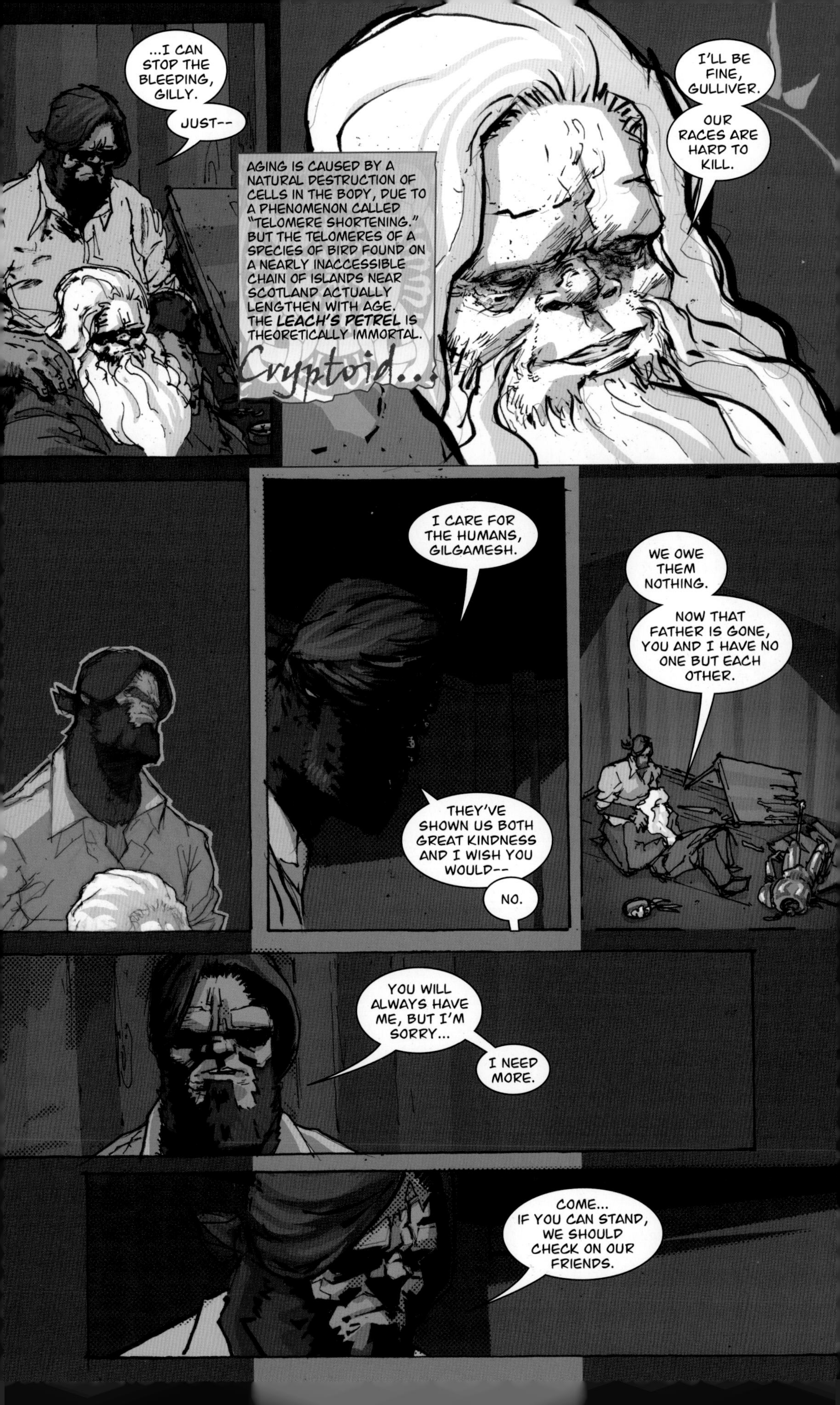

...I CAN STOP THE BLEEDING, GILLY.
JUST--
AGING IS CAUSED BY A NATURAL DESTRUCTION OF CELLS IN THE BODY, DUE TO A PHENOMENON CALLED "TELOMERE SHORTENING." BUT THE TELOMERES OF A SPECIES OF BIRD FOUND ON A NEARLY INACCESSIBLE CHAIN OF ISLANDS NEAR SCOTLAND ACTUALLY LENGTHEN WITH AGE. THE LEACH'S PETREL IS THEORETICALLY IMMORTAL.
Cryptoid...
I'LL BE FINE, GULLIVER.
OUR RACES ARE HARD TO KILL.
I CARE FOR THE HUMANS, GILGAMESH.
THEY'VE SHOWN US BOTH GREAT KINDNESS AND I WISH YOU WOULD--
NO.
WE OWE THEM NOTHING.
NOW THAT FATHER IS GONE, YOU AND I HAVE NO ONE BUT EACH OTHER.
YOU WILL ALWAYS HAVE ME, BUT I'M SORRY...
I NEED MORE.
COME... IF YOU CAN STAND, WE SHOULD CHECK ON OUR FRIENDS.

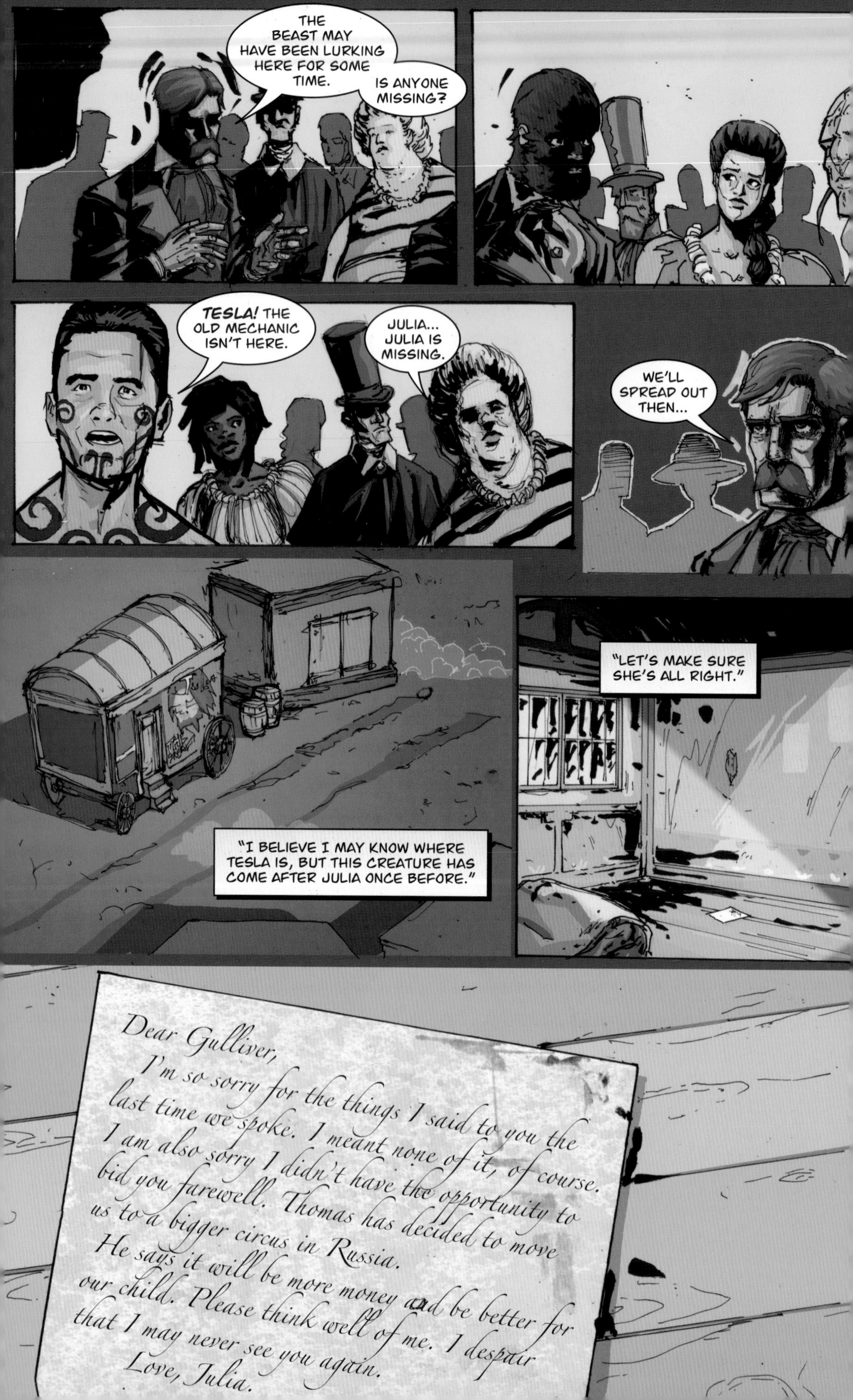
THE BEAST MAY HAVE BEEN LURKING HERE FOR SOME TIME.
IS ANYONE MISSING?
TESLA! THE OLD MECHANIC ISN'T HERE.
JULIA... JULIA IS MISSING.
WE'LL SPREAD OUT THEN...
"I BELIEVE I MAY KNOW WHERE TESLA IS, BUT THIS CREATURE HAS COME AFTER JULIA ONCE BEFORE."
"LET'S MAKE SURE SHE'S ALL RIGHT."
Dear Gulliver,
I'm so sorry for the things I said to you the last time we spoke. I meant none of it, of course. I am also sorry I didn't have the opportunity to bid you farewell. Thomas has decided to move us to a bigger circus in Russia.
He says it will be more money and be better for our child. Please think well of me. I despair that I may never see you again.
Love, Julia.

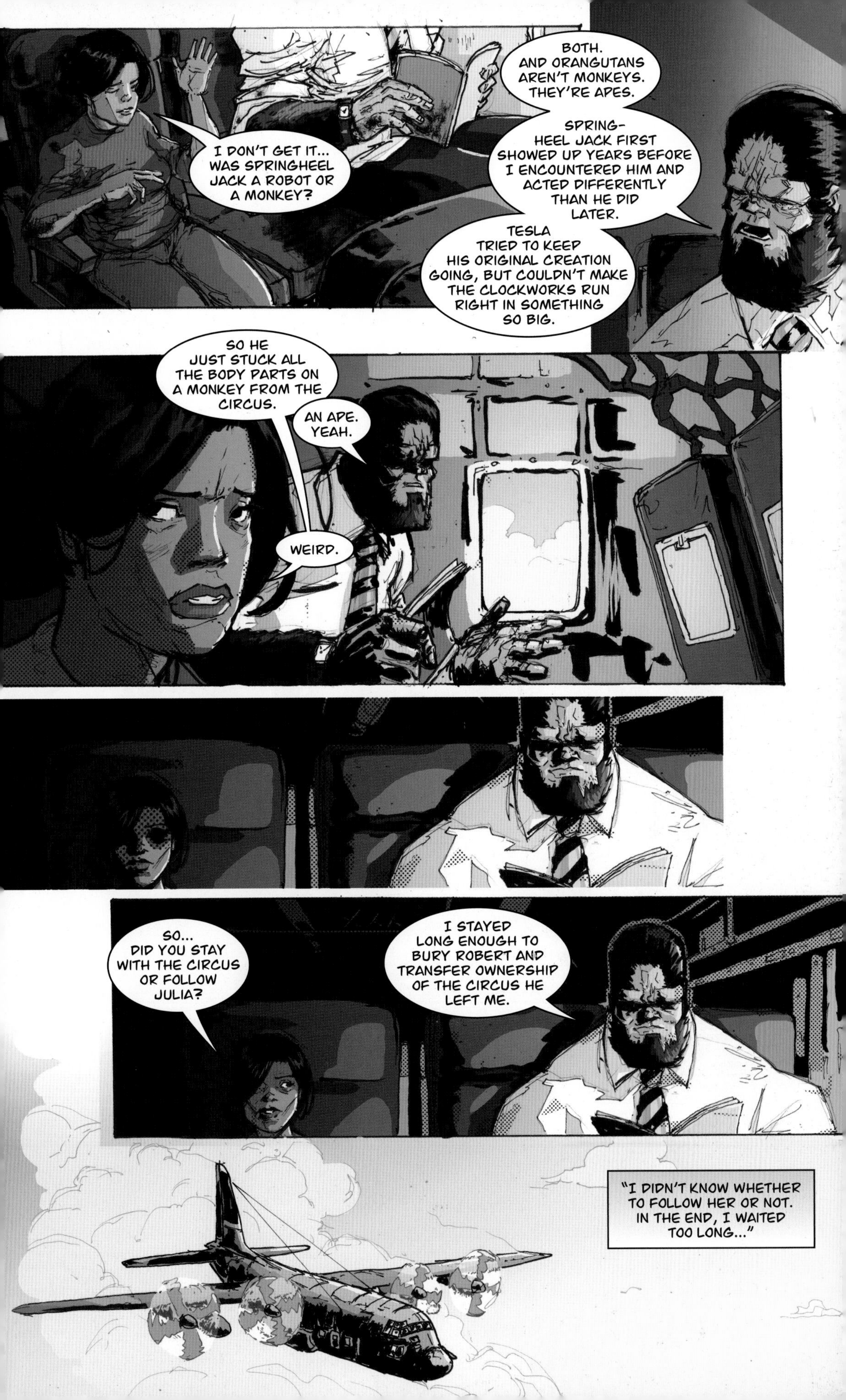
I DON'T GET IT... WAS SPRINGHEEL JACK A ROBOT OR A MONKEY?
BOTH. AND ORANGUTANS AREN'T MONKEYS. THEY'RE APES.
SPRING-HEEL JACK FIRST SHOWED UP YEARS BEFORE I ENCOUNTERED HIM AND ACTED DIFFERENTLY THAN HE DID LATER.
TESLA TRIED TO KEEP HIS ORIGINAL CREATION GOING, BUT COULDN'T MAKE THE CLOCKWORKS RUN RIGHT IN SOMETHING SO BIG.
SO HE JUST STUCK ALL THE BODY PARTS ON A MONKEY FROM THE CIRCUS.
AN APE. YEAH.
WEIRD.
SO... DID YOU STAY WITH THE CIRCUS OR FOLLOW JULIA?
I STAYED LONG ENOUGH TO BURY ROBERT AND TRANSFER OWNERSHIP OF THE CIRCUS HE LEFT ME.
"I DIDN'T KNOW WHETHER TO FOLLOW HER OR NOT. IN THE END, I WAITED TOO LONG..."

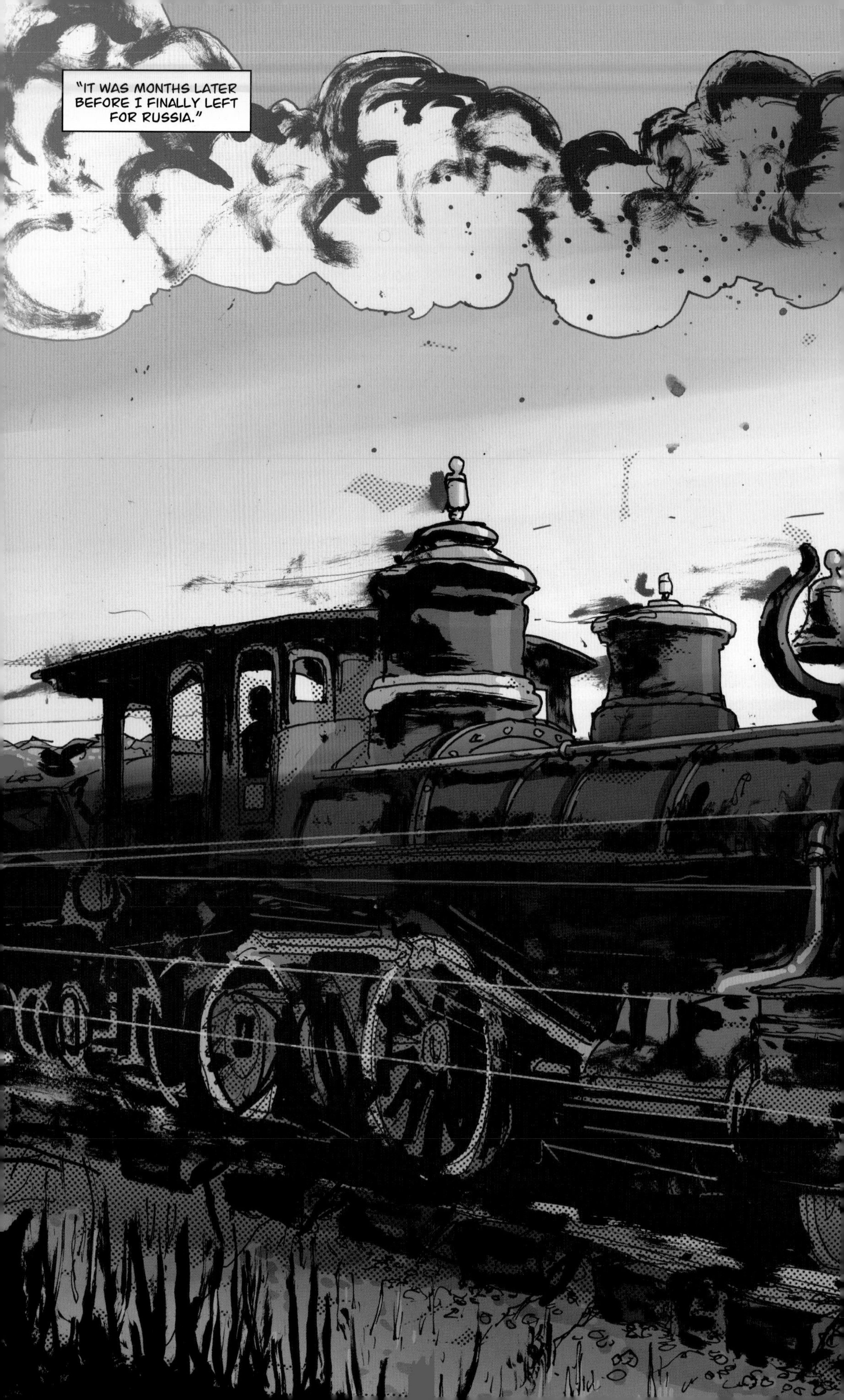
"IT WAS MONTHS LATER BEFORE I FINALLY LEFT FOR RUSSIA."

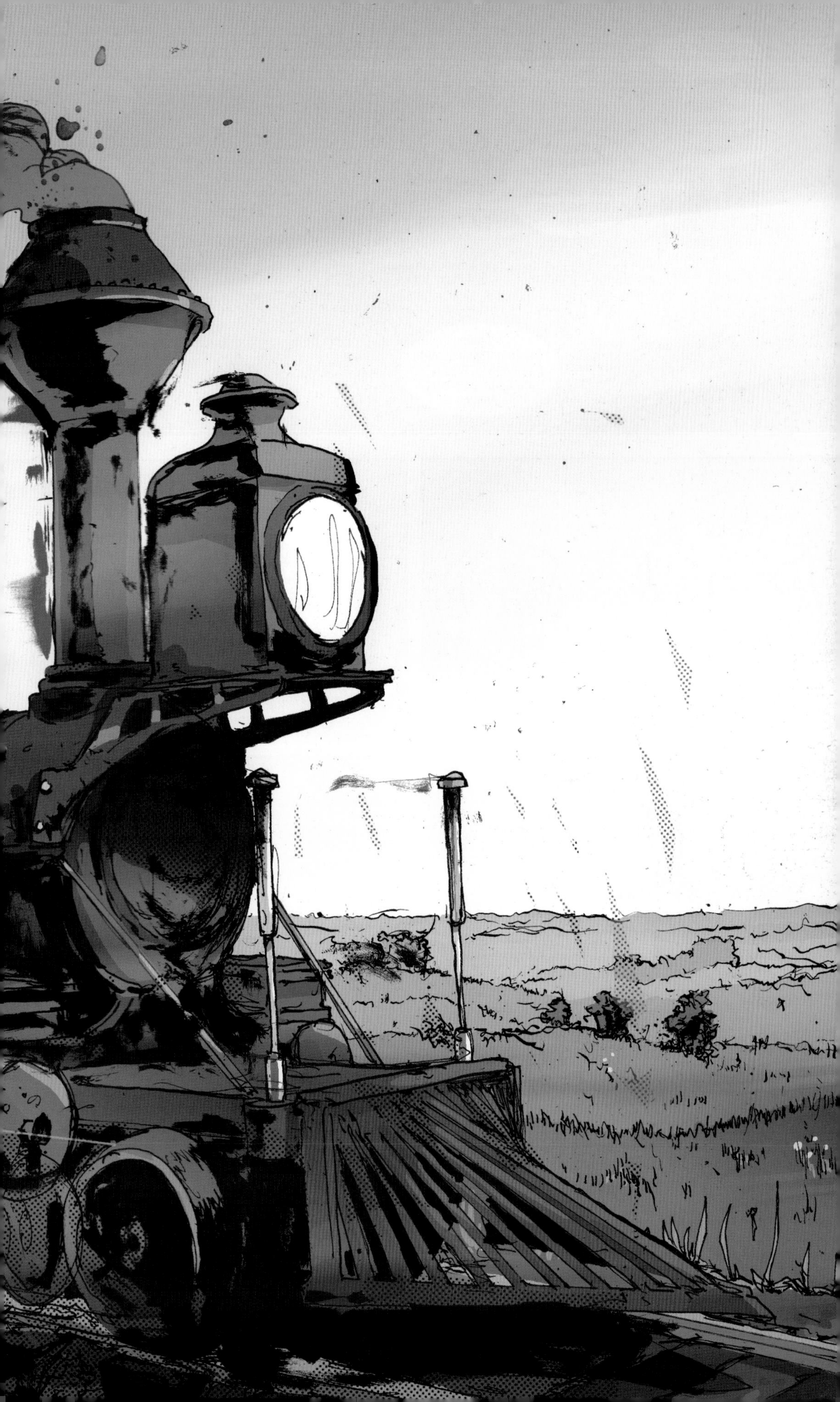

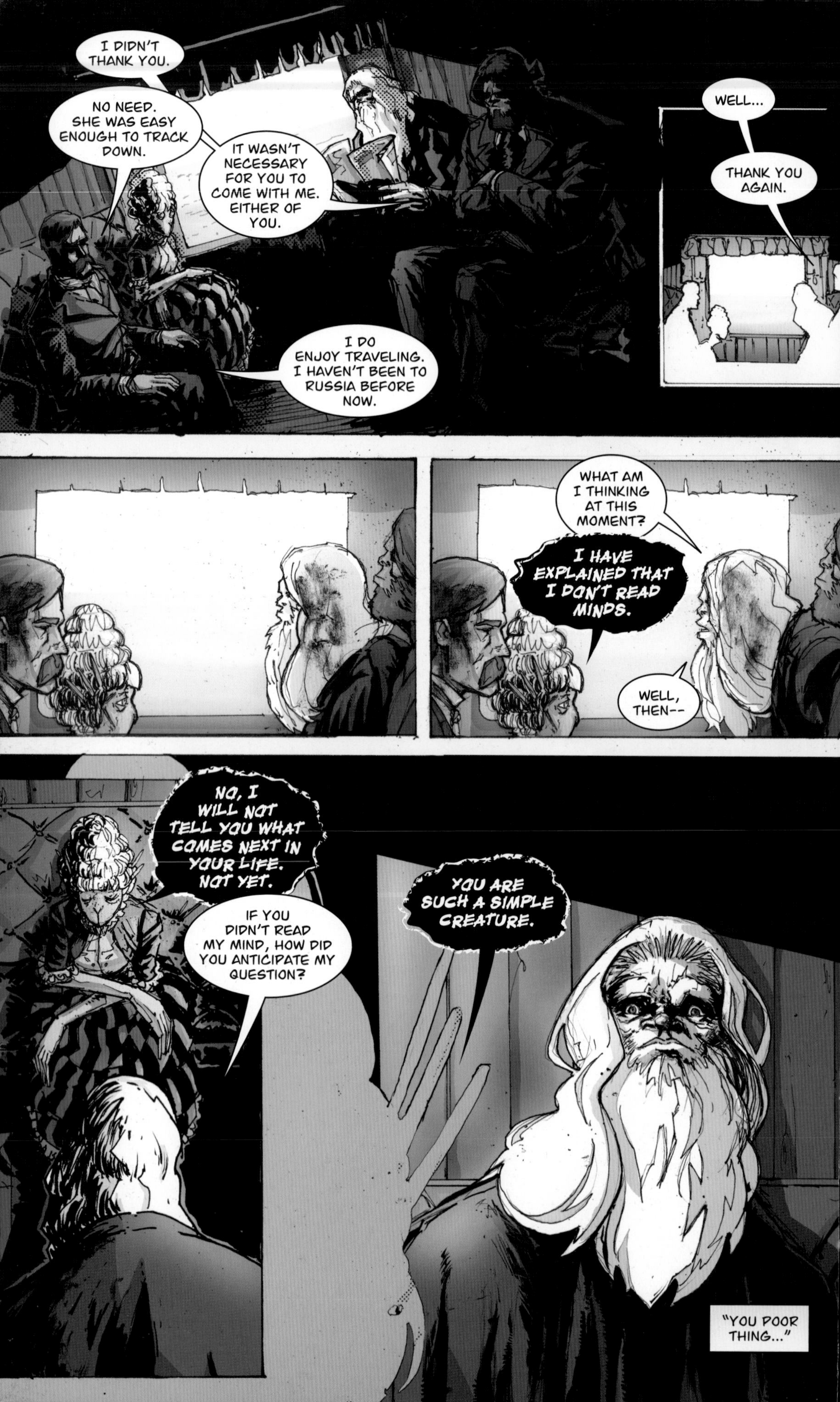
I DIDN'T THANK YOU.
NO NEED. SHE WAS EASY ENOUGH TO TRACK DOWN.
IT WASN'T NECESSARY FOR YOU TO COME WITH ME. EITHER OF YOU.
I DO ENJOY TRAVELING. I HAVEN'T BEEN TO RUSSIA BEFORE NOW.
WELL...
THANK YOU AGAIN.
WHAT AM I THINKING AT THIS MOMENT?
I HAVE EXPLAINED THAT I DON'T READ MINDS.
WELL, THEN--
NO, I WILL NOT TELL YOU WHAT COMES NEXT IN YOUR LIFE. NOT YET.
IF YOU DIDN'T READ MY MIND, HOW DID YOU ANTICIPATE MY QUESTION?
YOU ARE SUCH A SIMPLE CREATURE.
"YOU POOR THING..."

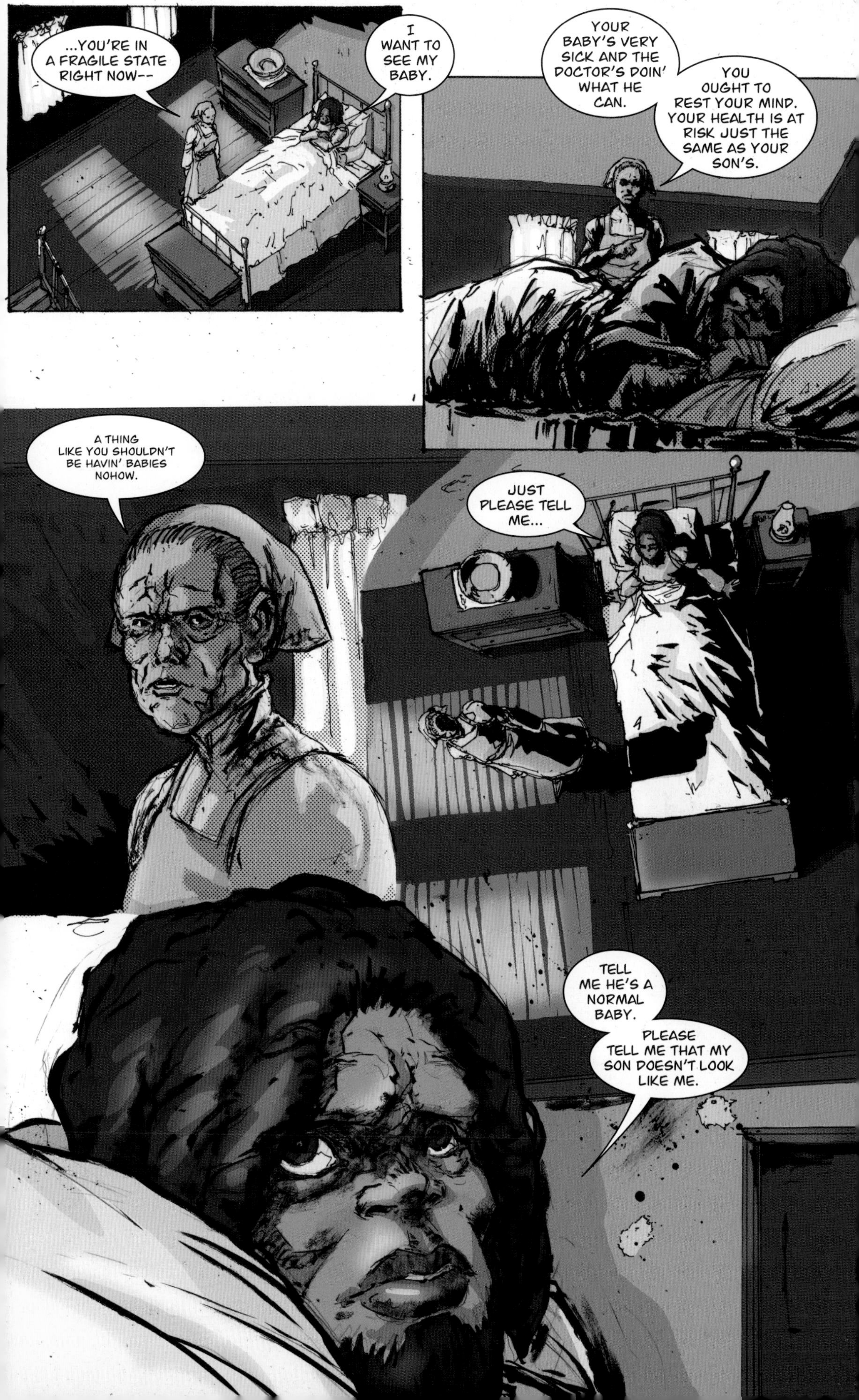
...YOU'RE IN A FRAGILE STATE RIGHT NOW--
I WANT TO SEE MY BABY.
YOUR BABY'S VERY SICK AND THE DOCTOR'S DOIN' WHAT HE CAN.
YOU OUGHT TO REST YOUR MIND. YOUR HEALTH IS AT RISK JUST THE SAME AS YOUR SON'S.
A THING LIKE YOU SHOULDN'T BE HAVIN' BABIES NOHOW.
JUST PLEASE TELL ME...
TELL ME HE'S A NORMAL BABY.
PLEASE TELL ME THAT MY SON DOESN'T LOOK LIKE ME.

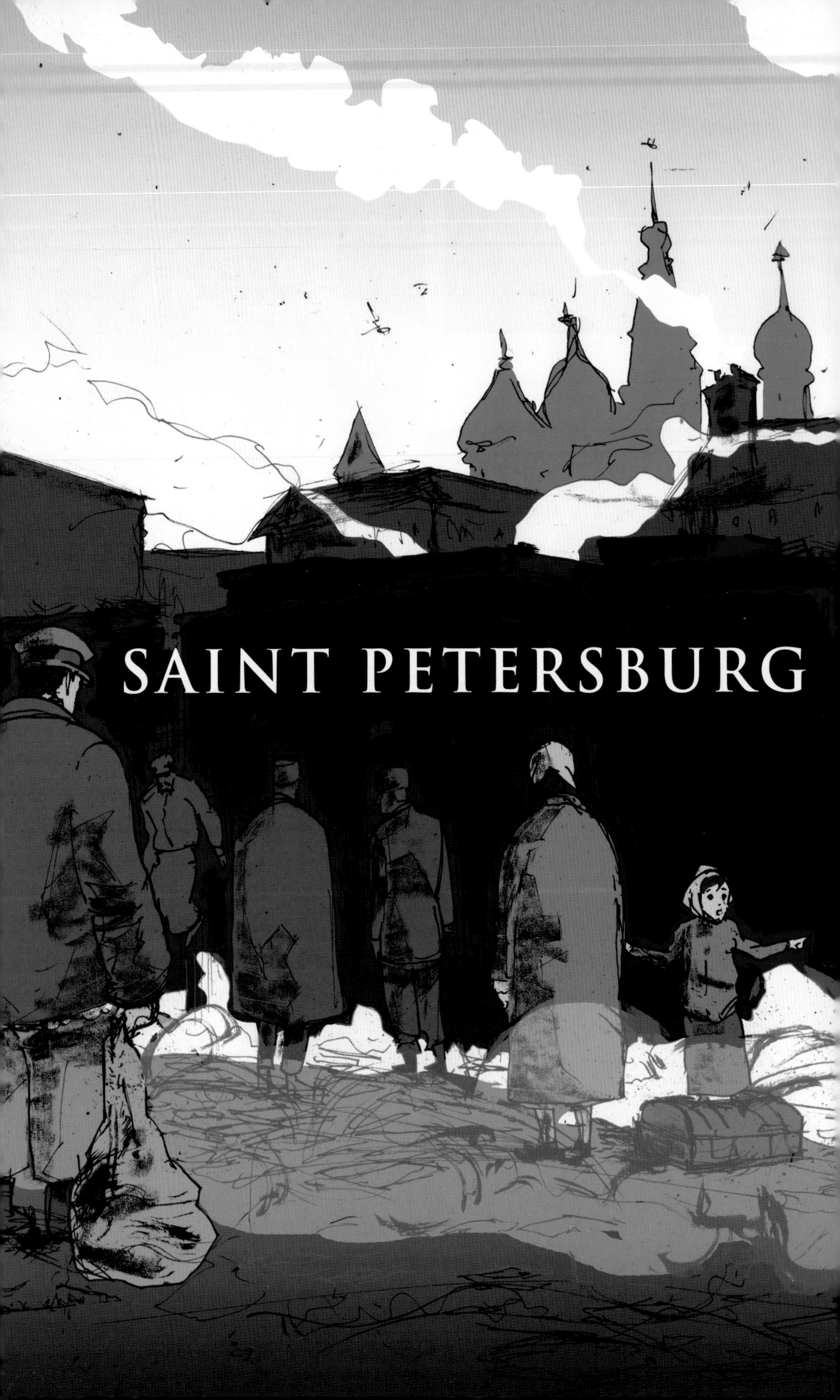
SAINT PETERSBURG

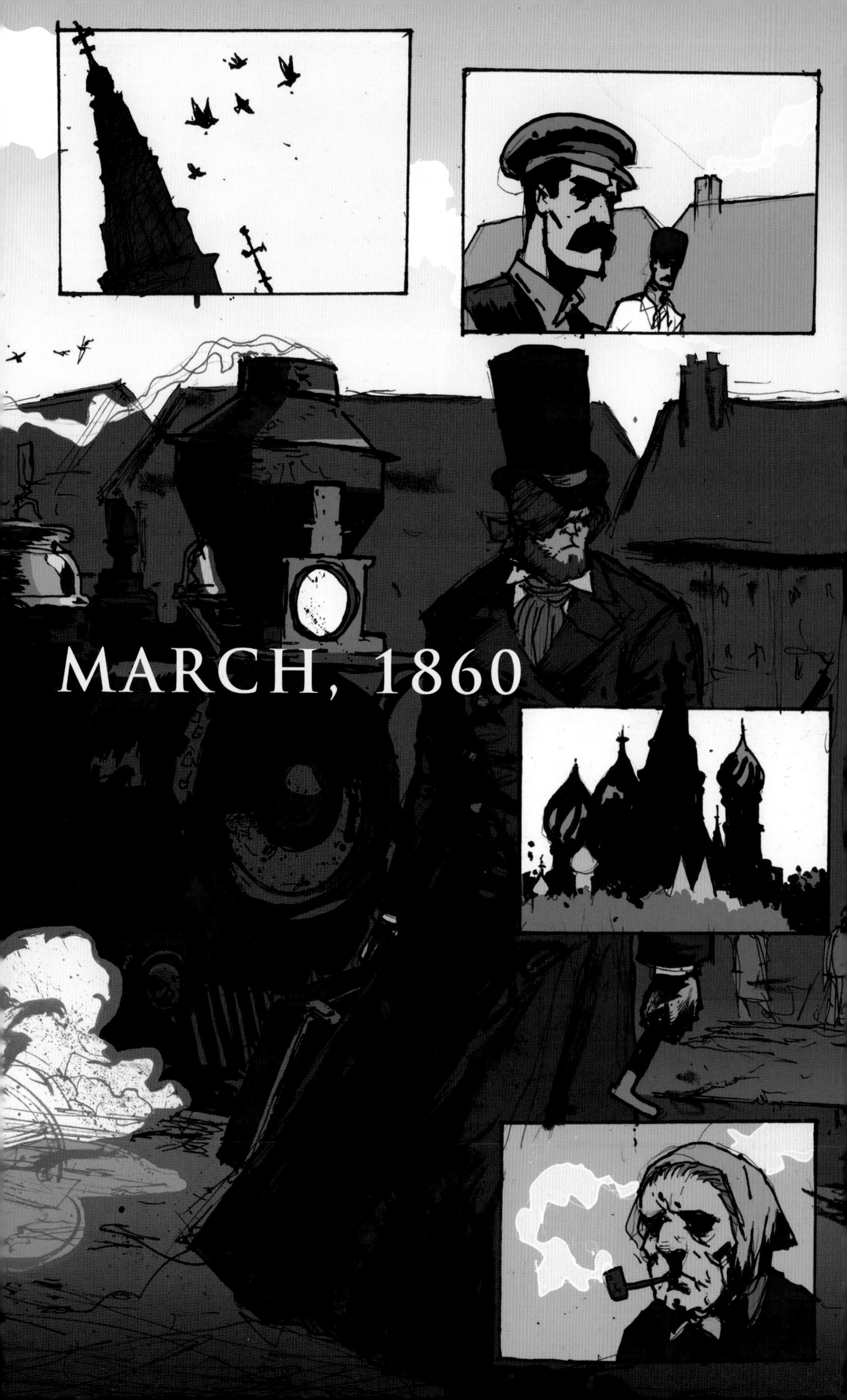
MARCH, 1860

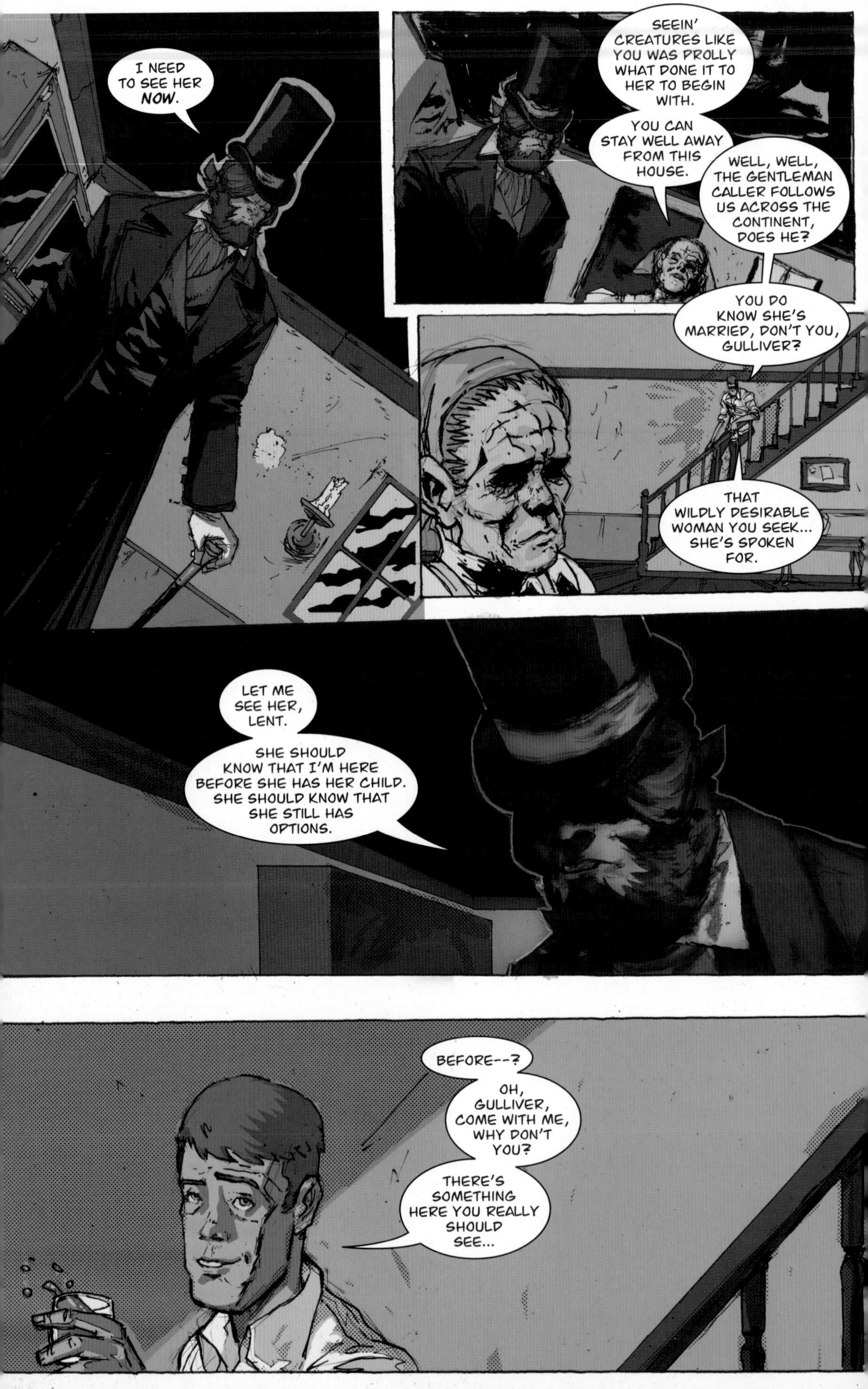
I NEED TO SEE HER NOW.
SEEIN' CREATURES LIKE YOU WAS PROLLY WHAT DONE IT TO HER TO BEGIN WITH.
YOU CAN STAY WELL AWAY FROM THIS HOUSE.
WELL, WELL, THE GENTLEMAN CALLER FOLLOWS US ACROSS THE CONTINENT, DOES HE?
YOU DO KNOW SHE'S MARRIED, DON'T YOU, GULLIVER?
THAT WILDLY DESIRABLE WOMAN YOU SEEK... SHE'S SPOKEN FOR.
LET ME SEE HER, LENT.
SHE SHOULD KNOW THAT I'M HERE BEFORE SHE HAS HER CHILD. SHE SHOULD KNOW THAT SHE STILL HAS OPTIONS.
BEFORE--?
OH, GULLIVER, COME WITH ME, WHY DON'T YOU?
THERE'S SOMETHING HERE YOU REALLY SHOULD SEE...

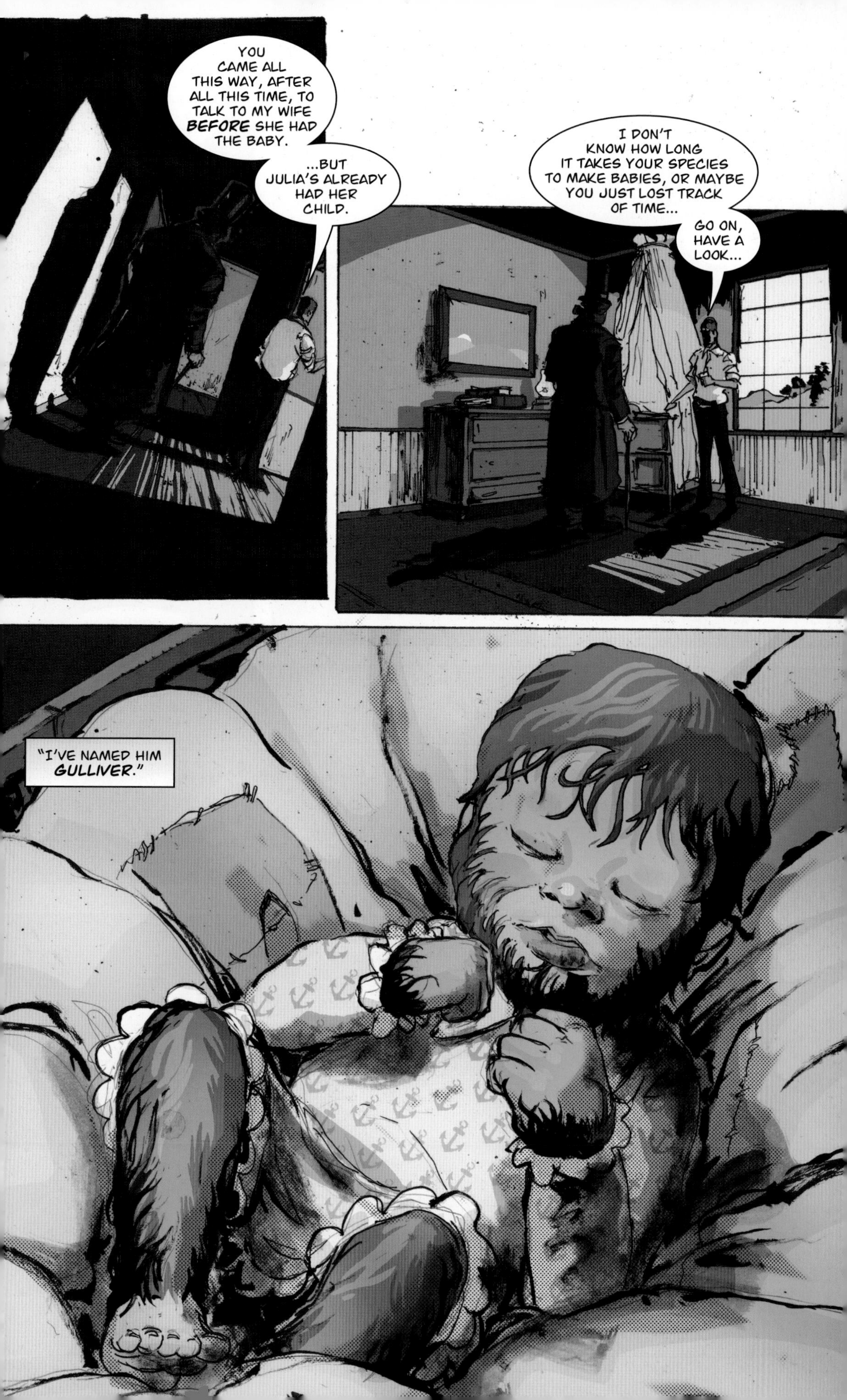

YOU CAME ALL THIS WAY, AFTER ALL THIS TIME, TO TALK TO MY WIFE **BEFORE** SHE HAD THE BABY.
...BUT JULIA'S ALREADY HAD HER CHILD.
I DON'T KNOW HOW LONG IT TAKES YOUR SPECIES TO MAKE BABIES, OR MAYBE YOU JUST LOST TRACK OF TIME...
GO ON, HAVE A LOOK...
"I'VE NAMED HIM ***GULLIVER***."

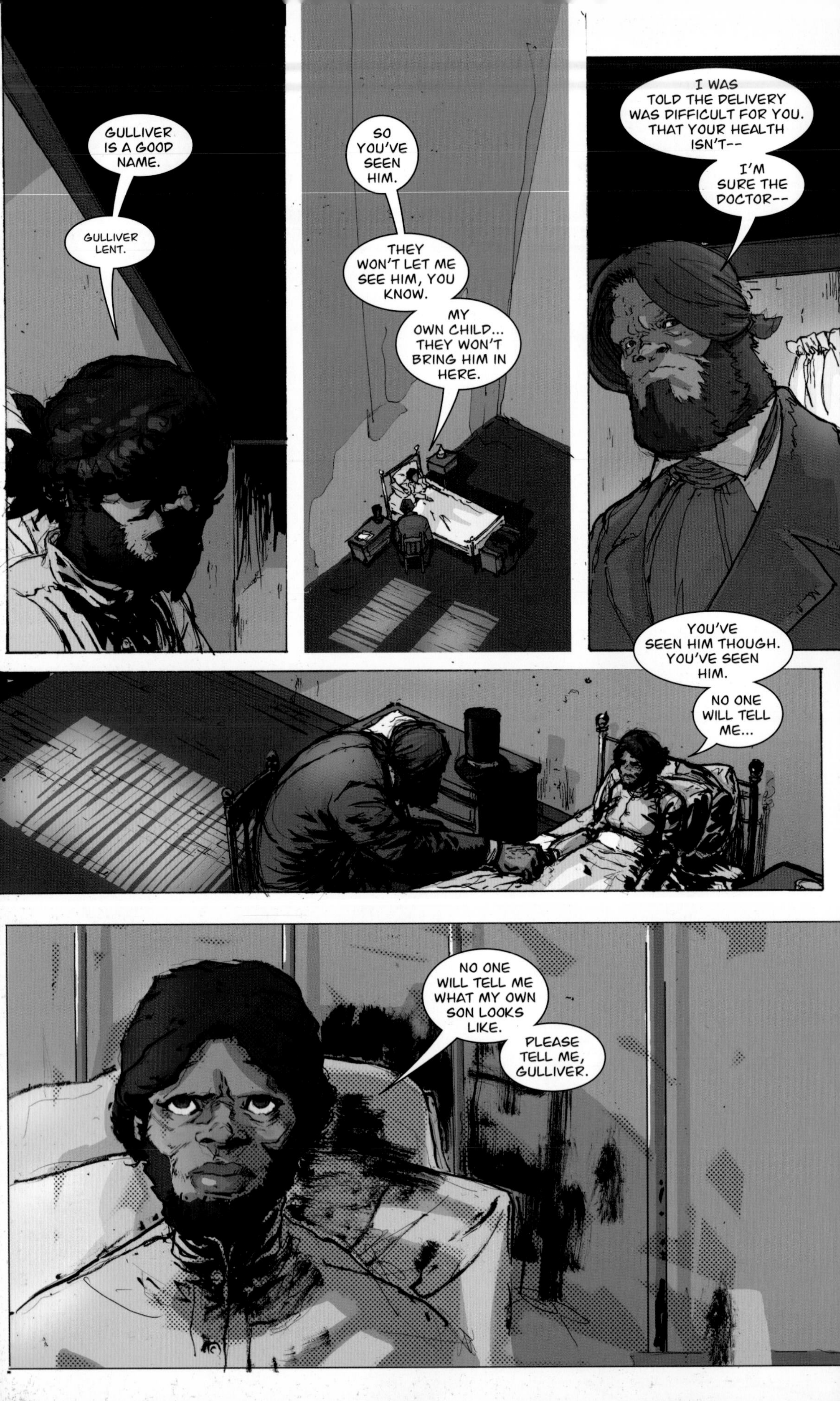
GULLIVER IS A GOOD NAME.
GULLIVER LENT.
SO YOU'VE SEEN HIM.
THEY WON'T LET ME SEE HIM, YOU KNOW.
MY OWN CHILD... THEY WON'T BRING HIM IN HERE.
I WAS TOLD THE DELIVERY WAS DIFFICULT FOR YOU. THAT YOUR HEALTH ISN'T--
I'M SURE THE DOCTOR--
YOU'VE SEEN HIM THOUGH. YOU'VE SEEN HIM.
NO ONE WILL TELL ME...
NO ONE WILL TELL ME WHAT MY OWN SON LOOKS LIKE.
PLEASE TELL ME, GULLIVER.

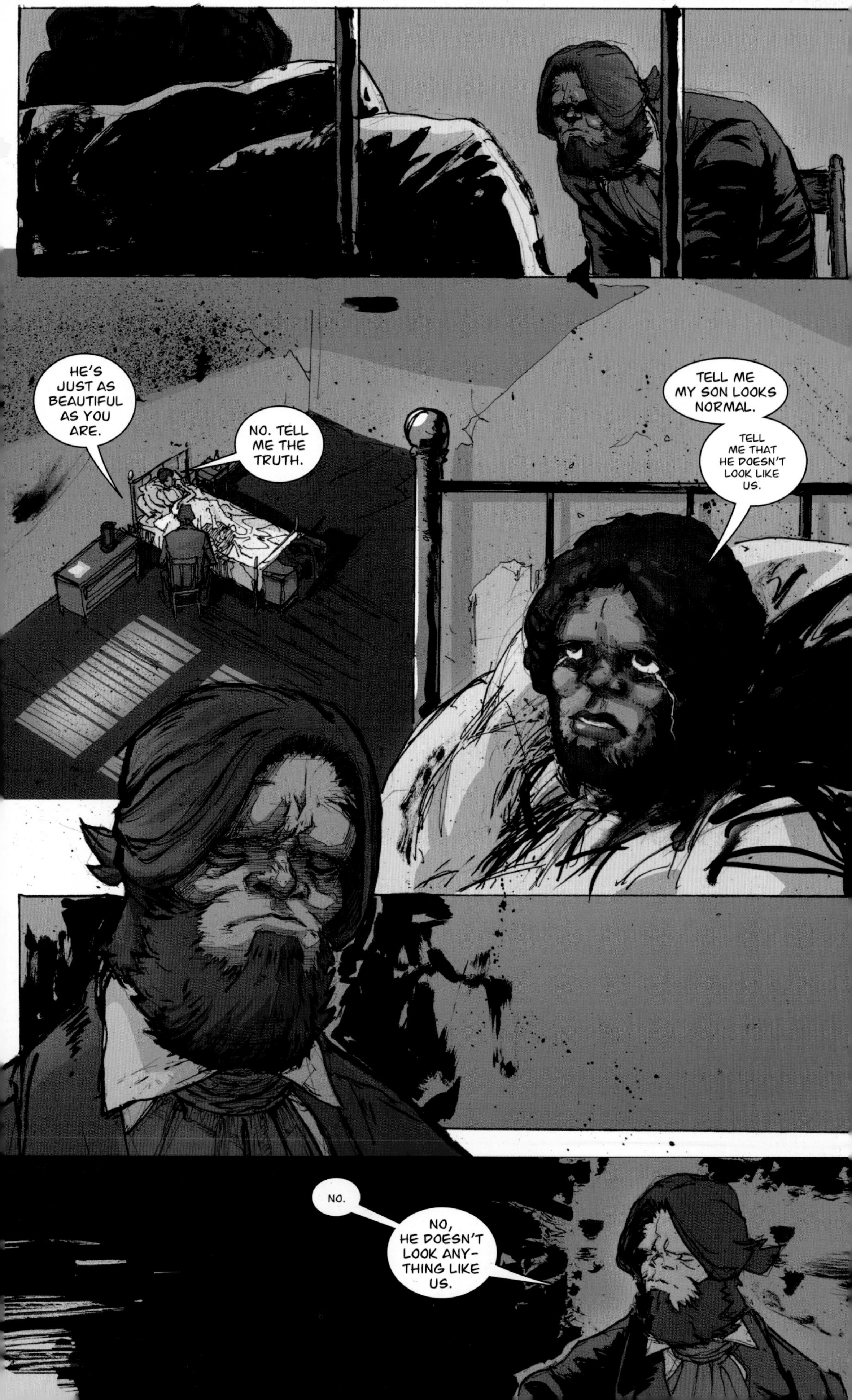

HE'S JUST AS BEAUTIFUL AS YOU ARE.
NO. TELL ME THE TRUTH.
TELL ME MY SON LOOKS NORMAL.
TELL ME THAT HE DOESN'T LOOK LIKE US.
NO.
NO, HE DOESN'T LOOK ANY-THING LIKE US.

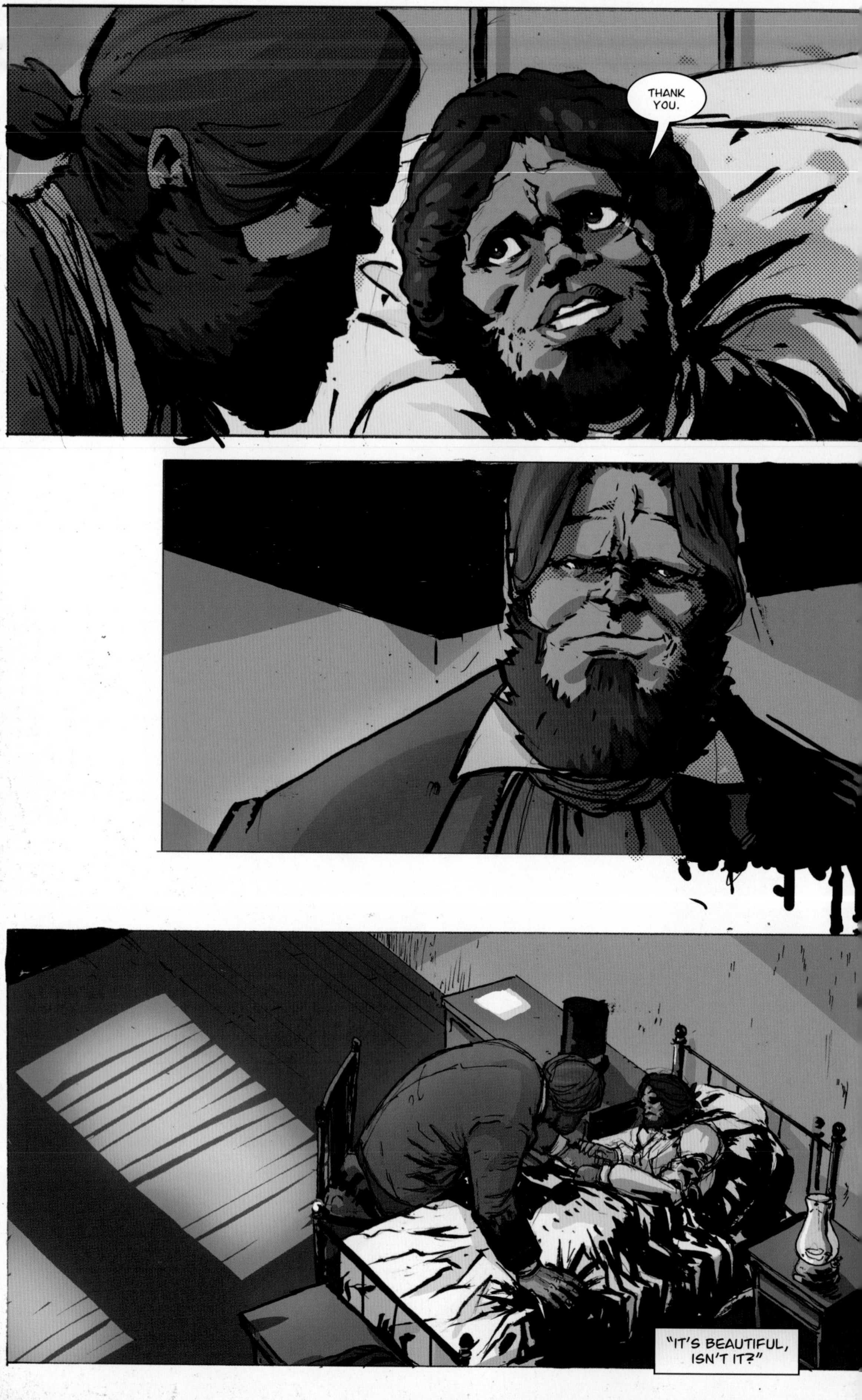
THANK YOU.
"IT'S BEAUTIFUL, ISN'T IT?"

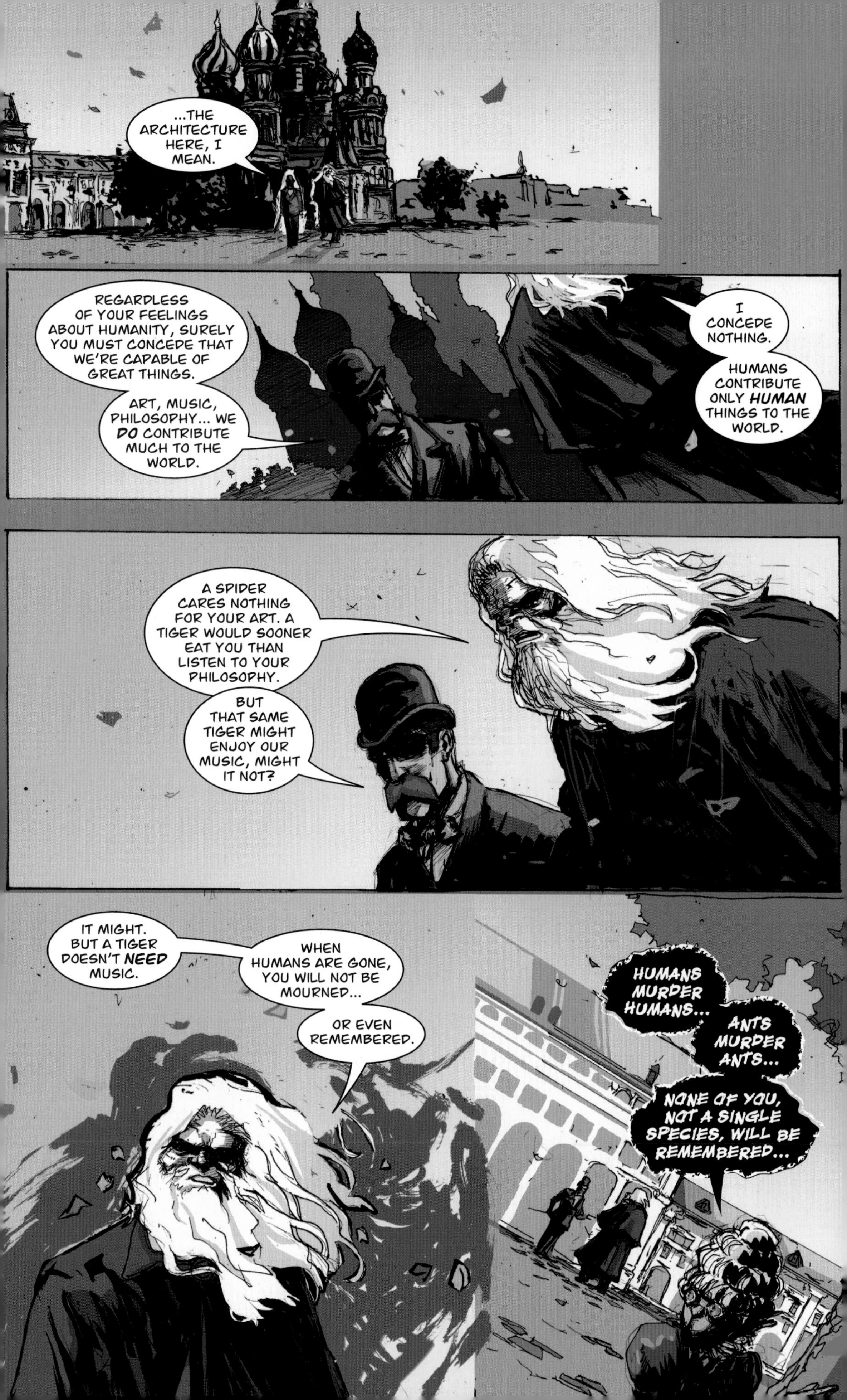
...THE ARCHITECTURE HERE, I MEAN.
REGARDLESS OF YOUR FEELINGS ABOUT HUMANITY, SURELY YOU MUST CONCEDE THAT WE'RE CAPABLE OF GREAT THINGS.
ART, MUSIC, PHILOSOPHY... WE **DO** CONTRIBUTE MUCH TO THE WORLD.
I CONCEDE NOTHING.
HUMANS CONTRIBUTE ONLY **HUMAN** THINGS TO THE WORLD.
A SPIDER CARES NOTHING FOR YOUR ART. A TIGER WOULD SOONER EAT YOU THAN LISTEN TO YOUR PHILOSOPHY.
BUT THAT SAME TIGER MIGHT ENJOY OUR MUSIC, MIGHT IT NOT?
IT MIGHT. BUT A TIGER DOESN'T **NEED** MUSIC.
WHEN HUMANS ARE GONE, YOU WILL NOT BE MOURNED...
OR EVEN REMEMBERED.
HUMANS MURDER HUMANS...
ANTS MURDER ANTS...
NONE OF YOU, NOT A SINGLE SPECIES, WILL BE REMEMBERED...

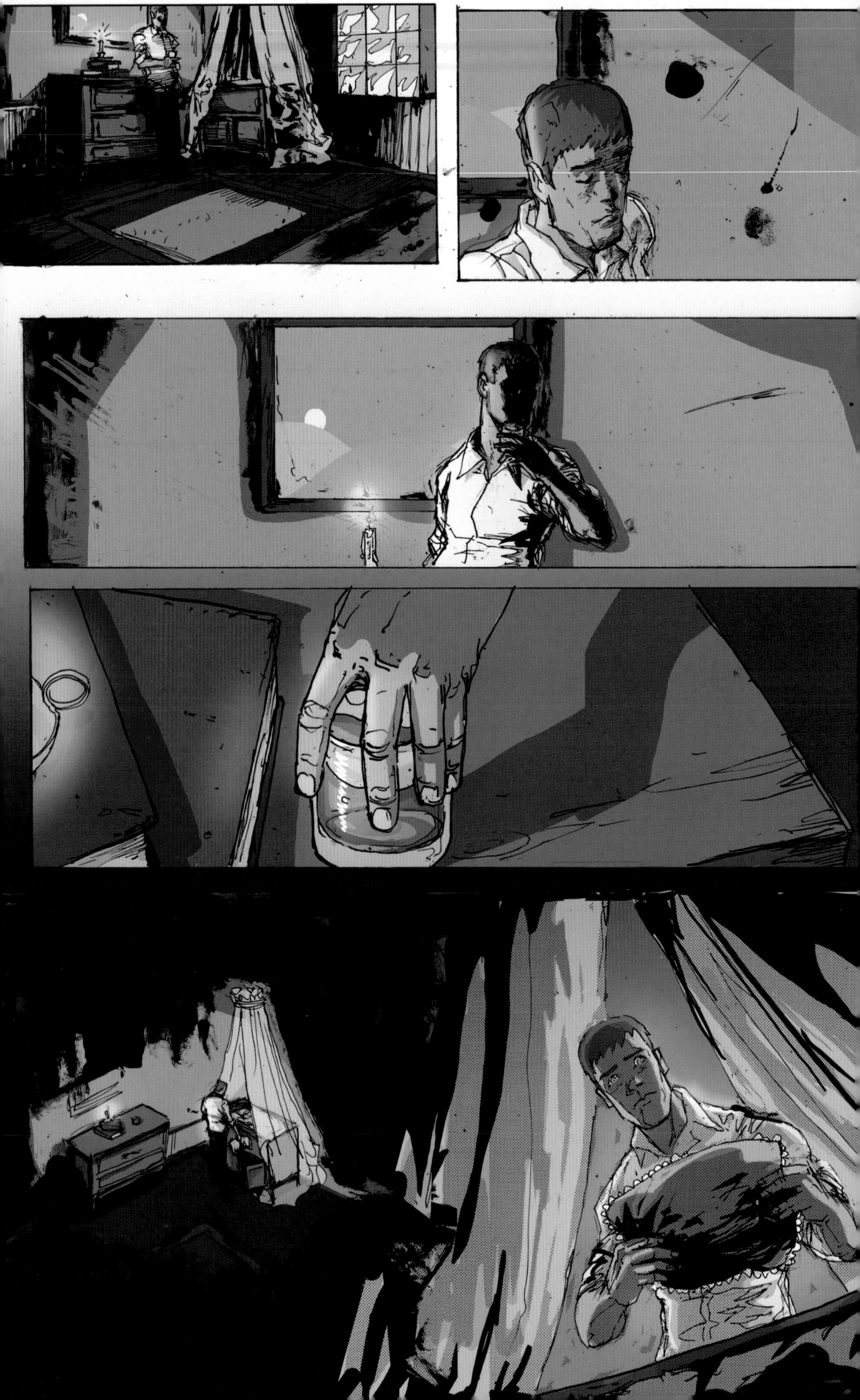

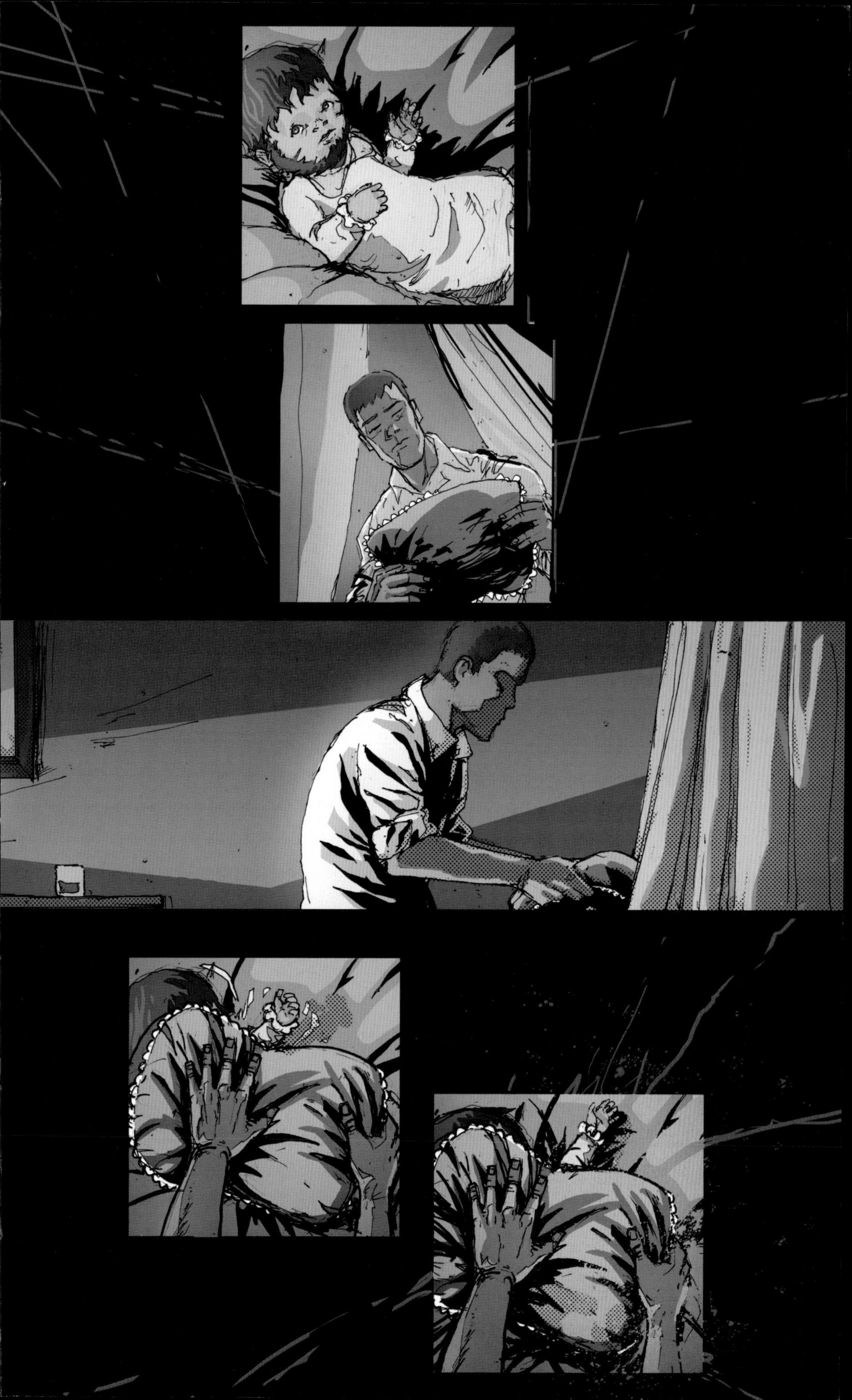

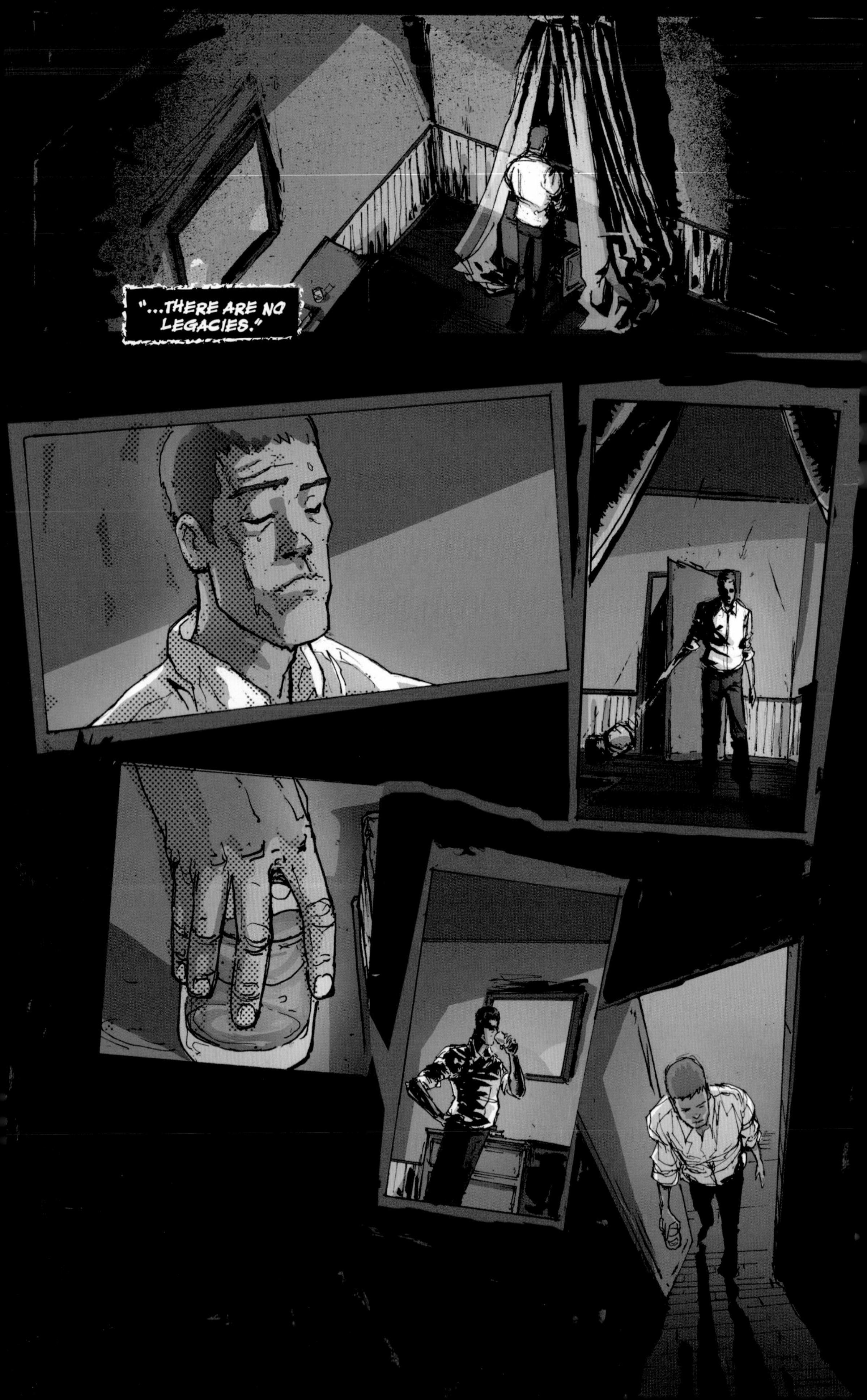
"...THERE ARE NO LEGACIES."

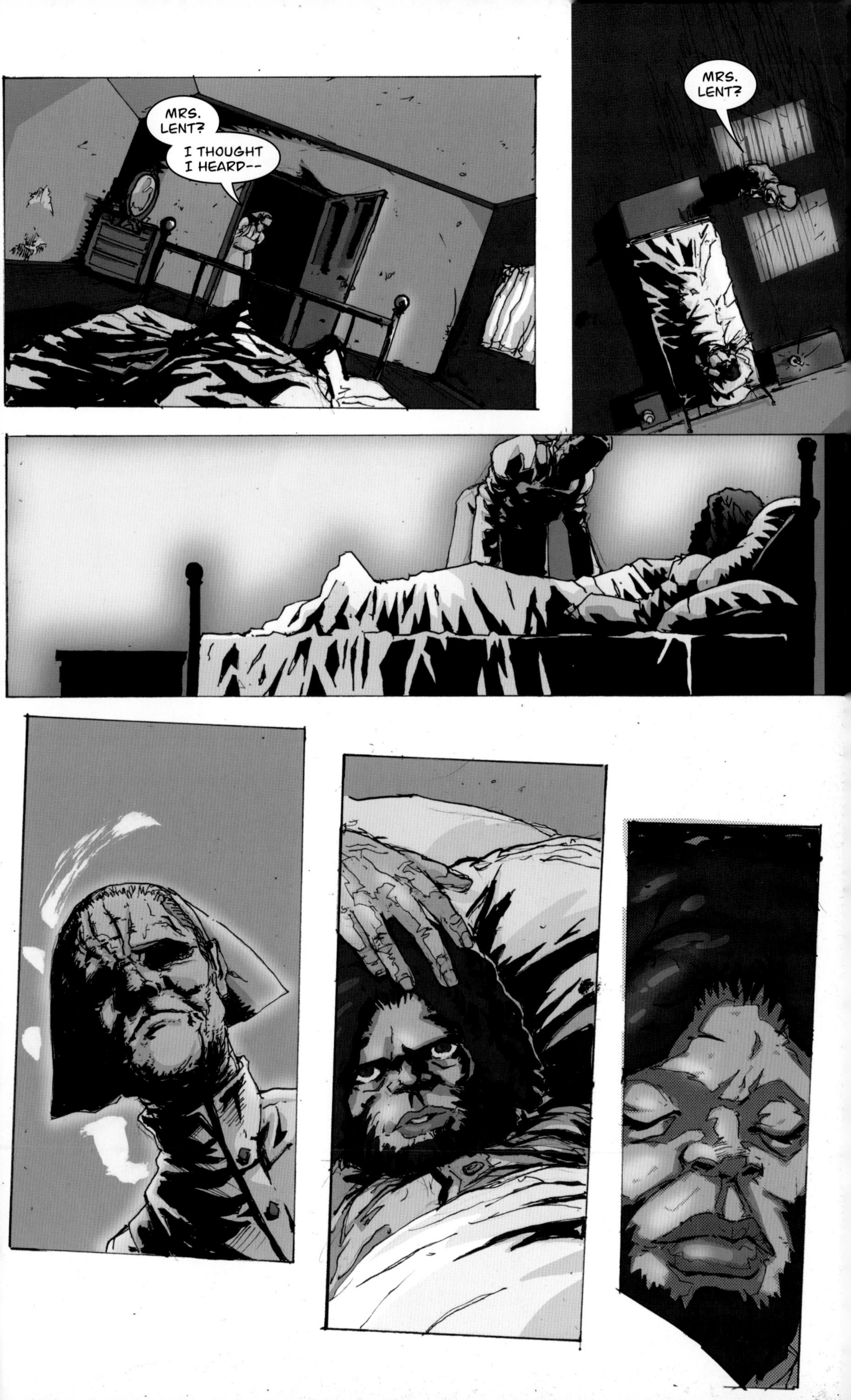
MRS. LENT?
I THOUGHT I HEARD--
MRS. LENT?

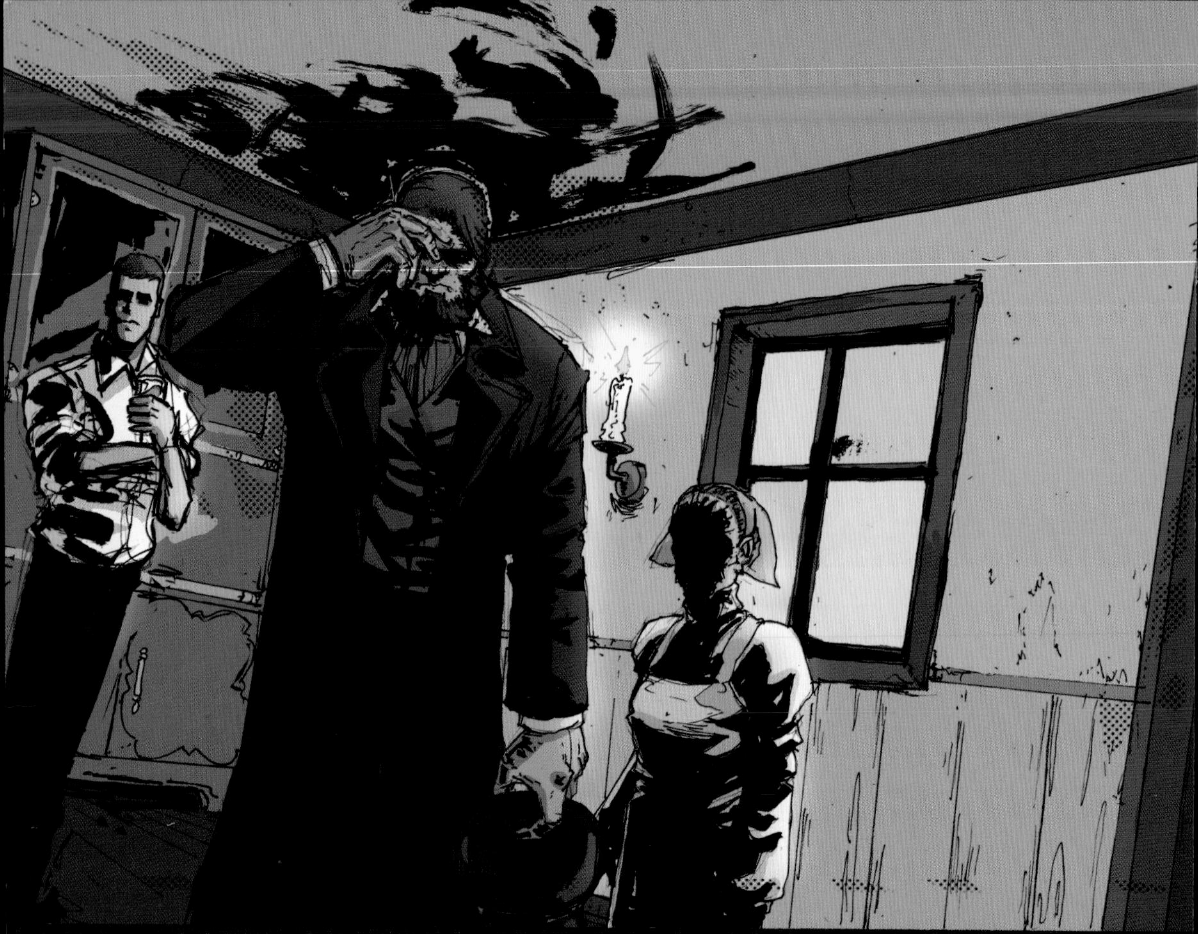

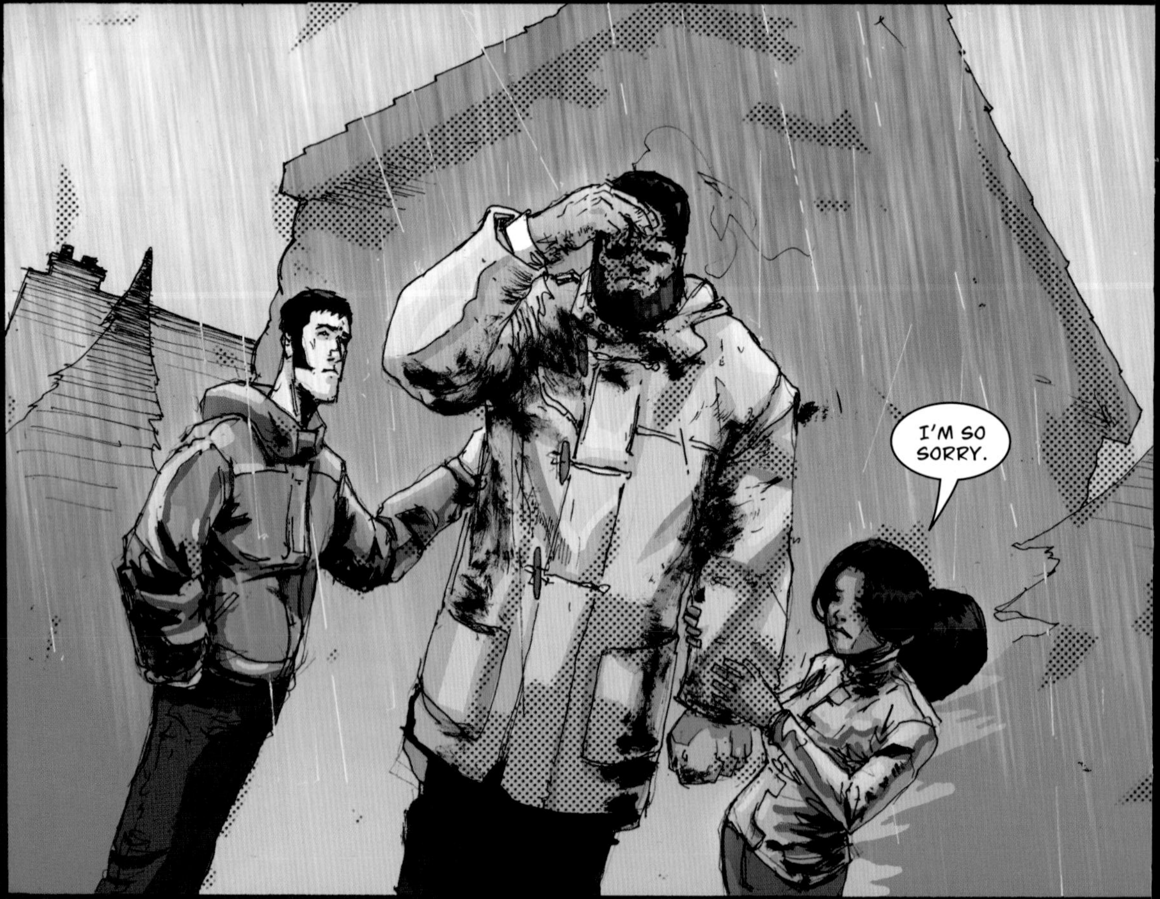
I'M SO SORRY.

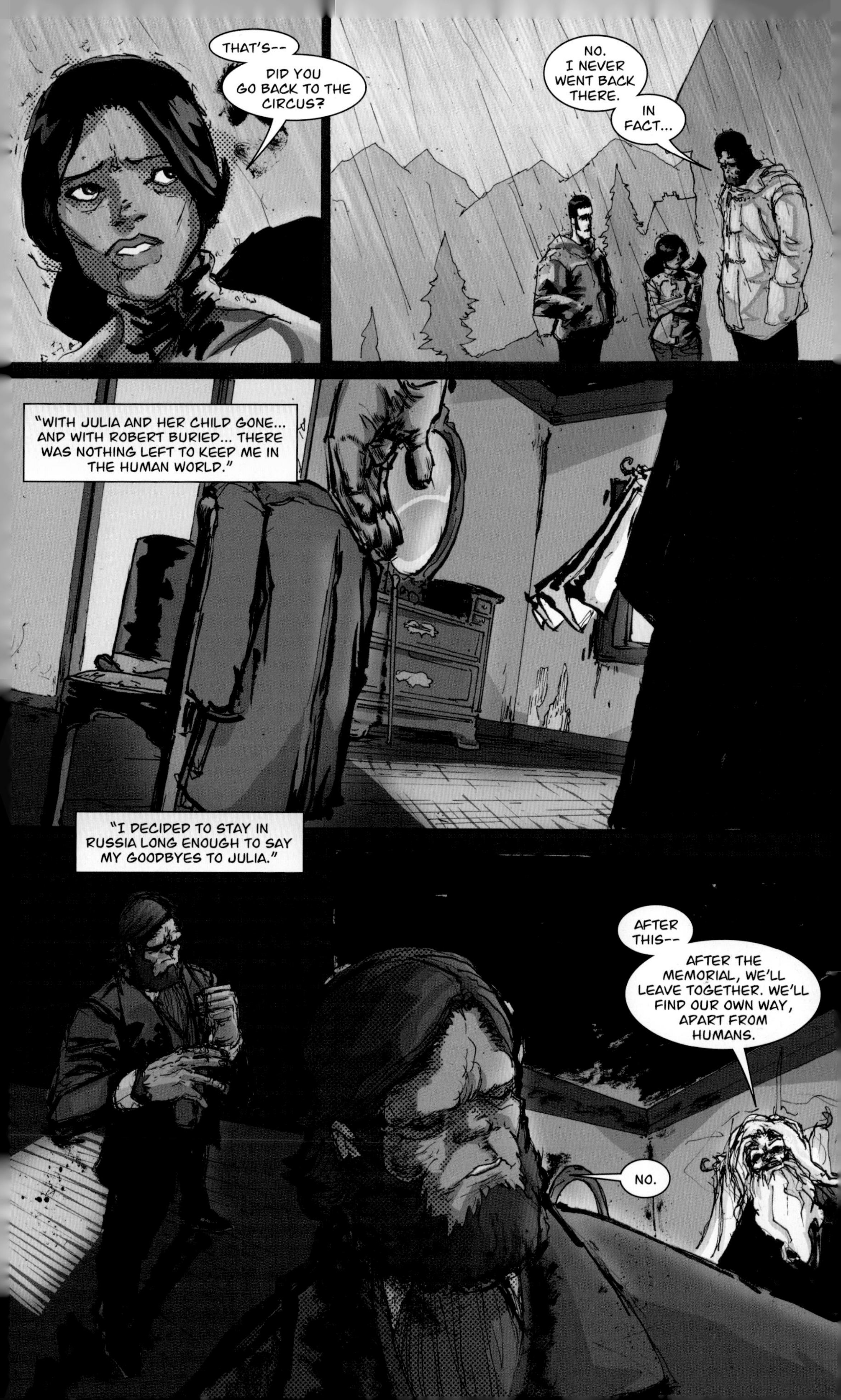
THAT'S--
DID YOU GO BACK TO THE CIRCUS?
NO. I NEVER WENT BACK THERE.
IN FACT...
"WITH JULIA AND HER CHILD GONE... AND WITH ROBERT BURIED... THERE WAS NOTHING LEFT TO KEEP ME IN THE HUMAN WORLD."
"I DECIDED TO STAY IN RUSSIA LONG ENOUGH TO SAY MY GOODBYES TO JULIA."
AFTER THIS--
AFTER THE MEMORIAL, WE'LL LEAVE TOGETHER. WE'LL FIND OUR OWN WAY, APART FROM HUMANS.
NO.

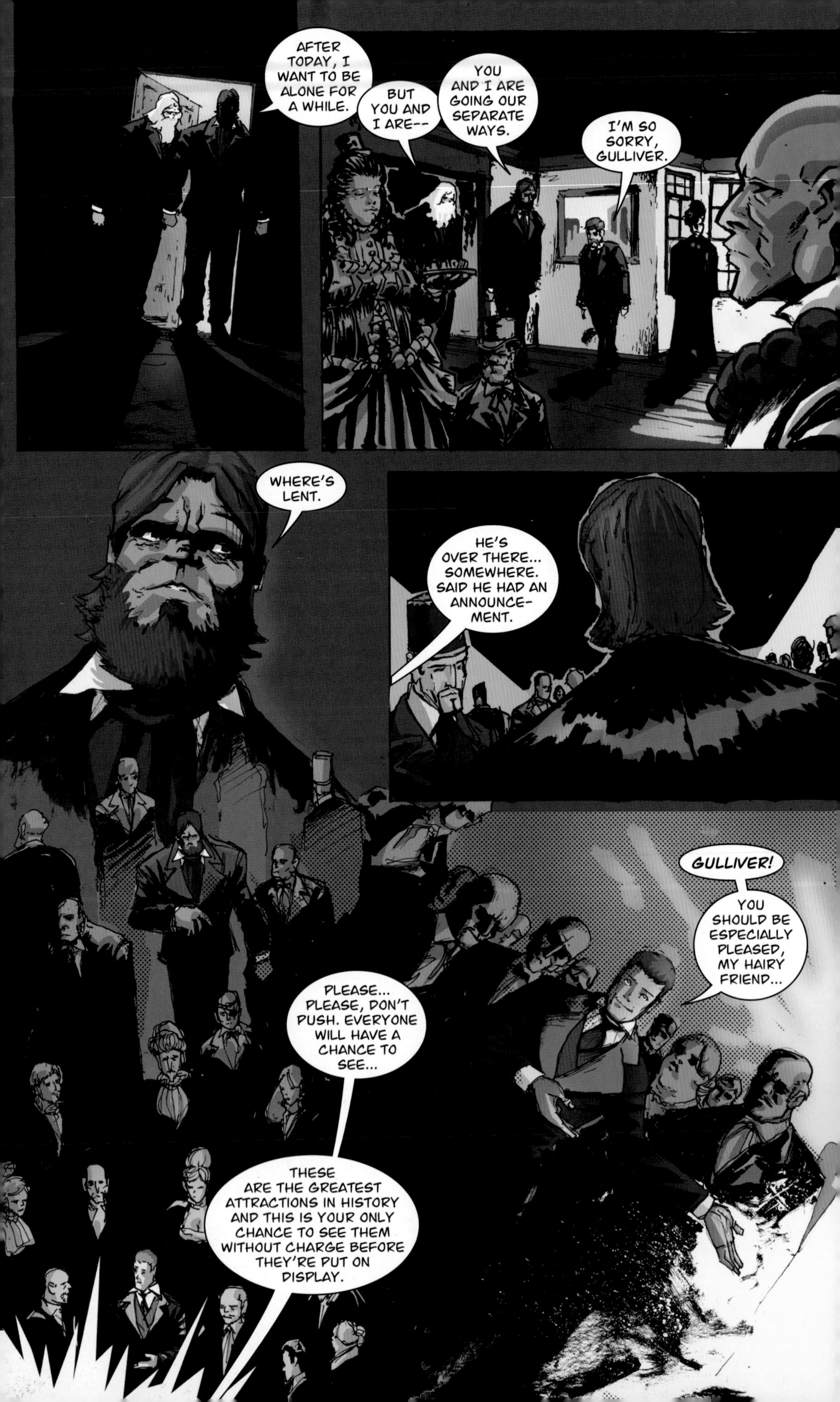
AFTER TODAY, I WANT TO BE ALONE FOR A WHILE.
BUT YOU AND I ARE--
YOU AND I ARE GOING OUR SEPARATE WAYS.
I'M SO SORRY, GULLIVER.
WHERE'S LENT.
HE'S OVER THERE... SOMEWHERE. SAID HE HAD AN ANNOUNCE-MENT.
GULLIVER!
YOU SHOULD BE ESPECIALLY PLEASED, MY HAIRY FRIEND...
PLEASE... PLEASE, DON'T PUSH. EVERYONE WILL HAVE A CHANCE TO SEE...
THESE ARE THE GREATEST ATTRACTIONS IN HISTORY AND THIS IS YOUR ONLY CHANCE TO SEE THEM WITHOUT CHARGE BEFORE THEY'RE PUT ON DISPLAY.

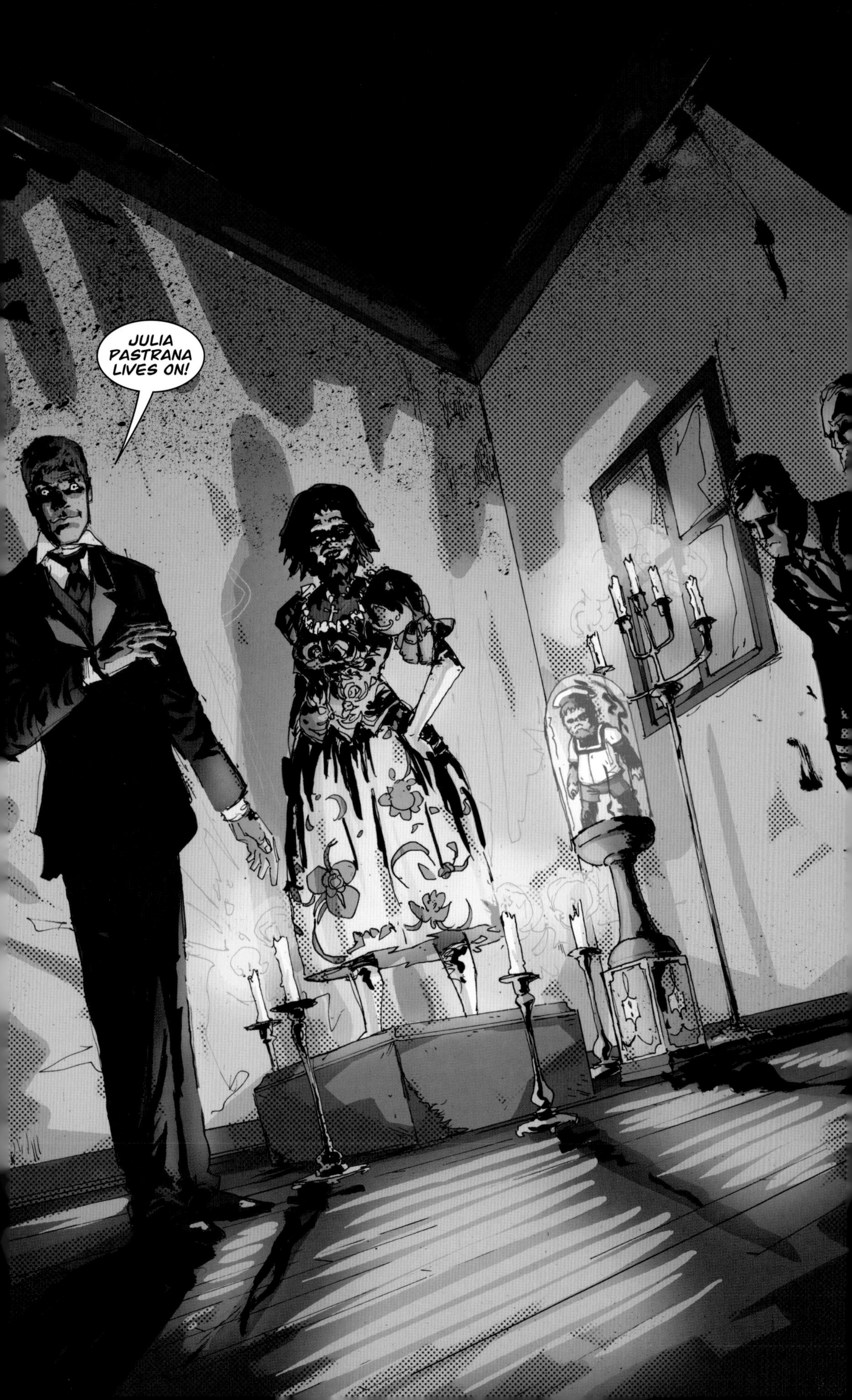
JULIA PASTRANA LIVES ON!

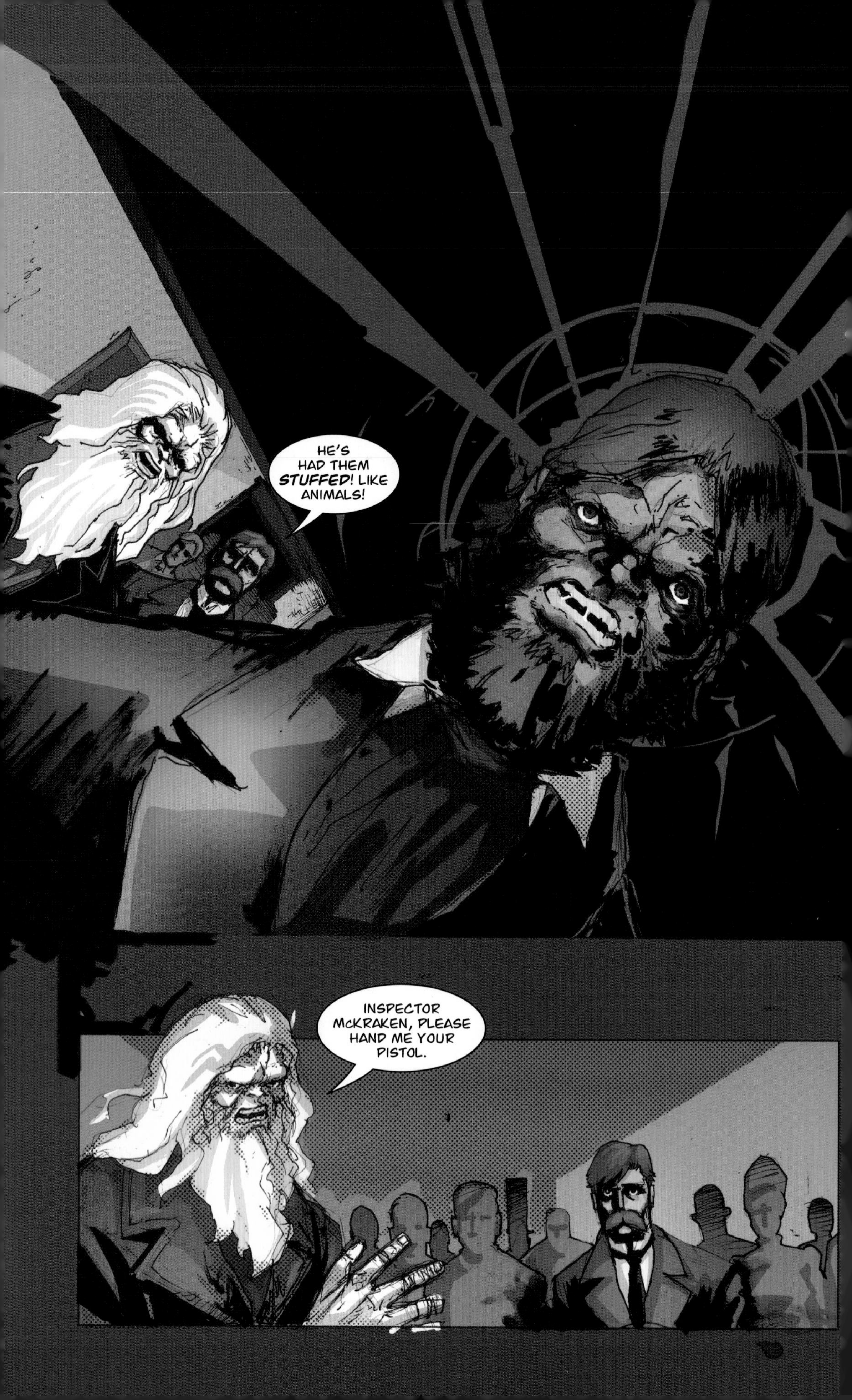
HE'S HAD THEM STUFFED! LIKE ANIMALS!
INSPECTOR McKRAKEN, PLEASE HAND ME YOUR PISTOL.

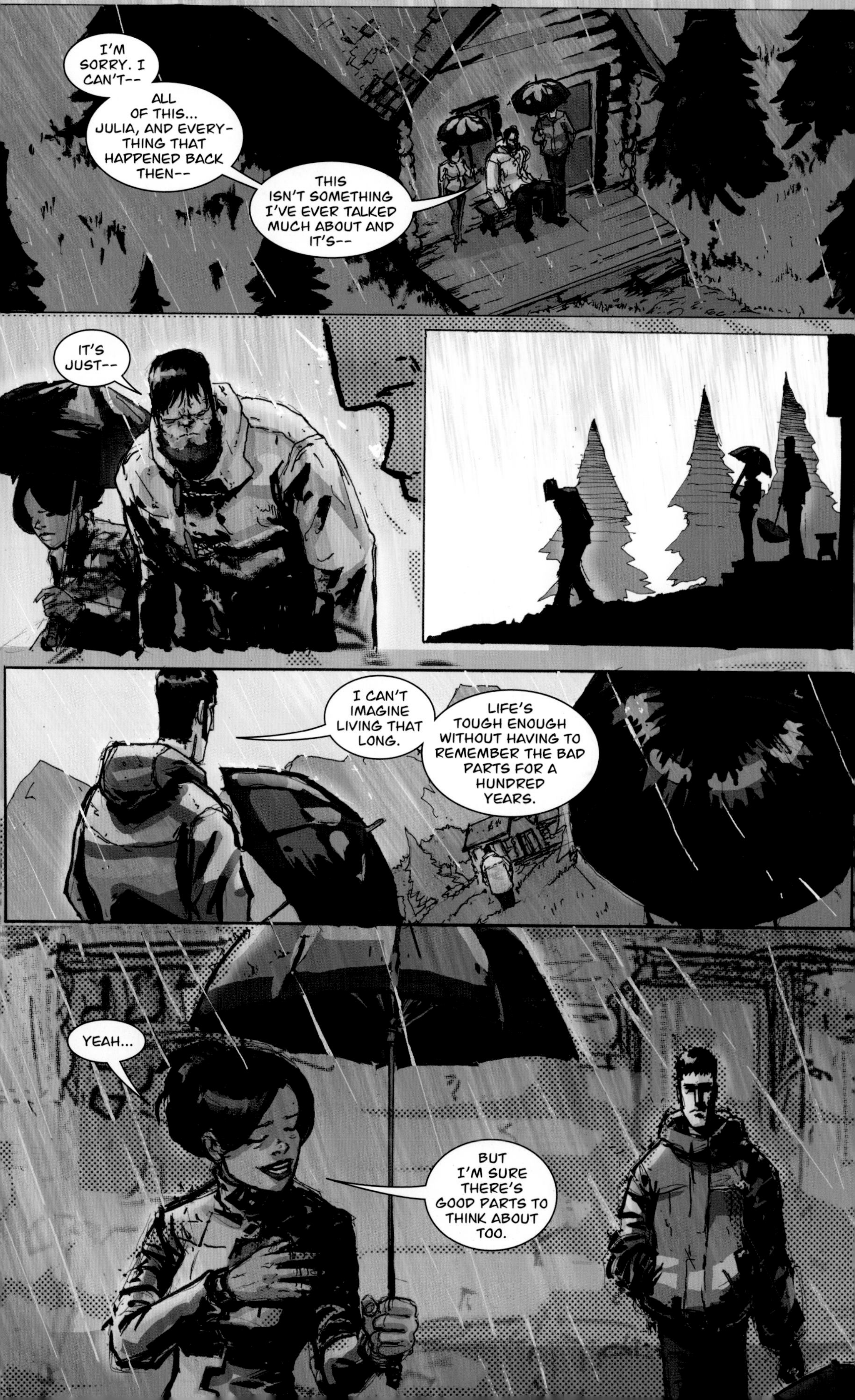
I'M SORRY. I CAN'T--
ALL OF THIS... JULIA, AND EVERYTHING THAT HAPPENED BACK THEN--
THIS ISN'T SOMETHING I'VE EVER TALKED MUCH ABOUT AND IT'S--
IT'S JUST--
I CAN'T IMAGINE LIVING THAT LONG.
LIFE'S TOUGH ENOUGH WITHOUT HAVING TO REMEMBER THE BAD PARTS FOR A HUNDRED YEARS.
YEAH...
BUT I'M SURE THERE'S GOOD PARTS TO THINK ABOUT TOO.

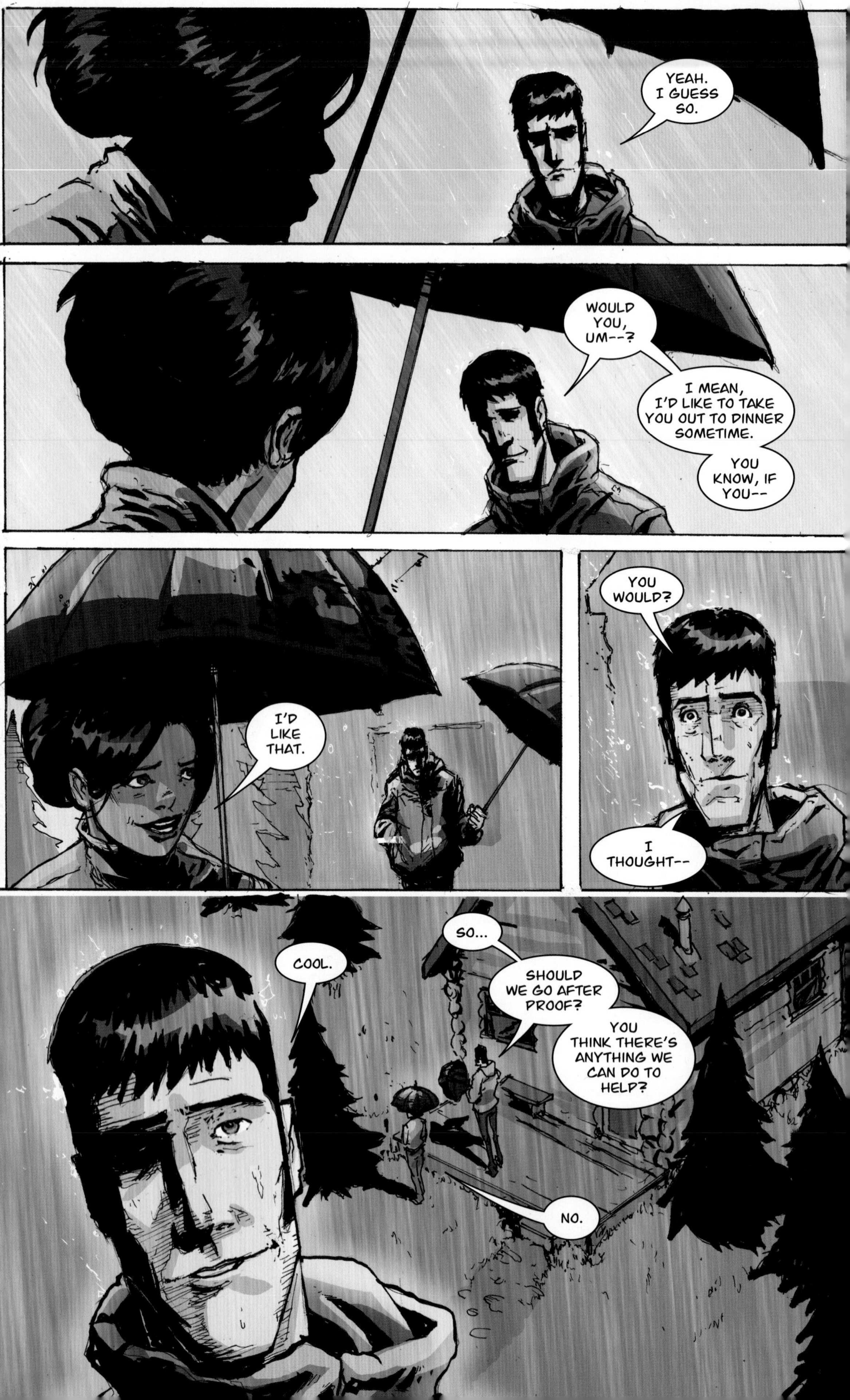

YEAH. I GUESS SO.
WOULD YOU, UM--?
I MEAN, I'D LIKE TO TAKE YOU OUT TO DINNER SOMETIME.
YOU KNOW, IF YOU--
I'D LIKE THAT.
YOU WOULD?
I THOUGHT--
COOL.
SO...
SHOULD WE GO AFTER PROOF?
YOU THINK THERE'S ANYTHING WE CAN DO TO HELP?
NO.

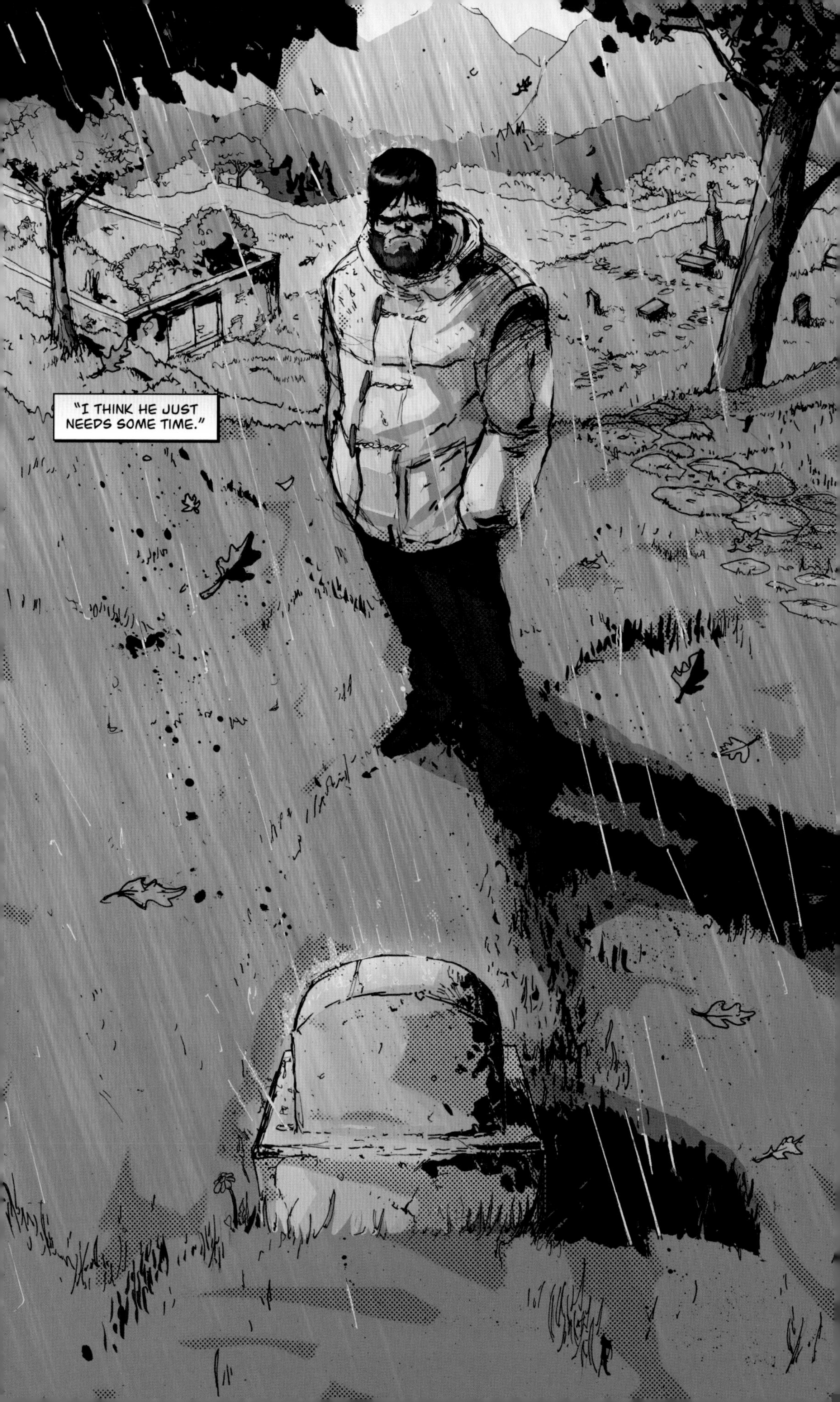
"I THINK HE JUST NEEDS SOME TIME."

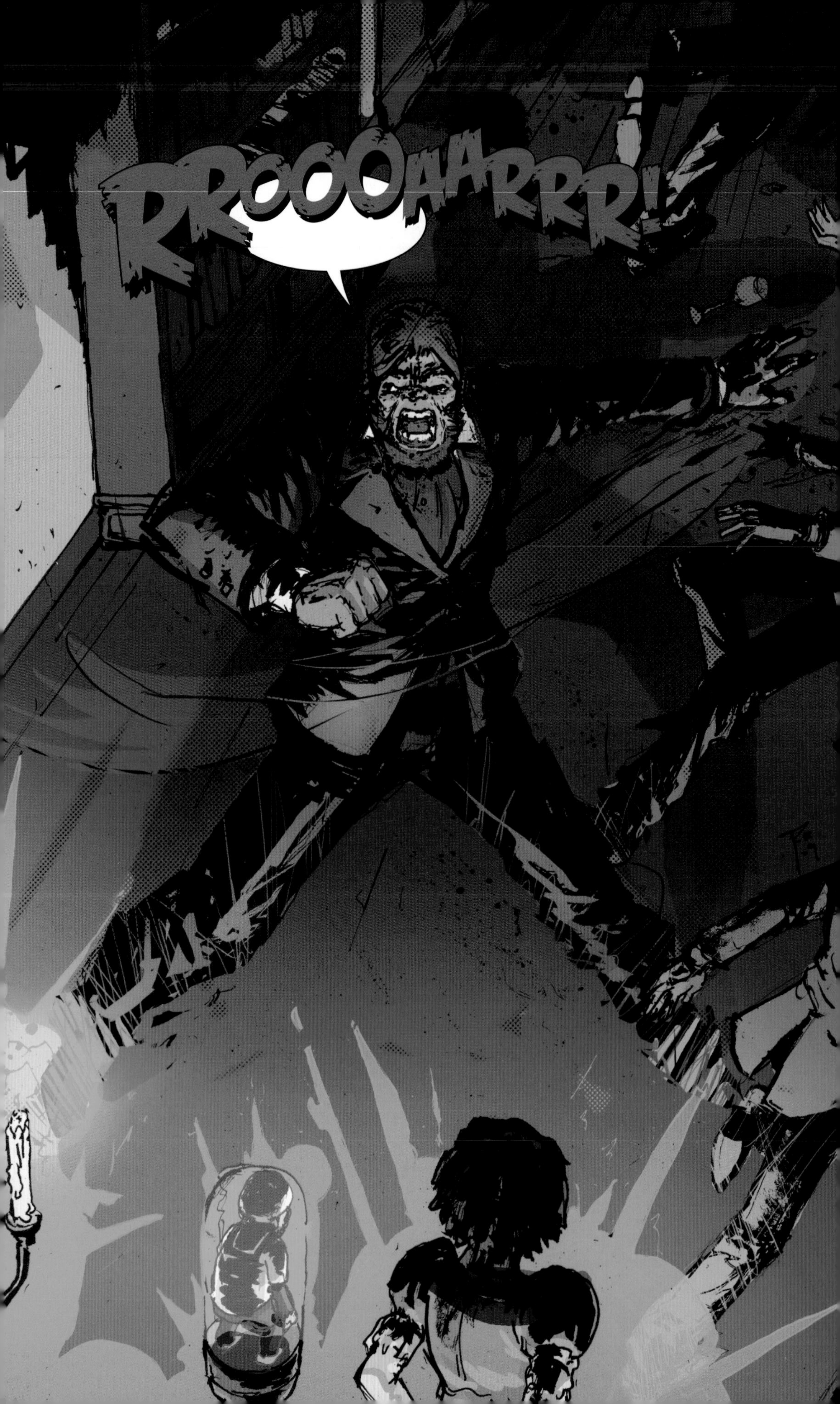
RROOOOAARRR!

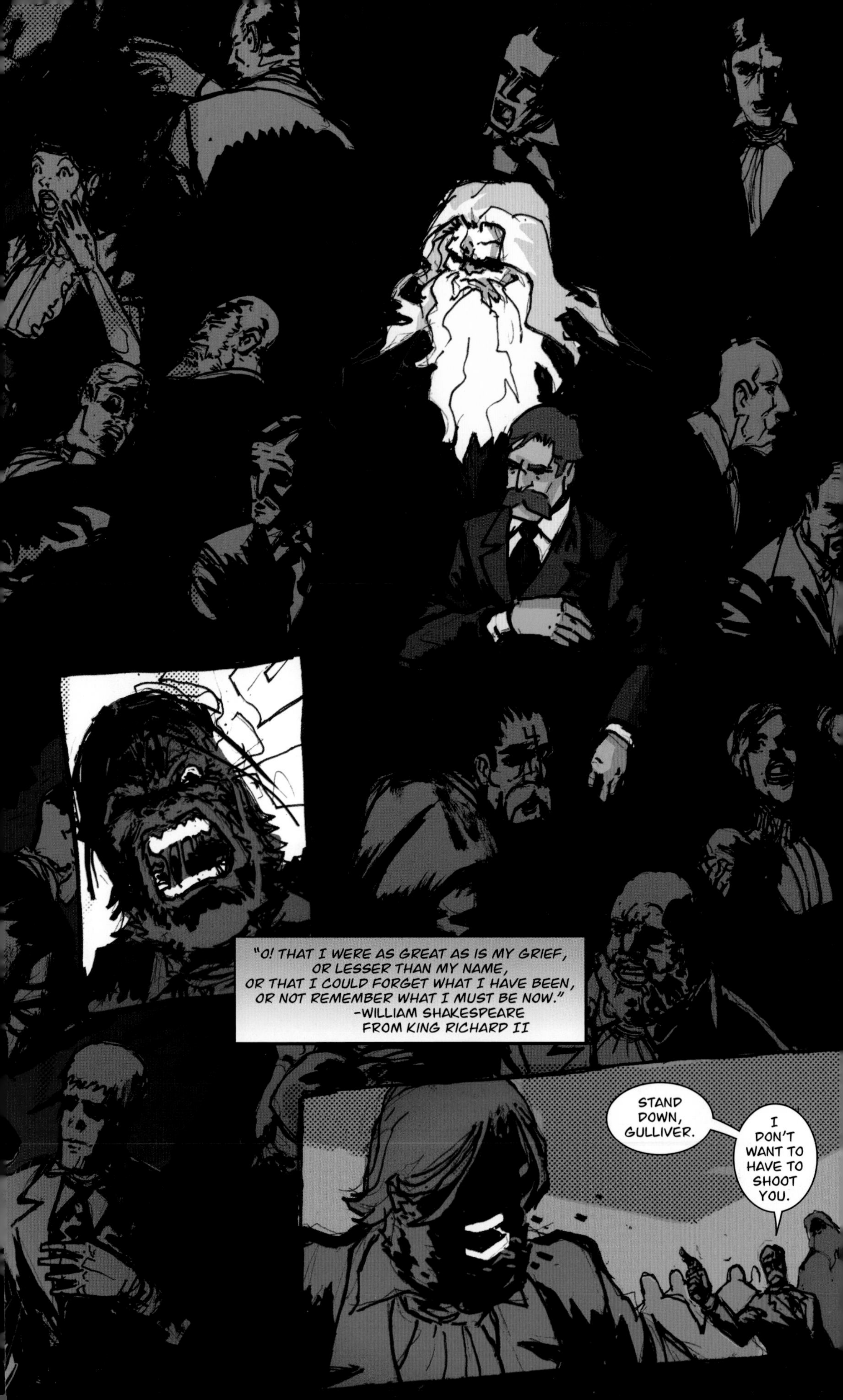

"O! THAT I WERE AS GREAT AS IS MY GRIEF, OR LESSER THAN MY NAME, OR THAT I COULD FORGET WHAT I HAVE BEEN, OR NOT REMEMBER WHAT I MUST BE NOW." -WILLIAM SHAKESPEARE FROM KING RICHARD II
STAND DOWN, GULLIVER.
I DON'T WANT TO HAVE TO SHOOT YOU.

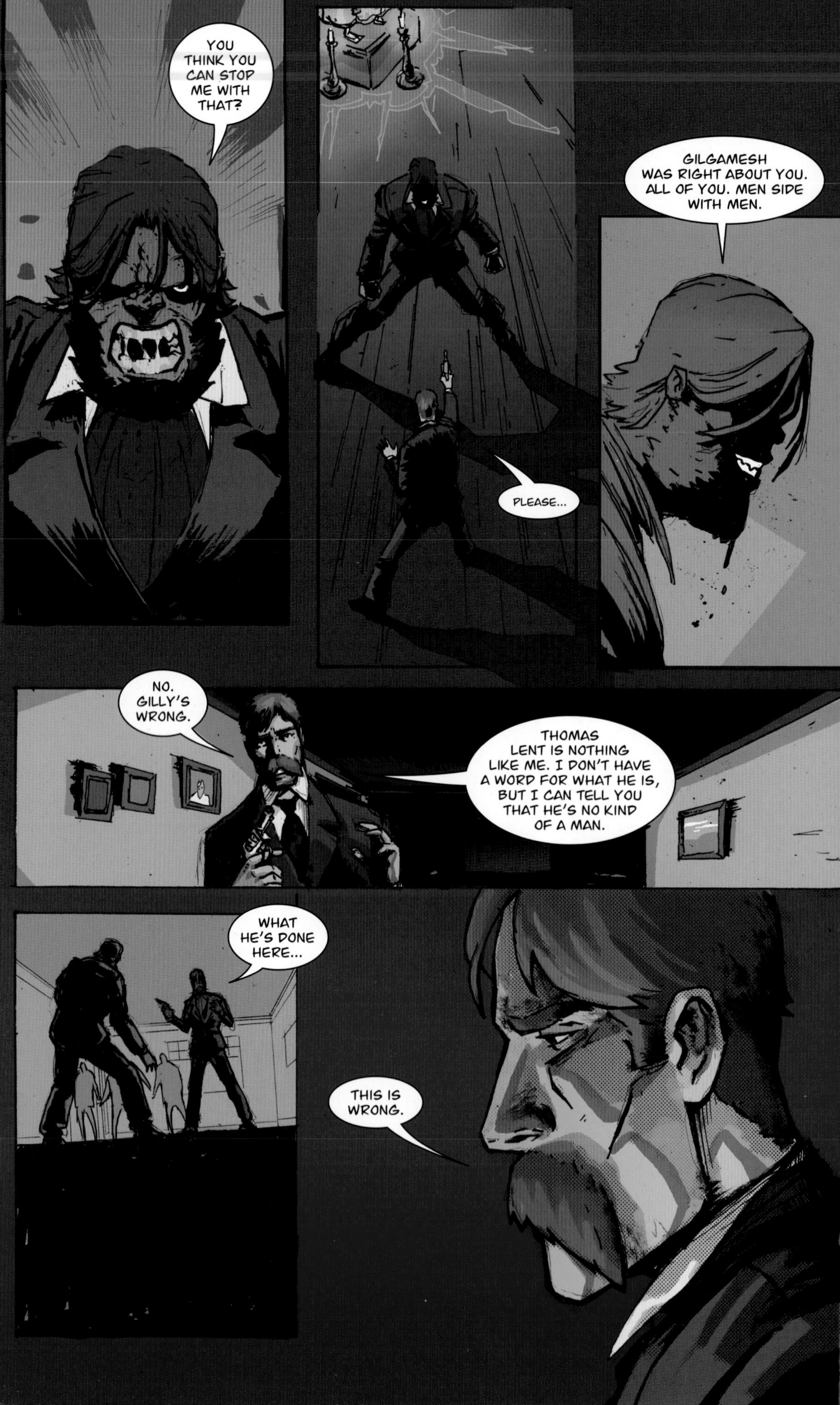
YOU THINK YOU CAN STOP ME WITH THAT?
PLEASE...
GILGAMESH WAS RIGHT ABOUT YOU. ALL OF YOU. MEN SIDE WITH MEN.
NO. GILLY'S WRONG.
THOMAS LENT IS NOTHING LIKE ME. I DON'T HAVE A WORD FOR WHAT HE IS, BUT I CAN TELL YOU THAT HE'S NO KIND OF A MAN.
WHAT HE'S DONE HERE...
THIS IS WRONG.

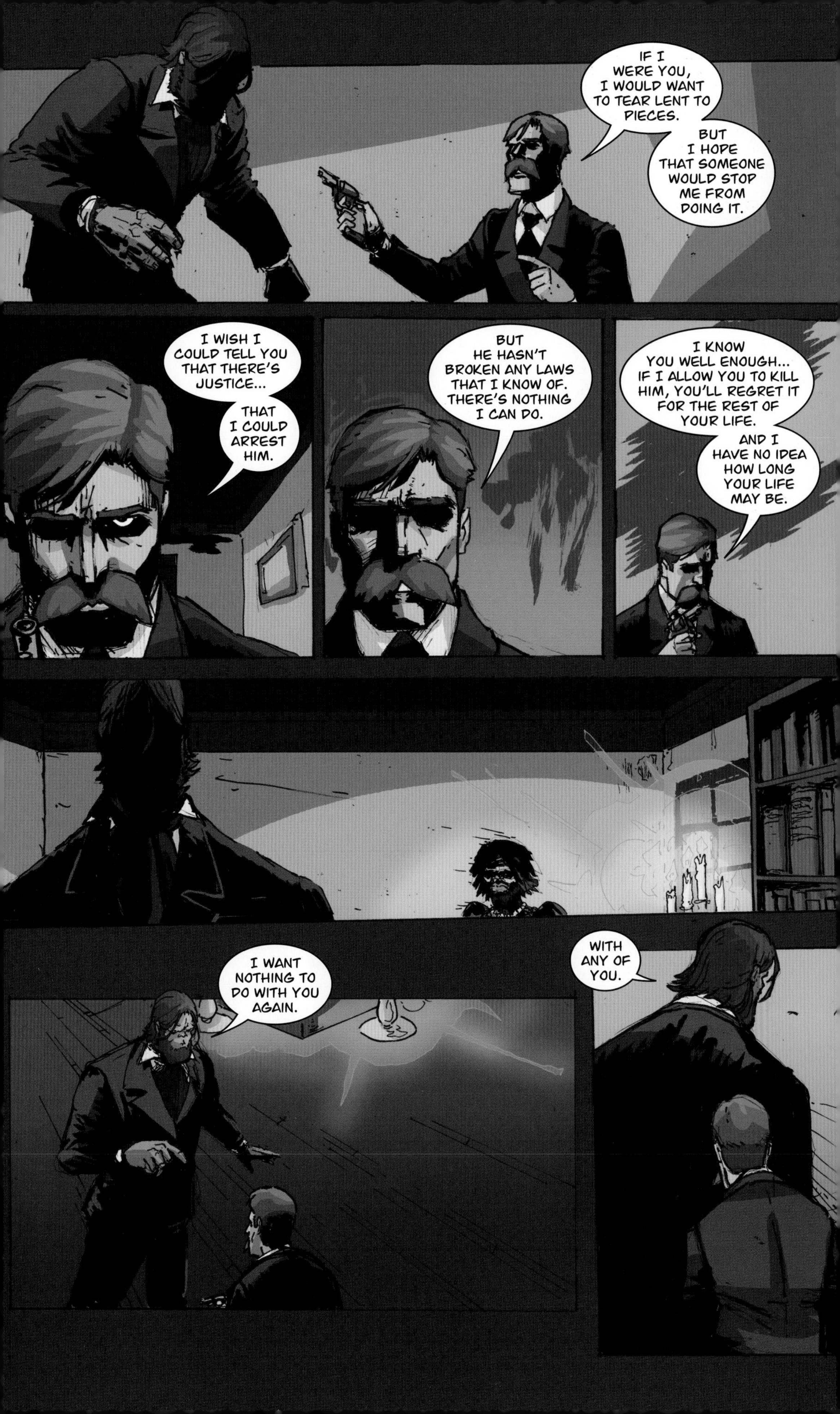
IF I WERE YOU, I WOULD WANT TO TEAR LENT TO PIECES.
BUT I HOPE THAT SOMEONE WOULD STOP ME FROM DOING IT.
I WISH I COULD TELL YOU THAT THERE'S JUSTICE...
THAT I COULD ARREST HIM.
BUT HE HASN'T BROKEN ANY LAWS THAT I KNOW OF. THERE'S NOTHING I CAN DO.
I KNOW YOU WELL ENOUGH... IF I ALLOW YOU TO KILL HIM, YOU'LL REGRET IT FOR THE REST OF YOUR LIFE.
AND I HAVE NO IDEA HOW LONG YOUR LIFE MAY BE.
I WANT NOTHING TO DO WITH YOU AGAIN.
WITH ANY OF YOU.

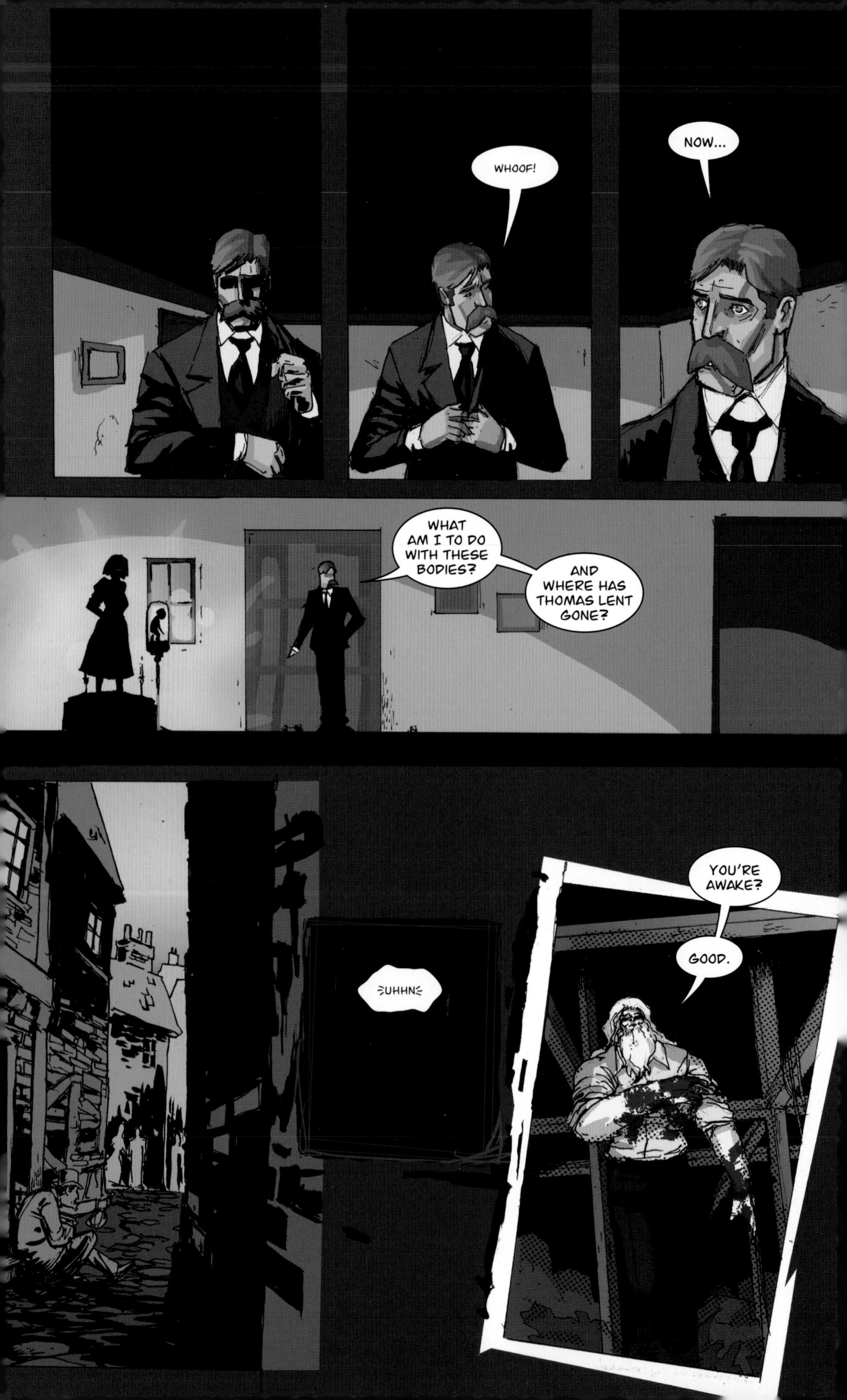
WHOOF!
NOW...
WHAT AM I TO DO WITH THESE BODIES?
AND WHERE HAS THOMAS LENT GONE?
UHHN
YOU'RE AWAKE?
GOOD.

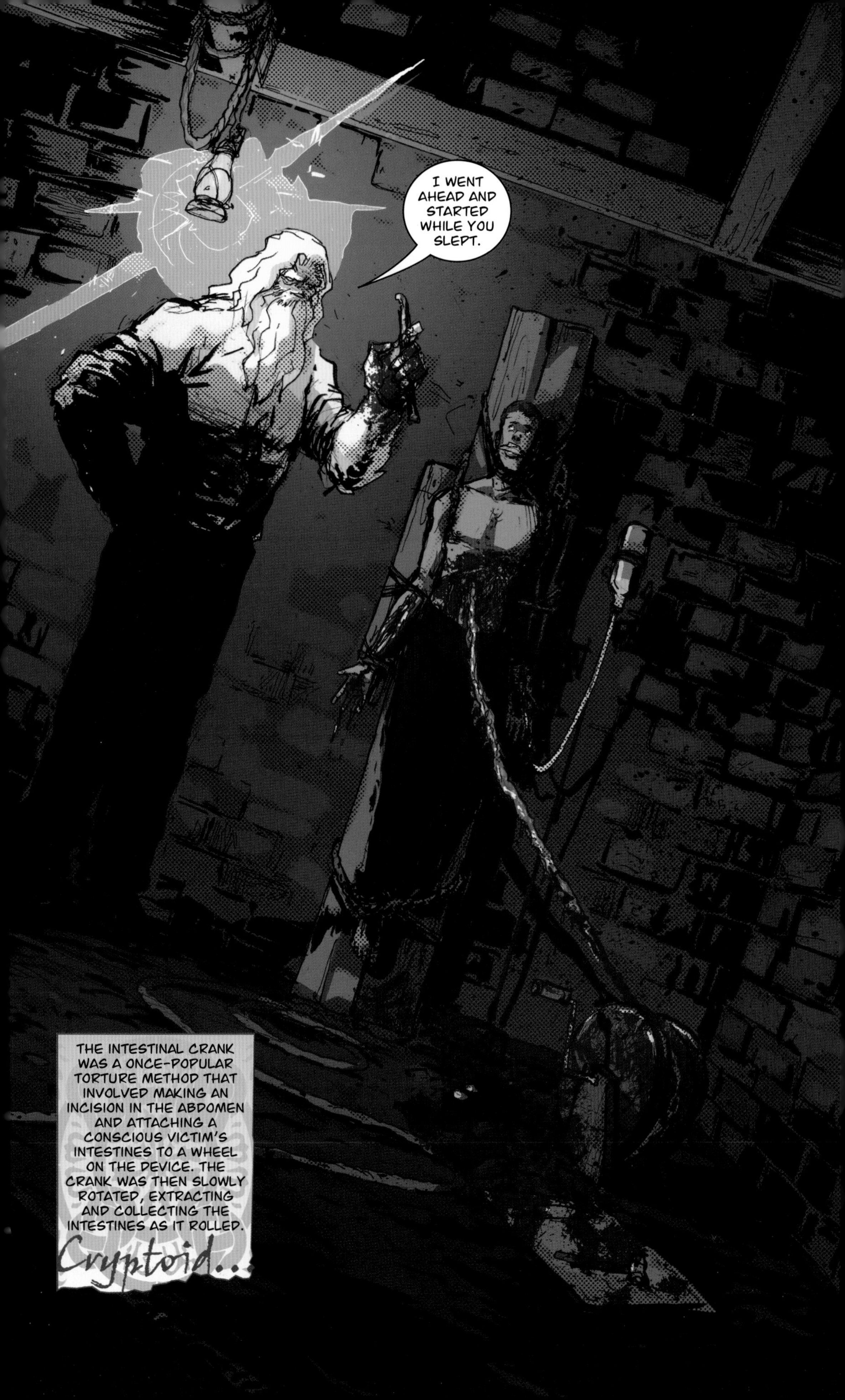
I WENT AHEAD AND STARTED WHILE YOU SLEPT.
THE INTESTINAL CRANK WAS A ONCE-POPULAR TORTURE METHOD THAT INVOLVED MAKING AN INCISION IN THE ABDOMEN AND ATTACHING A CONSCIOUS VICTIM'S INTESTINES TO A WHEEL ON THE DEVICE. THE CRANK WAS THEN SLOWLY ROTATED, EXTRACTING AND COLLECTING THE INTESTINES AS IT ROLLED.
Cryptoid...

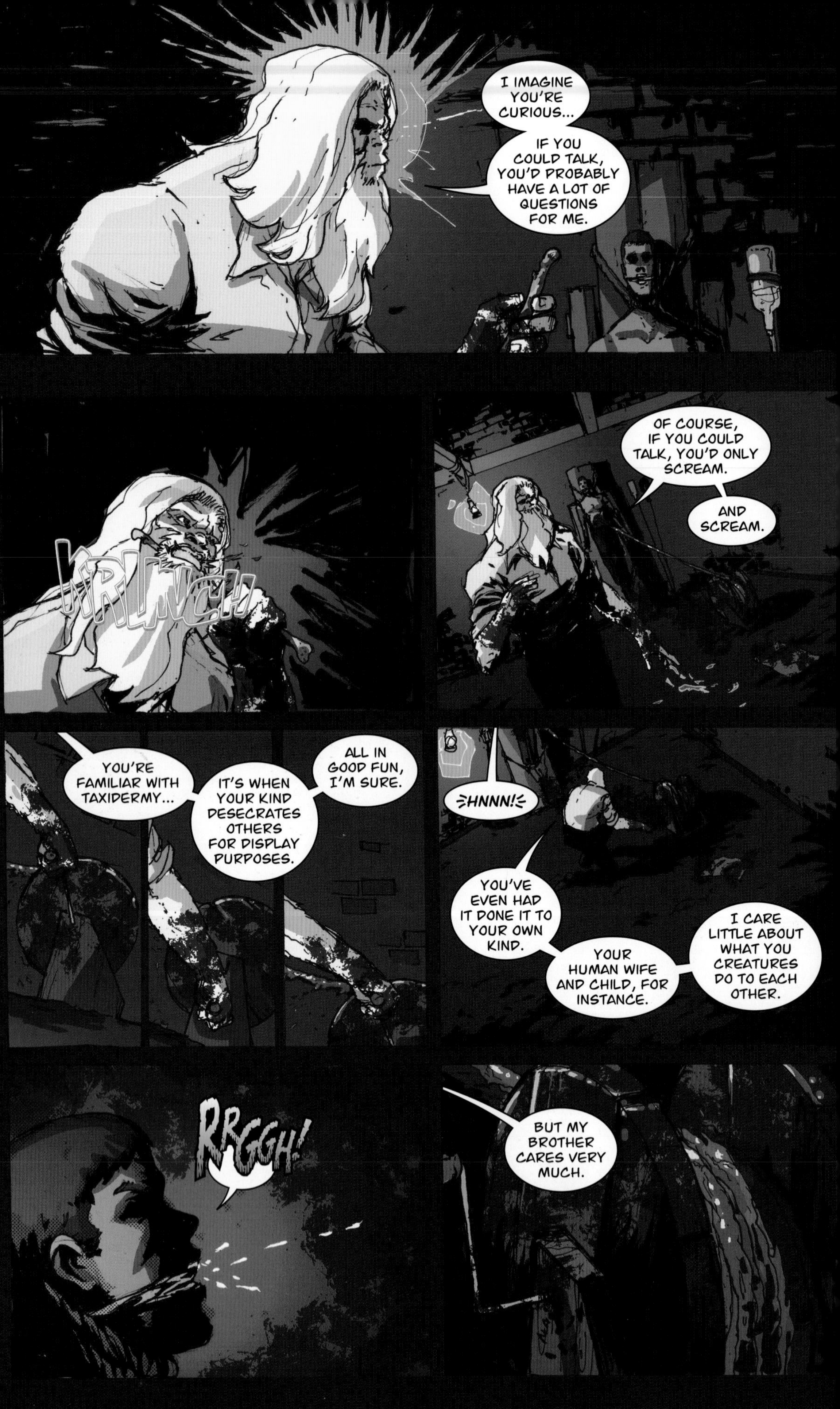

I IMAGINE YOU'RE CURIOUS...
IF YOU COULD TALK, YOU'D PROBABLY HAVE A LOT OF QUESTIONS FOR ME.
KRUNCH
OF COURSE, IF YOU COULD TALK, YOU'D ONLY SCREAM.
AND SCREAM.
YOU'RE FAMILIAR WITH TAXIDERMY...
IT'S WHEN YOUR KIND DESECRATES OTHERS FOR DISPLAY PURPOSES.
ALL IN GOOD FUN, I'M SURE.
HNNN!
YOU'VE EVEN HAD IT DONE IT TO YOUR OWN KIND.
YOUR HUMAN WIFE AND CHILD, FOR INSTANCE.
I CARE LITTLE ABOUT WHAT YOU CREATURES DO TO EACH OTHER.
RRGGH!
BUT MY BROTHER CARES VERY MUCH.

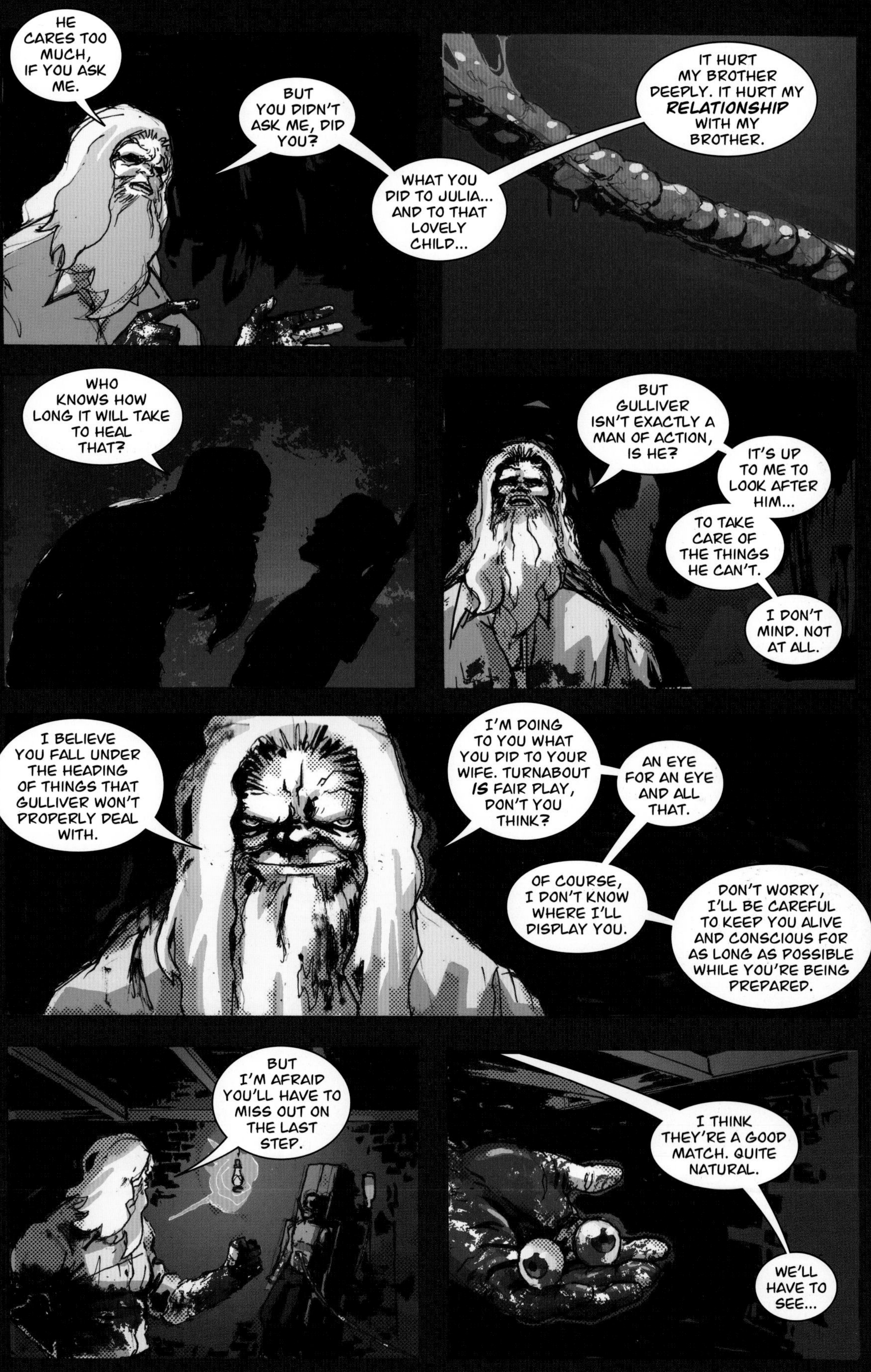
HE CARES TOO MUCH, IF YOU ASK ME.
BUT YOU DIDN'T ASK ME, DID YOU?
WHAT YOU DID TO JULIA... AND TO THAT LOVELY CHILD...
IT HURT MY BROTHER DEEPLY. IT HURT MY RELATIONSHIP WITH MY BROTHER.
WHO KNOWS HOW LONG IT WILL TAKE TO HEAL THAT?
BUT GULLIVER ISN'T EXACTLY A MAN OF ACTION, IS HE?
IT'S UP TO ME TO LOOK AFTER HIM...
TO TAKE CARE OF THE THINGS HE CAN'T.
I DON'T MIND. NOT AT ALL.
I BELIEVE YOU FALL UNDER THE HEADING OF THINGS THAT GULLIVER WON'T PROPERLY DEAL WITH.
I'M DOING TO YOU WHAT YOU DID TO YOUR WIFE. TURNABOUT IS FAIR PLAY, DON'T YOU THINK?
AN EYE FOR AN EYE AND ALL THAT.
OF COURSE, I DON'T KNOW WHERE I'LL DISPLAY YOU.
DON'T WORRY, I'LL BE CAREFUL TO KEEP YOU ALIVE AND CONSCIOUS FOR AS LONG AS POSSIBLE WHILE YOU'RE BEING PREPARED.
BUT I'M AFRAID YOU'LL HAVE TO MISS OUT ON THE LAST STEP.
I THINK THEY'RE A GOOD MATCH. QUITE NATURAL.
WE'LL HAVE TO SEE...

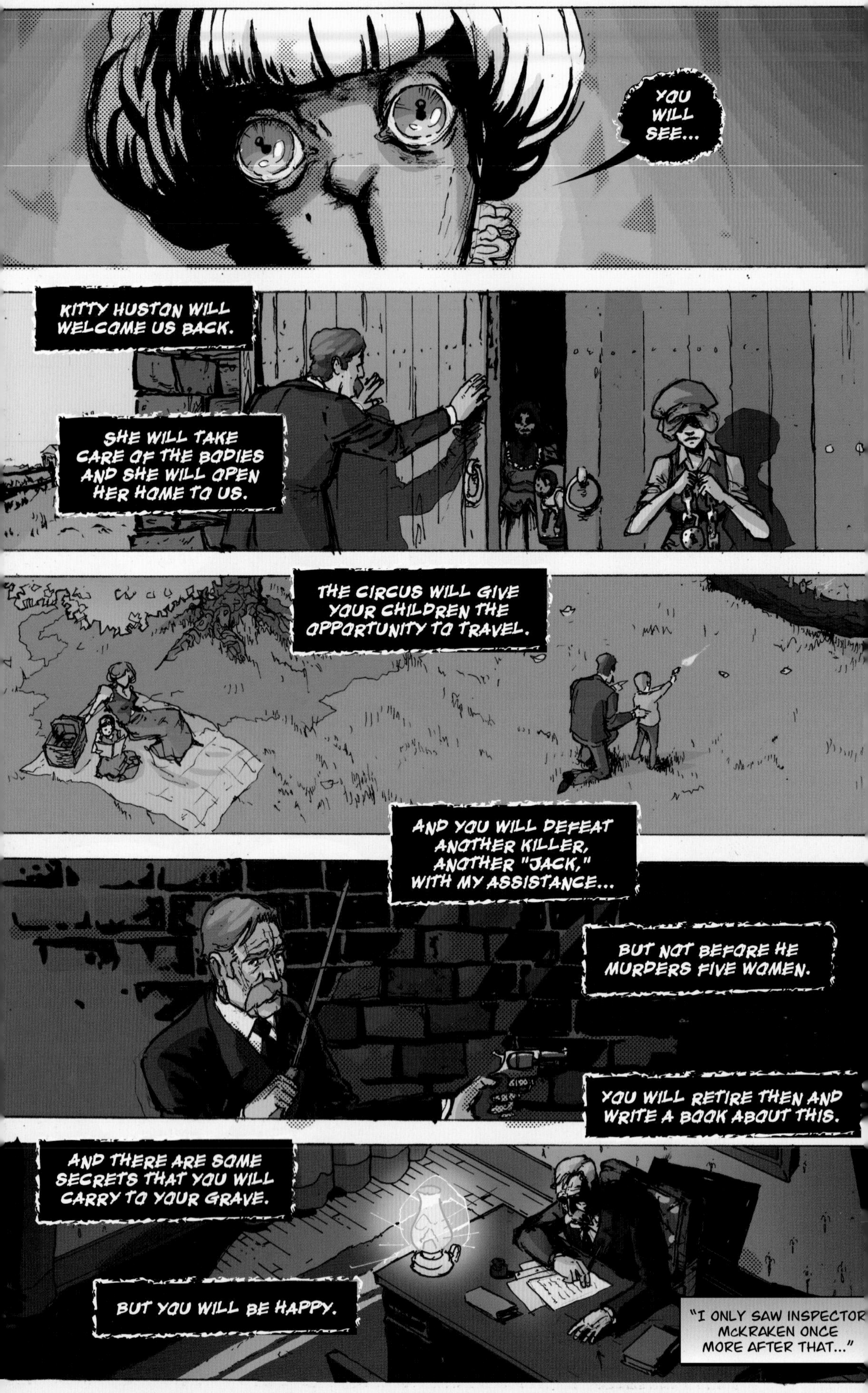
YOU WILL SEE...
KITTY HUSTON WILL WELCOME US BACK.
SHE WILL TAKE CARE OF THE BODIES AND SHE WILL OPEN HER HOME TO US.
THE CIRCUS WILL GIVE YOUR CHILDREN THE OPPORTUNITY TO TRAVEL.
AND YOU WILL DEFEAT ANOTHER KILLER, ANOTHER "JACK," WITH MY ASSISTANCE...
BUT NOT BEFORE HE MURDERS FIVE WOMEN.
YOU WILL RETIRE THEN AND WRITE A BOOK ABOUT THIS.
AND THERE ARE SOME SECRETS THAT YOU WILL CARRY TO YOUR GRAVE.
BUT YOU WILL BE HAPPY.
"I ONLY SAW INSPECTOR McKRAKEN ONCE MORE AFTER THAT..."

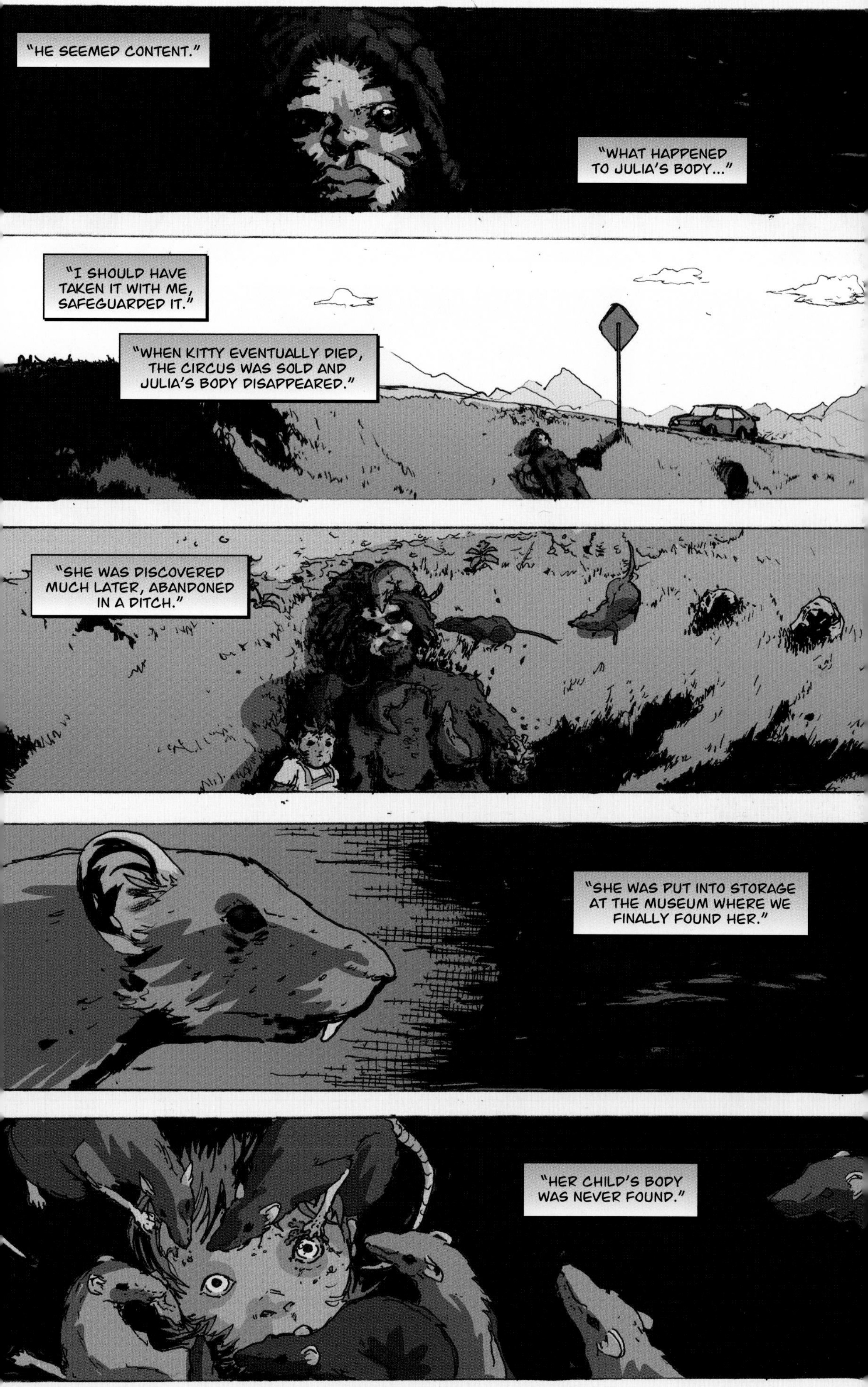

"HE SEEMED CONTENT."
"WHAT HAPPENED TO JULIA'S BODY..."
"I SHOULD HAVE TAKEN IT WITH ME, SAFEGUARDED IT."
"WHEN KITTY EVENTUALLY DIED, THE CIRCUS WAS SOLD AND JULIA'S BODY DISAPPEARED."
"SHE WAS DISCOVERED MUCH LATER, ABANDONED IN A DITCH."
"SHE WAS PUT INTO STORAGE AT THE MUSEUM WHERE WE FINALLY FOUND HER."
"HER CHILD'S BODY WAS NEVER FOUND."

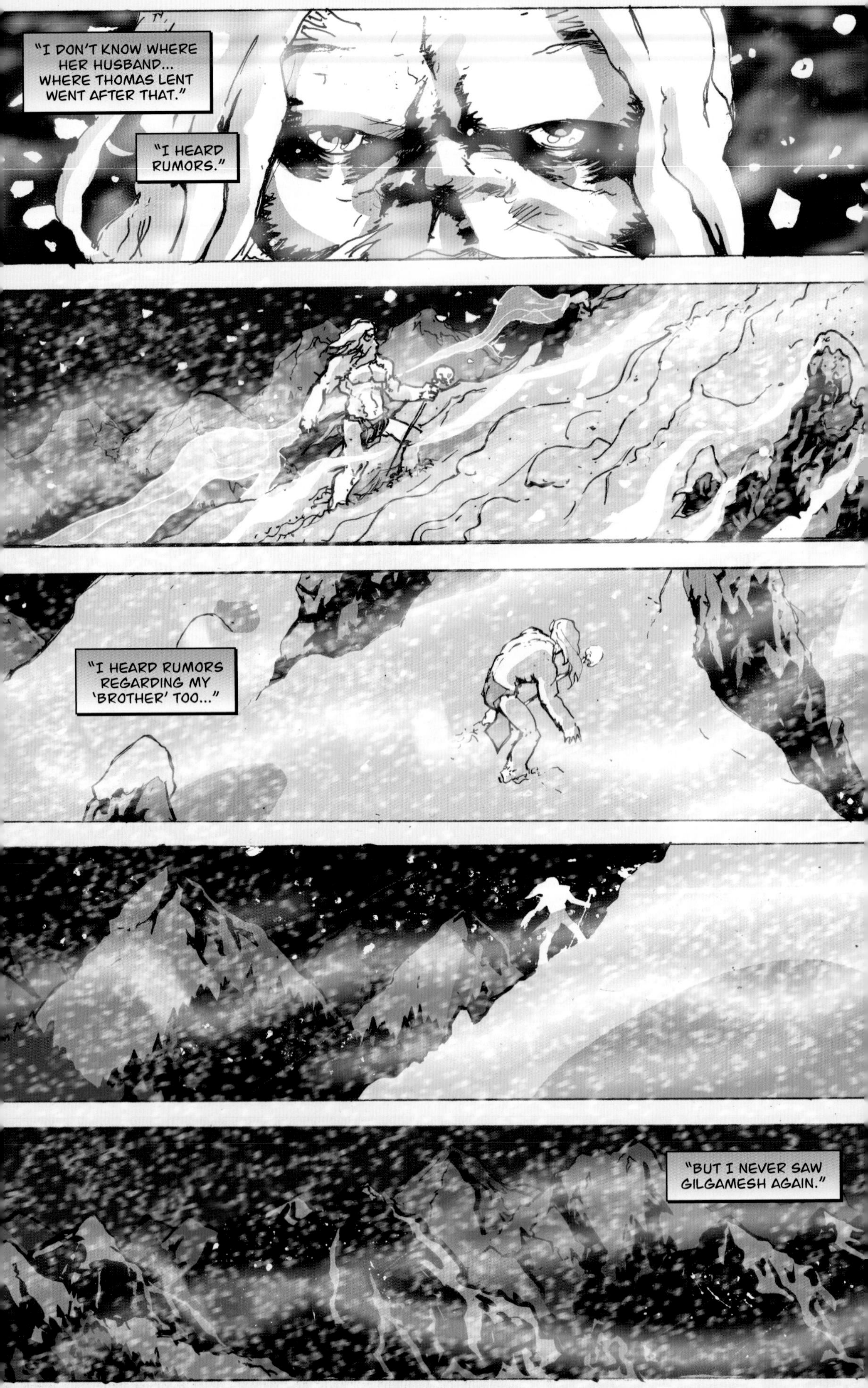
"I DON'T KNOW WHERE HER HUSBAND... WHERE THOMAS LENT WENT AFTER THAT."
"I HEARD RUMORS."
"I HEARD RUMORS REGARDING MY 'BROTHER' TOO..."
"BUT I NEVER SAW GILGAMESH AGAIN."

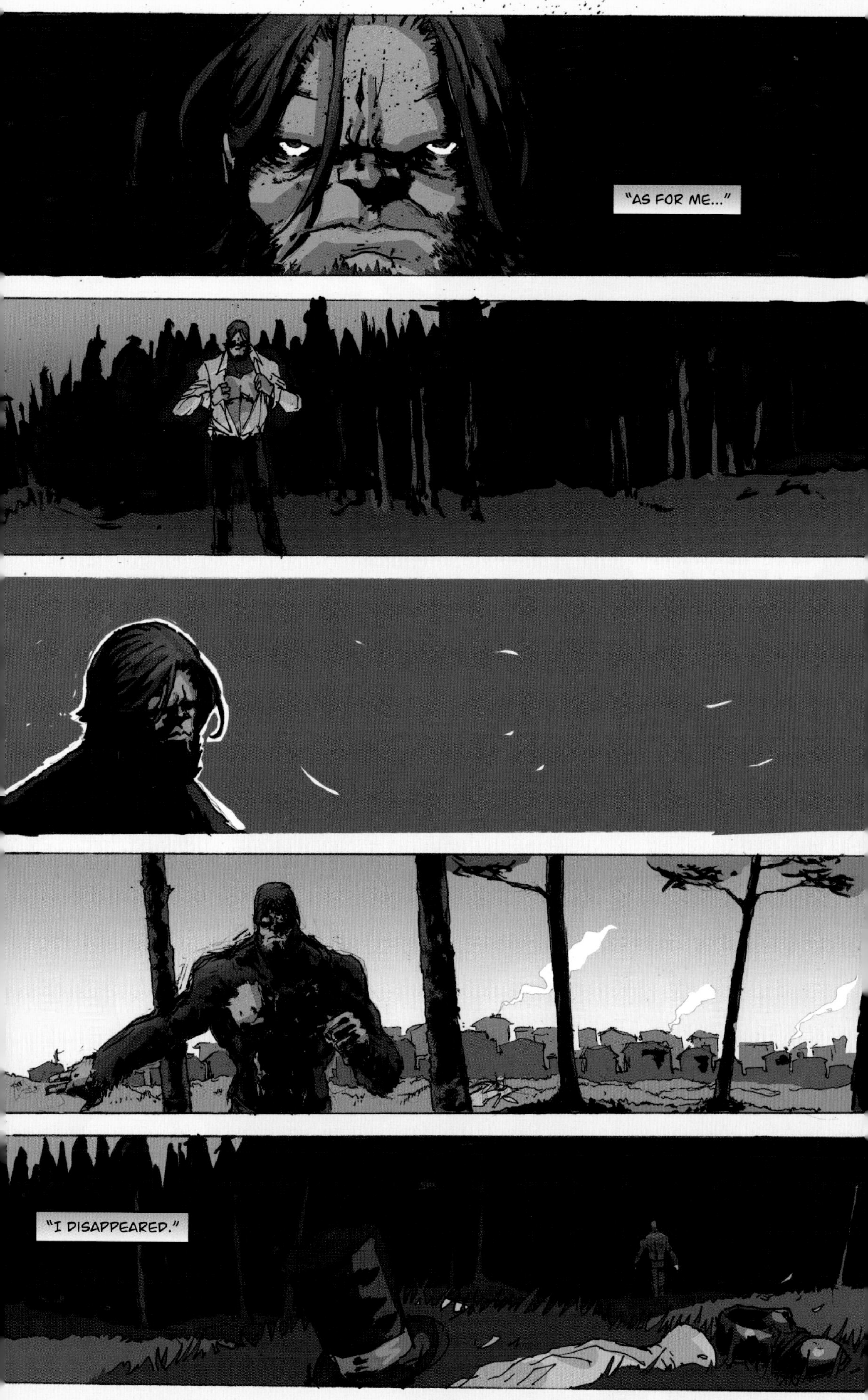
"AS FOR ME..."
"I DISAPPEARED."

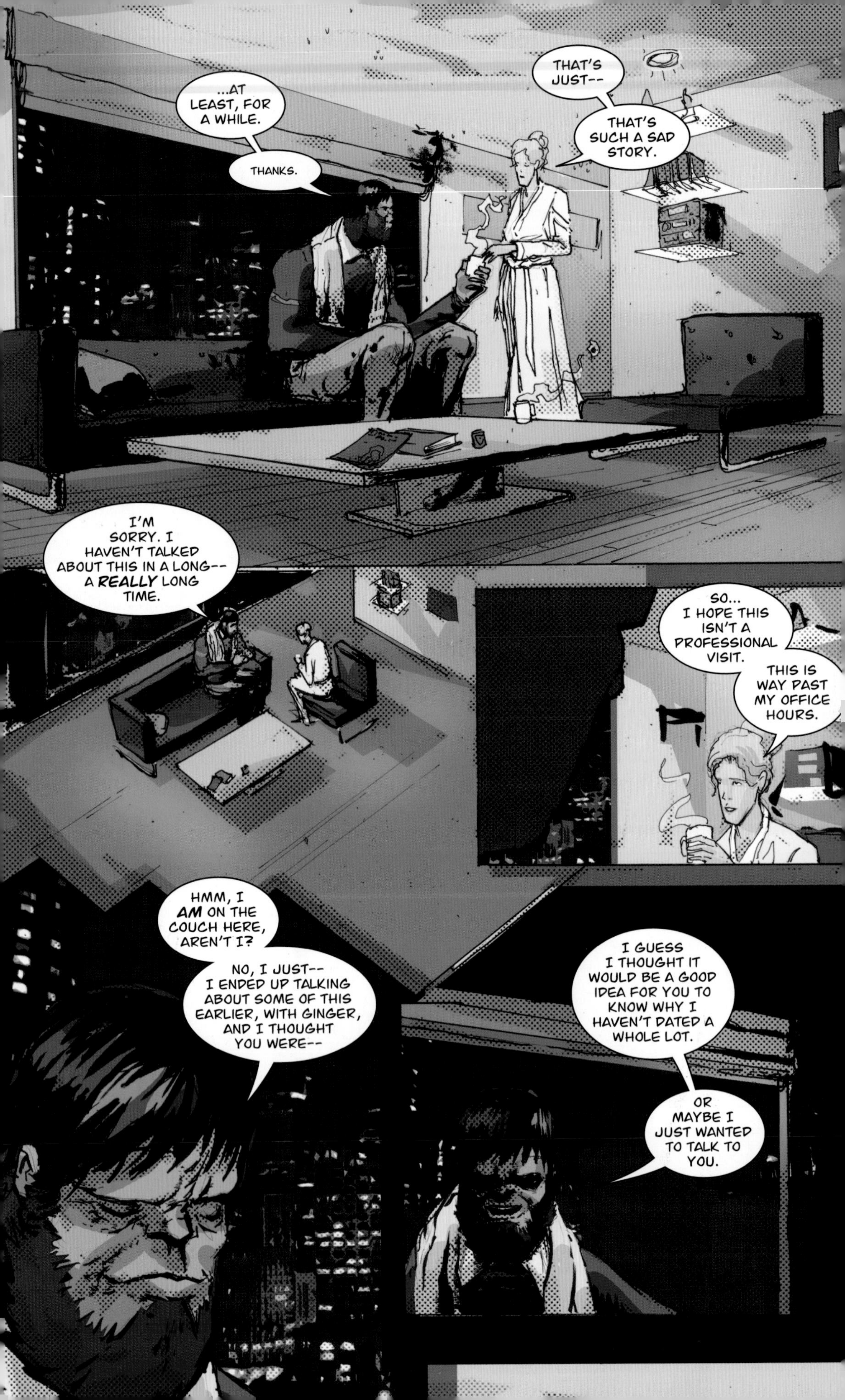
...AT LEAST, FOR A WHILE.
THANKS.
THAT'S JUST--
THAT'S SUCH A SAD STORY.
I'M SORRY. I HAVEN'T TALKED ABOUT THIS IN A LONG-- A **REALLY** LONG TIME.
SO... I HOPE THIS ISN'T A PROFESSIONAL VISIT.
THIS IS WAY PAST MY OFFICE HOURS.
HMM, I **AM** ON THE COUCH HERE, AREN'T I?
NO, I JUST-- I ENDED UP TALKING ABOUT SOME OF THIS EARLIER, WITH GINGER, AND I THOUGHT YOU WERE--
I GUESS I THOUGHT IT WOULD BE A GOOD IDEA FOR YOU TO KNOW WHY I HAVEN'T DATED A WHOLE LOT.
OR MAYBE I JUST WANTED TO TALK TO YOU.

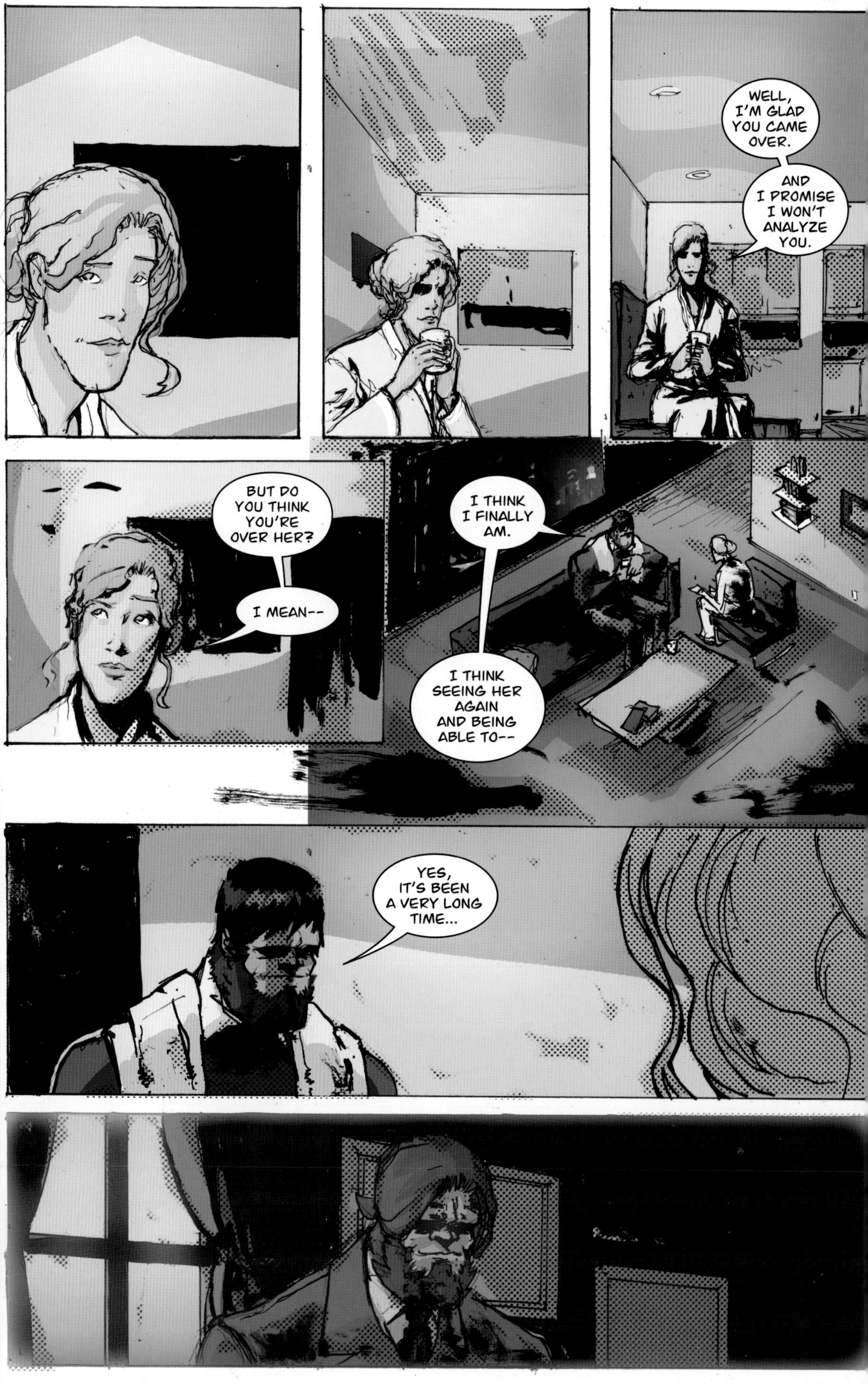
WELL, I'M GLAD YOU CAME OVER.
AND I PROMISE I WON'T ANALYZE YOU.
BUT DO YOU THINK YOU'RE OVER HER?
I MEAN--
I THINK I FINALLY AM.
I THINK SEEING HER AGAIN AND BEING ABLE TO--
YES, IT'S BEEN A VERY LONG TIME...

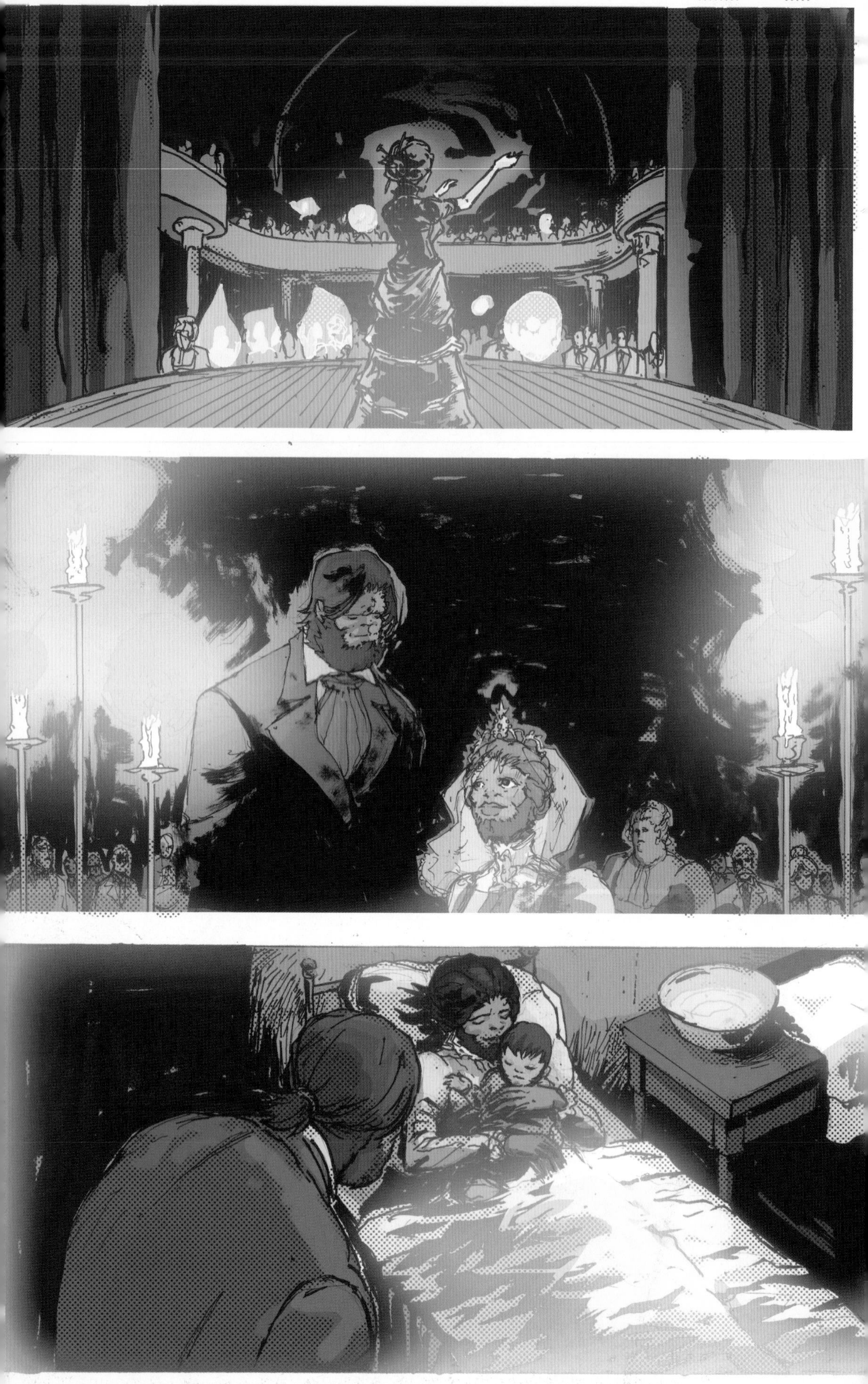

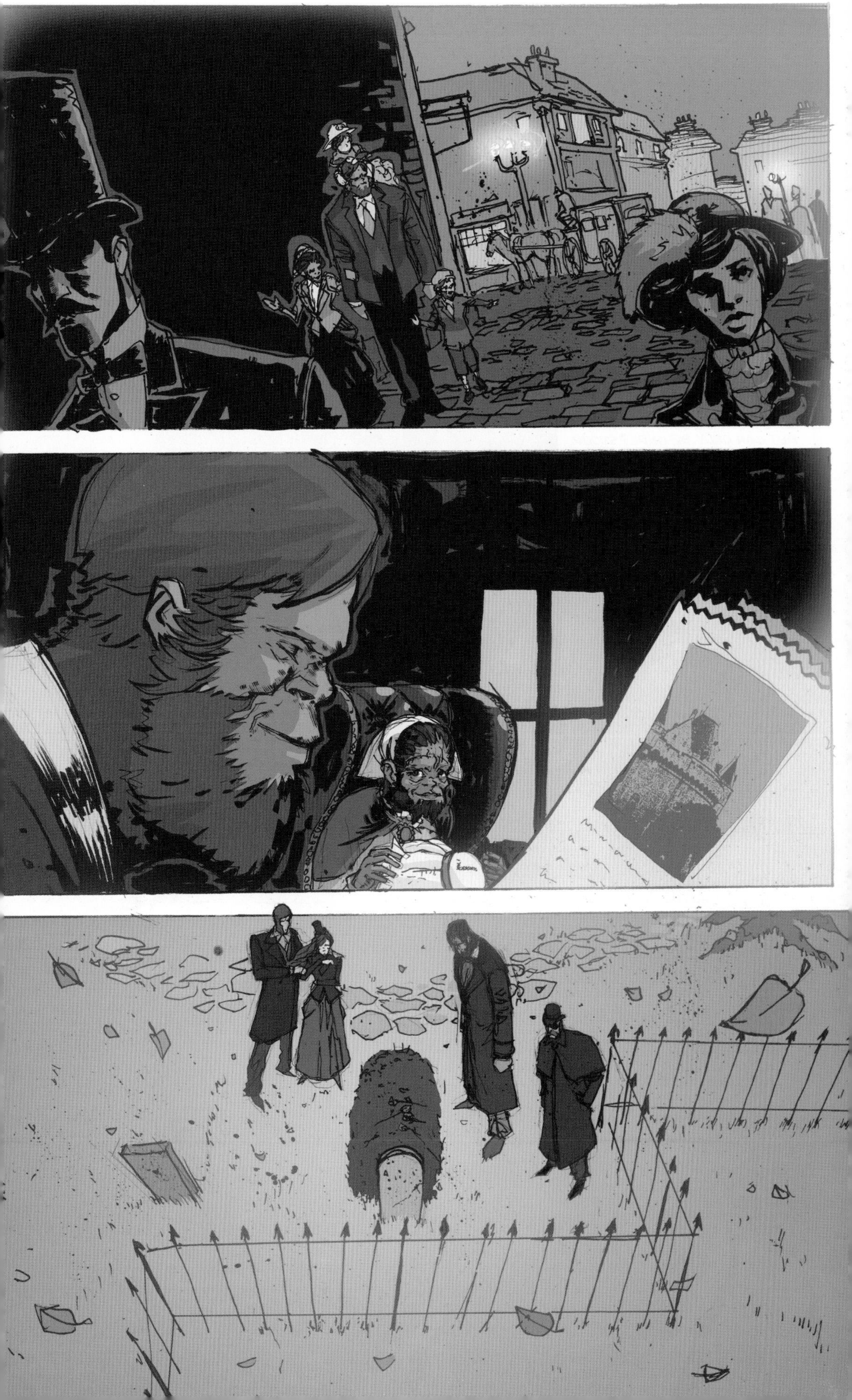

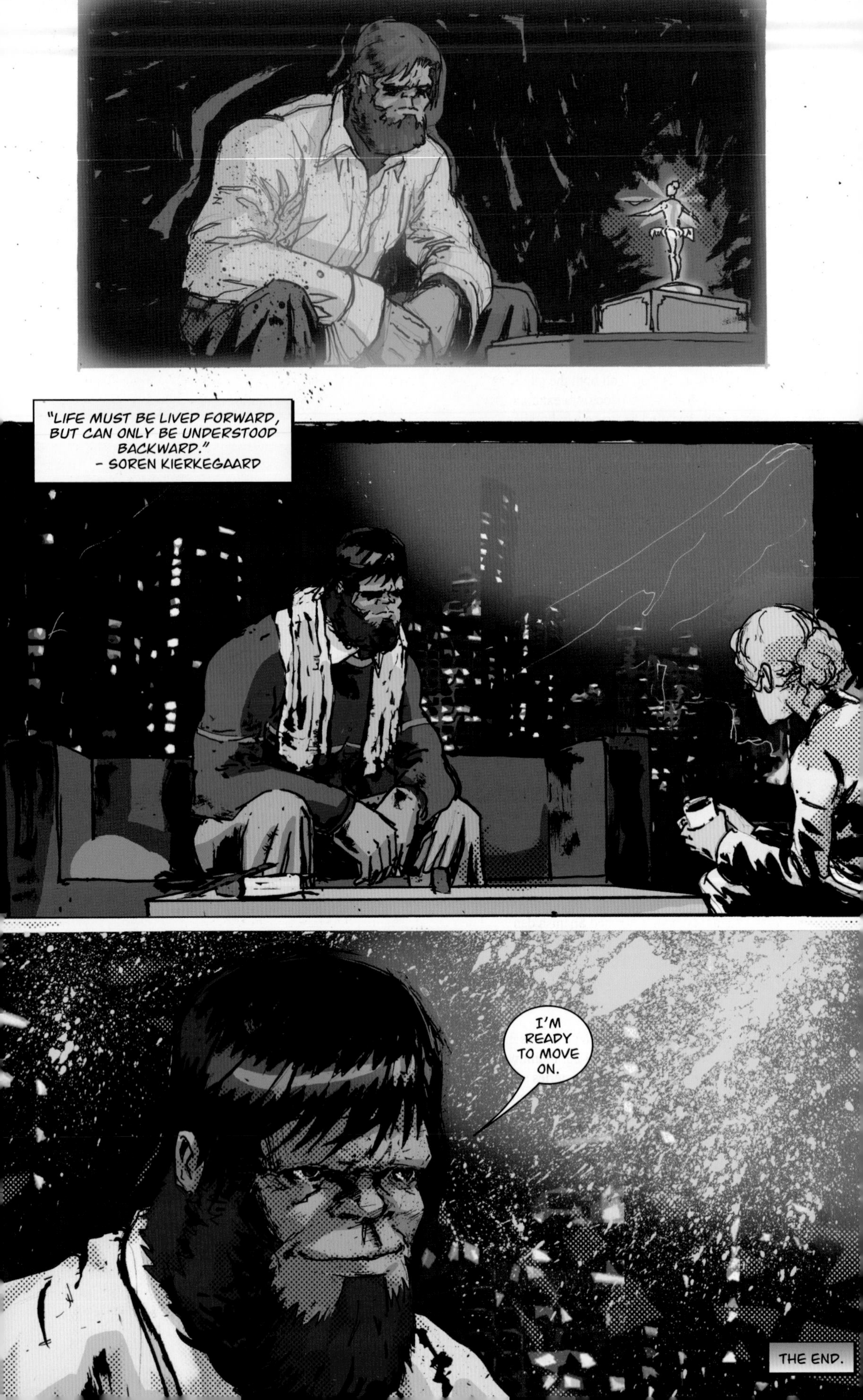
"LIFE MUST BE LIVED FORWARD, BUT CAN ONLY BE UNDERSTOOD BACKWARD."
- SOREN KIERKEGAARD
I'M READY TO MOVE ON.
THE END.

SEMI-HUMAN

Julia Pastrana was born in Mexico, in 1834. After her mother died, Julia's father sent her to live with the local governor where she worked as a serving girl and cleaned house. She was not treated well, more an object of curiosity than a bona fide member of the hired help, and she returned to her Indian village in April of 1854. There she encountered a traveler named "M. Rates" who persuaded her to accompany him to America.

After a brief stopover in New Orleans, Julia made her Manhattan debut eight months later at the Gothic Hall on Broadway. She was an immediate sensation with both the public and the scientific community. The first doctor to examine her, Alexander Mott, MD, declared her to be a hybrid between a human and an orangutan. Julia's bittersweet relationship with Victorian society had begun.

Julia soon found another showman (or he found her) and traveled across America with J.W. Beach. In Cleveland, another doctor examined her and declared her to be of a "distinct species," with "no trace of Negro blood." It wasn't until she was exhibited at the Boston Natural History Society that the curator of comparative anatomy, Samuel Kneeland, Jr., dispensed with hyperbole and pronounced her "a perfect woman." At the very least, a human being.

Julia was four and a half feet tall, had a wide flat nose with large nostrils, bulky lips, a double-row of teeth in each jaw, swollen gums, and a full beard and moustache. The sleek black hair everywhere on her body inspired her first official title: "The Marvellous Hybrid or Bear Woman." Later in her career, she was billed as a "Semi-Human Indian from Mexico," "The Baboon Lady," "The Ugliest Woman in the World" and, most frequently, the "Nondescript." (Although it seems somewhat counterintuitive now, "Nondescript" was a common term of the day for any exotic or unusual attraction.)

But she was of above-average intelligence, with a gentle disposition and a lovely singing voice. She enjoyed reading, learned three languages, and performed Spanish dances along with popular songs of the day. She was by all accounts highly spiritual and generous, giving vast sums to charity. And she earned a fortune touring three continents at a time when most women had few opportunities outside the home.

Based on anecdotal evidence, Julia's condition was misdiagnosed for decades, but recent analysis of her mummy has finally helped to crack many of the medical mysteries surrounding her. Congenital *hypertrichosis lanuginosa*, while rare, is seen frequently among human abnormalities, often called dog-faced boys or girls. But Julia is one of only *three known cases in history* to exhibit her unique physical traits. (One of the other two cases was Julia's own son.) It's now believed that she suffered from a combination of several genetic conditions: extreme congenital *hypertrichosis* with terminal hair (an extraordinarily unusual pattern of hair growth), severe *gingival hyperplasia* (swollen gums) and gross facial deformities. Victorian-era audiences knew that Julia was special, but nobody had any idea how unique she really was.

With the possible exception of Theodore Lent…

How and where he met Julia is unknown, but by 1857 Lent was advertising his new exhibit in London newspapers as "The Wonder of the World!" Under Lent's management, Julia was no longer allowed to go out in public without a thick veil covering her face, for fear of "giving away the show." She was, from this point on, a virtual prisoner.

But Lent did allow her visitors, people he apparently felt could give him free publicity. P.T. Barnum paid a visit, as did the famous naturalist Frank Buckland. "Her features were simply hideous," Buckland said, "on account of the profusion of hair growing on her forehead, and her black beard; but her figure was exceedingly good and graceful, and her tiny foot and well-turned ankle, *bien chaussée*, perfection itself."

Lent and Julia traveled on to Germany, where the "monkey-faced lady" caused a considerable stir. She was considered "obscene" and was banned from public stages for a time. There was much concern that pregnant women in Julia's audience might miscarry at the sight of her or, worse, bear children that looked like her. Lent was forced to find legal loopholes to allow her to perform. Still the money poured in and so did offers from other showmen. In order to keep his prize exhibit to himself, Lent proposed marriage and Julia accepted.

Whether Lent found her physically attractive or not, the marriage was consummated and Julia bore a son while touring Russia in 1860. It wasn't an easy birth and she was heartbroken that the infant looked like her, rather than resembling her husband. The hairy baby boy lived only a day and a half; and, five days later, Julia died.

Lent wasted no time in turning a profit from the bodies of his wife and child. He sold them to a Russian professor named Sukaloff who embalmed them both, using a fluid of his own invention. The process of mummifying the unnamed baby was quick, but Julia's body took months to complete. When he had finished, Sukaloff exhibited the bodies at the anatomical museum of the University of Moscow.

They were an immediate sensation, attracting the attention of students, scientists and, once again, Frank Buckland. "Having had some experience in human mummies," Buckland said, "I was exceedingly surprised at what I saw. The figure was dressed in the ordinary exhibition costume used in life, and placed erect upon the table. The limbs were by no means shrunken or contracted, the arms, chest, &c. retaining their former roundness and well-formed appearance. The face was marvellous; exactly like an exceedingly good portrait in wax, but it was not formed of wax. The closest examination convinced me that it was the true skin, prepared in some wonderful way; the huge deformed lips and squat nose remained exactly as in life; and the beard and luxuriant growth of soft black hair on and about the face were in no respect changed from their former appearance."

Buckland wasn't the only one impressed by Sukaloff's handiwork. Theodore Lent soon resurfaced and bought his mummified family back from the professor (who made a tidy profit from the deal).

Russian authorities refused to allow the bodies to be displayed for profit, so Lent moved once more to London, where people paid a shilling apiece for the privilege of seeing Julia and her baby. Lent dressed her in an elaborate Russian dancer's costume for the exhibit. He chose an ill-fitting sailor's outfit for his infant son, who was then placed under glass, on a tall pedestal next to his mother.

After taking them on a tour of America, Lent apparently felt he'd milked all he could from his dead family and, in 1864, lent them out to a traveling English museum of curiosities. Julia and her son toured Sweden while Lent went in search of a new exhibit.

He had heard rumors of another bearded lady, living in Karlsbad. He asked for the young woman's hand in marriage, but her father did not want her to be put on display. Lent won him over by promising never to exhibit her. After the wedding, however, he moved her away from her family, took away her shaving tools, and prepared for a grand tour of Europe.

To augment the new show, he reacquired Julia and her child. His new wife was christened "Zenora Pastrana" and she toured with the mummies, as Julia's sister. That arrangement didn't last long. Whatever the reason (Zenora may have refused to continue touring with the mummies), Julia and her unnamed son were once again farmed out. This time they went to the Präuscher Volksmuseum in Vienna, in exchange for an annual payment to Lent of 320 taler. There, Julia joined a large collection of human curiosities.

With his former wife out of the picture, Lent changed tactics, seizing one last opportunity to capitalize on her name. His fresh claim that Zenora *was* Julia boosted ticket sales.

Sometime in the early 1880s, Lent and Zenora bought a small waxworks museum in St. Petersburg and retired there. By 1884 Lent was often seen dancing in the streets, tearing up bank notes and throwing his money in the river. He was taken to a Russian insane asylum and died there.

Zenora reclaimed her "sister's" mummy and moved to Munich, where she exhibited it, and herself, for a final time at The Anthropological Society, thus proving to the world that she was not, in fact, Julia Pastrana, as Lent had claimed. Zenora then left show business, married a man 20 years younger than she was, and settled in Dresden. She gave the mummies to a showman named J.B. Gassner, who exhibited them briefly before selling them at a circus convention in Vienna. From there, Julia and her child were passed around until they disappeared from sight.*

In 1943, during the German occupation of Norway, Julia resurfaced and was put on tour once more, with all proceeds destined for the treasury of the Third Reich. (I doubt she would have approved.) Julia and the baby were put back into storage in 1953 and stayed there – except for a handful of brief exhibitions – until 1971, when they went on tour once again and made worldwide headlines.

(That tour may have been the reason for her inclusion in a big leather-bound book of human curiosities that I spent countless hours poring over as a child.)

Sadly, although the 1970s tour brought Julia thousands upon thousands of new fans, she was once again billed as a hybrid between humans and apes. Her picture was even circulated in racist pamphlets, in which she was described as the product of a union between a black man and an orangutan.

When the tour reached Sweden, the board of health closed it down, citing a 100-year-old regulation against displaying dead bodies. Julia and her son went into storage at a fairground.

In 1976, vandals broke into the fairground. They tore Julia's dress and shaved part of her face, then stole her baby's body and threw it into a nearby ditch, where mice ate it. In the summer of 1979, vandals again ransacked the fairground. This time they stole Julia's body.

Later that year, children playing at a dump in a suburb of Oslo found a mummified human arm. The police found the rest of Julia's body in an abandoned caravan near the dump. City officials put Julia into storage in the basement of the Institute of Forensic Medicine at the Rikshospitalet. According to eyewitnesses, her arm has not been reattached. Her dress is long gone and the right side of her face is torn open. Her right eye is missing.

In the late 1990s, a petition was brought before the Norwegian home secretary asking that Julia's remains be cremated or buried. The proposal met with overwhelming resistance from the scientific community, who felt that destroying Julia's body would be an act of shortsighted vandalism. Instead, it was decided that Julia should be kept in storage at the medical history museum, out of sight of the public eye forever.

Presumably, she's still there.

In 2003, Julia was the subject of a stage production called *The True History of the Tragic Life and Triumphant Death of Julia Pastrana, the Ugliest Woman in the World.* There was no attempt to replicate Julia's likeness using make-up. Instead, the entire play was performed in the dark.

Personally, I don't think Julia Pastrana was the "Ugliest Woman in the World." Nor do I think there was anything remotely "triumphant" about her death. Theodore Lent clearly suffered a miserable end, but not miserable enough. In *Proof: Julia*, Theodore Lent's stand-in, "Thomas," finally pays for his villainy and his wife's body is put to rest. That's the best we can do here for Julia, whose inner beauty continues to inspire us.

– Alex Grecian

* While researching Julia's story I came across multiple snippets of a poem that was published in 1909, decades after her death. I finally tracked down the entire thing and I'm presenting it here. This is, as far as I know, the first time it's seen print in a hundred years (special thanks to Cynthia Appl for her help in translating the final stanza). It's a cruel poem, but it demonstrates how Julia was perceived in her day…

PASTRANA

'Twas a big black ape from over the sea,
And she sat on a branch of a walnut tree,
And grinn'd and sputter'd and gazed at me
As I stood on the grass below;
She sputter'd and grinn'd in a fearsome way,
And put out her tongue, which was long and grey,
And hiss'd and curl'd and seem'd to say
"Why do you stare at me so?"

Who could help staring? I, at least,
Had never set eyes on so strange a beast
Such a monstrous birth of the teeming East,
Such an awkward ugly breed:

She had large red ears and a bright blue snout,
And her hairy limbs were firm and stout;
Yet still as I look'd I began to doubt
If she were an ape indeed.

Her ears were pointed, her snout was long;
Her yellow fangs were sharp and strong;
Her eyes, but surely I must be wrong,
For I certainly thought I saw
A singular look in those fierce brown eyes;
The look of a creature in disguise;
A look that gave me a strange surmise
And a thrill of shuddering awe.

But the ape still sat on that walnut bough;
And she swung to and fro, I scarce knew how,
First up in the tree, and then down below,
In a languid leisurely dance;
And she pluck'd the green fruit with her finger'd paws
And crush'd it whole in her savage jaws,
And look'd at me, as if for applause,
With a keen enquiring glance;

And she turn'd her head from side to side
With a satisfied air and a flutter of pride,
And gazed at herself, and fondly eyed
Her steel-bright collar and chain;
She seem'd as blithe as a bride full-drest,
While the strong cold steel, in its slight unrest,
Did jingle and gleam on her broad black breast
And under her shaggy mane.

But I must confess I was glad to see
That her chain was made fast to the walnut tree,
So she could not manage to get at me,
Were she ever so much inclined;
For I did not like, I scarce knew why,
That singular look in her bright brown eye;
It meant too much and it reach'd too high
To come of an apelike kind.

Perhaps she guess'd my thoughts and fears,
For she suddenly prick'd her large red ears,
And grinn'd with the grin of one who sneers,
And lifted her long rough arm,
And flung it about with a whirr and a wheel,
And scratch'd herself from head to heel
With a strength and vigour that made me feel
What power she had to harm.

There are very good reasons, we all know well,
Why an ape should claw its hairy fell,
But it seem'd to me I could surely tell,
By the grin on her hideous face,
That she did it to deepen my disgust,
And to make me think that she might and must
Be nothing higher nor more august
Than a brute of the simious race.

And, lest that proof should happen to fail,
She gave a blow like the blow of a flail
With the switchlike length of her muscular tail
To the branch whereon she sat;
The tail curl'd round it and gripp'd it tight,
And she flung herself off with all her might
And hung head downward, swinging as light
As a human acrobat.

So easily sway'd she, so easily swung,

You could see she was healthy and lively and young
And she toss'd up her head, and her long grey tongue
Shot out, as it did before;
And she caught the bough with her brisk forepaws,
And loosed her tail and tighten'd her claws,
And swung herself up, with her chain in her jaws,
And sat in her place once more.

Oh then, what masterful airs she took!
She gnaw'd her chain with an elfish look,
Till the long links dripp'd and foam'd and shook,
Like the curb of a bridle-rein
On either side of her rugged lips;
And I shudder'd and thrill'd to my finger tips
When I saw she had bent and and flatten'd to strips
A piece of the massive chain.

Perhaps she would get at me, after all!
If the links should break, I might well feel small,
Young as I was, and strong and tall,
And blest with a human shape,
To see myself foil'd in that lonely place
By a desperate brute with a monstrous face,
And hugg'd to death in the foul embrace
Of a loathly angry ape.

For the ape was nearly as tall as a man;
So it seem'd to me the safest plan
To leave her at once, ere her wrath began
To spread from her glowing eyes
To the long sharp nails of her powerful hands;
For the Lex Talionis and its commands
Are just what the creature understands
And just what her passions prize.

But what had I done to rouse her wrath?
I had simply stepp'd from the garden path
On to the soft sweet aftermath
Of the lawnlike woodland green,
And had stood, like a rustic clown, agape,
To study and stare at the fearful shape
Of the most uncouth outlandish ape
That ever mine eyes had seen.

Ah, perhaps that was the very thing!
She had never been used to communing
With man, who holds himself as king
Of the animals great and small;
She did not like my scrutiny,
And she meant to know the reason why
A human mortal such as I
Should trouble her state at all.
That was the reason I gave to myself
For the conduct strange of this angry elf.
As I put my doubts and fears on the shelf
And walk'd to my sumptuous inn,
Where I went upstairs and read and wrote,
And then came down to the table d'hote
With a fresh white rose on my spotless coat.
And an appetite within.

Fifty people were seated there,
Taking their pleasure with solemn air;
Gentles and simples, ladies fair,
And some not fair though fine;
And all of them ate and drank with a will,
For each felt bound to take his fill,
As the long procession of dishes still
Invited them all to dine.

None of the fifty cared for me
Nor for each other, that I could see;
Each of them felt exceeding free
To live for dinner alone;
And I too only look'd at my plate,
And thank'd my stars I was not too late
For that central portion of good white skate
Which I specially made my own.

But at last, we were weary of knives and forks,
And cloy'd with the popping of Rhinewine corks,
And the Oberkellner and all his works
Were seen with a languid eye;
We raised our heads, and look'd around
To see what guests mere Chance had found
To people our happy feeding ground
With a various company.

Ah, by the powers, a singular sight!
What is that lady opposite,
Sitting alone, with her back to the light,
Who has such wonderful hair?
She is comely and young? I do not know,
For her face shows dark in the evening glow;
But I wonder why she looks at me so,
And with such an elfish stare!

Sure, I remember those bright brown eyes?
And the self-same look that in them lies
I have seen already, with strange surprise,
This very afternoon;
Not in the face of a woman like this,
Who has human features, and lips to kiss,
But in one who can only splutter and hiss
In the eyes of a grim baboon!

And what is that white metallic thing
That shines on her throat, like the gleam of a ring
Now sparkling out, now vanishing,
As her shaggy tresses move?
I have had but a pint of Heidenseck
Yet I think of the collar and chain that deck
The broad black bosom and hairy neck
Of that monster in the grove!
Aye, and they rattle, indeed they do!
I look'd hurriedly round it was all too true
That the folk were gone, save only two,
That silent dame, and I;
But a third appear'd, was there anything wrong?
For the Oberkellner tall and strong
On the parqueted floor came gliding along
With an air of mystery.

His face was pale, as if from fear,
And he stepp'd so softly, it seem'd quite clear
That the lady was not to see or hear
Whatever he had in charge;
Perhaps he had some sad news to say?
Perhaps her mind had given way,
And it was not safe to leave her all day
Untended and at large?

Whatever it were, with an anxious mind
He reach'd her seat, and stood behind,
While she, still gazing at me, seem'd blind
And deaf to all he did;
He raised his hands, and suddenly shed
Over her shoulders and over her head
A thick grey web, like a shroud for the dead;

And she sat there, closely hid.

She would have sprung to her feet in a trice
She was no meek victim, bought with a price,
Ready and willing for sacrifice
She would neither yield nor spare.
But the Oberkellner knew his part;
His grasp was firm, and he had no heart;
He pinion'd her arms, with accurate art,
To the back of her stout broad chair.

What did she do, in that shrouding sheath?
She tried to tear the web with her teeth
I could see them snatch it from underneath
And she strove to free her arms;
Then she raised her voice and I must confess
It was not a voice to soothe and bless,
Nor such an one as is more or less
The best of a woman's charms.

No, 'twas a scream and a roar and a growl,
More like a cry of beasts that howl
Than the shriek of a startled human soul;
And it thrill'd me through and through;
For I thought, If she does contrive to get free,
She will fly at the Oberkellner and me,
And though I am nearly as strong as he,
She may prove a match for two!

But Fritz the waiter had heard that sound;
And he straight rush'd in with a spring and a bound,
And lifted my lady off the ground
With the aid of his artful chief;
She might roar and howl or scream and scold,
But he and the Oberkellner bold
Stuck to her chair, and kept fast hold,
To my very great relief.
As they carried her off, a cold damp sweat
Seized me all over, and yet, and yet,
I order'd my coffee and cigarette
As usual, in the hall;
And I did not even ask of Fritz
Whether the lady were subject to fits,
Or had gone quite mad and out of her wits;
I ask'd him nothing at all.

For in fact I dreaded to hear her tale;
That very word made me turn quite pale,
When I call'd to mind her long wild wail
Of anger and despair;
And my thoughts went back to the walnut tree,
And the creature who sat there and look'd at me
So fiercely, strangely, eagerly,
From under her shaggy hair.

The very next morning, I went away;
And I heard the Oberkellner say
(He had taken his tip, and wish'd me Good-day,
And he thought I could not hear)
I heard him say to that stern old Klaus,
Who keeps the keys of the garden-house,
"Lassen Sie es nicht gehen hinaus
Das schlechte schwarze Thier!"
["Don't let it get out,
That bad black animal!"]

– Arthur Munby
from *Relicta*